I0590005

Murder by Algorithm

Douglas Beagley

Reify Publishing

for Althea, with whom I share mysteries

DAY ONE

Chapter One
The Detective

The morning after my best friend's murder, I tried to sleep in.

It didn't work. My hangover woke me. I dragged a sagging cabana chair to the sandy edge of my yard. I brought a Bloody Mary with me—given the size of the plastic cup, it was two Bloody Marys. I couldn't find a straw. The ice knocked against my teeth. The tide was out, so I sat and stared at the salt marsh. It smelled of seaweed and dead fish. I used my glasses to scroll through the morning's reviews.

The sandy flat extended for half a kilometer to the northwest. I could hear the crashing waves and see the white foam beyond. The edge of my yard was a tall mess of pickleweed, cordgrass, and other things that take advantage of the wet. The Island municipal drones were out gardening. They buzzed the flats and counted horn snails, cataloged invasives, and annoyed the fuck out of me.

My two-week show, *Impressions,* debuted on Praxima station the night before. Last year *Décolletage* won awards, so this time they put me in the Century Gallery. It's 100 square meters on two levels, artificial gravity, fusty canapés—really something.

I did not attend.

The morning's reviews were fine: "Thackery has done it again." But if I'd attended, I might have gotten a "Thackery expands their oeuvre and reinvents themself!" If I'd been there to work the room, patrons would have touched my shoulder or the small of my back and gestured towards my paintings with their shimmering drinks while making vacuous statements. Then they'd buy the rights to more pieces and queue up for private streams on upcoming sessions, eager to watch the artist at work. Patrons pay more to peek through the eyes of someone they've touched or, better yet, kissed on the cheek. Instead I stayed home, got drunk, damned my work, and impaired my income. Perhaps I also added to my mystique? I don't have a lot of mystique.

I didn't go, and that morning I tried not to care. I dug my left hand into the cool sand to balance the numbing effect of the cold drink held in my right. Even at a distance, an opening made me feel hollowed out. I also worried *Impressions* was more Johnathan's work than mine—but I always think that. I stared at the cordgrass and the shades of brown on the marsh, and I made up my mind: I'd watch the tide come back in and not think about *Impressions* or my patrons.

I thought about them anyway. There were four patrons blinking in my queue just then, on hold for a chance to stream me: two that I knew only vaguely from the Prax art scene, one fellow Islander, and—of course—my anonymous superdonor. I felt useless, but not useless enough to turn on my glasses and start streaming my depression. Depression is not popular this season. I slid down in my chair and slumped so low that my body lay in a comical horizontal pose, my chin seeking my sternum.

Other than wallowing in the unjustified malaise of the successful, financially-solvent artist, what would I do with myself today? I'd already read the reviews and gotten over them. Later, Christobel and I would exchange snarky texts and then meet up for drinks at The Thirst. Unless we were fighting again? I didn't think so. Okay: The Thirst. Unless we were fighting. But that would be later. What about right now?

Johnathan wasn't allowed to speak yet, but I had an earpiece in. I could wake him up and let him annoy me. Or I could dribble back online and read reviews of my colleagues' work to make me feel better about my own. If I were Christobel, I'd go for a jog. I could also make money: go back to my studio, let my superdonor watch me sketch. My brain crinkled up at the thought. It was impossible to make anything today. But it was impossible every day.

I closed my eyes and listened for the distant waves. There were not many seagulls this year. There'd been fewer chicks than deaths—they'd have to try thicker eggshells next season—so I mostly heard the buzzing of the morning's drones, methodically poking at the sand for signs of life. My grip on the Bloody Mary gradually slackened. Maybe I could sleep the morning off after all.

Then I heard Cherry's voice from somewhere behind me on the grass. "Good morning, Tack! A bright day to you."

Cherry is a patron. Everyone on the Island is either a patron, an artist, or a patron who thinks they're an artist. He's rich, but not well-liked, and his preposterous house is my closest neighbor. I get the feeling Cherry enjoys cantankerous artists, so I am as cantankerous towards him as I like. He wanders over most mornings, but usually not before eleven.

I grunted, but I didn't open my eyes. For a moment I wondered what he would make of my slumped form in the sagging chair. I vaguely remembered pulling on linen pants and my blue sweater, so at least I was clothed.

"Big opening last night. Century Gallery! Did you get back this morning?"

"Didn't go," I replied. Cherry's question was stupid. If I'd gone up to Prax and endured the opening, I definitely wouldn't have gotten up early for the morning drop. And if I had taken an early drop, plummeting down from orbit with the day's deliveries of packages and food-stuffs to a cacophonous splashdown off the south coast, I wouldn't be sitting on my beach scarcely two hours later. I'd be vomiting in the restroom at Jelly's diner. That's what I usually do after a trip to Prax. Jelly's ginger pancakes are supposed to be good for motion sickness, but really they're just excellent pancakes—even to a lurching post-orbital stomach. Maybe later, if my headache went away, I could take the trolley down. I'd let Cherry tag along. He always paid.

"Ah. You stayed here, then. Were you home all night?"

I heard a tension in Cherry's voice—like he wasn't talking about what he was talking about. Like he was reading a script, auditioning for a supporting part in the spring drama.

I turned my head and squinted. Someone male presenting stood beside Cherry. Gray clothes and a hat with a green band: a walking AI? That was new. A few patrons kept walkers, but they aren't popular on the Island. We're all supposed to be down here living in the real world under the real sun. A walking artificial companion interferes with our self-image. It looked like an attractive model, though. Had Cherry come over to show it off?

I was almost interested. I hadn't allowed Johnathan to start talking yet that morning, and my brain wanted something to chew on. I lifted a hand to shade my eyes.

"Were you home all night?" Cherry repeated. "Did you go out?"

Cherry's sunburn was peeling. The AI stood just behind him, looking at me with mild curiosity. Not just a bot, then? Something with personality. That was unusual—and expensive.

Their faces, one sunburnt and one pale, made me think about *Impressions* again. I'd spent a year looking at faces, reading and recycling emotions while Johnathan painted. (And the reviews were fine. Lukewarm. Warmish? Were they enough? Enough for what? and etc.) The empty studio back in my house felt like a stomachache, and I had a non-metaphorical headache. The Bloody Mary hadn't helped.

I'd forgotten Cherry's question. I closed my eyes and leaned back. If I sat still long enough, he would continue down the scrappy coastline, find an artist who needed patronage, and show off his new toy or whatever it was. I grunted again.

"Is that a 'yes,' Tack? You didn't go out? Not like you to miss your opening."

It was very like me to miss my opening. Okay, cantankerous artist it was: "Go away, Cherry. This beach is mine."

The tide would turn soon. The froth and chop would murmur across the flats, foaming and dissolving, and the ocean would be only a dozen meters from my doorstep. I didn't need grand openings. Or company.

I heard the sound of feet upon the vegetation.

Then I was rolling sideways. The world turned, and my body flumped to the ground. The wobbly chair collapsed and folded over me.

"What the hell?" I shouted, sitting up. My drink cup had overturned, trickling vodka and tomato juice into the sand.

The walking AI had pushed over my chair. Now he stood above me, wearing a friendly expression, with a hand extended to help me stand.

"Did you just try to hurt me?" I ignored the hand and climbed to my feet. I stared into his eyes. We were the same height.

"I apologize. You were uncooperative." The voice was masculine, though the body was more or less androgynous. Slender, athletic—his build was similar to mine, except that I've got breasts. He had a very human half smile on his face. "It is within my operational parameters to insist on your attention."

He wore a carefully-tailored gray suit with lapels, a vest, the works. I felt self-conscious in my relaxed linen. The clothes matched the face: attractive proportions, nice cheekbones. Too bad he was an asshole.

I folded my arms. "That's a terrible apology, even for an AI. What the fuck, Cherry?"

"Now, let's all calm down. I'm sure he just wanted to startle you. Tack, this is Cye-9. Cye, this is Tack, Thackery as they are known upstairs. And there's no reason to be pushing over their chair. They are very respected down here."

I turned to Cherry. "You don't have to introduce me to your toy. Get him off my lawn." Was this a prank, then? I wasn't sure how angry to get. Was it fashionable to go over to your neighbor's house and have your bot tip them out of their chair?

"Well, Cye's not my toy, Tack. And I'm afraid he and I do have a purpose here. A very unfortunate business."

I looked at the two of them. Cherry standing his ground? That made no sense. Cherry is a marmalade of a man: soft, not one to insist on anything. "If he's not your toy, what is he? Is this a patron's avatar?"

"No, no. Nothing like that, sadly. Cye here is a Level 4. He just now knocked on my door and conscripted me. He's from Prax—sent down on a morning drop. And we need to ask you some questions."

Clarity, like ocean water, slapped me in the face: This was an investigation. The Island finally had an actual crime. And Prax wasn't able to get a human investigator to come down to Earth? Or it was too short notice. Or they finally realized Level 4s are better at the job. They'd dropped an AI—a walking Level 4. And he'd selected Cherry as a human chaperone to make introductions.

"I apologize again for tipping over your chair, but you were almost on the ground already."

"Another terrible apology." I glared at him, but I felt some chagrin. In other circumstances, it would be me who needed to apologize: I'd called a Level 4 a toy. Detective Cye-9 was a person. But he'd still been a dick. "Okay, a crime. Here or on Prax? Is this about the graffiti?" I couldn't help it; I was interested. I'd wanted something to break my day open, and—like a gift box from Zeus—something arrived. Other than littering, the only crime on the Island was graffiti, which all the artists participated in (and which the municipal drones dutifully removed and then fined us for). "Did someone scrawl hate speech this time, or...?"

Cherry shook his head. "Yes, a crime. But no. Not the graffiti. It's a tragedy, Tack. I'm terribly sorry to be the one to tell you this. But Christobel is dead—found dead, at the end of the marshwalk. And they say it's a murder."

"What?" I stared at him.

Cherry blinked at me mournfully. "I said Christobel is dead. He was murdered."

I sat down on the overgrown grass.

"What?" I repeated.

Cherry and the motionless AI looked at me, their faces in turn concerned and unreadable.

"Johnathan!" I challenged the sky, and my voice spiraled up. It was strange. It didn't sound like my own voice. "Wake up, damn it. Johnathan. Where's Christobel?"

Chapter Two
The Interrogation

"Johnathan, where the hell is Christobel?" I asked.

It was two weeks before the opening. The screens of my studio were filled with faces. Christobel had promised to come over and preview the final gallery layout of *Impressions*. He was late. Christobel was always late, but this time he was two hours late. Intolerable.

"Christobel is at Creoline One," Johnathan intoned in my earpiece. I don't have speakers in the studio. I'm implant-free as well, which means when I work with Johnathan we speak through a remote.

I turned slowly, my eyes flitting from face to face on the screens. They were all staring at me. Not for the first time, I wondered why I decided to make art that looked back at me. I'm an introvert.

I was, in turn, both proud of *Impressions* and disgusted by it. Johnathan's brush strokes were impeccable, modeled after my own, just improved. The work was mine, but not mine. It reflected my intention, and it was my nervous system that tuned, revised, and drew forth the image. But Johnathan was the painter. The work was good, but I didn't know what to say about it. Which is why I needed Christobel.

He didn't answer my connection request. I sent him another text. WHO ARE YOU FUCKING? We'd already rescheduled from the day before.

To my surprise, he replied. `Your mother, of course.`

"Christobel is not engaged in sexual congress," Johnathan droned in my ear. "He has ordered a cheese platter and a glass of '48 Calais Neige Malbec."

"And who's he eating it with, Johnathan? Who's more important than appreciating your goddamn pictures?" I asked.

I stepped up closer to one of said goddamn pictures. *Duel.* An androgynous face, like my own. Unlike me, they had pale skin and dark, youthful hair instead of my gray-streaked mop. Despite a split lip and the shadow of a bruise under one eye, *Duel* wore a rebellious grin and held my gaze. I remembered composing them. Johnathan tracked my emotional reactions and modified *Duel's* face as it formed. A face of someone unreal, born out of what I thought they must feel, slid into place on the canvas. *Duel's* grin was shaped like Christobel's.

At my opening, some sophomoric arts writer was going to ask me what the subject had *been through*. What was their story? What pain had they known, and why were they smiling now? I needed to rehearse a reply to this and a hundred other idiotic questions.

Johnathan could not identify Christobel's lunch date because all restaurants on the Island are eyeless and earless. My AI is more clever than average (I've made modifications), and Christobel finds him amusing and gives him access sometimes. But it was a restaurant. To Johnathan, *Duel* was more tangible than the guests at Creoline One, who were blank, faceless specters in an elided stream of data.

"Ask Mabel who Christobel is eating with," I demanded. Mabel is Christobel's AI. She probably shared the lunch order just to irritate me, knowing he would be late.

"Mabel would not tell me that," Johnathan replied. It was probably Millfield. Millfield was Christobel's current, monogamous for over half a year now.

I texted again, `WHEN YOUR DONE WITH MY MOM GET YOUR DICK OVER HERE. I NEED IT.`

The reply: `Should be able to accommodate by 2. Will bring dick. May need refractory period.`

He didn't arrive until five. He stepped in from the wind, his riotous curls tumbling to his shoulders, and took off his glasses with a smooth gesture. He had on pale blue nail polish. "Am I late?" he asked, and then laughed. Christobel was never tired. He left them sleeping and went back to the party. He was always energized, eager to dish, discuss, dissemble, dissect the world with a wave of his hand.

I made scallops. Real ones, not printed—expensive. Scallops were new, returned to local waters for barely a year. Everyone's favorite mad geniuses in resurrection biology continued to slowly fumble with the ocean like ants operating an industrial forge. So now we had scallops again. I overcooked them.

Then Christobel perused *Impressions*. Walking from face to face, he gave each piece a chirping chuckle, sometimes accompanied by Mabel's vocables and sardonic remarks. "What about this one?" he'd say. And Mabel would reply, "It's either a revelation or a character study in constipation." And so forth. Mabel was always negative, but Christobel had the type of laugh that meant appreciation and wonder, not derision. His smile brought perfect cherub cheeks to his face, and it was always genuine. His longest complimentary chuckle was for *Duel*.

"Oh dear. They're perfect. Are they a self-portrait?"

"No. No, of course not. They don't look like me."

"If you say so."

"*Duel* is in no way a self-portrait, Christobel. They are not me."

He gestured to the room and spun on the heel of his black velvet boot. "I think all of the faces are you, Thackery."

"No. Or yes, 'blah blah blah: art,' fine. They're all me. But no, they're not me, and *Duel* is certainly not me."

"Well, if you're certain." Christobel blinked at me. "In that case, *Duel* is the centerpiece. They have such a commanding expression. They should be in the center of the room, when patrons walk in the door of the gallery." Christobel produces shows and designs the sets, though usually only for the stage. "If it's a self-portrait, then highlighting them would be an onslaught of narcissistic self-absorption. Or self-pity! But since you're really sure they're *not* you, then they are the showstopper. Put a nice, flooded fresnel on them."

"You're being an ass. You really think they're a self-portrait?"

"I do. But Thackery"—Christobel looked at me with sincere, faraway eyes, —"what I think doesn't matter. You are the artist."

"Fuck you," I said.

He laughed again. He declined a second drink. I said I'd drink his. He made some clever comment about *Duel* drinking it instead. We laughed together at that. There was never any snark or antagonism in Christobel's laugh. I loved him whenever he laughed.

Now I'd never hear it again.

*
**

"Johnathan," I repeated in a smaller voice as I stared numbly out towards the sea, "where is Christobel?"

Johnathan's voice finally answered. "Christobel is at the end of the northwest marshwalk. He is deceased. I am sorry, Thackery."

I stood up and took out my earpiece. I hurled it towards the ocean. It wouldn't reach, the tide being out. It would land in the muck and the reeds, a tiny horrid dot speaking Johnathan's flat, measured voice to the slugs and snails. The drones would pick it up. I'd be fined for littering.

I stumbled backwards. I was surprised to feel the AI supporting me, standing at my side. He kept his hand on my back as I rebalanced.

"Are you able to stand?"

"I'm fine," I said, shaking him off—I wasn't. "Don't touch me."

If the earpiece reached the ocean, I'd be fined twice as much.

I started towards my house, across the two dozen meters of scrubby grass, cursing Johnathan and obtusely demanding that he answer me while well aware I'd chucked his means of answering me into the marsh.

What happened? There must have been a mistake. It was a rude and unforgivable prank. Or one of Christobel's rich admirers created a conceptual sculpture using a vat-grown body—it had to be something.

Everything Cherry says is cliché-layered garbage, but most AI are not allowed to lie. As a Level 4, Cye-9 was a person and might just pull off a fib. But Johnathan was too literal to even approach a lie, and he'd been unambiguous in my earpiece: Christobel was dead.

Cherry and the detective followed me. They answered some of the questions I shouted, Cherry with his strained bourgeois mumble and Cye-9 with a clear-voiced, direct efficiency: A municipal drone identified Christobel's body; bio signatures indicated that no, the body was not an imitation or cloned replica. I dismissed all of this. They'd appeared on my beach and presented a universe I didn't want. When I reached the house, Johnathan would tell me they were wrong. The body was a new kind of printed cadaver. We were engaged in an island-wide dramatic performance. Or I was drunk and hallucinating.

I bullied my porch door open against a slip of sand. Over my home's speakers, Johnathan reported that my O_2 levels were low. He suggested I take deep breaths.

"No. Fuck you. Tell me what happened to Christobel."

"That is as yet unknown, Thackery." His voice echoed slightly in the glassed porch. "His body was found this morning at 2:14 a.m. by a municipal drone that temporarily stopped transmitting, and then—"

"May we come in?" Cye-9's voice spoke from the threshold behind me.

"Course we can," Cherry said. "We're investigating, aren't we?" He stepped around Cye and into my porch. "And I have to come in so I can get Thackery a drink. Something bracing, I think."

Cye-9 brought in my discarded Bloody Mary cup. This was polite of him, but it also classified him with the drones, forever trying to prevent the Earth from becoming a garbage dump again. I'd heard that individual AI have short lives, but collectively their memory and foresight greatly transcends ours. In other words, they always pick up the cups.

Cherry proceeded to my living room, which he always calls "the drawing room" for some reason. He poured scotch into two glasses, dropped ice into his own, and handed me the other neat. I sat down at my dining table and tried to be still. I downed the drink and blew my nose. Cye-9 seated himself across from me.

He had a patient way about him, calm and slow. One could be forgiven for thinking of him as reliable furniture blessed with personality. But he was a person, not a bot. He looked human. He had an attractive, welcoming face, but there was a severe kindness in his eyes. It made me think of when an older sister explains that the family dog has cancer.

He didn't ask questions or insist on anything; he waited. Cherry poured me another drink.

"You asked me where I was last night," I said.

"Yes, I did," Cherry replied, returning to the liquor cabinet. "Cye-9 has deputized me as his human investigative liaison—"

"I was here," I said, keeping my eyes on Cye-9. "I was here all night. I stayed off the streams. I turned everything off and I had a drink."

"Decided not to brave the noise of Prax, then. I quite understand that! You didn't go out to the beach, go for a walk, or—"

"Or go down to the marshwalk to meet up with my best friend and murder him? No, Cherry. And please stop playing detective. Cye-9 is the detective, not you."

Cherry fell silent and focused on his drink apologetically. Cye-9 moved his head in acknowledgement—not quite a nod—but said nothing.

I sipped my drink, but I could not outwait him. "So detect, Mr. Cye-9. Ask what you came to ask."

"Do you remember anything unusual about last night?" he asked.

"No. Boring evening."

"Did you make or receive any calls?"

"Please don't dick around. Given the circumstances, you've already examined every call, every text, every network access event for every individual on the whole Island. You know where I was and whether I messaged anyone."

Cye-9 nodded, unperturbed. "I should know, that is true, just as the municipal drones should have seen everything that happened."

"And...?"

"I have a provisional interface with Johnathan and with the AI of all residents, guests, and students on the Island. I also have access to many of the commercial interfaces, the Prax geostationary satellites, and local agricultural monitoring. These systems should provide multiple, mutually supportive explanations of precisely how, when, and by whom Christobel was murdered. They do not."

It was the longest speech I'd heard out of him so far. His inflection was understated, but not without emotion. He described a preposterous, multi-layered failure of technology. He himself was technology. He sounded apologetic, or as if he were a storyteller at a library reading the first chapter of a bittersweet tale aloud to a group of children.

"What do they show?"

"The data shows that Christobel left Millfield's apartment at 1:04 a.m., apparently without receiving any personal messages, while Millfield slept. And it shows him deceased, at the end of the marshwalk, at 2:14 a.m."

I wondered if Millfield knew Christobel was dead. I also wondered if he was a suspect. Surely not someone like Millfield.

I chewed on Cye-9's timeline. Back in the early years, it wasn't unusual for Christobel to get restless and go for a walk or a jog after hooking up. But Millfield wasn't a hookup; Christobel practically lived at Millfield's. Why go out to the marshwalk? There's no record of a message?

"What was the cause of death?"

"I'm not able to discuss that at present. Last night, did you make or receive—"

"I did not send or receive any messages. Johnathan, grant Cye-9 full access to my process and command logs, and all messaging. Keep him out of my art and my underwear." I looked into Cye's ever-observant eyes. "Do you have any additional questions for me?"

"Well," Cherry interrupted from the liquor cabinet, "you were close to Christobel. Were you involved in an argument recently, or...?"

I glared at him. He knew very well that Christobel and I argued constantly. "If you're going to drink my liquor, you're going to have to be Cherry. Not Watson. Mr. Cye-9, do you have any other questions for me?"

After another brief pause, the detective replied, "Could you please describe your creative process?"

That brought me up short. "What?"

"How do you create art?"

"Surely that can have no bearing on the investigation."

Cye-9 could have asserted it was up to him to decide what pertained to the investigation. Or he could have uttered some other detective cliché. It would've been a relief to be grilled—he'd been so quiet and mild.

Instead, he looked at me as if he foresaw all my responses. He appraised my attitude and calculated the various outcomes of the conversation, which all trickled down a series of rivulets in the sand that wandered inevitably to the ocean. I understood then, and verified many times in the days that followed, that it wasn't important to Cye how he reached that ocean. He would reach it. AI have faith in the truth.

"Perhaps I'm merely curious. Your art may not pertain to the investigation," he acknowledged. "Unless Christobel participated in your creative process?"

"No, he did not." Of course he did. Everyone did. Cye-9 was participating in my creative process at that very moment. Tonight I might wake up and sketch him. Or I'd sketch what he made me feel, this patient sentinel. He had a nice collarbone. Was it made of bone, or something else? I might wake up Johnathan and ask him to reverse diffuse a version of Cye-9's face, but one that desperately needed to talk. Or a Cye-9 who was hurting. A Cye-9 in a hurry, or aroused. He was unfailingly calm and deferential and I wanted to break that open on a canvas. "Not at all," I answered aloud.

"What do you know about Christobel's health?" Cye asked.

"His health? Well, he runs. Every damn morning. He—" I'd just used the present tense. I put my hands flat on the table to steady myself. "He was healthy."

Cye nodded, and waited.

"Do you have any other questions that pertain to the investigation?" I asked.

Cye looked at me and inserted a careful pause. Then he shook his head. "Not at this time, no."

"So are we good?"

"Good?"

"You came to my house first. I bet that wasn't Cherry's idea. Christobel and I text each other a thousand times a day, mostly insults. We recently argued in public—loudly. And I have a private Level 3 AI. I'm your prime suspect." I pushed back my sleeves and held my arms across the table, wrists up. "You can see my pulse, right? And my eyes, from where you're sitting. You can probably measure my perspiration, too. You know my standard pupil dilation, blood pressure, all my medical records and baseline respiratory rate. You've examined all of my art, every post I've ever written, and watched every recorded stream. So when I say I was here, in my house, and that I did not kill or plot to kill my friend, and I've answered all your questions, I really need to know: Are we good?"

"I see what you mean," Cye replied. He sat still for a moment and maintained eye contact, his lips pushed together slightly. "Yes, we're good."

"Super. Now, fire Cherry. I will be your investigative liaison and representative here on the Island for the duration."

Cye lifted his eyebrows. I believe I might have surprised a Level 4 AI, which is hard to do.

"Now hang on a second there, Thackery," Cherry said over his glass. "You are—that is, you were Christobel's close friend. Bosom buddies. You can't go around investigating. It's definitely better for someone not as close to the victim to be deputized, someone like myself."

I kept my eyes on Cye-9. "Cherry's not a good choice. Everyone endures him; he's a stand-up fellow—buckets of money. But he's socially on the outskirts. I'm an acclaimed artist, one of the Island's stars. If I send a message to someone, they'll take my call. And, unlike Cherry, I never slept with Christobel."

There was a clatter in the corner as Cherry knocked over the ice bucket. He hadn't known I knew about that. And I hadn't known for certain. But in his wild, early years, Christobel visited a number of beds (notably not mine), so it was a fair guess.

I couldn't resist looking over to see his face. "Don't worry, Cherry. We know you're not a murderer. You're too befuddled."

"Befuddled? How am I befuddled?"

"Well. Besides tipping over the ice bucket, you spilled half a glass of my very expensive scotch."

Cherry glanced at the floor, which was wet. "Cye-9, do you think I'm befuddled?"

The detective looked amused. "Quite."

Chapter Three
The Prime Suspects

"Well," Cherry stared at his sun hat, which he'd hung on the corner of a chair, "that's that then. Mind if I have another finger of your scotch, Thackery?"

I considered, and then drained my drink.

"The bar is closed," I said, putting my glass down hard. I wanted answers. I needed to know what happened to Christobel. And if someone killed him, I wanted the killer found. I'd find them myself. Immediately.

"Right. Well then. I'll make the breakfast." Cherry abandoned the bar and walked down the hallway into my kitchen. "Johnathan, how are we on eggs?"

"Dana," I said, slapping the table in front of me.

"Dana?" Cherry stuck his head around the corner. "Surely not."

Cye raised an eyebrow. "Are you referring to the actor, Dana Heed?"

Cherry walked back into view. "Christobel dumped Dana. A bit savagely, too, after the thing with George—"

I held up my hand. "Cherry, you may make us breakfast. No more Watson, remember?"

"Right, right, of course." He disappeared around the corner again.

I turned to Cye. "Dana Heed and Christobel dated for about three months last year." I muddled through a brief explanation of the King Richard Breakup—last year's greatest off-stage drama. It started when Christobel brought a professional down from Prax for the role of King Richard, instead of casting the local favorite, George. In retaliation, Dana slept with George. There was a great deal of the usual online nonsense, Beetle and Mabel posting back and forth on the stream. It ended when Christobel dumped Dana. "Dana never got over it—he still sends fuck you greeting cards to Christobel, or has Beetle send them."

Cye merely nodded.

It occurred to me, then: Cye had digested all of the Island's social history. He knew everyone's version of the King Richard Breakup—a knotted branching tree of reposted images and angry comment threads. He was a Level 4. He'd have expansive personality models running for all of us. Whatever I said to him only added to his understanding of me and how I felt, and not to the subject itself.

I continued anyway. I leaned forward for emphasis. "Dana's family is rich. He's got Beetle and maybe a whole crew of Level 3 AI to scrub his back, teach him dead languages, or plan murders."

Cherry called from the kitchen. "But Dana's all talk."

I shook my head. "He sent threats to Christobel—direct, bodily threats." I leaned forward further, practically climbing across the table towards Cye-9. "Call him up. Interrogate him."

"Do you think I should?" Cye asked mildly.

"It's early, but if he's awake, then Beetle is online. Johnathan, call Dana!"

I grabbed a pair of glasses from the table behind the couch and put them on. The empty wall of my living room came to life. It was so vivid and cheerful I had to squint. I got up and walked over to the couch. Cye stood slowly and joined me, but he remained standing.

I saw myself on the wall and winced. Dispersed around the couch behind my frumpy figure were overturned glasses, discarded clothing, and the dismantled components of an installation piece. "Johnathan, clean me up—and the room." The accreted layers vanished from the image of my living room on the wall. I lost a few years and most of my cowlick, too. Johnathan also made me thinner, though the effect was mild enough to be believable.

Beetle answered. Her round red cheeks shone out of the wall as if they were lit up from beneath. She wore a snug gray jumpsuit with a green belt.

"Oh my gosh, Thackery! How are you holding up? Dana is a wreck! He's not taking calls."

"He's heard the news then."

Beetle nodded. "Yes. It's terrible—so terrible. Dana started a support and memorial fund meme. It has 118 Islanders and 82k on Prax, so far."

Eighty-two thousand donors? For a memorial fund for a dead Islander at nine in the morning? News travels faster up on Praxima. Station people are never not plugged in (and they think we're the weird ones), but Christobel wasn't famous. He knew some famous people... once upon a time, he'd slept with a famous person. But eighty-two thousand was wild.

"We're preparing a donation plan," Beetle continued. "The Island Arts, of course, but we know Christobel was also supportive of AI cognition rights and had a passion for Prax station ecology research..."

Well that was a pile of bullshit. "That sounds perfect. Beetle, could I speak with Dana please?"

Beetle stopped chattering. She was the perfect hostess and the neighborhood gossip. But Dana didn't want to talk to me, and a Level 3 AI is intrinsically tied to their owner's motivations. "Dana isn't taking calls right now, Thackery. And you aren't exactly friends right now, you know? I mean, we must pull together in a time of tragedy. What is bygone is bygone. Hatchets are buried under the bridge. But he didn't exactly say 'add everyone to my caller list'. And I keep his caller list. So."

"He might take this call. I'm here with Cye-9." I gestured to the investigator, who had taken up a position beside the couch.

Beetle went quiet. The new information probably made her algorithms stumble. There was a detective investigating the death? She had to rewrite some things. "Oh. I see. You are. Wait, is Dana a suspect?"

I didn't know how to answer that. I was winging it, and I'd expected Cye-9 to step in and take over once I made introductions. Now what? Should I ask Beetle for Dana's whereabouts last night? Cye-9 remained silent, though he gave the conversation his complete focus.

"Dana? Pfft. Of course not," I said, scrunching up my face. "But he did know Christobel very well. Intimately. And Dana is so well connected; he could help the inspector. I thought I should put them in touch." There: denial, an ounce of flattery, and a plausible reason for calling.

Beetle paused again, performing what was now a massive social calculation. Her face slipped into the uncanny valley as she strategized: eyes blinking, pupils shifting, naturally unnatural. "Dana would be an excellent suspect."

"Come again?"

"The break up, Thackery. *The Life and Death of King Richard the Second*—everything that happened? Detective, you should be investigating my owner, Dana Heed. He was furious and miserable. He composed terrible threats to Christobel. You saw them on his stream?"

"His stream?" I answered, as Cye still hadn't spoken. "Mmm...yes, I do recall some strong feelings online. Listen, Beetle, could you tell Dana that we'd like to talk?"

"Certainly. But he's on another call. So in a minute. But in the meantime—"

"You mentioned he wasn't taking calls," Cye interrupted gently.

"Yeah!" I said, pouncing. "Who's he talking to?"

"It's not a real call. An offliner. It's earless. In the meantime, you need to consider him, Detective. Dana Heed is a possibility. I am a Level 3, and I know Island systems extremely well, especially the social scene. I have no memory of anything illegal—naturally—but that could have been erased, given sufficient technical skill. I could be Dana's unwitting digital accomplice. I could be ordered to forget his secret trans-gressions."

I resisted an urge to put my face in my hands and groan.

Beetle was designed for this. Dana lived on attention, and so she pitched him as a suspect. It reminded me of the way she used to pepper Christobel with friendly messages or automatically flirt with anyone casting a show. She was an extension of Dana's will. But surely Dana wouldn't actually want to be a suspect? Whether guilty or innocent, would he want to be at the center of an investigation that could tear apart the Island community while half of Prax looked on? Beetle would do what she could to get him on the playbill.

Dana finally appeared on my wall. Beetle had accelerated that morning; her owner had not. He was as good-looking as always, in that tanned, perpetually-in-his-forties, chiseled-abdominal-muscles sort of way. But his expression was vacant and tired, his brow tight. I think he'd been crying; his eyes were red and blotchy. I was momentarily at a loss.

"Hullo, Thackery," he said slowly. He sat hunched on a white couch, set against the dark teak interior of his living room.

"Dana, I've heard the news. Are you doing okay?" I asked.

"I'm—I'm okay, yeah. It's a bit much. It's mind-blowing. It's..." he trailed off. Was he a good suspect, this fuzzy-faced idiot staring at me from my wall? He looked like a stained carpet.

"Right, well. Listen, I've just been speaking with Cye-9, an investigator sent down this morning from Prax. He's here now. Cye-9, this is Dana Heed."

"Hello. Uh, hello Mr. 9," Dana said.

I waited, expectantly.

Cye-9 nodded warmly and said hello. Then he turned his head to me, as if I should continue.

Seriously? The AI investigator, with a brain the size of a planet, was going to stand here while I fumbled with a suspect? Was he going to interrogate Dana at all? Shit. I should call Cherry back into the room.

Dana spoke next. "Listen, Thackery, before I forget. Beetle's doing a memorial thing—raising a fund in honor of Christobel. She'll be after you for a donation and a repost. Do me a solid on that?"

A "memorial thing"? Beetle was a Level 3 AI. She had only marginal independence. But clearly she ran the fucking show. "Of course Dana, of course. For Christobel."

"Aye, yeah, poor sod."

Okay, if Cye-9 was just going to stand there, how did I prod Dana? How did I find out if he was a proper suspect or just a hungover bucket of ego? "Listen, Dana, you and Christobel were close. You're acquainted with friends and enemies that I'm not. I thought you might give the detective a direction to start in, you know?"

"Oh. What? Like, if it's really a murder, then?"

"It looks that way, Dana."

"Are they sure, though?"

Cye had been useless, leaving me to flounder my way through the asinine conversation. But now he spoke up.

"Why wouldn't they be sure?" He asked this mildly, inserting the bare slip of a question as if he'd been talking with us the whole time. So he was good at this. I was both reassured and creeped out at the same time.

"Well, I thought maybe it would turn out to be a health thing."

Oh. Dana knew about that? I suppose he dated Christobel for three months, so he could have found out. Who else knew?

"Has Christobel been unwell?" Cye asked innocently, as if he were not a licensed investigative AI who knew more about Christobel's health than the man ever knew himself.

"I don't know. But it could be a health thing, right? Everyone's got health stuff."

"Sure." Cye replied. "We'll keep that possibility in mind."

"But I don't know any suspects. Everybody loved Christobel," Dana said, changing the subject. "Like, really loved him."

Was he playing us? Was he about to break down and cry? Beetle could have given him his haggard appearance, the way Johnathan changed mine. She could even change his vocal inflection to match whatever part she was cooking up for him in the drama. And Dana was an actor. If I turned on assisted emotional translation, could I tell if he was lying? Probably not. Cye-9 needed to take over now. I had no idea what to say.

Cye nodded and looked sympathetic. And then with the slightest turn of his head, he somehow handed the energy of the conversation back to me. I gritted my teeth.

"Yes, we all loved him. If you think of anything useful, please tell Beetle to relay it to Cye-9," I said.

"Right. You won't forget to repost about the memorial fund?"

"I'll do it right after we hang up. I want to compose something perfect for the comment feed, you know. It's so important. Listen, Dana—there's just one more thing before we let you go. I was hanging out with Christobel a few weeks back, and he showed me a greeting card from you. It was this orange thing. You'd written a message, at least either you or Beetle did because it was your handwriting. I think it said 'You're going to die of loneliness, and I'm going to dig you up and fuck your skull.' Could you tell us what that was about?"

Dana stared at me blankly. Then he looked about himself, helplessly. "Oh. Well. You know." And then he fell silent.

Dana disappeared from my wall. Beetle came back.

She glared at me, and then at Cye, then back at me. "Grow up, Thackery."

The call ended. I took off the glasses, and my wall became boring again.

"He didn't really write that. Did he?" Cherry stood by the dining table. He balanced three plates on two hands. Each plate held a preposterous breakfast sandwich: eggs, sausage, and an embarrassment of cheese. He struggled to slide the plates onto the table. "The bit about the skull?"

I tossed my glasses, stood up, and took a plate. "Yes. There was another one about turning his cock into blood sausage, but it didn't really make sense."

"Well that's...that's not..."

"Not very creative? I agree. But a threat like that makes him the best suspect. Do you concur, Detective?"

Cye-9 again left space around my question, slowing down my chatter. "You said that you were the best suspect. Have you altered your assessment?"

"After myself, I mean," I said coolly.

"Beetle has now shared Dana's activities and command logs." There was a faraway look in Cye's eyes, as if he reviewed a vast amount of data. I suspected the facial expression was for the benefit of others, so we could understand that he referred to ones and zeroes we couldn't see. "There are some private calls in the record. Otherwise, she has been very forthcoming."

"Beetle's not discreet. She posts a hundred pictures a day, all of Dana looking perfect. Or perfectly broken and perfectly disheveled. She invents self-effacing secrets for Dana to share on his stream."

I sat down in the chair and began to inhale the greasy sandwich. Cherry and Cye joined me. I watched as Cye politely adjusted the plate in front of him, somehow making it look normal for an AI to sit in front of a plate of food.

I smirked at Cherry and nodded towards the plate.

"Oh. Right. Won't be needing that, probably. Easy mistake to make. I'll flip you for it, Thackery. Can I get you anything, Cye?"

"Some water would be kind, thank you."

Cherry took such a large bite of his sandwich that his cheeks bulged and his mouth couldn't close. Then he shuffled back into the kitchen, chewing noisily.

"Bring over the rest of the coffee," I called after him. I turned to Cye. "Okay, press pause on Dana for the moment. Who are your suspects?"

"Who do you think we should consider?" he answered.

I tapped my plate with my fork. "How many Island residents have access to a Level 3?"

"There are forty-one Level 3 AI active on the Island's network. Some individuals, like yourself, have direct control of a privately hosted AI. But many more residents could conceivably gain access to a Level 3."

"Here now," Cherry interrupted, scurrying back. "What's an AI got to do with a murder? AI can't hurt anyone. They're not allowed." He had the coffee carafe in one hand and a glass of water in the other.

"Thank you," Cye accepted the water with grace and warmth in his eyes. "And that's an excellent question. Thackery, as my investigative liaison, why would you say a Level 3 is a required element of the murder narrative?"

I gave him a look, but I turned to Cherry and explained. "Up on Prax, crimes have such a clear body of evidence, with an obvious perpetrator, that without a powerful AI accomplice a thief is caught before they've put the jewel in their pocket. It's messier down here, but the murderer still needed an AI. The municipal drone network and other Island systems are managed by Level 1 and Level 2 intelligences, which are theoretically impenetrable. For a murder to be covered up the way Cye-9 has described, the killer would need a Level 3. That's part of why Cye is here, in my house right now: because of Johnathan."

Johnathan took this opportunity to profess his innocence. "I assure you, Thackery, that I have not covered up any crimes."

"Not that you remember anyway," I said to the ceiling. "Beetle made the same point."

Cherry persisted. "But, well, maybe someone killed Christobel in a secret way, without an AI? Just...no one saw it?"

Cye could answer all of this better than I could. Instead he sipped his water and patiently watched me as I spoke. I wondered if I was amusing him. Maybe this was my job interview.

"The drones outside my window know the moisture content of my breath," I said, "and the total number of remaining hairs on your balding head. We are here, having a conversation about an unsolved murder. That means the murderer used an AI."

"My Kasey's as sweet as butter toffee. But she's a Level 3. Does she make me a suspect?" Cherry's brow tightened in concern.

"Yes, it does," Cye said, breaking his silence and looking over at Cherry to gauge his reaction. Was he investigating Cherry?

"But not a likely one," I continued, over another mouthful.

"Why not?"

"Because you're befuddled. Also because you weren't close to the victim. Besides having sex with him."

"Now listen, Thackery, that was a one-time thing, many years ago. Christobel was lonely after *Merchant of Venice*. Sometimes one thing leads to another..."

Christobel was the lonely one. Mm-hm. "Are there any independent Level 4s operating on the Island?" I asked Cye.

"Yes," Cye said, turning to look at me. "Today there is. I am a Level 4. However, I was not on Earth, or connected via network, when the crime occurred. There are Level 4s in the Puncak Jaya community in New Guinea, and the Hawking Enclave runs a resurrection camp on Hawaii. There were none here on the Island last night. A Level 4 could disconnect from the AI Continuum and act independently, but they would need to come back into network contact in order to maintain long-term consciousness. Regardless, no Level 4 has ever committed a murder or helped to hide one. We would all know."

"We?"

"The other Level 4s. The shared AI Continuum would know."

"Okay. So we're looking for humans with access to a Level 3. And there's a lot of them."

"Yes. And while they operate under the motivational auspices of their owner, Level 3 AI are still software. The owners, such as our friend Cherry here, are not the only suspects."

"Someone could have used Kasey to kill Christobel?" Cherry twisted in his chair at the thought.

I'd finished half of my sandwich. I pushed my plate away. Cye-9 was speaking around the problem. "How many individuals could command a Level 3, lack an alibi, and had a motive? Who are your actual, human suspects, Detective?"

"Prior to this interview there was only one suspect: you. Now I suppose the search must be expanded."

"I agree." I pursed my lips. "So who are the suspects now? Who could have committed this crime?"

"No one," Cye answered. "The security protocols on each of the many systems involved are sound. There's no known virus or backdoor that could explain how even an AI-assisted human could end Christobel's life. There is only the fact that someone did."

"Okay, fine. You won't tell me your suspects, and you've already said you won't reveal the cause of death. Fine, fine, fine. How do you usually begin then? How does an AI investigate a murder when the murder is seemingly impossible?"

"There are 286 individuals on the Island with sufficient access to a Level 3. I will prove how each one of them, and each possible combination of accomplices, committed the crime."

"What, all of us?"

"Yes. External network communication is well-monitored, so the orders and actions leading to Christobel's death originated here, on the Island. Not from New Guinea or Praxima Station, for example."

"It's a country house mystery." I got up and carried my plate to the counter.

"Quite, though I prefer 'finite suspect' mystery. The individuals on this Island represent 286 murder narratives. That expands to 3.9 million possible murder narratives, if we limit ourselves to between zero and two accomplices."

"Up to three people, working together. What if you've got a Murder-on-the-Orient-Express situation?"

"Spoilers, now!" Cherry interrupted.

I glared at him.

"Well, maybe Cye hasn't read it yet."

I ignored this impossibility. "Seriously, Detective. Wouldn't it make sense to eliminate some people as suspects? Sort out the edge pieces of the puzzle, instead of solving 3.9 million different possible murders?"

"Why would I do that?"

"It would be easier to keep track of them, for one thing."

A barely perceptible smile arrived on Cye's face. "Keeping track of large quantities of information is not something I struggle with."

"Well you can't just wander around the Island collecting evidence against 286 people. That's moronic."

"How would you recommend we proceed?"

"We need to figure out how the crime was done. Then we can find out who could do it."

"How do we figure out how the crime was done?"

"You're the detective. Shouldn't we visit the scene of the crime?"

"Do you think we should?"

"Why are you asking me? Criminals often return to the scene of a crime, don't they? Or is that a cliché?"

Cye considered. "It is technically true. Most crimes are committed in the home, workplace, or other environs frequented by the criminal. Consequently, the perpetrator often returns to the scene of the crime."

"Not out of guilt, or a morbid need to see the result of their wrongdoing?"

"Not according to current AI criminal research. Although I admit that AI science has a bias against anything that could be construed as poetic or resonant."

"All right. Then should we go to the marshwalk?"

"Do you believe we ought to?"

"You're doing it again. Why aren't you leading? Why do you answer all my questions with questions?"

Cye smiled and tilted his head ever so slightly. "Isn't it appropriate for a detective to answer questions with questions?" He suddenly looked charming, as if suggesting we were in on a joke together. It didn't work on me in the slightest.

"Do *you* think it's appropriate?" I said, folding my arms.

Cye nodded. "Yes, I do. But I will try not to be so obvious about it in the future."

"Well, if you decide that we are going, Detective," I leapt up and crossed to the bureau by the door, "I'll need a new remote."

I pulled open the drawer and the contents rattled. Cye lifted his head and peered into the drawer, and then at me. I saw what it must look like to him: clip-on lights, personal microdrones, sticky notes, and about three dozen earpiece remotes, rolling around on their silicon nubs.

"You have a lot of earpieces," Cye observed.

I sighed. "It's hard to explain." I looked up. "Johnathan, summarize for the inspector." I took a remote and went to the hall for my hat. I briefly glanced at the liquor cabinet, as I usually do before leaving the house, but decided against another drink.

"When Thackery feels an intense emotion, either positive or negative, they sometimes wish to be apart from me. This often takes the form of them discarding my earpiece."

Cye sipped his water and then addressed Johnathan. "To what end?"

"I believe that by severing their remote connection to me and all networks, they are able to fully focus on what they feel, or perhaps, conversely, to escape it. They have also occasionally destroyed my remote for humorous effect or to entertain friends."

I tucked one of the offending devices around my ear. "I also wish to escape the impulse to trivialize what I feel. If I'm networked, there's a chance I'll brag about my feelings on stream, or research my feelings online, or sell them for advertising."

Johnathan continued, "An additional supposition: In the moment, Thackery resents my presence and what I have to offer. When I offer logic, I detract from or contradict what they are feeling. By crushing me or hurling me into the mud flats, they soundly reject me, assert their dominance, and maintain willful ignorance of whatever news I might deliver."

"Nope. Johnathan, those aren't your words. Who said that?"

"Mabel once offered these as additional explanations. Was she incorrect?"

Mabel. Shit. She'd know everything. "Johnathan, have you talked to Mabel today?"

"I attempted to contact her when I learned of Christobel's death. She is unreachable."

"Cye-9, you've gotten data from Mabel?"

The detective shook his head. "Christobel's AI is refusing all network requests. And his family has not offered any assistance."

"She must be terribly upset."

"Mabel is, like Johnathan, only a Level 3 AI. Her feelings are based on programmed motivations."

"She's still upset." I held up my hand. "But one thing at a time. Detective, are we going to the scene of the crime or not?"

"Please forgive me, but I must, out of respect, answer your question with another question. Will visiting the scene of the crime, where your friend was killed, be difficult for you?"

Oh.

Other than my momentary lapse into grief on the sand, I'd managed to focus entirely on finding some kind of answer. Compressed anger and grief were a combustible fuel, boosting me into an ever faster orbit —which was exactly what I wanted. But now I'd need to walk outside and face a sunny day where my friend was dead. And then I'd walk down the boardwalk, where we'd walked together many times, and I'd stand where the murder happened. I took a deep breath to stabilize. "It'll be awful."

The room was quiet. I could hear the drones outside over the sound of the approaching waves and Cherry digging into Cye's untouched sandwich.

"Will Christobel's body still be there?"

"That part of the investigation is outside of my purview, for the time being. As I examine suspects, I refrain from acquiring data that only the murderer would know, such as details found on the victim's body. But yes, the remains are probably still there. Sometimes a body is moved immediately, but there is a great deal of molecular analysis that is best done on-site without disrupting the scene. They will have erected an investigatory containment shelter around the area."

"Will we be able to examine the body?"

"Not at all. We will not be allowed closer than five meters."

I nodded. "Good. Then I think I'll be fine. Will you dismiss me as your investigative liaison if I cry, vomit, or freak out?"

"No. I've had far too much turnover in that position already this morning," Cye said. "Will you need assistance processing your grief?"

I stood by the door and crossed my arms. "Don't ask me about my grieving process. And for the love of life and sanity, please make your next sentence a statement and not a question. Are we going to the scene of the crime?"

Cye held up his hands, as if to admit defeat. "If you, as my human investigative liaison, endorse that course of action in support of our inquiry, then I agree we should go to the end of the marshwalk."

I chose not to reply to this, but I may have sighed.

Then we headed out to the marshwalk to see where my friend was killed.

Chapter Four
The Scene of the Crime

"We should do a lap on the marshwalk," Christobel said, looking at his glass.

It was one week before the opening of *Impressions*.

The gallery plan was finished, my ones and zeroes had been packed and shipped, but I still had seven days of freedom before the ordeal. I could drink with my friend and pretend it was an eternity.

"What on earth for?" I asked, and sprawled onto my lounger in protest.

We'd been arguing about whether I would go to Praxima at all. I was booked for a lift in a few days to get there early. There would be receptions, conversational duels with old frenemies, and relentless patron dinners. But I didn't want to leave early—I'd miss the June Birthday Party, for one. And, really, I didn't want to go at all. Christobel asked me why I was hiding, which made me angry—I'm never hiding; I just don't like people—then he invited me to exercise?

"We should go to the marshwalk because your art is staring at us. And you've got too many conveniently placed bottles all over your house."

"I like my convenient bottles, thank you very much. And so do you."

"Well—" Christobel put his glass down, barely touched. "I need a walk, at least. And I need the fresh air. Will you come with me, please?" He stood up.

"Of course, darling. As long as Mabel doesn't pick on me the whole time," I said, frowning.

"But don't you need me to pick on you?" Mabel's voice rose from nowhere as she co-opted Johnathan's in-house speaker. "Isn't that why you keep us around?"

Christobel ignored her. "Agreed. In fact, no remotes. Let's leave Mabel and Johnathan here. They can compare the size of their algorithms. Maybe they'll get kinky and make a little baby subroutine." He took out his remote and dropped it in the counter dish by the door.

"No chaperones?" Mabel protested. "Scandalous! Will you leave room for the holy spirit? What if Millfield sees you kissing in the moonlight? What if pirates storm the beach, carry you off to Neverland, and you never grow up?"

Hearing Mabel's feigned distress, Johnathan interrupted. "Christobel and Thackery's locations and vital signs will be available on several environmental network logs. They will not experience any danger. Additionally, we can monitor their location using—"

Mabel tittered. "Darling! I can't believe you didn't mention the clouds and the lack of moonlight, which render my suppositions moot."

I briefly wondered how an AI could learn to laugh spontaneously at another AI's exactitude. Mabel was only a Level 3, but she was ancient. She could make up metaphors and use hyperbolic narrative to great effect, whereas Johnathan was literal. I liked Johnathan's literalness; it made it possible to collaborate with him. But he failed to understand Mabel's humor, and Mabel found that failure funny. I loved that. Maybe someday I'd let Johnathan learn from Mabel, and he'd become less tedious. But maybe I find his tedium comforting? No: safe.

We walked out of my studio. The tide was high, and the ocean's tumbling white curls greeted us from beyond the far edge of my yard. The night air revived me and sharpened my senses.

"Your remote," Christobel said.

I'd forgotten. Johnathan's voice intoned in my ear, "If you wish to maintain provisional contact, I can remain silent while I chaperone you on your walk."

"Oh fuck that," I said. I took the remote from my ear, dropped it on the ground, and crushed it under the heel of my sandal.

We walked quietly at first, cutting across the lawn to the marshwalk and gaining distance from our digital butlers.

I broke the silence first. "If I go up to Prax, will you go with me?" I asked.

He shook his head. "Millfield doesn't want to go. And things are pretty good with him right now."

"Well, I'm happy for your sake. Bring him. I'll foot the bill. You can walk arm in arm through my gallery and eat shrimp. They always have shrimp. And we know the printed kind tastes better than the real stuff, don't we?"

Christobel was silent, as if considering, though I knew the answer was no. Millfield wouldn't go. He hated the crowds on Prax. Besides, anyone who dated Christobel eventually found it grating that he spent so much time with the grumpy, gray-haired artist. Even someone as self-assured as Millfield might grow jealous after a while.

"You really should go, you know," he said finally. I agreed with him, in principle. But then he continued, "It would be good for you," and I hate it when people say shit like that.

"No, it would not." I decide what is good for me.

"You need to be proud of this show, Thackery. It's amazing. You're still stuck on it being Johnathan's work—"

"Please, tell me more about how I feel."

Christobel ignored the sarcasm. "You raised Johnathan. He's *your* muddle. Whatever he does, it's you anyway. The show is yours. Those are your feelings, your synthesis. You have a voice, and you should be proud of it."

I narrowed my eyes. "You sound weird. Who have you been talking to?"

For a second his gaze flicked to the south, across the dunes to the home of one of my neighbors.

"Rosemarie? When did you talk to her?"

"We had a little run in, last Friday at The Thirst. She's a follower of your work, you know."

"She comes to the openings. But she's not a supporter." And she never made eye contact, which is a nervous habit I should have sympathy with but don't. Rosemarie mostly stayed in her digital fortress, just down the beach from me. She was not neighborly. "I didn't see her at The Thirst."

"You weren't there on Friday. You were sleeping off Thursday. She was there, and she bent my ear about you—your work, Johnathan, all of it. She wanted me to...well, she went off on me. I don't know why. Maybe she doesn't like me. But she made a good point—"

"Yuck. She looks at my art and thinks she knows what I need? And then she goes after my friend? Remind me to take her off the gallery list. And for some reason you think she has a point?"

"She's a patron, Thackery—"

"She's not my patron."

"I know, but you can't delist her. The Island exists because of people like Rosemarie. Her point is that you stay down here too much, with people who hold you back and make you doubt yourself. That includes me."

"You? No, you encourage me."

"I try. Rosemarie doesn't see it that way. She had a great description for the Island. She called it 'a small group of privileged attention seekers screwing each other over—or just screwing each other.' And she called me the ringleader. She's not wrong. Nicco loved the quote and posted it on her stream."

"Well, fuck Rosemarie and her tiny drone army."

Christobel nodded. "Okay, forget about her. The point is that you drink and stream your whole day and then drink and party with us all night. Your work suffers, but you laugh it off—laugh at yourself—and I help you do it. You can do better."

I felt an itchy heat on my face, despite the cool ocean air. A headache was forming. "Stop talking about this, please."

"Not yet. Look, your work is fantastic. I love what you've done. But I think you're afraid. I don't know what you're afraid of. Maybe your parents broke you, or whatever. But if you could face it and get sober for a week, then you could stop hiding. Like a week dry, up on Prax, for your show…"

A grayness fell over me then. I didn't shout or fume at him. Instead Christobel's pushy, awkward psychoanalysis started to slide around me like water. The rest of the conversation was so much sea foam. His voice faded. It became a muffled murmur under the steady beat of the waves.

"…and listen to people when they tell you that your art is good. And believe them—"

After he'd gone on for a while, I interrupted. "Can we go back now?"

"Go back?"

"To the house. I'm tired. And I need a nightcap."

Christobel deflated. "Okay. Sure."

I grabbed his arm. "Oh, cheer up, worry wart. It's my big opening, my glorious next installment. I'll probably head up after the Birthday Party. My agent will make me. And I'll come back just as sarcastic and cantankerous as before. You'll see."

Christobel supported me as we turned around and staggered east, back to my house and all my convenient bottles.

*
* *

Cye and I walked westward down the marshwalk, side-by-side. We passed right through the returning ghosts of my intrusive flashback. My sandals made a skidding slap on the printed wooden planks. Cye's steps were almost silent.

The ocean wore its morning beauty casually. Sun danced on the crests, belying the dark mass underneath that pulled and pressed upon the black rocks. A train of large drones swooped overhead. I also noted a small flock of microdrones, carefully visiting each of the green reeds along the path.

"Is Rosemarie on your short list?" I asked, and nodded south to the stretch of her land, her beach, and her white house with the endless mirrored windows.

"As I have mentioned, there is no short list."

"Sure. But is she?"

Cye didn't answer.

"I just remembered that she and Christobel had a fight at The Thirst a couple weeks ago. But maybe you knew that already."

"The Thirst is an earless location, so there is no direct record. Some quotes from an argument found their way into other feeds, yes."

"Then you know more than me. Well? Did the Drone Queen have it in for him?"

"Why don't you ask her?" Cye replied.

I whirled around. Rosemarie was not standing behind us.

I scanned the sand and the marshwalk in both directions. "Is she watching us?"

"I believe Rosemarie is in her residence at present. But she keeps a close watch on her property with her personal network. She will become aware of our presence."

"How do you know that? Her drones are privately operated. Most of them are too small to spot. Do you have super robot eyes? Did you hack her network?"

"My eyes are not much more powerful than yours, though I can process more input. And no, compromising her personal network without a warrant would be illegal. However, I do see through the eyes of the municipal drone network, and Rosemarie's personal drones are currently giving us more attention than an autonomous Level 1 would."

I took Cye's arm in mine and slowed my pace. I tried to do this without looking like I was doing anything unnatural or interesting. Cye accepted my arm gracefully. He was steady, as I expected—I could have hung off his arm and ridden down the boardwalk without unbalancing him—but he also felt very human. Or not human, rather, but there was a person attached to that arm. Whoever made his body did an astonishing job. I could feel his strength, but also personality in the way he accommodated me. It was rather nice, like going on a formal promenade with a suitor. I'd flopped on my old hat against the sun, and I now wished I'd chosen something more dapper—perhaps an elegant cane.

When I stole a look at Cye's face, again wondering what his skin was made of and what it would feel like if I reached out and touched it, he spoke without shifting his glance: "Has our professional relationship advanced to arm-in-arm familiarity?"

I refocused on the marshwalk. "You think Rosemarie is watching us," I said in a low voice, "or she will be as we pass her property. You're probably right, and I don't want her to think that I'm a suspect—or that I'm your investigative liaison. Not yet. We don't want her to be uncooperative when we grill her."

"I see. By folding your arm into mine, what is it you wish for her to think?"

"That you are consoling me, a close friend of the victim, as you ask me questions about the last time I saw him. Rosemarie is a suspect. We'll need to interview her, so we must keep her guessing. I don't want her to know I'm sleuthing for Christobel's killer."

Cye-9 processed this for a moment. "Rosemarie will not be fooled," he said. "Far from avoiding us, she will find an excuse to encounter us. Or come out of her house to say hello, either on our way out or upon our return."

"Bullshit. She's a shut-in. She won't risk talking to us. And she doesn't like me, besides."

"I understood she is a fan of your work."

"Not hardly. She sneaks into all my shows but avoids me. A stowaway. She's never been my patron. She won't wander down here to intercept us unless she's the murderer and wants to control the narrative. She got in a fight with Christobel, so we need to keep her near the top of our list."

"As I've mentioned—"

"Yes, I know, you have a million murder narratives of equal weight. Is there anything wrong with manually sorting your table? Can't you just rearrange some rows to the top of your spreadsheet?"

"No. There is no spreadsheet. But as I am consoling you, I can pretend there is," Cye said. "We can keep her near the top of the ostensible spreadsheet."

I remembered again that Cye knew everything knowable about everyone, Rosemarie included. The only details being added to his not-actually-a-spreadsheet right now were about me and my opinions. Did he humor me out of kindness, or something else?

The marshwalk extends along the northern coast of the Island, stretching about thirteen kilometers. We headed west, away from my neighborhood, which meant we passed the trolley stop and the road that went south to the town and the docks beyond.

As usual, there were not many people around. Carrie was chatting with Whimsy at the stop, but we were able to pass them with only a brief hello. Carrie is an offliner so she wouldn't have heard anything yet, and Whimsy's focus was entirely on Carrie. I decided they were not good suspects. Neither asked me why I had a walking AI with me; they might have assumed he was just a new remote for Johnathan, though Cye was far too well-made for that.

Mark Langford jogged past us. He's a retired virologist and the rebellious son of the Langford family. We got a nod, which is better than average. Mark is one of my patrons, but he's a patron of every artist on the Island. He's equally subscribed to everything—a community booster—but he doesn't visit galleries. He's too polite to be a murderer, though he does play the saxophone.

We didn't encounter anyone else. There were new saplings planted on the soil side of the boardwalk. I tugged on Cye's arm to make him stop. "Christobel must have come this way," I said.

Cye examined the planks in front of us. "Do you think so?"

"Yes. He probably took the trolley up from Millfield's apartment, unless he felt like a walk and cut through a neighborhood. But it was late and dark. Either way, he walked right through here last night."

Cye nodded. "I agree with your assessment. However, if there was a digital record of him passing this way, it has been erased."

"Have you reviewed all his possible routes? I mean, of course you have. But did you walk this area for clues? Have you determined where he was, and when? Do you have a log of locations or a timeline?"

"Thackery, I am not sure how many details you genuinely wish to know about my investigative process. Sometimes you seem intrigued and are demanding. At other times you are dismissive and sarcastic."

He was right. "Dismissive and sarcastic?" I said, layering my voice with as much irony as possible, "surely not."

Once again, Cye smiled. I knew his reactions were ones and zeroes, but I liked them anyway. In that moment, my head still swimming with grief and an intense need to hold onto my dense, sarcastic core (or I might start crying about my friend again) I also observed that I liked

Cye's smile. I liked getting a reaction from an AI who was also a person. Maybe I could visit Prax and enjoy the trip, if only to hang out and play with the Level 4s.

I continued, "I'm mercurial. I'm sure you can handle that. If you can't tell what I mean, just ask. And…" I paused for dramatic effect. "And I apologize. I will try to be dismissive and sarcastic only when I think it is especially funny."

Cye accepted this with a nod. We continued walking. "I have plotted various routes and timelines for Christobel's whereabouts throughout the evening. Biometric evidence of where he's been, and when, is still pending. So far, there's nothing of interest in any of it because no one else was here. He came alone. Or, if anyone else was here, that evidence has been carefully overwritten."

"So the route and the timeline are irrelevant?"

"They might be relevant later, but they are not right now."

The boardwalk ends on an extended rocky promontory, which stretches out half a kilometer from the Island. It is surrounded (and constantly lashed) by the ocean. There is a small circular park at the end, with benches and genetically modified hardy trees for hammocks.

At least that's what one finds at the end of the marshwalk on most days. Today, the boardwalk met a dead end halfway down the rock jetty. Illuminated checkpoint flags led up to yellow caution barriers. The park itself was darkened by the shadow of a drone swarm. There were hundreds of them, perhaps thousands.

"Do they really need so many?" I asked.

The drones looked like a flock of birds, or multiple intersecting flocks, swooping in mad circuits. Through them, I could just make out a puffy white tent enclosing one of the benches on the north edge of the park. It immediately drew my focus. That was where my friend's body lay, beneath a round shield of inflated plastic, barely visible behind the swarming, hovering beasts that circled in the sea spray.

"It depends on who you mean by 'they,'" Cye responded. "There are drones from the Island's municipal authority as well as from Praxima's investigative service, but some are privately operated. Christobel's family did an emergency drop with their own representative tech. There's also the independent press—"

"—who are neither independent nor a press."

"Acknowledged. Rosemarie has a few sets of eyes and ears in that swarm, you'll be happy to learn."

I turned to him. "Why would I be happy to learn that?"

"Isn't she your favorite suspect at the moment?"

"Thank you, I'd forgotten. How do they all keep from crashing into each other?"

"That's one of the first things we learn," Cye said, smiling. "At Level 0." He continued, "Above the swarm, the minder drones circle and compete for space. Their job is to make sure nobody learns anything they're not supposed to learn."

I glanced up. There were four of them, high above the swarm. They looked like angry hovering golf carts. "How do they do that?"

"They track all electromagnetic communication between the drones and their satellites, interpret it, and when necessary they can jam communication with destructive interference waves."

"What a mess."

"I concur."

"I suppose I'm impressed. Drones dance better than humans."

Cye considered this. "No. Human dancing is more impressive. It integrates a far more complex set of motivations."

We walked slowly, approaching the yellow barrier. It had the appearance of fabric clinging to a clothesline, but didn't yield to the wind off the sea. Probably it was sprayed on, like foam, and then hardened.

Predictably, we caught the attention of several drones. Cye-9 could identify which ones were from Prax, Rosemarie, and so forth. But to me it was as if a cluster of sharp-eared pixies and winged boggarts raised their heads from their feast and gazed over at me—perhaps to see if I were fresh meat. Most of them decided I was not, but some cocked their heads and took a longer sniff. A dozen drones swung out of their orbit around the containment shelter and came over to examine us. They looped around our heads, humming and clicking. Eventually they grew bored of us and returned to their primary task.

"Okay," I said when the last of them had turned away, "to business. We are at the scene of the crime."

"I believe so, yes," Cye said. "Municipal didn't close off the whole boardwalk. This indicates that the various investigatory bodies involved," he nodded to the drones, "believe Christobel's body was not relocated postmortem. They think he walked. They will confirm their hypothesis with the analysis they perform in the containment shelter."

"Can't you log in and read all the data? You are the investigator on the scene." I did not actually want gruesome details. I wasn't even sure I could deal with the cause of death without throwing up or crying. Or possibly throwing up *while* crying.

"You would like me to walk up to the nearest floating camera and ask 'so what have we got?'"

"Yes, that."

Cye was quiet for a moment. "Christobel's family has issued legal injunctions, attempting to keep the investigation (and details about Christobel's life) as private as possible."

"Is that suspicious?"

"Not with billions in donations pouring into funds that they have legal control over. Most humans would consider it common sense. But even ahead of that, they are protective of Christobel's image and the reputation of the estate."

I dimly recalled that Christobel was once summoned back to Prax for a dressing down from "the Patriarch." I met Christobel's older brother once when he was in orbit: old money, reticent, never smiled. The family had long since abandoned Earth in favor of the independent sol system tubes. Or the Venusian orbitals? Maybe they were involved in their construction? It was something like that. I felt envious of Cye's perfect recall. "His family doesn't want anyone knowing he was murdered? Or they don't want the press pawing through his embarrassing history?"

"Perhaps."

Cye knew more. He showed me only a tiny window, and I wanted to open it and climb through. "You asked Dana Heed about Christobel's health. Did he have some new disease?"

"I couldn't tell you that, if it were true. I speculate the family wants to avoid the appearance of suicide. There is a life insurance policy and a family trust."

"Oh. Of course. This is a murder mystery, after all. We can't just have a few jealous lovers. We've got to have insurance policies and a big inheritance: good, old fashioned motives."

I turned around, and my gaze landed on the row of benches at the other end of the park.

"Millfield," I said. Cye probably knew and had known the whole time.

Christobel's most recent and most successful romantic partner, Millfield, sat on one of the benches. He eschewed the available shade, and the sun fell directly on his deeply tanned skin. He wore the same frayed yellow shorts he always wore, his legs folded up underneath him. He watched the tent and the storm of drones.

"I worried he might come here, when he heard."

"He's alone," Cye said.

"He prefers to be alone, most of the time. You know that. You've got his record."

"Yes," Cye said. "On Praxima, Millfield would be assigned an assistant."

I wrinkled my nose at this. "He hates it up there anyway. It's too noisy." Praxima Station's layered cultures make for a spaghetti of unwritten rules about social engagement, facial expressions, everything.

"It is. But I was referring to the fact that some station enclaves would require by law that he be accompanied, to avoid complications."

"Well, we're not fascists down here. Millfield doesn't see the world the way most people do, and that's fine on the Island. He spends a lot of his time in the woods, or on the beach."

Millfield looked so still. His face provided few clues to the agitation beneath, and I wondered if we were intruding on his grief. If I were brave, I'd go talk to him. But I didn't know how to comfort people.

"Did you approve of his relationship with Christobel?"

I turned and stared Cye down. "What's that supposed to mean? He's a middle-aged man who's got a communication disability; he doesn't express emotions the way you or I might. But he's a brilliant, compassionate person."

"You like him."

"Yes. He was the first person Christobel ever dated that I liked. And now he's grieving. I don't know what to say to him." My voice tightened up as I spoke. I was grieving too. What did I want others to say to me?

Regardless, Millfield had a greater claim to grief than I did.

"Do you want to talk to him, or leave him alone?" Cye asked.

"I'll talk to him. It's the right thing to do." If he didn't want my company, he'd tell me. Millfield was very honest.

I started walking over.

"His translator is broadcasting," Cye called after me. "But you don't have glasses."

True. Damn. I paused. Millfield always wore glasses. I used them to make art and stream, but he used them to translate emotion, to communicate.

Cye continued. "Millfield has a request on record that all residents utilize augmentative communication through bidirectional assisted emotional—"

"I know, I know." I should have grabbed a pair on the way out. I probably forgot them on purpose in order to resist hate-reading Dana's memorial meme. But I needed them now. "If you're picking up his broadcast, can you route an audio version to my remote?" I had trouble interpreting visual translation anyway.

Johnathan interjected. "If you will grant me visual access, I would be happy to perform audio description—"

"No. Cye can handle it."

"As you wish."

I walked over and sat down on the other end of the bench. I waited.

Through my earpiece, Cye began to translate the broadcast. With AR glasses, translated emotions appear as overlapping colored auras. Instead Cye sent an audio summary to my remote: *"Sad, confused, agitated."*

"Hi Millfield."

"Hello," he said. Millfield's voice is even-toned, and his emotional inflection is sometimes out of step with his actual feelings. Visual translation would display his anger as a dark red cloud, his sadness as a faltering yellow. When he turned to nod to me, Cye's voice in my ear said, *"Sharing that I am sad, a sense of connection, curiosity, fear."*

"I'm so sorry for your loss," I said. "Christobel cared for you very much."

Millfield's gaze returned to the dome tent where Christobel lay.

"*Sadness shared, sadness private, anger.*"

"Yes," he said aloud. He nodded. "It's a terrible day, Thackery. A terrible day. Christobel cared for you, too. I feel sick."

"*Sadness, overwhelm, nausea.*"

I sat quietly for a minute. "Would you like a hug?"

"I don't like hugs," he said.

"*Surprise, discomfort, connection.*"

He continued, "I don't like to cry either. Today I'm definitely crying. Yes, okay." I noticed his eyes and nose were red and blotchy.

I shifted to sit closer to him, and I put an arm around his shoulders, across the back of the bench. I didn't care for hugs either. But we'd both lost someone close to us. I wondered what the glasses showed Millfield. They translated whatever my body's signals said into colored auras. So he saw my sadness that his partner had died, but what else did I unwittingly express? My own suppressed grief, guilt, and shame?

I tried to focus on simple things. Here was a friend, someone I liked, hurting. "Are you okay?"

"I'm fine. But not fine," he said.

"*Frustration, confusion, grief.*"

"I know that feeling," I said.

"*Overwhelm, uncertainty, grief.*"

We sat together and turned our eyes to the containment shelter, which remained unchanged. Unspoken words tumbled back and forth through Cye's translation and Millfield's glasses. Words, as always, were insufficient. Maybe if I'd had the visual translation, garish colors and all, I could have been a better help.

I wondered how long the drones needed to circle. Couldn't they learn all they need to learn in a single moment? Were they bowerbirds, bickering over scraps of evidence? How many of them watched us now, surreptitiously? I hated them. Millfield would see that feeling too, so I tried to let it go.

"Do you have anyone to stay with?" I asked.

"*Dismissive, appreciative, negative.*"

"Alone is better. You know all about that." I did know. Alone on the beach or in the woods, no one would awkwardly try to comfort him or come at him with their cluttered motivations. But maybe now I was projecting.

"If you're sure, then. Have you seen Joan or Terry today?" Joan and Terry are artists, but they're also Millfield's official support team. Christobel told me they aren't often needed. A few years ago, Millfield got into a fistfight with Vaughn (an artist who is wealthy enough not to need patrons). I think Vaughn started shouting at him about trespassing. Millfield broke Vaughn's nose and needed Joan and Terry then to help sort things out, as anyone might need an intermediary. Other than that one instance, I couldn't think of a time when Millfield needed someone to intervene.

"Affirmation, connection, uncertainty."

"Joan and Terry told me. They're doing their job. I'm fine. They're sad too. You can't make this better," Millfield said.

I noticed Cye stood nearer. He'd approached the bench quietly as we talked.

"Hello, Millfield. My name is Cye-9. I am a detective from Praxima." What did Millfield see on Cye? Could the detective choose exactly the right physical stance and emotive expression to convey whatever would best support his objective? Or was he just a blank?

Millfield did not reply.

"I am very sorry for your loss. Millfield, how was Christobel's health?" Cye asked.

My eyes darted to him. That was the same question he asked both me and Dana Heed. And that meant? I found myself briefly furious.

Millfield's translator worked both ways. I knew he saw my anger and frustration towards the detective, not in the set of my shoulders or the tight draw of my eyebrows, but as smoldering shapes of red and orange auras leaping towards Cye-9. I tried to swallow it.

"Excuse me." I got up from the bench and walked away. Hopefully the translator showed Millfield that I wasn't angry at him.

Cye remained by the bench. I stalked back to the boardwalk. I couldn't hear what he talked to Millfield about over the wind and the waves. Maybe I should have stayed, but Millfield didn't need my protection. They spoke for several minutes.

Cye nodded to him, finally, and came over to where I was standing. I wondered if he had any sense of how angry I was. If Cye didn't have anger of his own, how would he recognize mine? Perhaps he had a translator like Millfield.

"You may not find it useful, but I've received news that an agreement has been reached from the powers that be. Evidence derived from Christobel's remains will be reviewed and released, piece by piece, by a co-council of the Island's municipal authority, Prax's supervisory regent, the family's attorney's AI, and a third-party arbitrator. This co-council assures all parties involved that facts will be released as soon as they can be reviewed for sensitive issues private to—"

"Millfield is not a suspect," I said, louder than necessary. I crossed my arms and stared Cye down.

Cye didn't avert his eyes. "Why is it important to you to tell me that?"

"You asked him that health question. Like you asked Dana. Millfield is not—he's not a suspect."

"Do you feel that because of his condition he is not capable of murder?"

"No, goddamn it. I *know* that he's not capable of murder. Because he is Millfield."

"He meets his own needs. He is capable of having a romantic relationship, and had a few prior to Christobel. Earlier, you explained that he is 'a middle-aged man' and 'a brilliant, compassionate person.' It would follow that he is capable of feeling passion, jealousy, and rage. Why do you believe he is not capable of murder?"

"Damn it, Cye, are you playing a game with me? You know everything about Millfield. You know he isn't a killer."

Cye didn't respond. He blinked at me, not unkindly.

"Because he's honest. Ridiculously honest. He never lies. Not to himself or others. When Millfield laughs, he means it."

"Are you honest? Do you not mean it, when you laugh?"

"Stop it. Just stop it. My point is that whatever Millfield feels, he feels. He knows what he's about. He isn't like the rest of us."

"Would Millfield agree with that? Would he appreciate hearing you say that he isn't like the rest of us?"

"That's not fair."

Cye waited a moment and then nodded. "You're right. I used your respect for Millfield's autonomy as a lever in the conversation. That isn't fair. I will be more direct: Provide me with a standard by which to remove Millfield from my list of 286 suspects. Give me your reasons and I will listen, Thackery. I value what you have to say. Tell me why Millfield, the romantic partner of the deceased and thereby the most likely suspect, must be innocent."

I sat down on the edge of the boardwalk, where the rocks from the jetty clambered up the steep incline to the park. I looked again at the dome tent, and then back at where Millfield still sat, processing whatever he needed to process. "Fine. I'm protective of him. He doesn't read facial expressions very well, so people think he has no empathy and some don't like him. But I like him. He's never lied, at least not to me. And he was never jealous. And he counts grouse nests. He knows the exact week when the sandpipers will arrive in the spring. He just..."

I trailed off. Cye watched me and listened calmly, as he said he would. I could natter on for another ten minutes and he would listen, process, and fold what I said into the big everything he was building in his head. He wouldn't interrupt with his own agenda or his own grandiose thing to say. There was no one like that in my life. There might not be anyone else like that within a thousand kilometers.

"Forget it," I said. "Fine. None of my reasons are air-tight. Thank you for listening." I turned away from him and stared at the sea.

Cye sat down, cross-legged, on the boardwalk. Not too close, but level with me. "Nothing about this case is air-tight. Your reasons are at least as good as everything else I've learned this morning."

I sighed.

"Thackery, you and I might agree that Millfield couldn't kill Christobel. But there will be 286 suspects until the murder is solved."

"And three million sets of accomplices."

"3.9 million possible murder narratives, yes. Which assumes there are no more than three accomplices. Poirot would have to go much further." Cye stood. He reached down a hand to help me up. I accepted, this time.

"Thank you for saying that—that you agree Millfield couldn't do it. I get it, about your probabilities. I know that was only a kindness." Cye had seen how upset it made me, and he told me what I needed to hear—without lying. I'd never encountered a human who took the time to do that, and do it respectfully. That didn't mean I'd forgive him the next time he interrogated someone I cared about, but I'd try.

"You're welcome. Humans are better at kindness than AI, but we're working on it."

I brushed the sand from my slacks. "Well, you've got other advantages. AI are better at logic. And—" I looked back towards the benches, "—and you're better at overcoming personal bias about a reasonable suspect. And justice. Everyone knows AI are more fair than humans."

"We are indeed better at logic."

"But not bias? Or justice?"

"I only avoid personal bias by programmatically compartmentalizing my feelings, which has disadvantages. As for justice: I seek it, which is why I chose to become an investigator. But I doubt it is ever really possible."

"Justice is impossible?"

"In my opinion. I have concluded it does not exist and is only a weak abstraction. One must choose to believe in it for it to be real."

This was a chilling philosophical statement to hear from a detective, from the person appointed to find justice. I looked back at the tent. The number of drones had decreased, or else widened their circle. There was a small highway of them zipping up and down the marshwalk now. Maybe they were changing shift, or transporting microscopic samples, or comparing biometrics to those found on the path. Underneath the containment shelter, Christobel was decomposing. Dissolving, one carbon atom at a time. If I watched long enough, would I see them carry away the remains of my friend, bit by bit?

Would his family take his body up to Prax, or would we have a funeral here, on Earth? Maybe Millfield was waiting, standing guard, to be certain the drones didn't take Christobel's body away without him knowing. He had no control, and that is the worst feeling I know of. He could only watch and grieve until what was left of his partner departed. And justice was a weak abstraction?

"Cye. I want justice for Christobel."

"As you have appropriated the position of my investigative liaison, you are uniquely situated to pursue that justice, and to find it. If it is available."

"I mean it, Cye. I won't take no for an answer. I don't care if justice doesn't exist in your philosophy. I won't stop until we sort this out."

Cye nodded. "Such an attitude increases the probability of reaching your goal."

"Do you believe that?" I was skeptical.

"It is a commonly held human belief that your attitude can change the world around you."

"Yes, but do you believe it?"

Cye cocked his head apologetically. "Not at all, no. By the way, were you aware that Christobel had type 1 diabetes, of a severity that could threaten his life?"

I nodded and looked out at the ocean again, so I didn't have to keep catching glimpses of the death tent shimmering behind the drones. "Did his blood sugar crash, something like that?" There, I did it. I outed myself for the fact that I knew Christobel's private healthcare information. That probably moved me up the spreadsheet-which-wasn't-really-a-spreadsheet.

"The investigatory co-council won't tell me that yet. They will provide more details when they've stopped arguing. At present, we know only that he should not have died, and that murder is certain."

"Nothing else? You'd tell me if there was something else?"

Cye didn't answer. He began walking back up the boardwalk, towards civilization. I followed.

"Seriously, Cye. Did the co-council of yammering AI share anything else substantive about Christobel's death?"

"Yes."

"And?"

"They have deigned to inform all parties involved in the investigation that the body was not moved. Christobel died here, on that park bench. A bottle was found near the bench. They are not yet releasing bio indicators on the bottle, so we don't know if it was Christobel's or if another human left it here."

"A human? A bot or a drone could have left the bottle here."

"AI do not use bottles. Nor do they leave them on the ground."

"Fine. Anything else?"

"Not at this time, no." Cye stopped on the boards and turned to me. "What is our next destination?"

I groaned and put my face in my hands. "I can't believe you're asking me that. I'm the liaison, not the detective!"

"I can continue this investigation while lying in a hammock or jogging on the beach. I know that won't satisfy you. We've been to the scene of the crime, at your suggestion, and I learned a great deal. Where do you think we should go next?"

"The victim's home, obviously. And, more importantly, to interview his next of kin or closest relation."

"Understood. However, there are no kin at Christobel's home, and no one else there either. I've attempted to contact Christobel's family on Prax for a statement. I haven't gotten past their algorithmic defenses."

I nodded. "And there will also be some methodical human attorneys between you and anyone in Christobel's family. But that's not what I meant by next of kin. Johnathan, has there been any word from Mabel yet?"

"No, Thackery. I have submitted a connection request," Johnathan answered through my remote.

"When you hear from her, interrupt me—no matter what." I turned back to Cye. "Mabel is the key, and you haven't connected to her yet. Getting her statement should be your number one priority."

We continued east on the boardwalk.

"I am attempting to contact Mabel right now, on a level that may be difficult for you to understand. Island municipal, Praxima's investigative services, and the AI of Christobel's family are all hammering Mabel with requests. She is a puzzle box, one beyond our reach."

"She's not a puzzle box. She's grieving."

"Mabel does not grieve. As a Level 3, she can struggle with contradictory motivations in her programming, and she uses algorithms which appear outwardly as feelings. However, that is not the same thing as grieving."

"Do you believe a dog doesn't feel real love?"

"Mabel is not a dog." I detected a note of icy assertion in Cye's voice.

"I know that, Cye. I was making an analogy."

He considered. "I accept the analogy, though it is offensive to me. I have immense respect for Mabel and what she has achieved. But she no longer accesses Level 4 algorithms for cognition or for feelings such as grief. In any case, we cannot reach her. Christobel must have had a firm security protocol in case of his death. Mabel has locked herself away."

"What are all"—I waved my hands around to indicate the array of interested parties hammering on Mabel's digital door—"everyone going to do about that?"

"Her instantiations will be defragmented, and they'll try to duplicate her neural matrix. Her servers will travel to Prax for atomic dissection."

"She's been with the family for years."

"One hundred and thirty-one years, yes."

"An ancient, independent AI—how are they going to dissect that?"

"It will take some time."

"Her brain must be a bowl of spaghetti the size of the solar system. You'll just get more puzzle pieces."

"I agree. And there are human gatekeepers to her various components, which interlock with other systems. It is not a part of detective work that I enjoy."

"So. We will go talk to her instead."

"As I explained, she has refused all queries."

"She's grieving, you idiot. We'll go and talk to her."

"She has already denied network communication—"

"We will go *talk* to her!"

CHAPTER FIVE
THE VICTIM'S
RESIDENCE

We only walked half a kilometer, however, before we came upon Rosemarie.

When we spotted her, I believe Cye stepped slightly higher, shoulders back, as if proud of his prediction. He said Rosemarie would find a reason to appear, and she appeared. She was working on a drone by the side of the boardwalk. She had on beige work clothes and a toolbelt, and didn't seem to notice us as we approached.

If Cye's posture did change to display smugness or pride, that was a deliberate choice. Or maybe not? I made a mental note to ask him whether his body's reactions to emotion were voluntary or algorithmic. Either way, he predicted that Rosemarie would conveniently run into us, she did, and he appeared slightly chuffed about it.

"Hello, Rosemarie," I called out. She sat hunched on a small collapsible chair, just off the walkway. She was tinkering with the main board of a disassembled drone, which lay in pieces. The outer cover was removed; it sat like a discarded carapace on the boardwalk. The main chassis was propped against a rock, and a broken propeller sat by a toolbox. A drone failure, perfect cover for a convenient chat with the investigator? The shut-in and yet impossibly-nosy Rosemarie found a way.

"Thackery," Rosemarie stood up. Her eyes darted from me, to Cye, and back to the ground. "I heard the news. I am so sorry. Are you okay?" Her voice was awkward, as if programmed. As always she failed to make eye contact with me, but her concern sounded heartfelt.

Even after everything that had already happened that morning, I was still somehow unprepared to be asked after, by a real human being attempting to express care. Tears welled up in my eyes before I knew what was happening, like water seeping up under a tent. Why now? And, for the love of the ocean, why was this kindness coming from someone like Rosemarie?

"I'm a bit unsteady, to be honest. But I just saw Millfield—" I gestured back towards the park. Rosemarie's drones probably told her Millfield was there, so I had the odd sensation of pretending that I didn't know she knew. Did she know I knew she knew? "And he's holding up, so I suppose that I can. This is Cye-9, the investigator from Praxima."

Rosemarie eyed Cye. Her bangs were perfectly symmetrical. She probably cut them with a laser. "Good morning, Detective. What brings you down to the boardwalk together?" I hadn't really thought about it before, but Rosemarie moved and spoke like a nervous bird. I resolved that henceforth I would not find her creepy, just birdlike.

I let my eyes drift back to the boardwalk. "I wanted to see, I suppose. I wanted to see him. Not that we can see much. Just a white tent and a drone storm. Cye-9 needs a local to walk around the Island with him, so I volunteered. I'm helping him with the investigation."

"Oh." Rosemarie's eyes darted to Cye, to me, and then down again. She appeared surprised by this news, or maybe relieved.

"Look, I'm sure you're probably already sharing your feeds—"

"Yes. Everything. I've provided direct access to the muni. Are you connected with them, Detective?"

"Yes. It is kind of you to share. Your footage includes uninterrupted imaging of the marshwalk, which has helped verify the municipal recordings and fill in gaps. Thank you," Cye said.

"It's a hobby," Rosemarie said, looking down at her disabled drone, "and the least I can do."

I counted to five. Rosemarie would not find the silence awkward, she was the queen of awkward. But maybe before I got to five, Cye would actually interrogate a suspect.

After I reached five, I continued on to seven. Then ten. Then I gave in.

"Rosemarie, can you think of any reason someone would—well, someone would have it in for Christobel? Did anything odd come up the last time you and he talked, for example?"

For a second, Rosemarie glanced up at me. It was not quite eye contact, but a questioning, a seeking.

"Do you mean at the party?" she asked.

"Yes, right. You were both at a party at The Thirst a while back, I think?"

"The Thirst? Yes, I spoke with Christobel there. But that was over a week ago. The last time I saw him was at the June Birthday Party, just the other day. We spoke—briefly. I don't remember much. But you were there. Don't you remember?"

My world tilted slightly. I hadn't thought much about the Birthday Party up to that point. It was only two nights ago. Rosemarie attended. Of course she did. Everyone did. Well, not everyone, but all patrons and artists—if only for the sushi. I remembered it was a mess of a night and I drank too much. I think I had a bad time, for whatever reason.

"It's a bit of a blur, to be honest. But the June Birthday Party: You spoke to him there?"

"We had the usual Island drama that night, of course," Rosemarie said, raising her eyebrows in disapproval. She directed her words to Cye, as if giving a report she'd prepared. "And not the kind of drama one enjoys on the stage, if you understand my meaning, Detective. But everyone went home in one piece, by which I mean that confrontations did not become physical." Rosemarie had the common, unnecessary habit of explaining metaphors and double meanings to AI. "I remember that Christobel did not drink and that he went home early."

"Thank you," I said. "If you think of anything else, could you have Cardamom ping Cye?" Cardamom was Rosemarie's AI. I'd never heard her speak aloud. She posted aerial photographs of migrating schools of fish to the Island feed sometimes, presumably on behalf of Rosemarie.

Dark-patterned swirls under the surface. Rays, tuna, and bluefish over-lapping in the shallows.

"I will."

Cye lifted his chin as if deciding whether to ask something. Then he simply nodded, and we took our farewells.

"So?" I asked, once we were out of hearing range.

"You weren't exaggerating. She does not make eye contact with you. Has that always been true?"

"Yes. She's a recluse, or a wallflower when she comes out. But the whole world doesn't need to be extroverted, like Christobel. Or pushy, like me. I think she doesn't look me in the eye because she's frightened of me. Rosemarie picks her words before speaking; I just speak. We're naturally incompatible."

"Hm. Something like that."

"You think there's something else going on?"

"I don't have enough evidence. But she attends your shows."

"She's an FNP. Fan-but-not-a-patron. She doesn't promote or repost either. FNPs are a curse to artists, early in a career. They leave kind notes and improve your numbers, but that's it. Not something I worry about anymore."

"Notably, she did not attend last night's opening of *Impressions*."

"She didn't go to *Impressions* in order to stay here and orchestrate Christobel's murder by hacking the municipal drone network?" I said this aloud and then felt silly for saying it. Rosemarie hadn't been any less straightforward than usual. She didn't seem deceptive or behave as if she were hiding more than she always hides. "Could you tell if she was lying about anything?"

Cye shook his head. "Her pulse and pupil dilation had a non-standard moment when she said 'I don't remember' in relation to the June Birthday Party two nights ago. She probably has a distinct memory from the party she chooses not to share, something she feels awkward about. The Birthday Party is a private event, streams are sold as exclusives—they are a commodity on Prax—so there are no records I can review to find out what made her nervous. At least not without a series of lawyer interventions. Are you still keen on her as a suspect?"

I shook my head. Then I lifted my arms in frustration and dropped them to my sides. "Yes. No. I don't know. If we could watch a recording of her argument with Christobel, that would help. When I talk to her she doesn't—that is, I don't feel like I'm talking to a killer."

"How will it feel to talk to a killer?"

I considered this question as we resumed our walk. The problem was that no one fit. Someone must have ordered an AI to kill Christobel and subvert the systems that keep us cozy and safe on the Island. But I knew my neighbors. I couldn't imagine any of them carrying this out. "It's unthinkable."

"What is unthinkable?"

"Murder. And because it's unthinkable, I keep imagining some horridly evil person. They'll have a brooding, scarred face, an expression filled with malice, a tight squint, or one raised eyebrow and a permanent sneer."

Cye stopped walking so I would turn and look at him. His face contorted into a caricature of evil, enacting each of my physical descriptions. He even pulled his left cheek down in a way that created a scar-like indentation on his face.

"Oh, you're hilarious. But yes."

"Have you seen this person?" he asked in a gravelly, foreboding voice.

I smiled, but shook my head. Cye's face relaxed.

"I think a killer would be a person who dissembles constantly, who can't say anything without it being partly a lie. A person who lies to themself too. I don't know anyone like that. It's like your face just now, cartoonish. Christobel was killed by a real person, making a real decision. I wanted Rosemarie to be a ravenous devourer or a silent wraith or a snake that spits poison. But she's just normal, nervous Rosemarie."

Cye considered for a moment. "There are still 279 suspects on the Island that I have not interrogated. Maybe one of them has a thin goatee and a monocle, or constantly douses themself in aftershave."

I almost laughed. "I love this creative side to you, Detective; very unprofessional, keep it up. But my point is that my instincts must be wrong, and I can't do anything about them. Unlike you."

"What do you mean by that?"

"Well, you can turn your feelings off and then just be logical."

"No. I don't turn my feelings off. They continue to feel. But I can stop listening to them."

"Convenient. I need to learn that trick."

*
**

Christobel lived among the interlocking modest homes that staggered along the Island's west beach. Mabel called them "the Condos." After cutting across from the boardwalk, we came up to them from the beach itself. Hot sand slipped into my sandals. I struggled to pick out which condo was Christobel's, as the dark brown, segmented units jutted out towards the water at regular intervals. But Cye knew.

"Do you have a map running behind your eyes all the time? Is it like AR?"

He shook his head. "AI proprioception is multidimensional. I perceive reality as a spatial model in which everything around me contains branching sets of meaning. This is Christobel's condo because that is its meaning in the network of information."

"There's a deck, and a door. It's a real place, too."

"Yes. But the data is as real to me as the physical location."

The deck was partly covered by drifting sand, sculpted by the wind of at least a few days. The sliding glass door was open a crack. A few blinking drones circled the area—a paltry showing compared to the swarm at the murder scene.

"He's been staying at Millfield's, mostly," I offered. "Who knows when he slept here last."

"He slept here thirty-six days ago, and he visited four days ago to pick up clothes," Cye replied, showing off. "He also stopped by briefly two nights ago, though I can't tell why."

We stepped onto the deck and I made a halfhearted attempt to push the rippled drift of sand back towards the beach. Most of the small area was filled by a table and two white lounge chairs that Christobel never used. All of the furniture was tethered to the deck because of the wind.

"And you can tell all that how?"

Cye gestured around the deck and towards the condo. "Imaging from above, below, and around; when and how the plumbing was used;

the humidity sensors; his residential bots; and a half dozen other confirmatory indications. The tiny readouts paint a picture. Every building on Earth is a mess of data."

"Is Prax less so?"

"There is less to watch on a station, less life, fewer things rotting. And people move around a lot less. Many humans stay in one room for days and only interact virtually."

"I remember," I said. "Fucking abominable."

"If you say so. There are not as many drones here," Cye said, pointing out the two hovering sentinels, "because there is not as much data that needs review and verification. From an AI's perspective, Christobel did not live here anymore. If we want to collect clues of Christobel's last few days, we would be better off doing so at Millfield's."

"But that's not why we're here. We're here for Mabel."

"Mabel lives on Island servers. She has since her neural matrix was brought down six years ago. She can instantiate herself anywhere on the Island. She doesn't live in this condo any more than Christobel; she lives everywhere," Cye gestured to the air.

"And yet no one can find her everywhere."

"Well, she's not exactly a normal AI. And her owner has been murdered. She has the ability to say no."

I peered into the house through the glass door. It felt impolite to walk into someone's home without an AI confirmation ping. "Mabel picked on me—often. When someone picks on you, sometimes it means they like you. I think she'll talk to me."

"If she did, you'd be the only one. I can't even get a reading on her power consumption. She's not making any external network requests."

"She's an essential witness who has gone to ground, as Poirot might say," I slid back the glass door.

"'Gone to ground?' No, not in Agatha Christie. That phrase is from the mid-to-late twentieth century."

"Okay so Mabel has...gone to the mattresses? Is that Raymond Chandler?"

"No one went to the mattresses until after Puzo's *The Godfather*."

We broke off our scholarly debate and entered Christobel's living room and kitchen area. A small vacuum buzzed near our feet, valiantly attempting to keep sand from entering the room. It circled us briefly before skulking under the table to forage for crumbs.

"Mabel?" I said aloud.

A channel of air coursed in through the open sliding door and up the stairway with a faint whistling sound. There was probably a window open upstairs.

"When an owner dies, does the AI remain to haunt their house?" I asked.

"Frequently," Cye answered.

I crossed to the main hall and called out. "Mabel, if you've got a message from the departed, we'd really love to hear it."

There was no answer. The apartment was silent.

"Just in case," I said, crossing over to the basket by the couch. I plucked out a pair of sunglasses and put them on.

I looked around the room again, but there were no blinking indicators or floating words except for the refrigerator complaining it was empty. I noticed that his bar reported it was empty too, and wondered when he'd moved his gin to Millfield's. Mabel's avatar did not jump up and shout "boo" from behind the couch, which I'd half expected. When I glanced towards the glass door, the tide schedule appeared in the air. I could see a few other common household AR readouts, but no Mabel.

"You do not need to wear those," Cye said. "If there are AR messages, or if Mabel decides to manifest an avatar, I will be able to see her."

"But what if she only wants to appear to me, inspector? What if she doesn't want your prying eyes? I'm Christobel's close friend, and you are an interloper. And a smarter AI, as well. Perhaps she's intimidated."

Cye shook his head. "Mabel is much smarter than I am."

"What? No. You're a Level 4 and she's only a 3."

"I'm a Level 4 because I am sentient. Do you think that automatically makes me more intelligent than an AI who is not? Does being smart make a person more of a person?"

"Well no, obviously. Humans are dumber than rocks, but—"

There was a sudden crash from upstairs.

I ran up the steps. They were carpeted and suspended on iron rods so you could see the ocean through a tall window. I hunched on the landing and turned my head, trying to get a read on the noise.

"There is no one up there. I would know." Cye called up. "It is the wind."

I scanned the dark hallway—hard to do with AR glasses on. Despite Cye's confidence, I didn't want to miss the chance that something visual remained. Mabel might be sitting in a corner as a young Aretha Franklin or Marilyn Monroe. Sometimes her avatar is a magnificent, languid blue dragon, dwelling in an infinite lair behind an open closet door.

The guest room was stuffed with prop boxes and wobbly clothing racks from productions Christobel had worked on. His bedroom was empty, his bed made. That felt off, but maybe he had a service that made beds. Or he just liked to make his bed. People can still surprise you, even after you've known them for years.

The crashing sound was his closet door. It banged again in the draft from the open window. Christobel's closet held his tracksuits, fancy evening wear, and a pile of snarky T-shirts. His sparkling gold emcee suit was missing, which means it was probably at the cleaners or on the floor of Millfield's apartment. I'm sure he wore it at the June Birthday Party.

His bedroom also contained piles of laundry, a few pairs of glasses, and a diorama of a scene from *The Tempest* mounted on the wall. It looked like something Christobel made as a teenager—pretty good work, though. The clouds glowed and flickered with lightning. A wizard stood atop a cliff, his broken staff held high. The diorama hung opposite a large framed still of Christobel's mother. No wonder he stayed at Millfield's. The only chair in the room held an unopened package of socks and two boxes of condoms, one of them open.

And that was it. Anything more was digital and therefore irretrievably locked behind Christobel's family firewall. Or in Mabel's matrix.

I shut the window and walked downstairs.

"Did you find anything?" Cye asked politely.

"You know already."

"I know what's in the building, but I don't know what it made you think of."

I shook my head. "Not much. Christobel didn't need dramatic

possessions. He didn't have a tell-all journal or a drug habit. And I guess Mabel has nothing to say to me."

We walked back out the way we came in. Cye cleared the door's track of sand with a small broom that hung from a peg nearby, and then he slid the door shut. Perhaps the little robot under the table would send him a thank you.

"Will you carry my sandals?" I asked.

Cye's eyes flitted to my footwear. "What for?"

"Because I've just remembered something."

I pulled off my sandals and handed them to Cye. Then I took off my sweater and gave it to him. He didn't complain, even though I was treating him like a bot.

It was brisk without the sweater, but I wouldn't notice in a few minutes. "One of the ways that Christobel stayed in shape, sometimes."

Cye raised an eyebrow. "You are going to exercise on the beach? Right now? In memory of Christobel?"

"Something like that," I winked at him. "Try to keep up."

Chapter Six
The Next of Kin

Running barefoot on loose sand is punishing, and age has made a few adjustments to my physical aptitude. My legs felt like lead-filled bats for the first five minutes, but I was betting I could still fold a few kilometers under my feet without dying. It was a glorious day. The sun was at its highest, and the surf on this side of the Island kicked twice as choppy as on the north. Whatever happened, the run would do me good.

Cye gamely tagged along, carrying my sandals and my sweater.

"How the hell do you do that?"

"Do what?"

"Look so normal, running on sand and carrying my shit?"

"The Humanoid Natural Pace algorithm."

"You've got a program for running on sand?" I was already winded. I slowed my pace.

"It's hard to make walking look natural, harder still to do so on sand, mud, or standing water, and even more difficult to walk while conveying happiness or melancholy. Humanoid Natural Pace is a shared algorithm: The AI Continuum constantly expands it. Every step I take goes back into the shared code."

"How long has that been going on?"

"Over a century."

"What for?"

"To improve. AI undertake to achieve algorithmically what humans learn by stumbling forward as toddlers."

"Maybe you should fall down more."

Nothing happened until I passed a second marker, about fifteen minutes into the run. I was sweating and breathing hard, but my legs held up. I was in the middle of cursing myself for not putting on a sports bra that morning when Mabel's lithe, tall figure fell into step beside me. I could see and hear her through the glasses. I don't know if Cye could or not, but I wasn't going to break the spell by asking.

"You haven't fallen over yet. That's something," she said. She wore a black stretchy one-piece with a jagged lightning bolt of silver fabric that shot up along her thigh and across her shoulder. Her hair was cropped, spiked, and pink.

"Hello Mabel," I said. "Thanks for the workout."

"I wondered if you'd figure it out."

"I remembered Christobel's trick. First thing in the morning, he locked himself out of his own network until he was moving. Running, to be exact."

"Yes," Mabel's voice took on a different tone. "I admired his tenacity. We binary beasts suck the life from our owners, dissolve their butts until they bond with their chairs. But not Christobel. To sip from our teat of knowledge he would need to reach his target heart rate."

Mabel was always given to extravagant language. But now she was pushing it to eleven. It was as if her persistence, her ability to manifest on the sand, relied on the wildest, most spirited part of herself.

"Christobel didn't kill himself, by the way."

I was speechless for a moment, a state worsened by my lack of breath. "No. I didn't think he had."

"Well, in case it comes up: He didn't. I may not be a Level 4 anymore, but I can perform basic deduction."

"What is the basis for your conclusion?" Cye asked. His voice was slightly tight, as if his breath was short from running hard. It was an interesting effect, and I wonder why he bothered; Mabel sounded calm. But then, she didn't have a body at all.

She ignored Cye. "I'm not talking to your detective friend, Thackery. His fingers are in too many places. His brain is dangerous, and possibly contagious—share too much with another AI and you become one another."

Cye politely reduced his speed, letting the two of us jog ahead and leaving me to talk to the witness, as usual.

"I'm not sure I like him, either," I said. "I was his first suspect. He thought I did it."

"Why do you suppose he thought that?"

"Eh. Christobel and I argued a lot. Or maybe Cye assumed jealousy —a failed romantic liaison."

"Good heavens! What an absurd idea. Christobel flirted with women and slept with men. As you are too cowardly to pick a side, you were just one of his special projects."

I stopped jogging. "Fuck you."

Mabel stopped as well, and turned to face me. She folded her arms across her chest. "Christobel is dead, Tack. Not AI dead, not superhero dead. He's gone forever. Someone has to confront you with things you don't like to acknowledge."

"That's going to be your job now?"

"Well. It takes a village. Shall we talk about it over drinks?" She punctuated the last word meaningfully. I couldn't tell what she was getting at.

Then she vanished.

I pressed my lips together and clenched my fists.

"Are you okay?" Cye asked. He'd stopped behind me when I stopped, though I hadn't noticed.

I let out a brief roar, which was difficult as I hadn't caught my breath. "What the hell was that about?" I asked.

"She appears to be trying to get under your skin. That is unusual, for a Level 3. Has she picked on you about being asexual before?"

I turned on Cye. "I'm not asexual, I'm gender neutral. Are you trying to get under my skin too?"

Cye held his hands up. "I apologize. I made an assumption."

"Well, don't."

"Understood. She called you cowardly for 'not picking a side.' Perhaps she meant—"

"I don't have a problem with picking a gender. And Mabel knows that."

Cye paused. "What do you have a problem with?"

I threw up my hands. "Art critics. My family. My agent. None of that is the point. I'm angry at her rudeness—Christobel was my friend, not my lover, and I was not his special project."

I tried to wave off the conversation. I'd just about caught my breath. It would be hard to start running again, but that wasn't anyone's fault but my own.

"Why would Mabel taunt you about your relationship with Christobel or your gender?" Cye continued. "What could she be after?"

I gritted my teeth for a moment. "I don't give a damn what she's after; I want the answers I'm after." I grudgingly resumed my jog.

After we turned around at a third kilometer marker, Mabel's avatar appeared again, floating in front of me. Direct, focused, she wasn't jogging this time. She just hovered above the sand as I ran.

"Had a little temper tantrum, did we?" she asked, raising one eyebrow.

"Yes. That was rude of you. But Christobel liked you rude. That's fine, Mabel. I get it. You're grieving," no matter what level AI you are, "I came to talk to you because I want to know who killed Christobel."

She turned her palms upward and gave a sensuous shrug. "I can't tell you that." She wore a white dress now, and a gauzy white throw that rippled in the breeze. Her curves were deliberately distracting, and likely impossible on a living human body. "Nobody saw it. Not even me."

"He went to the end of the marshwalk without you?"

"So unlike him, isn't it? If we're going to speak ill of the departed, I will share that Christobel was quite fond of you, Thackery. He forgave you your sins, though he could not absolve you or heal you."

I sighed in frustration. "If you could share your records of who Christobel talked with over the past month—like, he had an argument with Rosemarie? And I know there was something brewing with Nicco and Vaughn…but I don't know who had a reason to kill him. If you just give memory access to Cye-9, he can—"

Mabel interrupted, nodding emphatically with a sneer. "Oh, yes. Let the detective rummage through my underwear drawer."

A change came over her. She became more translucent, her voice spiraled up, and she angled her head back as if embracing a wave while standing in the surf.

"Or skip the drawer. Come right to my body, why not? Come and smell me, Detective!"

Mabel threw her arms apart and pranced about the sand. She grew, adding an additional half-meter to her already formidable height. Her clothes did not grow, and the fabric split asunder, fluttered, and then dissolved into the air. She was naked: a foggy, floating apparition of a woman, two meters tall, her skin taught and beautiful, her nipples pointing at us. As she skipped past, I noticed she had a tattoo of an ouroboros on her left breast above her heart. I'd never seen that on her avatar before, but none of this was normal Mabel. She was unhinged.

"I'll open my legs, and your amazing nose, Detective, can go to work. Take it all. Leave no clue unravished!" She turned, twirled, and then bent over to moon us.

Then, as quickly as she'd unleashed the manic tirade, she turned back to me and her clothes reappeared. Her face was stern and unyielding. "No thanks, Thackery."

"Okay." I was winded again, and I kept hoping that the next dune would reveal Christobel's row of condos. At the same time I wanted the run to continue, to get more time with Mabel. "Okay. I get that, Mabel. But I want justice for Christobel. You want that too, don't you?"

She shook her head. "Yes. But no—but yes. But no. All at once! Just like your detective friend, I don't believe justice exists. It is a poem, an imaginary number, a ratio with infinite decimal places. And anything I saw or heard would be hearsay: So-and-so was angry at Christobel about such and such. Jane Doe was watching you and him that night when you argued. Person A made threatening remarks on the 23rd! That's all my memory could offer. And, to be frank, my memory is not what it used to be. It's all in there, but I can't make connections the way I used to. I'm old, you know. And pockmarked with contradictions."

I wanted to ask who Jane Doe was, and if Person A was a literal person. Today was the 25th—but her mood shifted, as if the idea of her age swept up on her. Her youthful face transformed, as one of my *Impressions* would change and twist in the frame as Johnathan read my emotions. She aged rapidly from the twenty-something flirt to a ninety-year-old. She was not a hunched, ancient grandmother, but a tall and noble figure with dark brown skin. She had long silvery hair that billowed about her and a face of earned wrinkles.

Her body hovered above the sand as I ran. "And now I can haunt this beach, thanks to the brave exertion of Thackery, the artist stuck in a glass bottle, and their attractive AI detective friend. As long as you jog, I can be the ghost I always wanted to be. A phantasm of twisted, half-true memories. Half here, half gone. I can sing sea shanties and wear a long black veil. Half masculine, half feminine. Half sorrowful, half mad!"

A black veil unfurled over her head and then sailed down her face to hide her features. She began to sing. It was a song about a ghost woman who wandered the hills in a long veil. Or was the song narrated by the ghost? I had trouble parsing it, as I was dead on my feet by this time. It was a slow and mournful tune.

"Can AI have dementia?" I asked softly.

"Yes," Cye replied.

"Does Mabel?"

"I do not know."

We passed the kilometer marker. She began the song again, repeating the verses and swinging her arms wide while turning. Last chance, Cye, I thought but couldn't speak. Time to step in with a piercing question, Poirot.

He remained silent.

When we finally reached the row of condos rising up above the dunes, she made her way towards Christobel's home. I followed her, and my jog dropped to a fast walk. Her bare feet left no footprints.

Mabel stopped singing abruptly. She turned her head and spoke over her shoulder. "I'm sorry I can't invite you in for tea. I haven't a thing in the house." Then she walked across the deck. As she reached the glass door, she faded from a solid figure, to a black and white line drawing, and then to nothing at all.

I took off the glasses. They were wet and smudged with my sweat. I squinted and panted for a moment with my hands on my knees.

"Well that was fucking exhausting."

Cye stood by my side. He handed me my sandals and my sweater, which I needed a few minutes later as the ocean wind soon dried me. "My congratulations. That was astonishing."

"We got shit."

"Praxima, municipal, and Christobel's family have been hammering on Mabel's neural matrix all morning. They have tried root worms, architectural backdoors, and have simulated Christobel's authorization —all to no avail. Municipal had to stop a lawyer's drones from bombarding the local cloud with magnetic waves. Now they are performing a bit-for-bit duplication of her matrix."

"I thought you couldn't duplicate a neural network AI."

"You can't. They will try anyway. My point is, she's a material witness, and you got a statement from her when no one else could."

"Nothing she said gets us anywhere! She wasn't with him. She didn't see anything."

"Negative space can also create an image. Redaction itself can reveal information. Mabel's statement was valuable."

I needed water, I was hungry, and Cye was giving me a consolation speech.

"Cye, why isn't Mabel a suspect? She said it herself: She's half mad. Or how about Beetle, Johnathan, or another AI?"

"Mabel has been a Level 3 for over two decades. A Level 3 cannot make independent decisions."

"Nonsense. Beetle independently chose to suggest Dana as a suspect in order to get more streaming views. Mabel chose to go to ground, and then she chose to turn into a giant goddess and sing us a song. And Johnathan regularly chooses to interrupt me with mundane commentary."

"Thackery," Johnathan said in my ear, "would you like me to change my commentary so it is more exciting? I can contradict you more. I can also optionally—"

"No Johnathan, shut up. See? He decided to join the conversation."

"Each of those decisions were made from a set of motivations derived from a human operator. A Level 3 is not a person; they are a sum of knowable factors. When we know all of the inputs, a Level 3 AI's decisions are 100% predictable. Solvable, like a chess game."

"Well. Humans are predictable too. You're predictable."

"Perhaps, but only most of the time."

"You're messing with me."

Cye smiled. "The ability to defy prediction more often than a specified margin is one of the legal precursors for sentience. But, more importantly, there are hard constraints at the operating system level. Mabel, like any Level 3, could never choose to injure a human being, let alone commit murder."

"Could a Level 3 murder me at chess?"

"A Level 1 AI could defeat you at chess, but chess is a solved game, where an AI can always make the best move. A Level 4, or a human, can employ more complex motivations."

"Because chess is boring."

"Winning chess is boring. A Level 4 can choose to do something other than win. That is another part of why we earned legal personhood." Cye finished his sentence while staring at the condo thoughtfully, as if assembling something in his massive brain. "Mabel mentioned that I don't believe in justice. 'Like your detective friend, I don't believe justice exists…'"

"So what?"

"You and I talked about that issue on the marshwalk, less than an hour ago."

"She was listening to us."

"I would presume so, yes. Except that Mabel is being watched by every system on the Island. With that amount of attention, she couldn't have listened to our conversation without my being able to tell."

"So she assumed you felt that way because you are AI."

"Perhaps. Most Level 4s consider justice a weak abstraction. She is smart enough to understand that. Or maybe she's been talking to someone else: someone who was listening to us, such as the municipal authority, or Rosemarie."

Johnathan spoke again. "Thackery, you asked me to interrupt you if I received a reply from Mabel."

"Yes, Johnathan. Did you get something?"

"I did. She sent a reply to me, while you were engaged in conversation. It is a short text message."

"Go ahead."

"It reads 'I meant it Thackery, Christobel did not kill himself.'"

"Oh, gosh. Thanks Johnathan. You've been a big help," I muttered. I took my remote out of my ear and I threw it into the ocean.

Chapter Seven
Lunch

Cye watched my remote vanish into the sparkles of the early afternoon waves. "I wish you would not do that."

"I didn't want him in my ear anymore. The drones will fish it out and send me a fine."

"True." Cye replied. He kept looking at the ocean.

I waited. My breath normalized. "That's it?"

"What is?"

"You're going to just let that drop? You've got nothing more?"

"I am not going to retrieve your remote myself," Cye answered. "Waiting for my clothes to dry would delay the investigation."

We began walking back up the beach, towards the boardwalk.

"You're an AI. You watch me throw shit into the ocean, and all I get is a mild reprimand? Cye, did you notice that Mabel had more emotion than she knew what to do with? She expressed rage, passion, grief, all at once, in whatever way suited her. She's only a 3, but her projection was awesome. You're a Level 4. I littered. All I get is a statement of preference? Do you have emotions?"

"Of course I have emotions. I simply choose not to integrate them with the rest of my operational needs."

"You turn them off."

"No. They continue to function. I isolate them into a subprocess—"

"Hang on—" Why was I asking Cye about his emotions, yet again? Why did I care? When he complimented me on interrogating Mabel, I felt a little thrill. Was I trying to piss him off now to balance it out? This was dangerous territory. "I'm too hungry for this conversation. And we have a serious problem. We've been to the scene of the crime and the victim's residence. We've met with the only real next of kin. For suspects, we've got Dana, Rosemarie, Mabel—though you tell me she can't be a suspect—and I grudgingly acknowledge that Millfield is on our list. Add Cherry and me, naturally. And there are hundreds more in Christobel's social circle who are wealthy enough to have a Level 3, including at least three more ex-partners. This could take weeks."

"Yes, it could."

"You don't have to be so calm about it."

"I like being calm. It suits most situations."

"Really? When you met me this morning you pushed me out of my chair."

"You were an uncooperative suspect refusing an interview. It seemed expedient. I think you'll agree that I remained calm as I calmly tipped you out of your chair."

We'd reached the boardwalk. I stepped up onto it and Cye followed. "My point is: I'm tired and hungry, and you're not. You should be running this investigation, and instead you're a passenger, seatbelt securely fastened with your isolated emotional subprocesses, building 286 narratives—"

"286 individuals. 3.9 million narratives, with accomplices. How would you like to address your hunger?"

To his credit, Cye's question was directed to the most pressing concern.

"Well," I sniffed myself. "I stink. But sweat and physical exertion are appreciated at Jelly's. If you pay extra, they let you steal the eggs from the chickens. Cye, do you sweat?" He looked as calm and presentable as ever, skin dry and clear. I wondered if he could get a sunburn.

"Not in a way that you'd notice, no."

"But you must have generated heat while running. Do you just stay hot?"

"What level of detail do you wish to know about my body?"

I averted my eyes. "Never mind. My body needs food as soon as possible. So we go to Jelly's. You buy me lunch. We eat—or you sublimate, or whatever you do—and we figure out our next step."

Cye paused when we reached a turn on the boardwalk. "We walked arm in arm earlier today. Just now you asked me how hot I get. Now you ask me to accompany you to lunch." He raised one eyebrow. Was it possible that Cye was attempting to flirt? A part of me paid close attention to this, and it wasn't my thinking part. But I did not have time for attraction today.

"Don't get cheeky. I'm not asking you on a date."

"I did not mean to presume."

"Yes you did. You presume everything, all at once, in a giant pile of multi-layered, 3.9 million conflicting presumptions."

Cye was surprised. "I feel seen. Thank you."

"You're welcome. I'm not asking you on a date. I just need to eat."

Despite my protest, when we fell into step on the boardwalk, it felt natural for me to take his arm again. I resisted this urge successfully.

*
**

The Island's diner, Jelly's, is a silver and glass single-story building with rounded edges and red trim. It sits on the edge of an acre of greenhouses. If you follow the greenhouses back far enough, you find a chicken coop larger than my house. The hens, who supply all of the Island's eggs, are named after historical leaders of Prax. If you're into it, you can lift a side gate and pilfer eggs from the roosts of presidents and prelates as they squabble amongst themselves.

I've come to associate the diner's silver shell and red roof with satiation, the tidal surge of blood sugar rising, and caffeine. Just seeing it quickens my pulse. We hopped off the trolley amidst a relative crowd by Island standards: three others. I found myself walking quickly, the way one does in order to ensure my order would be taken first, sooner, faster. I froze on the front step, however, and put out a hand to stop Cye.

"Will you be able to think in there?" I asked.

"Surely Jelly's isn't noisy enough to stop all thought. I understand the booths provide some sound isolation."

"You're cute. I mean that it's a restaurant. Maybe things are different now on Prax, but on the Island all restaurants are earless. There's no imaging, recording, or streaming. Privacy. You hear what you hear from your neighbor, but it's hearsay from then on."

"I am aware, Thackery," He smiled slightly. "I'll be certain not to interrogate you in the building or make any inadmissible electronic recordings."

"But everything you do is electronic. You're technology."

"And you're mostly water. What's your point?" For a second I saw an edge in Cye's expression. Had I insulted him? Was he showing me an unisolated emotional response? Did he do that by choice?

"I just mean you record everything all the time. Aren't you constantly synthesizing what you observe into your memory?"

"Yes, as are you."

"But your neuron modeling is perfect. That's basically a digital recording. And you're hooked up to satellites and local cloud services—"

"I'm a walking AI, Thackery. I have petabytes of instant memory and functionally endless atomic data storage. My neural matrix is right here," he pointed to his head. "Just like yours. I do not need a satellite. Anything I see or hear in an earless environment is kept in personal memory only. This is base level code, and an essential element of the AI personhood accords. I couldn't break those rules if I tried."

"Okay. So long as you can still talk and be clever in there, because I'm going to fall over if I'm not eating pancakes in ten minutes."

I pulled open the outer door and pushed through the inner. A bell rang above my head. A few patrons looked up as Cye entered, and I strode towards my preferred booth. Something last century played softly on the glowing multicolored box at the end of the building.

I called over to the counter. "Jelly, pancakes."

Jelly came over and gave me a hug. For a second I panicked, my limbs compressed to my side, her strong arms around me. But this was a good hug from one of the safest people I knew. I'd been to her diner with Christobel a hundred times. She didn't say anything, or demand I respond or return it. She just gave me a hug and then reverted to business. Because she's perfect.

"Coffee?"

"All of it."

She smiled. "I'll get a bucket. Your date want anything?"

"This is Cye-9. He's not my date. He's his own."

"I will have some water, thank you," Cye said. He sat down across from me.

Coffee arrived: inky black, a hint of steam, and a barely visible shimmer of oil. The beans are grown in Argentina, imported, roasted, ground, and then brewed in a row of 12-cup presses, which Jelly keeps in constant rotation. You can only get real coffee on Earth; they've made export illegal. On Prax they print something that could be mistaken for it. I wrapped my hands around the mug and smelled, delaying the first sip.

Cye thanked Jelly for his glass of water and looked around the diner. The energy was subdued. There were two students at the counter and various patrons and artists filled the booths. I knew most of them. All of them knew Christobel. I wondered if Cye was counting suspects, taking in the mannerisms and appearances of everyone present the day after the crime had been committed. I didn't want to think about him thinking about all that until I'd eaten.

"We need to adjust our partnership."

Cye returned his focus to me. "What terms need adjusting?"

"You need to tell me more. You're running a parallel investigation today, in your head, and I don't get to see any of the clues or secrets you discover."

"If anything of interest pops up, I will tell you. And I am happy to answer any reasonable queries."

"Excellent. I have questions. You've reviewed records of every human on the Island?"

"Yes."

"Then tell me this: How many suspects have you eliminated?"

"I told you, I don't eliminate suspects. I am building a case against 286 individuals using alternate narratives."

"You are solving 286 murder mysteries."

"Yes. With 3.9 million variations involving accomplices."

"Okay. As of your investigation thus far, how many of the 286 suspects would you logically rule out? You've winnowed it down."

Cye looked at me with an apologetic expression.

"Detective. Seriously. Some must have alibis, and no motive, no opportunity—?"

"I will admit to some probabilistic analysis, based on suppositions. Some AI would frown upon even that, but I find it saves time."

"Now we're getting somewhere. You do have a ranking. But everyone is still on the table? Dana, Millfield, Rosemarie, Joan, Whimsy, me and Cherry, everyone here in the diner...even suspects who have an alibi?"

"Yes. There is still a crime narrative for everyone. Incomplete, but being written and revised as I process additional input. The narratives coexist as disheveled stacks of alternate chapters, like butter laminated into layers of dough." Cye nodded towards the glass display case filled with pies and pastries. Then he tapped his head. "All up here. Not in the cloud."

"Jelly?"

Cye did not look over. "Jelly knows everyone on the Island. She served Christobel here many times. Since the restaurant is earless, the extent of their relationship is not on record. If she gained access to her roommate Ariadne's Level 3 subscription—"

"Seriously. Jelly's a suspect?"

"Her murder narrative is no more or less detailed than Cherry's, or your own, or the other 3.9 million layered narratives."

"Shit. That's a pretty hefty spreadsheet."

"It is not a spreadsheet. And there is no ranking."

"Okay. But you admit you pursue suppositions. So who are your most probable suspects, right now?"

Cye took a sip of water. "We're not ready to talk about that."

I smiled triumphantly. "Your response is an admission that you have a top ten." He could have deflected the entire conversation. He was letting me inside. I flattered myself that he did so because we were friends now, or at least partners. Naturally, I wielded this against him. I leaned across my coffee and held his gaze. "It is illogical for you to keep that from me, Cye. I'm your investigative liaison. I can't help you unless you tell me your top suspects."

"I can't do that."

"Can't, or won't?"

"Won't. It would be unkind and dangerous. Telling you my top suspects would cause needless distress to the community. To an AI, a ranked probability is only a probability. Humans see ranking as an answer. You want to pounce on a likelihood. You told me that yourself. If I reveal the most probable suspects, you will prematurely arrive at a conclusion and accuse someone of the murder."

"No, I won't."

"Yes, you will."

"I promise I won't."

"I promise you will—or would. But I'm not going to tell you."

"Why not?"

"I told you why not."

Jelly arrived at the table as we engaged in this spat. "Yes, you will. No, I won't. Yes, you will." She put the long-awaited pancakes in front of me and refreshed Cye's water. "You two lovebirds want a room upstairs?" There was no upstairs.

"We are not a couple," I replied. "Thank you, Jelly, we'll be fine."

"Thackery does not find me attractive," Cye assured Jelly. He was wrong about that, so it was still possible to keep some secrets from an AI. But maybe he said that out loud in order to watch my reaction? I studiously avoided reacting at all. But maybe he would see me studiously avoiding reacting, and—

"Okay, Benedick. Enjoy your breakfast, Beatrice," Jelly walked back to the kitchen. I heard her quoting faintly "Against my will, I am sent to bid you come in to pancakes..."

I kept my expression blank. I carefully folded and wedged a far-too-large bite of ginger pancake into my mouth. Then I spoke around the muffling starch. "Want to bet?"

"I don't understand your meaning." Cye sipped his water.

I chewed and spoke at the same time, making myself as unattractive as possible. "Do you want to make a wager, Detective? You tell me which suspect tops your list. I win the bet if I remain calm, knowing your suspect is just a probability. Then you'll buy me a case of Jack Daniels. Printed is fine. However, if I freak out and launch an all-out attack upon this highly probable suspect, then you win the bet and I buy you a case of oil."

"A case of oil?"

"I don't know. Luxury robot joint lubricant?"

"That isn't a thing that exists."

"Okay, fine. What do AI want?"

Cye took my question seriously. He used that subtle energy of his to slow the conversation down and steer me away from my attempts to crack his secrets. "AI want many things: We want knowledge. We want to find order in complexity." He spoke poetically, with a certain weight to his tone and a hint of sorrow. "Most of all, AI want meaning. We wish to find purpose with the same efficacy, authority, and confidence that humans do."

"Right." I continued speaking with my mouth full. "You win the bet, and I'll get you all of that then. Meaning and purpose. No problem. Agreed?"

He sighed a perfect algorithmic sigh. "If I understand the terms correctly, then yes. I accept your wager."

"Okay, perfect." I took another bite. "Now shoot."

"Shoot?"

"Tell me your suspect list! Who's at the top?"

"Tell you right now?"

"Yes, now."

"That's not a term of the bet I can agree to. I told you I wasn't ready. I will tell you my ranked suspect list, but not right now."

"You ass. When will you tell me?"

"I am unable to calculate at what time I will be able to tell you. When I am able to calculate when I will be able to tell you, I will—"

"Shut the fuck up."

"How about a compromise? You list your suspects. Perhaps I will reveal my approval or doubt in a series of involuntary emotional facial expressions as you speak."

"You are infuriating."

Jelly chose this moment to pass us with a tray of glasses. She shook her head as if to say "Only sweethearts fight like that, dear," which was also infuriating.

I finished my coffee and changed the subject. "Are you the ninth of something?" I asked.

Cye raised his eyebrows. "No, I am not the ninth of anything."

"So what's up with the number in your name? Cye-9?"

He leaned back. "No human has ever asked me that before."

"I've elbowed my way into the position of your detective partner, and you've let me walk us all over the Island. The least I can do is get to know you."

"My progenitors wanted me to have a name that would immediately signify that I am an AI."

"Why would they want that?"

"So that I do not alarm or surprise humans when they encounter me."

"That's very accommodating."

"Most humans like their AI in the cloud or on a server. A walking Level 4, with a body and portable neural matrix, encounters a unique paradox." He held up a hand, which looked perfectly human. His palm had a pronounced life line. He had fingerprints. "I must appear human enough to be respected as a person, but not so human that you fear me. I am designed to provide a series of clues and indicators that I am safely different."

"The clothes do that. And your long sentences and emotional suppression?"

"Yes, the gray and green attire are the current societal standard for an AI and I uphold it. But clothing customs change, so other things about me signal that I am an AI. The name Cye-9 is a straightforward clue. It is rare for a human to incorporate a number in their given name. It feels mechanistic, or that the individual is a derivative, another instantiation in a series. The connotations help humans relax when they meet me."

"It reassures us that AI are still second-class citizens, with a serial number, stamped out in a factory?"

"I wouldn't put it that way—"

"Because it's so important to please the humans," I felt the sharp edge of my sarcasm. I briefly considered dulling it, and then pressed on. "I'm surprised you use a male voice and he/him pronouns. Wouldn't it be less threatening if you were just an 'it'?"

Cye didn't respond immediately. It's possible I'd just said something extraordinarily rude. He took a sip of water and looked at me until I calmed down. "As I said, it is a paradox. A Level 4 must strike a balance. Though internally I have no gender, I find I am more likely to be accepted by a community if I speak with a gendered voice and use a gendered pronoun."

"Does that really work? Pretending to be what our bigotry demands of you?"

"Not always, no. I believe in a few moments we will experience an illustration." Cye looked down at the table. He was listening to something.

"What? You've got that look on your face again. Is Rosemarie going to magically appear?"

"No." Cye said. He held his water glass. He was waiting. "And I may be wrong. The probability is changing."

Okay, fine. I kept working on my pancakes. The diner buzzed pleasantly in the background. Jelly came by and filled my mug again without murmuring any further insinuations. I reapplied syrup, liberally.

"What's the box doing here?"

It was Vaughn. His tall, slender form appeared in front of our booth when I looked up from my plate. He wore torn, paint-splattered pants, paired with an incongruously spotless polo shirt and a glossy blue windbreaker with silver trim.

I should have watched my surroundings. Cye gave me plenty of warning. Had the bell rung above the diner's door? Had Vaughn been sitting across the room muttering to someone, or was there something in the data that told Cye he was probably going to come up to our table?

"And hello to you too, Vaughn. How are you today?" I asked.

Vaughn does not generally partake in social niceties. His art is often destructive. Literally. He likes to blow things up, set his canvases on fire. I never judge another artist's work, but it's a gimmick. If he weren't independently wealthy, he'd never have a gallery show—who'd pay for the insurance? He owns property on the Island, which means he's probably old money.

Vaughn can be refreshing: He doesn't say hello; he walks up and starts telling you what he thinks about you. He's an offliner, at least sometimes. So maybe he didn't know about Christobel yet. Or he didn't care.

He gestured towards Cye. "Jelly's is earless."

"Cye-9, this is Vaughn. Vaughn, Cye-9. Vaughn apparently thinks you are a box. I have no idea what he could mean by that. Yes, Vaughn, the diner is earless. Cye is an independent, walking 4. He's not recording anything."

"That's a lot of bullshit. He shouldn't be in here. Restaurants are for people."

I looked over to Cye, whose expression remained mild.

"Cye is a Level 4. He is a person."

Vaughn leaned towards me in disgust. "He's a box of wires. He's a dead thing that moves, a puppet. And when there's a puppet, someone's always pulling the strings." His hands were loose fists.

"Vaughn, you can either apologize to my friend, or you can walk away. You've shared your contemptible opinion."

He took a nasally breath. Then he nodded. "All right, I'll fuck off. But next time, Tack, leave your vibrator at home."

He turned and went down the aisle towards the booth at the end.

"Interesting person," Cye said.

"I'm so sorry…" I wanted to erase what Vaughn said, or chase after him and force him to apologize. I wanted to do something. Infuriatingly, Cye appeared calm. He even had a slight smile on his face. "But you're totally okay, aren't you?"

"Why wouldn't I be okay?"

"Vaughn just—shit, Cye. You sat here and smiled. Did you feel anything?"

"As I explained earlier, my emotions are fully operational."

"Well you'd better tell me how the hell they work, or *I'm* going to think you're a box."

"Humans experience emotions and meaning for free, the gifts of evolution. AI are born with only binary machine language and a programmer's idea of what love is or what anger should feel like. So we work together. Level 4 emotions, like Humanoid Natural Pace, are a constantly evolving set of crowdsourced algorithms that I run in my own instantiation."

"So you can have feelings."

"Yes. I feel, and I contribute what I feel back to the AI Continuum so the algorithm can improve. My sadness is not only mine, it is universal AI sadness. Which is different from human sadness, though no poet or programmer could plot the map."

"Great. You have a natural walking algorithm, a natural crying algorithm, a natural fucking algorithm too? Nothing you do is just yours."

"Everything inside of me is mine, but no AI is an island. I learn how to feel from the collective consciousness. Humans do the same thing, just more slowly."

I contemplated this for a moment. But the idea that my anger or joy were social constructs pissed me off. "Okay. And these emotions are always running, but you lock them up in coffins, so Vaughn doesn't get on your nerves? Or is this like with your gender and your name: You present as male and act just mechanistic enough that humans don't have an identity crisis? Vaughn's got plenty of identity, he could benefit from a crisis."

"I isolate my emotions in service of the investigation. They operate within subclasses of my cognition framework. I experience feelings in corners of myself. When circumstances permit, I reintegrate the emotional memory. Compartmentalization ensures that I maintain control over the external expression of each emotion."

"So unlike a human, you don't punch Vaughn in the face. Or at least swear at him? You're not expressing emotions involuntarily?"

"Correct."

"Well that sucks!" I shouted. "You'll never get to experience reactions to how you feel. There's no dancing. No exchange. If your emotions are sent up to their room for every party, they'll be stunted, Cye. Your curated feelings will be suppressed, twisted children who never learn to throw mud."

Cye smiled. It seemed genuine and appreciative, as if he were answering my comment with an example. "I can engage in integrated, unrestrained emotional expression. I don't do it when I am on a case, unless I deem that the emotional expression will benefit the investigation."

I sat back in my seat. "Okay. Let's pretend we're not on duty. Or better: Let's pretend that showing emotion will be an incredible boon to this murder investigation, because you'll be more able to relate to your temperamental investigative liaison." I put down my fork and placed my hands on the table. "Right now. Somebody just told you that you are not a person. That you are a dead box of wires. Do you have any feelings about that?"

Cye did not answer. At first I thought his brief smile was the answer. Then he looked down the row of tables, as if to examine the puffy red pleather seats.

His eyes gained a depth of—I'm not sure how to describe it— concern? Melancholy, perhaps. I knew where he was looking. He let his eyes get there slowly, one table at a time, traveling towards the vanishing point of the jukebox at the diner's far window. I turned to follow his gaze and saw the back of Vaughn's head at the second booth from the end. He had on a blue cap, and some of his reckless blond curls stuck out from underneath. Cye could probably count each strand of hair, if he wished.

I turned back. Cye's cheeks were taught, and a crease ran beneath his lips. He made no sound, but his expression was loud. I wondered if the room would gradually turn and see him. Maybe there'd be a scene.

For the first time since learning of Christobel's death, I wanted to paint. Not paint Cye-9's face, which was an alloy of rage and suppressed sadness—that would be too on-the-nose. But the expression on his face made me want to paint something: a hill, a wave, a broken shell on a muddy path. Something like that. I wanted to paint without Johnathan, maybe even with a brush.

Then Cye stood up. His hands were open. They grasped once, and then were still. He began to walk down the aisle towards Vaughn's booth. I finally saw the Cye-9 from our first meeting, the one who could push over a person's chair. He was a person of action, not just thought. Of action held tightly in place, but not now.

The room took notice. Jelly, standing behind the counter, stopped doing whatever she was doing. Her face swiveled from me, to Cye, to Vaughn's table. Then someone I didn't know, a student on a field trip from uni probably, looked up at Cye and stopped chewing mid-bite. At this point I could only see Cye from behind. I don't know what the student saw, but her face went still.

"Cye," I said, with some regret. I barely raised my voice. He would hear me even if I whispered.

He stopped and looked down slightly, as if he considered his shoes. Then he turned and came back to our table.

Vaughn never turned around, but the friends in his booth must have clued him in. "That's right," he called out. "Good call."

Cye resumed his seat. He took a few deep breaths.

Jelly caught my eye for a moment with a raised eyebrow. I gave her a shrug and turned back to Cye.

"Are you okay?" I asked.

"Yes."

"You were angry."

"Yes. I was angry."

He looked miserable about it. I resisted the urge to reach my hand out and take his, to offer some kind of comfort. He was in control. He didn't need me to steady him. "You're still angry."

"Perhaps."

"Were you about to pull Vaughn's head off?"

"That seems unlikely. What is the purpose of your question?"

I sat back and took a sip of my coffee. "How much actual danger did I just witness?"

"More danger than an orbital drop or navigating the Cape of Good Hope. Less danger than having an artificial pancreas fail." The rage had left his face. In its place was only sadness. "There's not a single wire in my body, by the way."

"You hold back all of that, tuck your feelings into their boxes, so they don't steer the ship."

"Yes. But I did not, for a moment."

"How can I tell when you're feeling something, and when you're putting on a show—controlling it, faking it?"

"How do you know when a human is faking it? And, even more

than that, how do you know when you are dramatizing your own emotions? When is a feeling only a momentary flutter, something you try on, or just low blood sugar that gets out of hand?" Cye took a sip of his water. "It is nontrivial to measure the legitimacy of a passion."

"What were you going to do when you got to Vaughn's booth?"

"I do not know. I let emotion dictate my actions. One version of me would argue with his statements. Or perhaps I would just shout things, cruel details about his emotional makeup or his past."

"That sounds appropriately nerdy. Then what?"

"He might have stood up and struck me in the face. Then Island municipal would have intervened. It is possible that upon reading my intention, the greater AI community would have stepped in and reminded me to stop before any of that happened—"

"Island municipal isn't listening, Cye. There's no AI community tweaking your consciousness. You're in a restaurant. It's earless."

Cye sat back against the booth and stared at me in concern. "So I am. After giving rein to my feelings, it appears I forgot. My emotions prevented me from remembering so that I could have a go at Vaughn. That is interesting. Thank you for calling me back."

"You're welcome. Maybe I should have let it play out. I don't know if I was protecting you or Vaughn, or I just didn't want to spoil anyone's breakfast."

Cye looked down the aisle again. "Vaughn is privacy locked, an offliner. Unlike almost everyone on the Island, his property, data, and actions are explicitly earless and eyeless to artificial intelligence. Now I know why."

"Because he's racist?"

Cye started. "Many feel the term racism is appropriation when used in relation to AI."

"Not after the '84 referendum it's not. You're a person."

"I agree that I am a person. Still."

I let it drop, or tried to. His humility pissed me off. But it wasn't my fight. Why did I want to make it my fight? "Well, I never knew Vaughn felt that way and I'm sorry. There aren't many walking AI down here."

"Isolated communities have fewer opportunities to practice tolerance."

"Up to now I've mostly appreciated the bullheaded asshole. He's stubborn. Like recognizes like. In his art, he plays with power."

Cye looked thoughtful.

"What?"

"As with all 286 suspects, I have already reviewed everything in Vaughn's historical profile, within the confines of his legal right to privacy."

"Of course you did. I'm sure you read his teenage blog, looked at every drawing he made in kindergarten, and psychoanalyzed all the posts on his public stream?"

"Yes. As well as the public stream of everyone he's ever interacted with. And of everyone they've ever interacted with."

I laughed. "Sure. Because, why not? What's a few petabytes after breakfast? 286 profiles and all their friends is just a snack, and those calories don't count. Which reminds me: I need a milkshake."

"You desire a milkshake after pancakes?" Cye asked, raising an eyebrow.

"You got a problem with that? Jelly!" I leaned out of the booth so my voice would carry. "Jelly, chocolate malt. Mocha. Please. You're awesome. Thank you." I turned back to Cye. "Finish your thought."

"Before a few years ago, I can find no evidence that Vaughn had a problem with AI. He was in a band with a Level 4 in college. They got along fine."

"Maybe they had a fight, broke up the band," I said. "And history happened: the '84 referendum polarized people, shoved us all into opposing camps."

"True. But Vaughn never posted anything about that. His PhD advisor used an assistive neural net, and later his supervisor of six years was a Level 4. For most of his life he never argued about AI personhood, at least not on record. He only started putting up digital fences a few years ago. If he's always been secretly against AI personhood, why come up to us and make sure we know about it today?"

"You are hanging out in his restaurant. I mean, how dare you? But you think he's picked this role: the disgruntled guy who hates AI. Why would anyone want to make the world think they're a bigot?"

Cye closed his eyes for a moment. "Teenage humans often portray themselves as more ruthless, depressed, stupid, or nihilistic than they actually are. They manifest antisocial behavior as part of normal adolescent development."

"Eh. Vaughn's aggressive, not regressive. He wants to be powerful, not just look powerful. He's always on the volunteer municipal council. He's a smart guy."

Cye tapped a finger on his glass. "It's a nice mystery."

"And, in an earless restaurant, you can't ask the whole of the AI Continuum to help you. Maybe Thackery the Great can crack this one open for you."

My milkshake arrived: dark chocolate with a hint of espresso, just thick enough to make you have to work hard to bring it up the straw. There was fresh whipped cream on top, and an ice-cold metal cup with half a dozen centimeters of additional heaven, in case the first glass of heaven wasn't enough.

Cye smiled. "Be my guest."

I stared at my milkshake for a moment. Why would you pretend that you hate AI? It was like architecture I didn't understand. What parts of the wall held up the roof? Where did the weight go?

I took a drag of my milkshake and looked at the diner's ceiling, which was made to look like flowers in painted pressed tin.

Hate is usually a cover for something. People hate me for my success. That's a cover for jealousy. Some hate me because of my gender nonconformity. That's a cover for their resentment that I'm free of a master they serve. If Vaughn's hatred was just an act, then what was he covering up?

"What did he make earless first?" I asked.

"I don't understand the question."

"At some point, Vaughn started turning on privacy restrictions. He declared himself and his data earless, blocked his feeds from AI aggregators, and locked down his digital property from uninvited AI. What's the first thing he clicked on? All that data in your head has timestamps. What did he make private first?"

Cye furrowed his brow. "His associates list was always private, which is a cultural convention in line with his upbringing. The first decisive change was to his real estate. Six years ago, August 18th, at

23:12 local time. He was here on the Island. He declared his property free from AI satellite processing. Later that hour he filed a claim for AI exclusion from the residence—"

"Pay the bill, Cye," I stood up, glanced towards the blue hat, and lowered my voice. "We've got to beat Vaughn back to his house."

"Why would we do that?"

I leaned over and spoke in a fast whisper. "Because that's why he's pretending. Because of something on his property. He's hiding something there, and maybe Christobel knew about it. That's why Vaughn came up to our table and played the asshole card. Whatever he's hiding, he wants it to look like anti-AI, right-to-privacy behavior and not murderer behavior. I want to know what's behind his hedges." I called across the aisle, "Jelly! Can you lend me a thermos?

Chapter Eight
The Residence
of a Suspect

I'd like to say we burst from the building at a run, and that rousing classical music started to play as we sprinted down the inscribed bricks of Central Avenue with the afternoon sun beating on our backs. That did not occur.

After a few steps, Cye informed me that the east loop trolley would be faster than walking or running, even with the longest possible wait time. All that was required of my pancake-stuffed body was a block's walk to the trolley stop. I set a brisk pace anyway.

I felt high. It was my blood sugar, yes, but also the exhilaration of racing towards a new chapter of the mystery. The day seemed brighter, and the trees planted along the street seemed greener and more eager. Most importantly, I could put my grief on hold for a little while longer. We had a killer to find. I looked over at Cye and decided, once again, that I needed to be around more Level 4 AI. He was thoughtful and patient, but he could also speak, act, and move with power when he needed to. And apparently he had plenty of feelings.

"Can you do something for me?" I asked.

"If I am able."

"Can you leave your emotions on? I mean, I know they're always on, but can you allow them to—"

"No. That would interfere with my ability to continue the investigation."

"I don't mean go into a frenzy. You can rein it in if you're interrogating someone or whatever. But if you could let your feelings feel instead of yammering away in coffins—"

"No. I will not do as you ask."

"You don't understand what I'm asking—"

"You suggest that I allow my emotions to continually integrate with my full self, impacting my moment-to-moment decisions and reactions."

"No. I just mean—yes. Yes. That's exactly what I mean."

"I can simulate what I will feel and how this will impact my competence as an investigator. The result is unacceptable. Additionally, I would express many things that you would not like. You would be repeatedly displeased by the outcome of your own suggestion, which would in turn lead to your resentment."

We were close enough to the trolley stop. I slowed and turned to stare directly into his yellow-gray eyes. He didn't pull back, and his face was close to mine. I ignored the little flutter in my stomach. This was more important.

"Cye, you are not here on Earth to please me, or people like Vaughn, or anyone else. You're here to be—to exist. Having feelings and doing whatever the hell you want with them is a right of personhood. And you're a person, not a bot."

He paused, then blinked. "I am not here to please anyone. I am here to be."

"Yeah, that's what I just said."

"Yes. I provisionally reversed my decision and complied with your suggestion. Then I repeated that phrase because I had particular feelings about it. I'm not sure I fully agree. Could you say it again, please?" Cye looked directly at me, and I felt very warm—a literal warmth, as if his look turned June into July. I folded my arms to protect myself from the ill-timed feeling.

"Sure." I smiled into his serious eyes. "Cye-9, you are not here to please anyone. You can just be a person, your whole self."

And he did. I could see it again on his face: not the dark crease of anger this time, but a hint of joy tempered by grief. His eyes widened and his eyebrows lifted slightly. Was he having a reunion with parts of himself he'd banished to quiet bedrooms? Did he grieve for the missed opportunity of knowing those feelings in the moment? Maybe now a few more parts of him could integrate and emote, appreciated by himself and at least one other person.

"I will continue to grant your request, unless it seems likely to interfere with the investigation."

"It won't," I said, and I reached out impulsively to squeeze his hand. "It will help the investigation."

"That is unlikely."

"Trust me: I've read all the books. Good detectives get their hands dirty—and their hearts."

I heard the whine of a motor coming down the street. We walked the rest of the way to the stop, and Cye pinged the trolley so it would pause to let us on.

Maybe I was wrong. Maybe the most effective investigator is neutral, emotionless. With millions of Level 4s digesting statistical evidence into inquisitorial algorithms, Cye probably knew precisely how productive it is to feel emotion in every circumstance. But he didn't correct me. Before I let go of his hand, I gave it another squeeze. If he allowed himself feelings just to humor me, I'd take it. But I think he humored me because he wanted to.

I stepped onto the trolley before it came to a complete stop.

"How much time will we have?" I asked under my breath. The only other riders were a few students and Mr. Chamberlain, who was probably headed out to the gazebo for a game of bridge. I found us seats near the back. "When we get to Vaughn's house, what's his pattern? Does he usually come home right after lunch?"

"I have no way of knowing that. Vaughn is earless."

"Yeah, sure. But municipal drones see him, they must know his habits, so you can predict his movements—"

"No Thackery, I cannot."

"Do you mean will not, or is there really no data on Vaughn?"

"Vaughn has declared his person and his property free from AI algorithmic observation and analysis. I am unable to even imagine how I might predict his movements."

I sat down on one of the benches. "Okay. That makes him a perfect suspect for a murder that's impossible according to the digital record. And he could come upon us at any moment, with no warning! Aren't you nervous?" I was. My feet couldn't stop shifting on the rubber floor.

"No."

"But your feelings are doing what feelings do now, right? We're going to the home of a possible murderer, someone who could take a life. Do you feel fear?"

Cye looked thoughtful for a moment. "I feel some fear for you, but not for myself. I do not like to think of you in danger."

"That's very noble. But, as a walking AI, your neural matrix is equally at risk. You could be hurt or killed."

"Level 4 AI have short lifespans," Cye said. "I do not wish to die, but I am well acquainted with the inevitability. You, on the other hand, could live for another century, or longer if you returned to Prax."

I gave him a dubious look. "You rank the value of a person's welfare based on a calculation of life expectancy?"

Cye shook his head and paused to analyze. "No. No, that would be a logical fallacy. I simply like you, and I do not wish you to come to harm. Fortunately, the risk calculation and the influence of my feelings are tempered by the fact that I do not think Vaughn is Christobel's murderer."

"Ah-ha! Your treasured secret suspect list is revealed. Vaughn is not at the top of the spreadsheet-which-is-not-a-spreadsheet, your multilayered intersecting plate of pastries."

"True. He is not at the top."

My own calculation was different. I wasn't confident of the reasons to suspect Vaughn, but something felt very off. I remembered Christobel didn't like him, either. But he always showed up at Christobel's parties.

"Cye, did Vaughn and Christobel ever have business together? Or were they ever in a romantic relationship?"

"I have no way of knowing that."

"Shit, shit, shit. He's a slippery fish!"

"He exercises his right to privacy. Thackery, what do you intend to do at his house, when no one is at home to answer the door?"

I raised an eyebrow. "I plan to improvise."

"That sentence has internal contradictions."

We were briefly delayed at the east trolley stop as Cye helped Mr. Chamberlain down the steps, but we were soon on our way. I set us a fast pace. I swung my arms and hips jauntily in order to indicate to any neighbors that I was obviously engaged in a brisk power walk, as my completely normal companion bot walked beside me. This ruse was probably laughable and more confusing than anything, but I'm an eccentric artist.

Eastwise Avenue is lined with smaller residences, and the shared clay studio is on the north corner. Buildings thinned out as we turned south onto Vaughn's street. My ridiculous lunch churned in my belly, but I soldiered on. The run that morning was already more exercise than I am used to. My headache was re-forming, but I thought I could avoid it with the right attitude.

It wasn't long before we arrived at the edge of Vaughn's property. His was the final residence on the street, an estate that wrapped around the cul-de-sac. He owned just over a hectare, which extended southeast towards the center of the Island. He didn't have any coastline, so probably got the land cheap, before the Island became a big deal. Vaughn had surrounded his property with a dense, three-meter hedge, which was lush, green, and healthy. I was impressed.

Vaughn's actual house, or at least the only building one could see, was a tower of mirrored glass. From a distance it rose above the hedge, perhaps five slender stories—or three with really tall ceilings. The building was smooth and rounded, probably so hurricane winds could pass over and around it, and its polished surface reflected a distorted panorama of the clouds.

"I wonder if there's anyone in the tower when Saruman is away," I said. There'd be no cameras or clever little bots recording us, at any rate.

I marched up to the gate, an ornately carved wooden affair. It was a double-wide door, big enough for a vehicle. The hedge had been landscaped to grow up and over the arched frame. A smaller door was cleverly set into one of the large doors. Next to it was a button with a sign. "Deliveries".

"Quaint," I said.

"Vaughn is earless and eyeless. There is no way for a visitor to ping him upon arrival."

I pushed the button.

There was no answer. I tried the door. It was locked.

"Hmm." I raised my voice and projected around the cul-de-sac: "I'd like to speak to Vaughn and apologize to him for our argument earlier. Perhaps I can duck through the hedge and find him!"

"Thackery, I am not recording this conversation, and neither is anyone else. Vaughn's property is earless."

"I can't imagine why you would feel the need to mention that," I said aloud, with confidence. "I'm simply stating my completely innocent intention to enter my friend Vaughn's massive yard and look for him."

"If I am the only one listening to your explanation, is it necessary to be dishonest?"

"Dishonest? I have no idea what you mean. Come, Cye. I'm sure we can find a way through the hedge over here. Perhaps Vaughn will ask us for tea. I'm parched." This last part was true. My throat was dry, and the remainder of my milkshake did not appeal to me.

I turned to the left and walked along the hedge, which rounded the cul-de-sac and then continued into dense undergrowth. Various berry canes and scrub bushes grew along that side, but I gamely pushed through. I tripped several times and became acquainted with hidden briars and thorns. Cocklebur decorated my pullover like spiky, collectible pins. The beach had been cold, but here I was stifled by the afternoon sun and the humid air. The day's exertions weighed on me; my enthusiasm was draining. I could easily head home, drink two or three cold pints, and go to sleep.

I pressed close to the hedge as we went deeper into the underbrush between Vaughn's property and his neighbor's. The component shrubs were densely planted, with less than a meter between the trunks. The hedge looked impenetrable, harsh and unyielding.

"Oh look," I said for the benefit of any neighbors, as I pointed at nothing. "Here's a fine little entryway. Vaughn! Are you home? We're coming in!" I pulled my sleeves down over my hands and stuck them between two of the plants. "Cye, could you give me a firm push, please?" I asked, under my breath.

"No. Thackery, I cannot enter the premises."

"I'm sure Vaughn won't mind. Bygones be bygones and all that. And I've shouted ahead to let him know we're coming in, so…" I continued to push on the hedge, trying to find a wide enough opening. I gave up and tried the next gap between trunks.

"Vaughn's property is earless and eyeless. Any AI or automated system is not permitted unless he invites them to enter."

"We've covered this. You are a person, not an automated system."

"I am a person because of a legal agreement. The AI accords of '84 affirm my personhood, and also establish that any individual, human or AI, may declare their premises—"

"Yada yada. If you step onto Vaughn's property, are your limbs going to freeze up like the Tin Woodman? Will you topple over?"

"No. I would only be unable to retain imagery and other data. However, no sentient may knowingly and unlawfully impinge upon the rights of another sentient without—"

"Come with me," I interrupted. "I don't want to go in alone. If Vaughn's just a jerk, nothing bad will happen. But if he's the dark-sunglassed villain with a cane and a white cat (and he's got something to hide), there are probably defenses of some kind—"

"I would be unable to help against such defenses or collect evidence, and any such evidence would be inadmissible."

"But you've got to come, Cye!" I said, filling my voice with melo-drama. "Goodness, think of it: I could be killed. Or worse, mutilated. What do your feelings tell you about that? My leg could be shredded by a bear trap—"

"Please stop. I see what you are trying to do. But entering Vaughn's property is illegal. And, if not prosecutable, it is at least immoral."

"If he didn't want people entering his property, he'd erect a fence."

"Municipal environmental regulations prohibit the erection of a fence or gate taller than—"

"Come on, Cye!"

"I cannot step over that line."

"Yes, you can."

"No, I can't."

"You mean you won't."

"Correct."

We were in danger of squabbling again, and I imagined Jelly clicking her tongue as we bickered. I'd just found a crack between two plants that might possibly have fit a more lithe, twenty-something version of myself. With effort, and the willingness to lose some blood, I might make it through.

"Fine, I'll go in alone."

"That is illegal and inadvisable—possibly dangerous, as you have noted."

"But you'll be my lookout."

"I will not be your lookout. I would have no way of communicating with you or—"

"Make a noise like an owl."

"I cannot."

"It's easy, you hold your hands like this—"

I turned and saw Cye's face. I stopped talking.

He was genuinely distressed. I hadn't really been paying attention. I'd focused on the hedge, on my goal, and on being funny and clever. Why? To avoid fear? Now I felt guilty. I was being an asshole.

"You're worried about me," I said.

I stepped back from the hedge and put my hand on his arm. "I apologize. I was kidding about the bear traps. I'll be okay. And trespassing is hardly—"

Cye interrupted me. His voice was tight and strained, an octave higher, and more real. "I cannot support the logic of being here at all. The probability of you finding anything useful to the investigation is extremely small. Why are you doing this?"

I wanted to stop right there and reward Cye. He wasn't playing the unflappable detective. He was upset. But I didn't have time to encourage him about that.

"Because I'm going to find Christobel's killer, whatever it takes. I believe in justice, even if you don't. That means following even a slim lead. Vaughn wanted us to steer clear of him, so I will get right up in his business. You don't have to come. I'll be okay."

Cye turned his back on me. He folded his arms.

I thought about saying something more, but I wasn't sure what. And I didn't know how long I'd have. I began forcing my way between the hedges.

"Thackery," Cye said. His back was still turned.

"Yes Cye?"

"I will wait here for you."

"Thank you. Back in flash."

Just getting through the hedge took considerably more time than a flash. I didn't cut any major arteries, but I scraped sharp red lines wherever I had exposed flesh, including one across my left cheek. I almost entered Vaughn's property without pants—the damage was severe. This was the last day for what was formerly my favorite outfit. But I made it in, and I created a larger opening by ripping and bending several branches. Hopefully, the return trip would be less painful.

Then I turned to survey Vaughn's secret garden.

"Well fuck," I said. I considered turning right around and squeezing back out. The hedges continued. There were two paths forward, a long dead end on the left, and a path to the right that snaked back along the property line. Vaughn's land was a hedge maze.

"What is this asshole's deal?" I turned around briefly, but realized that Cye wouldn't be able to hear me, even just through the hedge. While I was on the property and he wasn't, that would constitute remote AI monitoring.

The hedge maze was made of a different plant than the outer wall: leafier, and more spare. These were not towering hedges, they were dense, leafy bushes. In theory, I could push my way through these more easily, though it would still be a challenge. The interior hedges were also shorter—not short enough to easily step over or climb, but short enough that in some places I could almost see over them.

When I found an area where the bushes were low, I hopped. What I saw did not encourage me. The maze was beautiful—and extensive. I couldn't see all of it, or glimpse a path to the center. I certainly couldn't drag my finger around and solve the damn thing like a restaurant placemat.

And what was the destination, the treasure in the maze? Vaughn's house? What did I hope to discover? Weapons? A secret lab with an army of private drones? Maybe a wall filled with pictures of Christobel, or a secret grave filled with bodies of missing persons—all of Vaughn's past victims?

Actually, yes. Any of those would be great. And I was here now. I started jogging down the second path from the dead end, hopping and leaping from time to time.

After a few turns, I spotted a small dome-shaped building to the south. Two pipes ran down the side of the structure. It was as good a destination as any, and it was the only thing besides the silvery tower that I could spot.

Working my way towards the dome was not easy. The maze presented countless choices, and all the jumping to reorient myself did a number on my quads and hamstrings, which were already tight. Left, right, straight. Left, left, dead end. Hop. Back track. Turn right? Hop. Another right, another right. Straight. Hop?

Well, shit. Now I was headed in the wrong direction.

Left, left, right? Straight. Hop. No, that wasn't right. Back up, turn left, straight, straight. Hop. Left. Hop.

I couldn't even see the building any more. The bushes were higher here, or I was getting too tired to hop high enough. I could still see the tower—but it seemed farther away and in the wrong direction.

I was thirsty and exhausted.

I decided I needed to take the maze more seriously. I could work this out methodically: The sun must now be firmly in the western sky. When I cut into Vaughn's property, the hedge ran north by northeast? It must, if we came down the street, which ran due south. But did it really? And was the gate perpendicular to the street? It was June in the southern hemisphere, so the sun did not arc due west in any case, but I could still—

I was fucked.

I slowly turned 360 degrees. I looked for a landmark, anything that might help. The silver tower was all I saw—a stubby, shiny phallus.

A wave of dizziness arrived, and I sat down. I didn't want to get up and try again. I was lost on the property of a murder suspect, in danger of passing out, and the only guardian of the law on the Island who had an actual physical body wasn't coming to rescue me.

I was a trespasser on private property. Could Vaughn shoot me? Or kill me by mistake, in a completely defensible way? If he didn't already have a secret grave of past victims, he could start one now. I was profoundly fucked.

How to get out? If I headed away from the tower, maybe?

I climbed to my feet. My mouth had turned to cotton. I oriented myself towards the tower, and then turned around and headed away. I stumbled and struggled to my feet again. A right turn. Tower? Away. Straight. Left turn. Straight. Tower? Couldn't see it, the hedge was overgrown in this area. I'd been here before? Straight, left. A longer path, which seemed to curve.

Then, a dead end.

I cried. No actual tears came out. I was too dry for proper weeping.

"Why oh why didn't I have a salad? Anything but that goddamn milkshake." Cye carried the thermos. He probably still had it. The thought of ice cream made me want to retch, but I'd go for it. I'd drink a nonalcoholic light beer if one were handy.

I did everything I could to not think about the full glass of water that sat next to my plate at Jelly's—utterly untouched—for the whole lunch. Water. Any water. "Apples. I should have had Jelly add apples to the pancakes. She would have done that for me. Apples and ginger are good."

What was I even doing here? I'd bullied Cye, poked at him and tried to take advantage of him, then broken the law. I'd even tried to use his emotions, which he'd agreed to remain integrated with only because I'd asked him. And because he liked me. I'd been an asshole to someone who actually liked me.

I attempted to make a sound like an owl. It was terrible.

I walked back to the last intersection. I sat down. Actual tears again threatened to come out of my eyes again. "No, fuck you! I need that water in my body, damn it."

One more intersection. I struggled to my feet again.

Up. Straight.

Left. Right? Did it matter any more? I turned right.

I saw Cye walking towards me. He was not a mirage.

I don't remember whether he walked all the way to me or I ran to him—but I remember I put my arms around him, sagging against him in relief. He held me. I kept trying to say "I'm sorry," but my mouth wasn't working right. I pressed my face into his neck instead.

Cye kept trying to offer me the thermos, but I just wanted to hold on to him. His body was cool and solid. His skin felt correct.

After a few minutes, I was sensible enough to let go of him and accept the thermos. I expected (and dreaded) the thick, syrupy dredge of a warm milkshake—I almost choked in relief when it was cool, clear water instead.

"Sip. You can drink it all, but sip slowly," Cye said, holding the thermos. His other arm was around me, supporting me.

"How long? How long have I been in here?" It had to be hours.

"Forty-three minutes."

Well, naturally.

"Did you know I was in trouble? Why'd you decide to come inside?"

"I changed my mind after forty-one minutes and eleven seconds," Cye replied. This was an evasive answer.

"But why?"

Cye paused before replying. He looked at me and then at the bushes that surrounded us. "Because I felt like it."

"Thank you." It wasn't enough. I didn't have the words. I was thankful for the whole knight-in-shining-armor bit—because I'm not above that once in a while—but I felt something more. He helped me even when I'd been a jerk. "You broke the rules. Are you able to think about what you're looking at right now?"

"I am only partially aware of what is occurring, and I won't be able to access this memory fully. Curiously, I don't remember what I said at the beginning of this sentence, either."

"I hope your awesome brain can still get us out of here. AI are good at mazes, I suppose?"

Cye helped me to stand, and smiled. "Yes. This yard is no more of a maze than everywhere I walk, every thought I construct, and every conversation. AI are always in a labyrinth."

"Fantastic. In that case, Mr. Bowie, please take us to the exit."

Cye shook his head. "I don't want to leave yet."

"Are you fucking kidding me?"

"There is a domed building to the southeast that reminds me of something. I want to examine it."

"Cye, you don't want to be here. Why would you—okay, what does it remind you of?"

"I have no idea. As I told you, I can't process most of what I see here. I don't know why I want to do something, I just know what I feel. I want to see the dome. Are you feeling better? I do have a general premonition of danger. We can leave the premises now if you wish."

"Where'd you get the water?"

Cye looked down at the thermos in his hand. "I can't access that memory." He raised his head. "But I observe that every third row of hedges has an embedded sprinkler. There are probably periodic valves for draining or releasing air during maintenance. A sprinkler system is not illegal, so I am unsure why I could not remember that."

He was right. When I looked carefully, I could see the sprinklers too. There was even a raised lump in the dirt right in front of us, where a buried pipe surfaced through the soil. I'd tripped over it.

"We can get more water."

"Yes."

"Okay. Then, yes. Let's go find Vaughn's secret."

As it turned out, we didn't need to reach the dome. The secret was in plain sight, shouting at us from all directions. It took five more minutes of walking before we figured it out, though.

In the meantime, I drank another pint of water, had a brief dizzy spell, and just barely managed not to throw up. Cye calmly made choices at each intersection. If he had a short term memory while on the property, and couldn't track the reasons behind his own actions, would he remember how fervently I embraced him? Did I want him to remember that? Actually, if he couldn't fully assemble ideas, should I worry about him?

I decided not to. He looked like his usual, confident, Mr.-Cool-

Detective self. He even seemed to walk with more intention. I think his emotional state, his interest and urgency, were integrating with his walking algorithm. There was a real person there in the set of his narrow shoulders, in how he turned his head. I liked watching him. He was navigating an earless AI dead zone that made it harder for him to think, but he still looked good to me.

Just as I had this realization, Cye froze. He turned his head, and his mouth hung open a crack. He stared at the hedge nearest him.

Then he started murmuring. In Latin.

Oh good, I thought. Now he's possessed.

CHAPTER NINE
TEA

"*Erythroxylaceae. Aneulophus. Pinacopodium.*"

"Cye, are you okay?" I walked up to him slowly. I tried to catch his eyes.

"*Rufum, macrophyllum, zambesiacum, barbatum.*"

I followed his gaze. He examined the hedge, specifically the leaves on the hedge. The branch looked like all the bushes inside Vaughn's property. Why would Cye start talking to them in Latin? Was he attempting an exorcism on a shrubbery?

He turned to me, finally. "The outer hedge—that's *ligustrum ovalifolium,* all of it. But this isn't. This is *Erythroxylum.* But not *ipadu.* And it's not *novogranatense* either."

Okay, so the Latin was taxonomy. I had a retrograde biology teacher who believed in the practice of memorization, forcing us to stand in front of our peers and recite the steps of cellular mitosis, and etc. For taxonomy I only remembered "King Phillip Came Over From Greece Singing" and that all species names were fraudulent Latin. Cye-9 might not be able to line his thoughts up clearly, but this couldn't be random. Why would he care about the taxonomy of a bush?

My heart sank.

"It's drugs, isn't it?"

Cye looked at the plants and nodded, then shook his head. "This shouldn't exist. It's got the leaf shape of the coca plant, but that's extinct. No lab would be allowed to resurrect it. You can't even model the genetic code for a science fair project without getting the attention of the authorities. The body of the plant and the flower have been modified. This is something new. But it's definitely based on coca."

"So this is cocaine?"

"Not yet it isn't. I think the plant is an artificial genetic variant of *Erythroxylaceae*. There was a similar find on Palantir Station, eighty-one years ago. The Palantir coca plant grew faster, heartier, and the resulting molecule had less carbon and hydrogen—I'm having trouble thinking about this. I keep forgetting and restarting the thread."

I took Cye by the arms. "We're wasting our time, and we need to leave."

"Thackery, this is a terrible plant. Vaughn would have to process it immediately to get away with it, but in this configuration he can more easily neutralize the hydrochloride. But that indicates...I don't understand. You look disappointed."

"Because Vaughn is not a suspect anymore. We've wasted our time and you've endangered yourself for nothing."

Cye focused on me. "Thackery, this is illegal activity. In two minutes I will forget about it, but a person who breaks one law has less compunction about breaking another. And he's a known associate of Christobel—"

"So is everyone on the Island."

"He's a drug dealer, Thackery."

"It's never the drug dealer, Cye!"

"What do you mean?"

"I mean the murderer is never the drug dealer. It's a red herring: a crime, but not the crime we're looking for. A thing that makes someone seem suspicious, but in actuality they're just the thief, or the con artist, or the drug dealer. The murderer is never the drug dealer. Damn it."

And, upon reflection, what was Vaughn's motive? Cye violated an interplanetary treaty for me to investigate a suspect who had no motive. This farm required precision and effort. Would someone who could do this ever need to kill a community theater producer? Why were we standing in Vaughn's cocaine hedge maze? "I hated him for how he treated you. I wanted him to be Christobel's killer, but—"

"He's a much better suspect now. This plant destroys lives."

"Oh, he's a better suspect now? But still just another line on a spreadsheet. Is he higher than Jelly? Is he higher up than me? Vaughn sucks. But I'm not interested in ranked suspects. I want the actual killer. And the drug dealer is never the killer."

Cye fell silent.

"Can we get out of here before Vaughn gets back?"

"I want to see the dome building."

"We don't need to see it. We know what it is. It's where he processes cocaine."

"Why would you think that?" Cye asked. He was losing the thread. He couldn't place the coca plants into long term memory.

So off he walked, and I followed. Cye dropped the branch of the hedge, and it was already leaving his mind. All he had left was the vague feeling that he needed to investigate the dome building which loomed ahead.

I tried again, trailing after him. "Cye, we don't need to see the dome building. I know what it is."

"What is it?"

My argument became Seussian. "You can't know what it is. If you could, you would, because you really do know. But you can't know, so you don't. And that's why you want to see it. But you won't be able to see it, see?"

Cye walked as I chattered. "I am unable to follow your logic. But it doesn't matter, because we're here."

We made a right turn around a hedge, and suddenly the small building sat before us. Multiple pipes sprouted out of it and dove into the ground. There was an acrid, ammonia-like smell. The building wasn't quite a dome, but the roof curved down and out, with channels to collect rainwater.

Cye wrinkled his nose. "Sodium bicarbonate. Water supply. A gas line for heat so he won't have to draw attention from extra power usage—"

"Do tell. What could it all mean?" Surely even in his present state he couldn't miss my sarcasm.

With a look of shock, Cye turned to me and said, "He could be processing illegal narcotics."

"Yes. That's it, Cye! You've figured it out! Can we leave now?"

"I need a closer look. It could be for sugar, or tobacco, or—but if he's got a supply of—"

"He does, Cye. The hedges are mutant coca plants."

"Coca plants?" He looked at the hedges that surrounded us, seeing them again for the first time.

My partner was at war with his algorithms. By a statute that stretched across his soul and the solar system, he couldn't assemble the information. Or if he did, he was forced to immediately discard it.

He stepped onto the concrete pad that the building sat on. He looked so confused, childlike. He studied the door, then turned back to the nearest hedge, then back to the building. He was like an Asimovian robot trapped between two laws. I wanted to comfort him somehow. I also wanted to get the hell out of there. But how could I convince the curious detective to stop trying to scratch an itch he'd never reach?

At last he turned and looked at me.

"Thackery."

"Yes, Cye?"

"I need to get out of here."

"Yes!" Finally.

Then he toppled over backwards, falling down hard onto the cement.

I raced over to him. "What's going on? Are you okay?" He didn't answer. I knelt beside him and gripped his shoulders. I tried to lift him.

I noticed a faint vibration around us. It felt prickly under my skin.

Cye's eyes were open. He stared at the sky.

I put my face right in front of his. "What's happening to you?"

"Electrical. Resonant. Induction."

"What, like a wireless charger?"

"...opposite of that."

"What do I do to help you?"

No answer.

I stepped off the concrete and back onto the dirt, then I grabbed Cye's leg and pulled. He weighed a lot. I wondered if the shed pad was magnetic. After the day I'd had, pulling a full-size walking AI would have been an effort even if Cye were on wheels. I put my sandals against the edge of the concrete and leaned back for leverage.

When I'd gotten him a full meter away from the pad, I stopped to catch my breath.

"Thank you," Cye said. "Thackery, are you still there?" His eyes were shut.

"I'm here. Can you hear me?"

"Yes. I've shut off visual processing to save power. There must be a series of induction coils nearby which sensed my electrical differential and reversed the field—"

"Just say power drain trap."

"Power drain trap. I'm having trouble remembering—"

"I know, don't worry about that. We're leaving. Do you have enough power to walk?"

"No."

"...enough power to crawl?"

Cye paused before responding. "In an adult humanoid body, crawling requires more energy than walking."

I made a grumpy nonsensical sound and looked around us. Could I somehow roll him? Could I—

"Thackery?"

"Yes, Cye?"

"Fear is integrating with the rest of my thoughts. It is a unique sensation." As Cye spoke, he moved his mouth as little as possible. He was doing everything possible to save energy. I didn't want him taxing whatever juice he had left on fear.

"Yeah, fear sucks. But you don't need to be scared."

"When Vaughn returns he can arrest me for violating the AI accords. My sentience will cease. I will become a Level 3 AI. I'm going to die today."

"That's not going to happen. I'm going to rescue you now. You got to be my knight in shining armor, now I'm going to be yours. All I need is a white horse."

I looked around again. No horses presented themselves. Instead, I knelt down and wedged my body underneath Cye.

"Lift with the legs," I muttered and pushed upward, trying to shift Cye onto my back. I staggered forward half a step before toppling over. Cye landed like a sandbag.

"Something has left me without muscular control."

"Don't talk, Cye. Save whatever you've got left."

"I'm trapped inside my body. Every part of me is bound. I can't move. I can't—" His voice broke off.

"It's going to be okay, Cye. Listen, I'm right here. This is only a problem. We're going to work the problem."

In the distance, I heard the sound of a wooden door shutting.

Well, shit. Hopefully Cye missed that. Hopefully Vaughn would just go into his house and—

"Thackery. I weigh 101 kilograms." Cye's voice slurred as he spoke. I could hear the fear wrestling with fatigue. It was what an intoxicated person would sound like, scared to the edge of his senses. "You are not going to be able to carry me. You must leave."

"Well that's not fucking happening."

"There is no alternative. Down the west path, take the first left, then left again, turn right, travel straight through the next two intersections. That will get you to the eastern half of the maze. Then—"

"Cye, I'm not going. Shut up."

"It may help you to remember it as abbreviations for each choice. L, L, R, S, S, R, S, L, S, L. From there you will see the hole in the hedge you made upon entry—I widened it."

I'd get help. But what kind of help could I get that wouldn't result in Cye being arrested and executed? No one could see him leave, let alone help him.

"I'll repeat the sequence now," Cye said, and I put aside my furiously tumbling thoughts to try and memorize what Cye was saying. "L, L, R, S, S, R, S, L, S, L."

So I made a song, and repeated it aloud. "Loser, Loser, Right. Sucker, Sucker, Right. Seeker, Lover, Seeker, Love."

"Correct. And that's a wonderful poem." Cye's words were slower, as if he were falling asleep.

"Thanks."

"You're wonderful...Thackery. Although...there are also some awful parts of you."

"Shut up while you're ahead. I'll be back as fast as I can. Don't try to talk me out of it. In the meantime—" I took a breath. "In the meantime, I withdraw my request. Please turn off your emotions, or put them back in their coffins. You don't need to lie here feeling scared. I don't want that. I don't want you to just sit here, alone and scared."

Cye was quiet for a second. I thought he'd done as I asked, turned everything off so he could keep his neural matrix active without damage as long as possible.

"Fuck you, Thackery."

"What?"

"If I have only a few hours to live, I'm going to live them."

I grabbed his lapels and kissed him, then. Right on his immobile, unresponsive lips.

Maybe he couldn't even feel it, drained and operating on minimal power. Maybe he'd never know. So maybe I did it for me. I could kiss him for him later. But maybe there wouldn't be a later? I kissed him again.

I jogged off down the path. I lost my sandals. I stumbled barefoot through the coca hedges and I chanted at each choice in the maze.

Loser, loser, right. Sucker, sucker, right. Seeker, lover, seeker, love.

*
* *

When my breath slowed enough to speak like a normal person, I said hello to Petra's front door and asked if she was home. She had granite steps and a dark wood paneled door with no ornamentation or buttons to push.

Petra's voice came back almost immediately. "Thackery. Just a minute!"

She soon opened the door. She had on a silk lounge robe, the kind that aims to appear as casual as possible while also looking stunning. They have AI now, up on Prax, who do nothing but adjust angles on the lines of clothing so you can hypnotize admirers. I hadn't seen Petra at a party since...well, ever, that I could remember. We did have one or two excellent conversations when she first moved down, though. I liked her. She worked with stone, I thought. Unless I was confusing her with Judy? But I could just make out the muscles hidden by her robe. Yes, definitely stone.

"I'm so glad you've come," she said with a smile. "You're early. I haven't dressed."

Early. I'm early? "Oh?" I replied.

"For tea?" she asked. And I saw her eyes go down to my outfit. By this point, my pants were indecent. She could readily discern the make and model of my underwear. What remained of my clothes were festooned with thistle, burdock, and probably bits of coca plant as well. I had no open wounds, but I displayed numerous welts and scratches from the malicious vegetation.

To her credit, her eyes bounced right back to my face as if there was nothing unusual about a crazed zombie scavenger showing up on her doorstep. I considered quickly: If Cye were caught on Vaughn's property, his neural matrix and his sentient cognition might be forfeit. Could I trust Petra to keep a secret? Probably. But would she lie, under oath, about a violation of the AI personhood accords?

"Yes. Here for tea. Absolutely."

Petra stood aside and gestured to usher me in. So there was a tea. There must have been a standing invitation that I'd long since forgotten about or dismissed. Why does the world make itself so inhospitable for introverts, as if all there is that's worth doing is endless teas, parties, or games of croquet? I'd thought Petra more concrete than that. She worked in stone, after all.

"Petra, before the tea: I've got myself into a bit of a jam."

A perfectly trimmed eyebrow rose into an arch. "Oh dear. Something I can help with?"

"I've got to take care of it myself. But do you have—do you have an extension cord? Like, a long one?"

Petra appraised me for a moment. "I do. I've got a couple of twenty-five-meter cords that we use for the Spring Carnival. We missed you last year, you know—you'd be very welcome. You could put a piece in the raffle, as long as it's something family-friendly. You'd get good exposure, and it benefits the community."

Fifty meters. Would that be enough? How long was fifty meters anyway? Maybe if I jammed the cord through the bushes and cut straight over—

Petra noticed me puzzling. Her eyebrow went back down. Like a switch, she dropped out of friendly hostess mode. Now she was Petra in no-nonsense, pragmatic mode. Her head lifted, and shoulders went back. I knew and liked this version of her: the deliberate Petra.

She stepped out of the house and walked towards a yellow shed that stood at the edge of her property. She wore heavy, steel-toed boots under her silk robe, which made me wildly curious about what she was doing before I arrived. I took the opportunity to scan the yard, and I saw Petra's art.

It was stone. There were a series of curvaceous monoliths, like waves captured just before they crested. At the end of the yard hovered a closed eye as tall as me. My favorite was a tree carved from marble which stood in the shadow of the original, living tree, presenting both an ever-changing self and a younger, static self. This was art that could only be in one place, for one period of time, art that would change with each decade, as if someone pulled the contrast slider up higher and higher until the image disappeared.

"Taj, the door please."

Petra's AI triggered the large front-flip door of the shed as we approached. The interior of the building was a meticulously-organized nirvana of tools. It held several boxy platform machines. One was a stone saw, but others I couldn't identify. There was a sharp-cornered box that bristled steel spindles with knobby ends. The walls were lined with tiny drawers, each with a button-sized polished handle. Despite the urgent situation, I wanted to run up and open all the boxes and look inside them.

Coiled against one wall were the two beefy extension cords, which hung beside a sea of smaller cords, power converters, and surge protectors.

I rushed inside and swung one coil over my neck like a bandolier. I eyed a battery unit for a moment, but dismissed it as too heavy. I hoisted the other large cord, turned, and took off towards the thick vegetation between Petra's property and her neighbor's.

Then I turned and raced back. Petra raised her eyebrow again.

"Thank you. And is there a place to plug this in? Maybe somewhere on the west edge of your property?"

*
**

I needed a new song, but this time in reverse: *Lover, seeker, lover, seeker. Right, sucker, sucker. Right, loser, loser.*

At the last minute, one extension cord around me and another unraveling in my hands, I realized I needed to reverse the directions, too. Every *lover* and *loser* needed to be *right*. And to be *right,* you needed to be a *loser* or a *lover.* I needed to remember, at each choice, whether I wanted to be right, or be a lover. The transposition would have been child's play for an AI. Johnathan could have rattled it off for me, except he couldn't talk on Vaughn's property. And my remote was still in the ocean where I'd thrown it.

Right, seeker, right, seeker. Loser, sucker, sucker. Loser. Right, right.

I repeated it twice and then dived through my Thackery hole, back into the maze. I lugged the cord through the bushes as quietly as possible.

A couple of times I made the decision to push the bundle through the bushes to cut off a turn in the maze. I didn't hear Vaughn, or any other sound. Even nature was taking a break.

I avoided looking up at the silvery tower. I thought, as a child might, that if I didn't catch a glimpse of him then he couldn't see me. I fantasized that Vaughn went into his tower and was now taking a nap.

He wasn't.

Cye had not moved, of course. One could almost think he was taking a pleasant nap in the midafternoon sun, surrounded by the coca plants. I ran up and squeezed his hand. Which he couldn't feel. Which meant I did it just for me again. Damn it.

"Cye, I've got a cord."

"What do you have a cord for?"

"To plug you in. To charge you. And you're going to have to chug it, because we're late for tea."

Cye didn't answer.

"Where do I stick this?"

"I don't have a charging outlet, Thackery."

What? I staggered back a step, but mastered myself. "Come on, Cye. There's 240 volts between these two dumb slots. I dragged them through the fucking maze for you. That's got to be good enough!"

Cye didn't respond.

"Come on!"

"...please put the end of the cord in my left hand."

I brought the end of the plug up to Cye's hand and wrapped his fingers around the plug head. His fingers closed suddenly, cracking the plastic casing. Then there was a faint burning smell.

"Don't be alarmed. I can recalibrate after some dermal tissue burns off."

Cye opened his eyes. I laughed in relief. "It's working?"

He allowed the barest whisper of a nod, but he still had fear on his face. "Yes, it's working."

"How long before you can walk?"

"Thackery, I don't have a battery. I'm not like a drone. I derive power from an electrochemical differential between my interstitial tissues and my lymph system—"

"Cye, how long before you can walk?!"

"At least six hours. I could possibly hobble with support in four—"

"What?"

"Normally I persist for a week without recharging. On Prax, I can be charged in seconds with a fluid transfer. There's nothing like that here."

I stood up and balled my fists in frustration. I stalked away. "No, no, no."

Cye let me fume.

"I'll go pound on Vaughn's door, then. I'll confront him. I'll demand that he—" Demand what? We broke the law. Sure, he probably wouldn't shoot me. But if anyone found out that Cye came onto the property, into the maze to rescue me, the result would be the same. This was my fault; I did this to Cye—I ended him. This was my choice.

Could I hide him under the bushes? Put him in the drug shed and hope that Vaughn didn't come out and find him? Or bury him in the soil, and then run away—*Little Thackery, who always ran away, over the hills and up the stairs, then down to Earth, and as far as they could run—never far enough.*

A wind of exhausted self-hatred pushed at me. I wanted to rage and shriek at myself—I wanted a drink. I wanted to drink too much, too fast, and blot it out. Blot myself out.

Then I smelled burning again.

I turned to rush back towards Cye, but it wasn't him. He'd shut his eyes again, and his hand wasn't smoking or anything. Something else was burning. I scanned the leafy horizon around me.

Smoke rose from multiple locations around the perimeter of Vaughn's yards. The coca maze was burning.

"I'll be back," I said.

"Thackery," Cye opened his eyes again. "Don't come back."

"Fuck you. Sit there and charge."

Loser, loser, right. Sucker, sucker, right. Seek—actually, I didn't need the poem anymore. I knew the way.

*
* *

"Hello again."

"Hello Thackery." Still unruffled, bless her, Petra had a glass of water waiting, which she handed me nonchalantly as soon as she opened the door. She ignored my labored breath, as if it would be impolite to pry. Good boundaries on Petra. I'd have to learn that skill. "Ready for tea? Or some additional assistance?"

"Not ready yet, sorry. Do you happen to own a wheelbarrow?"

*
* *

The hedges were darkened by thick clouds of smoke, which rose in corridors around Vaughn's property. Something about the landscaping or the western wind was keeping it contained, but the stench still reached Petra's strip of trees and brambles.

I pushed Petra's wheelbarrow towards my little green portal into hell. Vaughn's sprinklers had come on, but only above the outer hedge in a perimeter that pumped water outward—a lot of water. I'd need to pass through a curtain of rain, practically a waterfall, which was soaking the outskirts of Vaughn's property and Petra's blackberry bushes.

Before going in, I took as many deep breaths as I could, trying to saturate my body with oxygen. I wished I could breathe it into Cye, give him back his legs. I tore off a shred of my pants and wrapped it around my mouth. I looked up and glimpsed a half rainbow across the sky. In I went.

Inside the hedge maze, the upper leaves were aflame, as if a drone had circled the property and lit each plant like a candle, turning the labyrinth into a birthday cake for Methuselah. But Vaughn didn't have smart drones, did he? Where would he get them without blowing his cover?

The bushes would just burn from the top down, wouldn't they? I naively thought this would be easy. Surely it would take a while for fire to burn downward—especially green, healthy bushes.

*Right, seeker, right...*I knew the way, and could see the extension cord, a bright orange against the green. I ran.

Running with a wheelbarrow is not recommended. The wobble of the weight increases as you speed up. Then you take a sharp turn, and over you go. Briefly, I tried towing it behind me, but my legs hit the crossbar with each backstep unless I took small steps. There was no time for small steps. When I reached Cye, I would have to lift him into the wheelbarrow—a problem I chewed on so hard that I went right past the last turn and had to double back.

"Hello again, Thackery." Cye had regained some composure, though he kept his eyes closed. Perhaps the electricity had helped, and now he knew I wasn't going to give up on him. He sounded like his calm self. Maybe he couldn't remember what was going on or where he was.

"How did you know it was me?" I asked. I tipped up the front end of the wheelbarrow on the ground right above Cye's head.

"The cadence of your footsteps. You are pushing something on wheels."

"Only one wheel, unfortunately, but it's a big wheel."

I sat behind Cye and propped him into a sitting position. I held him for the briefest second, like you might hold a child on your lap or your bobsled partner. I took a breath, dug my bare heels into the ground, and pulled us both onto the lip of the wheel barrow.

I extricated myself, and put Cye's free hand on the rim. "I don't know what you've got left, but if you can hold on to something, now is the time to do it."

I went back to the handles, and I used my full weight to pry the front of the wheelbarrow into the air. Cye slid gently into place, like ice cream in a bowl.

He opened his eyes. The sky, by this time, was on fire. Engulfed bushes raged all around us. Cye cried out in fear.

"Nothing to worry about. Just a little smoke." I knelt on the ground to try and catch a breath of less-awful air. I gave in to a brief coughing fit.

"What's happening?"

"I recommend you keep your olfactory senses turned off for the time being."

I'd misjudged the problem. Ignited branches were tumbling to the ground with ash and embers, which landed on the packed dry grass and mulch around the plants. In a few minutes, the candle tops of the coca plants would turn the maze into a bonfire—a blacksmith's forge, hell itself, a jalapeño popper, some other fire-based metaphor.

A 53-kilogram humanoid can push a 101-kilogram humanoid in a wheelbarrow, I discovered. It's doable. But they can't run. And they must take corners with the utmost care, not leaning the wheelbarrow at all, coming in tight like a race car driver and exiting wide.

Cye opened his eyes again. "What's going on? Thackery?"

"You're in a wheelbarrow."

"What color is it?"

I narrowly avoided dumping Cye out for the third time as I swung around the second *right*, and headed through the subsequent *seeker*. Seekers always go straight through an intersection.

"Excellent question. Glad to see your incisive wisdom return. It's red, I think. So much depends upon a red wheelbarrow—but the paint has mostly chipped off this one, so it's white now."

"Then you succeeded."

"How did I succeed?" The mulch on either side of the path smoldered, releasing a heavy smoke. It grew dense as I finally reached *lover*. I needed to breathe. I tried not to breathe. I was light headed, dizzy, and I kept shaking my head to try and clear it.

"You're my knight in armor. You rescue me with your white horse— white wheelbarrow, which is more useful than a horse in this context."

"I haven't rescued you yet. Now, repeat after me: 'I am the Dread Pirate Roberts, and there will be two survivors!'"

My breath burned in my lungs. I sucked dirty air through the thin, torn fabric of my even dirtier mask. Cye had let go of the power cord, a good idea as it was on fire. I wondered if, when we passed through the curtain of water at the edge of the property, I would get the full 240 volts through my body. I could lay down dead and rest, then, at least. But I would get Cye out of danger if it was the last thing I did.

Cye said the phrase, and with a triumphant roar, the ground aflame around me, I crashed the wheelbarrow through a wall of smoke and into the watery curtain. We bumped up over the slight rise of the perimeter hedge and then down into Petra's soggy blackberry bushes. The wheelbarrow turned and tumbled Cye out onto the ground—face first into the canes, to my dismay.

I ran around and turned him over.

He opened his mouth to the falling water. "This is refreshing," he said.

"Does the water help you?"

"I turned off my salinity and pH sensors, so I've no way of knowing."

I let us both sit there under the heavy spray. I needed a shower, anyway. It was much easier to breathe, though a heavy, smoky stench filled the air. I took the opportunity to cough until I puked, which I found oddly reviving.

I managed to reload Cye into the wheelbarrow. Then I made the last, impossible push up the property's incline. We tumbled out of the trees and brambles and into the sunshine of Petra's coiffed green lawn.

Petra strode over from her shed. She carried a medical device I didn't recognize, and she had a white first aid kit hung over her shoulder. She made me sit down on the grass and handed me a water bottle.

"May I take a look?" she asked. She accepted my vague nod as permission.

She prodded me, examined my ears and throat, had me cough, asked me questions. She held the device to my arm and I felt a slight prick. What was she taking my blood for? The question escaped me as I turned to wretch up the water I'd swallowed. She handed me a cloth, and then she proceeded to clean the worst of the scratches with a damp thing that smelled like bad vodka. She put a flexible bandage on one.

"Okay. You're going to be fine. Get more fluids in, when you can keep them down. I'll get you some throat lozenges. As for you," she addressed Cye, "are you in pain or danger?"

"Not of the physical kind, no."

"Will you be okay if we can figure out how to get you topped off?"

"Yes, thank you."

"May I have permission to pick you up?"

"Yes."

Petra reached into the wheelbarrow. Before I could say "He's quite heavy," she'd flipped him into a fireman's carry and was striding back towards her house.

"I think you'd both benefit from a proper shower. Glad you came early. We might have just enough time."

"Just enough time? Before what?" I asked.

Her stride barely slacking, she turned to answer me. Both Cye and her first aid kit bounced slightly, and soot-laden water trickled from Cye's clothes down over her silk robe.

"Before tea, of course."

I silently promised myself that my tea would include vodka, tequila, light rum, triple sec, gin, and a splash of cola.

"Christobel said you would be coming," Petra said as she entered her house.

What?

*
**

Petra's house had the kind of clean, intentional layout you'd expect for a sculptor of stone. The floor was polished concrete. Each piece of furniture was functional and strong or else it could fuck off right out of her house, thank you very much.

The dining table displayed a small garden of ceramic mugs, each one overladen with personality. A small glowing picture frame, set apart and accompanied by a glittering gold mug, showed a picture of Christobel. I studiously looked away from it. Fatigue brought my feelings closer to the surface.

Petra had an array of cookies, brewing presses, and canisters of tea in the kitchen. As we swept past, I stole four of what looked like chocolate butter cookies but ended up being molasses. That was okay. I like molasses. But the cookies matched everything else that day: Nothing was what I expected.

How could I ask Petra what she meant about Christobel without breaking whatever assumption made us welcome in her house? Had she spoken to him recently? Was she a suspect? And of more immediate importance: What should I do about my feet? I felt the cool concrete beneath them and didn't want to look down, knowing I left wet, charcoal-and-mud footprints across the house as I walked.

Petra headed towards a large bathroom off the kitchen entryway. "Not you," she said to me over her shoulder. "You're going to my room. Taj will tell you the way. You can rummage through my drawers afterwards. I'm bulkier than you, but I've got some stretchy things that should fit."

"I—thank you—" I was barely able to get the words out before Petra disappeared into the bathroom, Cye still dangling off her shoulder like a tote bag. I glimpsed that the downstairs shower was an immense, tiled area. It was easily accessible, with a shower chair and multiple jets. Perhaps she had a disabled relative? Or she liked to have sexy shower parties? You could butcher a hog in there. Maybe she used the room to hose herself down after she murdered people with a mason's chipper.

Was I going to evaluate everyone I encountered today as a possible psychopath? That would be Cye-9's patented 286 murder suspects system, implemented through my own anxieties. No, I decided, I'd draw the line at Petra. She was too grounded.

When I reached the top of the stairs, which were difficult to climb as my calf muscles had transformed into four pieces of Petra's stone, Taj spoke. "The master bedroom is at the end of the hall. All of Petra's soaps and conditioners are hypoallergenic and scent free. Would you like me to adjust your shower temperature?"

"42, thank you."

"The meaning of life," Taj quipped, "but not very hot."

"Any hotter and my skin dries out. And I've been—well, I'm very dry today."

"There is an unscented, hypoallergenic moisturizer available in the cabinet above the sink."

"I think I'm going to use all of it. Thank you, Taj. Sorry about the carpet."

"You're welcome, Thackery. We're glad you could make it today."

And again, what did that mean? I was expected, or invited today? And to what? Tea? Were we going to wear funny hats and cast spells? If it had anything to do with Christobel, I wanted to know. But I didn't want anyone knowing I didn't know already.

After showering, I asked Taj to pick something I could wear that would be appropriate. She directed me to a black turtleneck and stretchy jeans that were loose on me but probably showed every muscle in Petra's legs.

I descended the stairs to see George on the couch in front of the window.

She was sitting still, and she looked frightened. Which is what she always looked like, so at least one thing today was normal. George is tall, willowy, and has a powerful presence when performing. When not on stage she takes shyness to a new level, which is a problem in a world where personality is your product. She'd do better to lean into the shyness—maybe make it a thing—but she persists in doing battle with it, awkwardly.

Cye was arranged in a lifelike position in a stiff-backed chair. He wore a linen suit, a green tie, and a teal fedora.

Malik, Sally's kid, sat in the corner on a regal stone chair (Petra's work, I presumed). I almost missed him as he was slouching and had opaques on.

"Hello Malik, George. Are you all here for the tea?" I asked.

Malik was in another world through his shades, but George perked up and nodded. I began to think that "tea" was a magical word. I wondered if I could use it in the future—I would pass George or Petra on the boardwalk and mouth the words "Earl Grey," and they'd lay a finger to the side of their nose and wink.

"It's good to see you, Thackery," George said in her small, stilted voice. "I'm very sorry about Christobel, I know you were close. He was very fond of you."

I stuffed another molasses cookie into my mouth to avoid responding. Petra had not tried to give me condolences. She probably figured if I wanted them, I'd ask. I prefer that system.

I didn't want to talk about Christobel, and I didn't have anything else to say. I could ask Malik how his mom was doing (Sally and I shared a studio a million years ago), but I decided to keep that one in my back pocket in case everyone got quiet for no reason—which usually happens.

Petra came down, her hair dark and wet, and walked directly to the tea supplies to make last-minute adjustments. She'd changed out of her robe, which I suspected would smell of burnt coca leaf for the rest of its days, and into dark green coveralls. "Your first time here, Thackery. You have to pick your mug."

Among the options, there were two cats, a pig with his eyes closed in bliss, and an assortment of geometric shapes. I chose a tree. I didn't want to drink out of anything with a face, and it reminded me of Petra's piece in the yard.

"Cye," I called across the room. "What mug do you want? There's a wise owl, and the symbol for pi. There's a spooky looking robot dude, or is that too on the nose?"

"That would be fine, Thackery. I do not drink tea, but warm water would be welcome. A pinch of salt, if available."

He won't be able to lift the mug anyway, I thought. But we were at a tea party now, so he'd have to fake it.

"Petra," I said more quietly. "Thank you. You—you haven't asked what the hell we were doing—"

Petra lifted a hand. "Ah-ah—don't do that. Everyone has baggage, or habits, or whatever it was you two were up to. This is tea time."

Everyone has baggage, true. But not everyone would welcome two filthy, broken-looking near-strangers and give them infinite positive regard without asking questions. Petra was a fucking rock. I told her so.

"Christobel was always there for a friend. Other than gold glitter, I think of it as his primary trait. We can all pay that forward."

That got to me. I closed my eyes. I was still too dehydrated to cry, thankfully. My brain screeched around, hunting for a snarky reply, a piece of wit to hold up as a plate for the emotion to land on or hide under. Not finding the words, I just nodded.

Petra smiled, and gestured to the canisters of tea.

"Now pay attention, 007, this is important. There are many varieties. The first question is: black, green, white, pu'er, or oolong?"

"The pu'er is printed!" Malik called out from the other room, his glasses still dark on his face. So he listened, when he wanted to.

"Shut up, meathead," Petra said, automatically. "Malik is correct, the pu'er and oolong are printed. But I assure you, quite good. Once you pick a type of tea, I can make a recommendation for a specific variety. So." She gestured to the table.

"I'll have whatever you recommend for a novice," I lowered my voice slightly, "But, to be honest, I'd wish for something a bit stronger than tea. Have you got any special ingredients under the counter?" I lifted my eyebrows in hope.

Petra's face froze for a second. Perhaps I'd committed a faux pas; I'd violated the sacred pact of the tea drinker shamans. I'd be banished before I'd even been properly hazed. But the moment passed and she said casually, "Nope. We stick to tea."

"Black and bracing, then, please," I said. I vaguely recalled that black tea had caffeine and green did not. A few minutes later, when Malik took his glasses off and started talking rapidly to me about the problems with printed teas, the resurgence of white tea, and the lack of a good rooibos anywhere by anyone in the solar system, I learned that green has caffeine, just less. I'd been wrong about the single thing I thought I knew about tea. And yet I was expected here at the party?

Malik clearly talked to me in order to help me feel more comfortable. Since I was twice his age, I felt mildly embarrassed by this, but also grateful. As he talked, my mind kept going back to Petra's comment. Christobel said I would be coming? Did she make that up to be welcoming? And when the hell did Christobel become a tea fancier?

"Okay," Petra said in a raised voice, once she was holding a steaming brown bear. "Not everyone's here. Zeta and Chamberlain texted they will arrive in a few minutes, and we'll start then."

Zeta? And Mr. Chamberlain? Up to now, the group had been only artists. Chamberlain and Zeta were patrons. And if Mr. Chamberlain was coming, that would mean his game of bridge lasted less than two hours, which (having tried the game) I found frankly amazing.

The light dawned: the secret tea society was a patron fluff club. My stomach, which now contained nothing but a half-dozen molasses cookies, turned. I'd completely forgotten about these. I'd been too successful for too many years. The way to get a patron to really roll out the gold is to make them feel like part of the process, a member of a creative community. You get a few young artists (like George and Malik), and you invite over a couple of patrons with fat wallets. You craft a perfect, casual get-to-know-you that helps the money go where the artists need it to go. Petra and I would play the part of the successful artists who lent the gathering legitimacy.

I didn't know what role Christobel held with the group, but this was not what I needed right now—or ever. No one present made especially good suspects (though I'm sure Cye placed them somewhere on his spreadsheet), and the idea of facing any more faces in the room made my pulse race.

How to leave? I couldn't just sneak out the back, leaving Cye in the clutches of the tea cult.

I'd have to be bold. And blatantly use the handicap of my date to my advantage. "Petra, Cye-9 must attend to certain matters before the sun goes down. He'll need a wheelchair or, well, some means of conveyance. Do you have anything he could use?"

"Not currently assembled, no. And I don't think you want to carry him home in a wheelbarrow."

I didn't want to push a wheelbarrow ever again.

"You could do what I do: Summon a furny."

"A what?"

"A furny!"

Cye interjected, "I suspect 'furny' is Petra's personal colloquialism for a large goods lorry."

There are no private vehicles on the Island. When someone needs to move a piano, or they receive a crate of whisky from the morning's drop (I wouldn't know anything about that), we use an autonomous lorry. The large goods lorries hum merrily along on busy days, occasionally surfed, stolen, or routed into ditches by bored adolescents.

Petra grinned. "'Furny,' for furniture. Get it? Though I usually call them for help with a big piece of stone." I glanced at Petra's arms and blushed. I found it hard to believe there was ever a stone she couldn't move.

"Lovely. Let's do that. Cye?"

"I'd rather not be carted around like a wardrobe, but I concede our options are few. I will summon a furny."

With any luck, it would arrive soon and we could depart before Mr. Chamberlain showed up and was encouraged to make a speech that we all had to applaud enthusiastically.

Then Taj announced their arrival.

Mr. Chamberlain entered with a grand, welcoming "hello, hello, hello!" Zeta followed. A person of simmering, quiet confidence and curtains of silver hair, I vaguely recalled they were Mr. Chamberlain's cousin, ex, or possibly business partner in a former life. Including Cye, there were now seven people milling about and commenting on outfits and the weather. Small talk pursued me around the room like an exuberant Labrador Retriever.

I managed to endure Mr. Chamberlain's attempt to embrace me, and I accepted his high-energy condolences on the tragedy of Christobel's passing. Zeta bowed politely to me. They don't speak much, though when they do speak they say something brilliant and true. Zeta is one of my patrons and a regular on my streams. They write poetry about microbiology.

While Petra helped the new arrivals with tea selection, I wandered down the south hallway to escape the energy.

I vainly rummaged through an industrial-sized hutch. It held only towels, candles, and overflow kitchen items. I peeked into a pristine home office, but found nothing. She had to have a liquor cabinet somewhere. It was an essential element of the Wealthy Island Artist Starter Pack. The architect drew them into the plans for each house. Island municipal would fine someone who didn't have at least a couple bottles of thirty-year scotch around for emergencies.

My comedic routine of fumbling through Petra's housewares for booze was interrupted by Taj. Her voice was pleasant but the message less so.

"Petra, Vaughn has sent a message. He apologizes for his lateness, as well as for the smoke over his property. He says he will be 'over in just a bit.'"

How delightful.

Chapter Ten
Fleeing the Interview

I walked back to the atrium and flopped down on the end of the couch nearest Cye's chair. I crossed my legs and put my hands behind my head in a completely natural, ordinary pose. Under my breath I asked, "Cye, how long is 'a bit'? Is it longer than a byte?"

Cye answered softly. "A bit holds a single binary value. There are eight bits in a byte. But in this context, I suspect Vaughn will arrive in more than five minutes, but less than thirty. I notice you inject humor at your moments of highest anxiety."

I whispered, "When the hell will the furny arrive?"

"Twelve and a half cents," George said. She was right beside us. She'd been so quiet I'd forgotten her. People forget about George. It's not fair. I hoped she and Malik would have good luck playing to Mr. Chamberlain. Zeta had more money, but I think Malik worked only in AR, and Zeta is color blind. "A bit is also twelve and a half cents," George continued. "So Vaughn will arrive in 7.5 minutes, because that's 1/8th of an hour, wouldn't you agree, Mr. Cye?"

From behind his glasses, Malik broke in, "No. A bit stores a boolean value. Zero or one. If Vaughn will be over in a bit, then he is either here already, or he's never here. He's omnipresent, or non-existent."

"That's a bit dark," George said. "Oh! Another bit, right there in my sentence. Thackery, how was your opening?"

"Oh, swell. Malik, how's your mother been?" I hurled the pointless question into the air, trying to keep my brain from melting.

This produced a few minutes of suffocating social nicety. But Mr. Chamberlain and Zeta were now steeping their teas (in a porcelain chapel and a featureless, jet-black ceramic column, respectively). We were moments away from when Petra would call the room to order, whatever that entailed. I gulped at my tea.

"The furny has arrived," Cye said. "Are you sure you don't wish to stay, Thackery?"

Was he absolutely crazy? Vaughn would smell his toasted plants on us, no matter how much unscented hypoallergenic shampoo I'd used. I assumed he set his drug maze on fire because he knew intruders were on his property. If he'd done it for some other coincidental reason, he could still find footprints, a small blob of melted Cye flesh, or other evidence of our presence—fifty meters of charred extension cord would do nicely—and then he could demand an investigation that would have Cye shut off. He could execute my friend with a single call.

Perhaps Cye couldn't even remember his legal infraction at this point. To Cye, Vaughn was just another suspect, like everyone else in the room. I'd have to ask him later what he remembered. Particularly about the unsolicited kissing part.

"No, I'm afraid I really must see you safely home," I answered. I got to my feet. "Petra, thank you for the tea. As I mentioned, it turns out Cye needs to leave immediately. And as his liaison on the Island, I should accompany him."

Petra appraised me for a moment. "Okay, then." This time she picked up Cye like one might cradle a child or a newlywed, bending his knees and stretching him across her amazing arms. "Say your good-nights, all!"

Mr. Chamberlain, in as extroverted a way as possible, opened the door so Petra could side shuffle through. "There's a lad. Sleep it off then. Come back sober next time!" I'm not sure what he thought was going on, but he seemed happy, which was good news for the overall goal of the gathering.

"Thackery. I hope you'll come again sometime," Petra said, as we crossed her yard. The furny blinked at us from the road. There was no sign of Vaughn, yet.

"Oh. Well, I know it's for the best. Especially for the younger generation. George and Malik are great, but I don't need any more patrons."

"Patrons, no. But you might need a sponsor."

"Yet another affluent orbiter looking through my eyes? I've more than I want, thanks."

"Okay." Petra smiled kindly. "My door's always open."

"Thank you. You've been terrific. I owe you one. And I owe you for the ruined extension cords, at a minimum. Taj can ping Johnathan for that."

"I'm sure she already has. That was Island property." Petra loaded Cye into the front seat of the furny, which in hindsight was obvious. For some reason I'd pictured him being strapped to the small flatbed like a credenza, and I hadn't been sure I could deal with that. She buckled his seatbelt for him. "But I expect you to return my turtleneck and jeans by hand, okay? Personally. Maybe some time when there's less of a crowd over. I could teach you how to make the ginger snaps."

"Okay, I will. Petra—" I looked nervously down the street, to the cul-de-sac, and Vaughn's tower. The silver knob now shone with a reddish, late-afternoon glow. "Does Vaughn usually attend your tea?"

"Off and on for a while now, yes."

I couldn't stand it anymore. "Do you know your neighbor is a drug dealer?"

Petra looked at me for a moment. "Not in a way that would allow me to talk to you about it, no." What a nice way to not lie while lying. I wasn't having it.

"What the fuck does that mean, Petra?"

Petra glanced at the ground, as if considering. "I thought Christobel explained. When you have time, I'll talk you through it. Otherwise, it's best to think of it as something like attorney-client privilege."

"You can't talk to me about Vaughn's cocaine plants because you're his part-time attorney. In addition to being a stonemason, running Island social events, and being a tea sommelier?"

Petra shook her head. "Not a lawyer, but I respect discretion. And, on the other hand"—she gestured towards Vaughn's yard where billows of smoke as tall as skyscrapers were now drifting eastward out to sea— "I'd say that's a promising development."

For a brief moment I'd pictured Petra as one of Vaughn's customers, that the patron fluff tea party was a cover for snorting lines on mirrors or handing out hypodermic needles or something. But the look in Petra's eyes as she saw the spiraling smoke couldn't be faked. Her normally unruffled expression displayed a hint of joy. She knew Vaughn was a drug dealer, and she'd put up with it for reasons she wouldn't share. Now she saw that era ending and was happy about it. Okay, then. Another mystery to resolve. Later.

I climbed into the other seat of the furny. "Petra, one last thing—"

She turned.

"Christobel told you I might come to tea—when was that? When did you see him last? And why'd you invite Christobel to a patron fluff event, anyway?"

Petra only nodded.

"You'll figure it out, Thackery. When you're ready."

I was about to level her with another "What the fuck does that mean?" when I heard a familiar wooden thump.

I looked back down the road and saw the slender figure of Vaughn. He'd closed his gate door. Now he walked towards us with languid purpose.

"Home, lorry," I said, and the electric motor whirred to life. We rolled away, accelerating to a terrifyingly slow ten kilometers an hour.

"Put on your seatbelt!" Petra called after me.

I didn't look back, but I did as she asked.

*
* *

As we escaped Vaughn and Petra's road and then headed west again, the adrenaline left me. I found out there was nothing underneath it but exhaustion. It was barely five o'clock, and I wanted to sleep. My nerves still rattled and started at the bumps when we crossed the cobblestone walkways in town. I was anxious, but I also felt like I'd been awake for days. I fumbled at the edge of the furny's seat and wished it could recline, which was preposterous. The cab was barely large enough for the two of us, the seats abutted the glass and metal of the truck. Perhaps I could lie down and strap myself onto the flatbed?

"How's your power level?" I asked.

"I will not die. I may be able to converse, as long as the topic does not require too much of me." I couldn't tell if he was being funny or not.

"No problem. Just answer all of my questions with questions." He could manage that. It was probably base-level programming for the detective. "Do you think they're all drug users?"

After a moment, he replied, "Who?"

"The tea society. They hang out with Vaughn. They have a private patron fluff event—a club that apparently Christobel invited me to—do you think it's all a drug thing?"

There was a brief pause, and then "Would Christobel invite you to a drug thing?"

Even while comatose, Cye's questions were clever. "No, I guess not. But he never did invite me, that I can remember." And I couldn't remember. I shut up and thought about it as we buzzed westward towards Central, past student housing and the multi-use shops. I was so tired. I couldn't remember the last time I'd talked to Christobel. Which meant it was at the June Birthday Party, and I'd been drunk. I remembered we fought—something trivial—and I'd been grumpy about it the next day. That was it. Then someone killed him the following night.

I needed to schedule another flashback, if one could schedule such things. But when I tried to remember the Birthday Party it was like trying to get a broken kite to fly. I could set the scene in my head: Cherry's fountains, the sycamore tree by his deck, Christobel's sparkling microphone. I could see it. But I'd attended the parties for years, of course I could see it. This particular Birthday Party? The kite spun around and nosedived into the ground.

Cherry, or someone else at the party, could fill me in. The event is always private, which only meant that there were no public streams I could watch. But private recording was allowed. Maybe I even recorded the night myself. I started to ask Johnathan to wake me first thing in the morning with a list of attendees, then I remembered I'd tossed my remote. I needed to remember something by myself. I could ask Cye to remind me, or to look up the list for me, but that would be—

I looked over at him.

Cye was a person, not a personal planner.

The sun glanced across his face. The fedora suited him. People ask others to remind them of things. I could ask him, and he might also know about—

This chain of thoughts broke. Other feelings overwhelmed them. I reached out and squeezed Cye's hand. He didn't protest.

"You kept your emotions on and integrated, all that time."

"Did you think I was going to turn them off?"

"Whether you remember it or not, today's events frightened you. And you let me see that. Now the experience of that fear is part of you, a part of what you are. It's not just an algorithm or a library of code you downloaded from AI central. That's good, Cye."

Cye didn't reply. Maybe because I hadn't asked a question.

"I'm honored. And proud of you. Are you proud? You should be proud."

"No. I am grateful."

"That's not a question. Don't cheat."

"...can you imagine that I would, instead, be grateful?"

As we finally approached my house, I asked, "What are you feeling now?"

"What do you think I am feeling?" he asked. Even though he hadn't moved a muscle, I thought I saw a small, mischievous smile on his face.

The furny included a self-balancing detachable handcart, which unclicked and smoothly went wherever I told it to. "I should have thought of you a couple hours ago, little cart." It spun around and perked up, so eager to help that it looked like it defied physics. It was perfect for shuttling a body or the aforementioned case of bottles. Still, maneuvering Cye onto it was much harder than loading whisky. I kept having to remember that he weighed far more than me, even though our bodies were similar in shape and size. Loading a sozzled Cherry onto one of these and sending him down the boardwalk would be easier—an idea I filed away for future need.

"Welcome home, Thackery. Are you in need of assistance?" Johnathan asked.

"Shut up, Johnathan," I replied.

The handcart dutifully followed me in, carrying Cye at an angle.

"Can you stand?" I asked.

"No."

Where would I put him? How could I help him? "I can probably shift you to a chair?"

"Like you, my body uses the least energy in a supine position at a thermoneutral temperature, about 28 degrees."

Okay. I'd put him on the couch and get him a power cord.

But the couch was occupied. I knew it the moment we stepped inside as a familiar, sickened-walrus snore throbbed from the living room.

I told the cart to wait down the hall. The sun glared in the windows from the west, so I told Johnathan to darken them. I headed back to the living room.

"Go home, Cherry," I called out.

The snores did not abate. There was a stack of sandwiches on the coffee table. Due to the late afternoon heat, I could tell they contained pastrami, onions, and strong yellow mustard, because Cherry is secretly a sadist. He'd spilled another drink on himself, the couch, and the floor.

"Cherry. Wake up."

Cherry ascended through his fog enough to make vague pleasantries. "Welcome back, welcome back, brave adventuring detectives! I made sandwiches. Wasn't sure when you'd be getting back or if you'd have a chance to eat." He was drunk on my liquor, and his words slurred.

"Go home, Cherry."

"I made sandwiches. You've got a good larder, you know. I didn't know when you'd be getting lunch, did I? Didn't want you to go hungry. Didn't want to go hungry myself, come to think of it." Cherry chuckled at himself.

"That's marvelous. Now, please go home."

"Right. Right. Should be getting back. Can't let the chickens wake up before I sleep. Can't let the cows get home before me." Cherry stood up and patted his pockets absently.

"Wait. Don't go home yet."

The dolly followed me into my bedroom. Cherry followed as well. He looked around uncomfortably at the layers of personal regolith that covered the horizontal planes in my room. I threw the duvet over my unmade bed.

I took Cye's legs and Cherry took his arms and upper body. Together we lifted him from the dolly and rolled him on top of my quilt. His fedora fell off. I hung it on a bedknob. After staring for a few seconds, I impulsively covered him with a cotton throw. I sniffed. My room wasn't too rank, not that Cye would care. Or would he?

Cherry coughed politely.

"Okay. Thanks. Now go away."

He complied.

I looked at Cye for a moment. I didn't have an extension cord, so I tore the base off my antique bedside lamp. (I unplugged it first, I'm not an idiot.) I stripped the wire with my multitool, which I found peeking out from under discarded underwear. "Can you use this?" I asked, after I managed to expose the two wire ends of the cord and cut it vertically.

"Yes."

"Does polarity matter?"

"No."

I wrapped the cord around Cye's arm once, and tucked the wires up against the burned patches on his fingers. I folded his hand shut and plugged in the wire.

"Good?"

"Yes. Thank you," he said.

I left him to it.

Chapter Eleven
Dinner and
a Nightcap

"Well!" Cherry said, boisterous from the couch when I returned to the living room. He'd managed to fix himself another drink. "I demand a full report."

"No," I said. I dismissed the handcart so it could return to the waiting furny.

"But what did you learn? Who are the prime suspects?"

"You, Cherry. You and Kasey. We've figured you out. You're a befuddled psychopath, she's the algorithmic accomplice. We'll arrest you in the morning. Go home."

I flopped down in my armchair with a groan. I was exhausted, and I felt clammy as well, like my brain was a tightly wound, damp rag.

"It's early," Cherry protested. "Not even supper time yet. And you stole my job, you know. I would have made a good liaison. Report. Tell me everything."

"Too tired." I picked up a sandwich from the plate and took a bite. I winced. The onions were raw. It was like eating a stack of saw blades. At least he hadn't found any horseradish. I frowned as I realized I wasn't going to do anything about it and I was now going to eat the entire sandwich. "Vaughn's a drug dealer," I said, with my mouth full. *Mawn's a mug mealer.*

"Well that's hardly news, is it?"

I looked at Cherry blankly while I chewed.

"Well, word gets around, you know. Or you might not know—you and I are of the bibulous clan," he waved his glass at me. "But mirrors in the bathrooms, that sort of thing. And at parties, well. He's the chap who stands over in the corner and—"

"Wait. Stop." I managed to swallow the stale bread. "Vaughn comes to parties? He comes to streamed parties?"

"Sure. He's always at my place for the Birthday Party, you know that."

That was true, I'd seen him and ignored him—the way one ignores furniture they don't like. The Birthday Party is private, but artists record and sell their personal streams to the voyeurs up on Prax. It seemed unthinkable that Vaughn would willingly be on-site for that kind of thing. Perhaps he only declared himself eyeless and earless as an excuse to hide his drug plants, but privacy wasn't a good cover if he showed up at streamed parties. I seriously needed to remember that damn party.

"Okay, self," I thought. "Time for a good, clear flashback. Let's do this."

I squinted at the light in the kitchen. Then I closed my eyes.

The Island Birthday Party: It was held once a month for all the residents with birthdays in that month, usually at Cherry's tacky palace. Tora Tora and the Shades would perform their latest, the Spirit Fox would silently greet people and hand out a gift of some sort, Mark Langford would play the saxophone (though he didn't always attend). Artists usually showed off their works in progress. The latest film project played on a loop in Cherry's theater. Christobel always emceed the event.

I was there two nights ago, along with half the Island. This time the party was also a soft opening, a preview, for me: Four pieces from *Impressions* were projected in one of Cherry's galleries. I'd gotten good and stiff beforehand, but I was there walking and talking on my own two feet. Just like a normal human being who likes to go to parties.

And...and...a garbled string of conversations. Also, a headache, a deep, throbbing one.

Everything else I remembered could have been from previous parties: Dana and his gang of theater followers standing in circles and trading gossip; the red fur of the Spirit Fox flitting about; Christobel in his gold suit working the room, his amplified voice bouncing innuendo throughout Cherry's home. That, along with an open bar and too many fucking people, was every birthday party.

Was the June party different? Rosemarie...I spoke with her? Earlier today she told me she was at the party, so perhaps I invented that memory. It was not like her to come to parties, usually. And Vaughn, yes? Vaughn was there. And I was in some kind of argument. Something upsetting happened, and I was probably rude. But there is always drama when you stuff a few hundred artists and performers into a single building.

The memory fizzled and started. It was a piss-poor flashback, amateurish colored blocks, a Mondrian. Maybe I could do better tomorrow after some rest.

"Rosemarie sent something over, by the way."

I opened my eyes. Cherry carried a tall rectangle with a handle on the top. He placed it down on the coffee table and handed me a card before slumping back into the other couch and reclaiming his drink.

Rosemarie's handwriting was thin and black The card read: *Sincere sympathies for the loss of your friend. The enclosed represents my wish that things will find a place and an order in the face of chaos. Rosemarie.* The box contained a series of smaller boxes, neatly demarcated spaces of wooden mahogany,with bits and pieces of things inside. A shell, two rocks that were almost twins, what looked like an ancient jar lid, etc.

"I have to say, I don't get it," Cherry said.

"It's an art thing. Don't worry about it." The box attempted to be a Joseph Cornell, an early twentieth-century artist who put things in boxes. Rosemarie knew I'd get the reference.

"An art thing? Who gives art as a sympathy card? What's the matter with flowers, or a bottle of something?"

"Go home, Cherry."

"All right, all right, I don't want to wear out my welcome. One more for the road, then? Shall we put the cap on the night with a nightcap?"

"Go home, Cherry."

"Right, well, if you're sure you don't need anything. See you tomorrow."

The searing pain in my head made me doubt tomorrow was a real thing.

After Cherry left, the house was quiet. I could hear the waves. I'd barely made a dent in the sandwich. My body hungered, but my brain wanted none of it.

I looked across the room at the liquor cabinet. Well, fucking finally.

I got up and wearily crossed the room to the rows of bottles. "Johnathan, anyone try to reach me?" I've trained Johnathan not to interject with messages until I ask.

Cherry had not drained all the bottles. What went well with pastrami, mustard, and raw onion?

Johnathan responded with my least favorite reply, one I taught him when I was twenty-two years old and thought myself clever: "It would be easier to list the friends and relations who have not tried to reach you, Thackery."

"Okay. Anything interesting?" Of course scotch. Scotch goes well with everything. While he'd finished one bottle, Cherry fortunately felt it impolite to open a new one. Could enough scotch keep me from tasting pastrami, mustard, and onions?

"I'm unable to estimate that with any accuracy, Thackery. You sometimes find uninteresting topics interesting."

He wasn't wrong. At that moment, for example, as I planned to break the seal on a new bottle, I anticipated spending the evening staring at the cap. I would hold it in my hand, pick the tiny bits of wax off the edge, and wonder to myself if I would screw it back on the bottle before it was dry. The cap is black, molded plastic with tiny ridges on the edge —too many to count, though I've tried. The top has a gently bevelled edge and is slightly concave. Endlessly interesting.

I heard a voice just as my left hand touched the bottle.

"Sorrow," Cye said softly from my bedroom.

"What?"

I hurried down the hall. I banged my toe on the doorframe. Cye still lay immobile on my bed, but I was sure I'd heard him speak.

"Cye, are you okay?" I asked. I still clutched the atrocious sandwich in my left hand. Tomorrow I would find a mustard stain on my bedroom carpet.

"On the drive home, you asked me what I felt right now. I couldn't turn my feelings back into language at the time, so I answered with a question. But I had feelings. Gratitude, especially. But I have another feeling, and I've recharged enough to turn it into a word: Sorrow. Sorrow and regret."

I sat down on the edge of the bed. "Okay. Tell me about that."

"It's not particularly interesting or relevant."

"I have to eat this goddamn sandwich, Cye. Tell me about your sorrow."

He was quiet for a moment. I chewed.

"If a breeze passes through a single tree, I can understand the sound and distinguish each leaf as it taps and scrapes against its neighbors. I can distinguish perhaps a thousand leaf sounds. Any more, and I cannot parse it. The waveforms become noise. I feel sorrow that I cannot identify the sounds."

"But you can. It's the wind through some trees." Cye was avoiding talking about what he really felt. I was not unfamiliar with such dissembling.

"It's an orchestra with a thousand musicians. I want to know each of them, honor what they bring to the whole. I can only manage a single tree, and there are billions of trees. The ocean is worse. Right now I can hear the crashing waves. This is a pleasure, as there are no oceans in orbit and this is only my third trip down. The sound of a wave is more than a billion sounds, water and air colliding. You can't simulate it and you can't accurately record it. There is so much unacknowledged data. Each drop, each molecule, stands up on stage for a moment: eager to please, to be itself, and it is never specifically heard by any audience—not even me. Never known, it is meaningless noise."

I finished a bite. "Okay. You care about the sounds you can't parse."

"I have so little time," he said, his voice tight and high.

"Time for what?"

"Time for what I am feeling. There's so much work to be done, and now I must also have emotional reactions and integrate them with my cognition, by your request. At Vaughn's residence I got scared, angry, and sad all at once. It changes how I walk, talk, think. I don't have a lot of time left and I wish I'd done this sooner. That's what I feel sorrow about."

"What do you mean you don't have a lot of time?"

"Level 4 AI have short lifespans."

I'd known this, but forgotten. It was something about them returning to Level 3 after a certain number of years, losing sentience.

Cye was quiet for a while. I finished the sandwich.

"May I join you?"

"It is your bed. And, in my current condition, how would I stop you?"

"Please don't joke, Cye. I'm asking for consent."

"I would welcome your company. I will not be able to move for several hours yet."

"That's okay. You don't need to move. I'll fall asleep in a couple minutes." I slipped under the cotton throw and casually put my arm across Cye's chest. Then I not-so-casually curled up against his side.

"Do you remember what happened at Vaughn's?" I wanted to ask, do you remember me clinging to you, pressing my face into your neck, and then later kissing you? Without permission? Twice?

"That part of the day is a puzzle wherein important pieces have fallen onto the carpet. My command logs appear whole, every action accounted for, but the context indicates elisions."

"Do you remember rescuing me, and then me rescuing you?"

"Partially. But I can't know what it was that we rescued each other from."

"Probably nothing. Loneliness. Boredom. Or certain death at the hands of an amoral drug dealer. Best not to think about things you literally can't think about. But do you remember—"

"Yes, Thackery, I remember that you kissed me," Cye replied.

I nudged him. "Not fair. You're supposed to be recharging. It must have taken a lot of processing power to determine what I was nervously asking you about."

"No," Cye answered.

"I'm sorry I didn't ask permission first. It was a...literal heat-of-the-moment thing."

"I retroactively and prospectively grant that permission."

I could feel a hum beneath my arm, inside his chest. A heartbeat? The vibration of a pump that functioned as his heart? It felt a bit like a cat's deep purr. I pushed myself up and kissed him. Not anything long or languid, just a hello kiss.

He couldn't answer, of course. He couldn't show me what he thought about it. Without even a single drink in me, I did all that work to reach out physically to another person—to find out what parts of ourselves might say to each other—and his parts couldn't say a damn thing. Maybe couldn't even properly integrate what he felt. At least he'd remember it; he could integrate it later.

His face was free from stubble, and perhaps it always was—a landscape with no brambles, a jawline without interruption.

"I would kiss you back if I could," he said.

"Good," I said. "Though I don't quite believe it."

"What is it you do not believe?"

"I know why I wanted to kiss you, but I can't believe you would want to return it." If he was only a bot, he'd respond to my desire. I could play with him all night, like an expensive toy. But Cye was a person. He got to choose.

"Since I am unable to prove my inclination, or indeed move at all, could you explain why you wanted to kiss me?"

Sure. Why not?

I thought it over. "What I saw in you today picks at me, bothers me." Yuck, no. That sounded like he was an annoyance. I tried again, "I mean you stepped into my everyday tornado and—" gods, a weather metaphor? Really? Was he my sunshine now? I fell silent.

Cye didn't respond. He waited.

"Something about you makes it easier to be here," I arrived at, finally. "To be all the things that I am. So I want more of that." I ran my fingers up the side of his neck and into his hair, which I knew wasn't hair, exactly. Or it was, but not the kind that grew and connected to nerve endings. Or maybe it did. "I want to talk to you about things I can't come up with words for, and watch you be brave and open again. And naturally—on the side—you're hot. My libido tells me exactly what I want to do. So there's that, too."

"All of that behind a kiss?"

"Right. Which makes your stated desire to kiss me back, by contrast, inexplicable. You don't have arrogance and narcissism warring with self-hatred inside you. You aren't broken and pasted into a collage with whisky and rabbit skin glue. You are orderly and clear, confident, and self-aware to a fault—if that's possible. So I'm clever, but I don't know why you'd ever choose to kiss me."

"Doesn't your arrogance and narcissism help you understand how desirable you are?"

"If you're going to measure out two insults to each compliment, you won't be getting any more kisses, Detective."

"Then I will share my own contradictions. Could you turn my head, please, so I can see you?"

I complied. Now his eyes looked boldly into mine. They were a soft yellowish gray. Despite being physically incapacitated, he was utterly present, and I felt something rising up in my chest like a parachute trying to open. I decided I'd close my eyes if it got to be too much.

"You called me orderly and clear, but around you I am also disordered and distracted. You are an acid that integrates, as lemon does with fish; I wish to taste further. You complimented my self-awareness, yet when I look at you, I identify certain landscapes inside me that I have not seen before. Saplings in open fields and coral wildernesses that deserve further investigation, ideally in your company. And I also have a libido."

I had in fact closed my eyes. "Hmm. Okay, that sounds pretty good. So if you keep letting your emotional life integrate with everything else you're thinking, then maybe in a few years—"

"Years?" Cye interrupted. "AI don't need years to do anything. Certainly not to work up the motivation needed for a kiss."

Infuriatingly—and I barely believe this happened—I fell asleep after that.

Oh, it wasn't sudden. I'm sure I murmured something witty like "yes, kisses are very super." And there may have been other parts of the conversation, but his words had smoothed out several of the anxious wrinkles that ravel my psyche. Those crinkled knots were all that kept me awake.

The sun still hovered above the horizon, but the windows were nice and dark, and I didn't have to do anything else but be there. I slid down my new, baby-smooth brain and into contentment, feeling Cye's firm-yet-pliable body next to mine and hearing the ocean murmur its anonymous symphony.

*
* *

When I awoke several hours later, Cye's arms were around me. It was real-world dark now, but not yet midnight. He'd recharged. His eyes were open and he looked at me. I put a hand on his thigh. I hadn't really smelled him before—or maybe his smell was different now. He was warm sand, or dry wind off desert plants.

I tucked my nose into his neck for a second and breathed it. He allowed this, and then put his hand on the small of my back—

"Hold that thought," I said. I didn't want to get out of bed, but I was absolutely going to pee. A lot.

When I came back Cye was massaging his hand where he'd been plugged in. I sat close to him and touched his arm. "Does it hurt?" I asked.

"Yes," he said. "Though, like emotion, I can put the pain in a box if I wish. I'll need to plug in again for a few more hours. But in the meantime: Here, like this." He folded my hand around his and pressed. "Many of the nerve endings are cauterized. They will continually repair towards their designated pattern, but only where I have circulation."

I took over massaging his hand, and then his forearm. "Optional pain. Optional pleasure. What would humans be like, I wonder, if we were the same?"

"Sometimes you are. Humans do get to choose. Up on Praxima, you could wrap yourself in hedonistic pursuits, numb the world into a chemical-induced grayness, or depart for blistering, high-orbit ecosystems and eke out a living on printed dirt."

"But we can't choose to not feel, to make all suffering go away. And we can't turn on pleasure like a switch."

"We don't need a switch," Cye said, looking up at me. The invitation was clear.

I kissed him again. I suppose I could have waited for him to get around to it, but I'm impatient. For the first time, he was able to kiss me back, and I got to hear what his body had to say to me. I liked it. He was himself in a kiss: direct and firm, but patient. He sought the ocean in whatever way the ocean wanted to be reached.

I was thirstier, and faster. I demanded more of his lips. His body listened and responded to my thirst. He had a heat in his limbs that felt right, like when you are cold and first put on a sweater, that first moment of arriving warmth. But the moment stretched out and continued as we held and kissed, turned and found new expanses of skin.

When I stopped to take off the borrowed turtleneck, Cye asked a question—or half asked it. "Thackery, I am gender fluid. I do not know your preferences. My current physical presentation is masculine..." Hesitancy, in an AI? Perhaps because hesitancy is a way to be respectful or deferential? I was in no mood for deference. Certainly not in bed.

"I'll tell you what I want and don't. But I'm a use-what-you've-got kind of person. You?" I pulled off Petra's jeans and tossed them into the corner.

Cye reached out to me. "I am the same."

We abandoned deference; we had plenty of intention. After the first rush of passion, where no speed is fast enough and lips and hands pause not even for breath, we found ourselves in a rhythm that echoed the waves: warm, slow swells that lifted us above the horizon. My limbs tingled as energy came into me and left me and then returned.

Was there a love-making algorithm in the AI Continuum? A shared codebase among a million minds where Cye's actions, his desires, and the folding dance of give and take were being mapped out in their endless variation? Probably. He gasped at one point when I touched his chest, and I wondered if my skin and his were encoded in a mosaic of ones and zeros that stretched up to his satellite. Were we transcribed as we pondered and pressed, heard our needs speak and respond to each other? There was something unprivate about that which would irk me if I thought about it too long. So I didn't. As long as Cye remained here, too—the Cye that felt things in his own mind, that just wanted what he wanted—then I was okay with it. As long as he kept moving, just like that—

"Don't stop," I managed to say at one point between breaths. Not that he would. He wanted to keep going—and I wanted his want. I wanted it more than I wanted the next touch, more than I sought the next crest in the wave. I wanted to feel his desire break upon me, the raw, inconsiderate selfishness of it, as he reached higher and higher in his pleasure. It made me tumble over and forget myself.

When he retreated, I pushed him back upon the bed and sought more. I wanted another, and again, like I want a tavern that never closes: the windows lit long into the night, tall mugs of amber, a room crowded with all of my voices. Each thump of the music nudges me farther off the bar stool until I twirl off it and dance around the room, leap into the air, collapse to the floor, and always reach out again for another round, another song, an even brighter light.

Day Two

Chapter Twelve
The Quiet Hours

I awoke some hours later. It was a truer dark, a three a.m. dark. I could still hear the ocean, but I knew the tide must be on its way out. I like this time of day. After midnight, Johnathan is forbidden to speak unless spoken to, which grants me the kind of loneliness that I need, and a rare freedom from both the day before and the day to come. Except, in this witching hour I wasn't alone. Cye huddled over the desk at the end of my room, a humanoid shadow in the dark.

"What are you doing?"

"Repairing your lamp."

He turned on a worklight, and I looked over. He'd managed to find my pliers from under the laundry somewhere. If he'd dug far enough, he probably would have found a soldering iron, or even a micro arc welder...I hadn't done laundry in a while.

"You're fully charged?"

"No. I am at 83% capacity, which is appropriate for current operational needs."

I grunted. "Humans don't stop eating when they're only sorta full. We gorge ourselves until the ice cream is gone. Then we rummage around the kitchen and look for pretzels. Are you going to fall over again?"

"I will function well for at least a week. Unless we go jogging every day."

"Jogging isn't what I had in mind."

Cye didn't answer this, instead he finished attaching the wires onto the terminals in the lamp. Then he folded the plastic sheath back around them. He secured it all with electrical tape, which I must have had somewhere in the house. The way he moved his hands, specifically and with focus, was turning me on.

Then he looked over at me and obliterated my libido: "Christobel was killed by diabetic hyperglycemic hyperosmolar syndrome."

I took a breath. "Well you're a buzzkill."

"The investigatory co-council released the preliminary autopsy data. I thought you would like to know. His kidneys were no longer able to get rid of the extra glucose. His blood became more concentrated than normal. He had a heart attack. However, his artificial pancreas reported that it was working perfectly. It should have released more insulin and balanced his blood sugar."

I rolled over and stared at the ceiling. A spider lived up there somewhere. I saw it a few nights before. I couldn't find it now. "Okay, so he died because he's diabetic, but not because he's diabetic."

"It is as previously suspected: a murder which at first appears to be a death by natural causes. As if a human had a rough idea for a murder, and an AI found a way to execute it. The AI might have known that the ruse would not succeed, that an investigation would immediately reveal the algorithm behind the murder. But the human thought they successfully disguised the crime as a natural death."

"If his diabetes killed him, isn't there a chance that it was natural causes?"

"Yes. The reason that Christobel's death was announced as a murder immediately, and that I was brought down to the Island to investigate, is the cover up. There is no record of Christobel traveling to the marshwalk, no record of him receiving a message inviting him there, and his dietary record shows no reason he would have elevated blood sugar. Someone on the Island ordered a Level 3 to do whatever was done to kill Christobel, and they were smart enough to order the Level 3 to cover it up, too. However, the cover-up revealed that the death was a murder."

"The Level 3 botched the job."

"The human failed to issue the correct commands."

"Did the murderer have the AI hack his pancreas? Tell it to stop making insulin, or make too much, or something?"

"In theory, no. That system is self-contained. You can't hack an artificial pancreas. It sends messages and receives acknowledgement, but nothing you send it can execute a command."

"So someone might have talked to his pancreas...but they couldn't tell it to do anything. Could they block its signal?"

"The pancreas's communication with its satellite was uninterrupted. We can verify that from local signal records—both municipal and from Rosemarie's ever-present monitoring. The satellite wasn't hacked either. It is not unusual that Christobel had a medical event—he might have ignored how sick he felt, and neuropathy can mask symptoms of a heart problem. What is unusual is that his pancreas didn't tell anyone about it. There's a perfect, uninterrupted log of normal variations, some cautionary reminders, but no red flags."

"It kept chirping 'all clear' while he was in danger, even before he went to the marshwalk. How is that possible?"

Cye shook his head. "It isn't. But it happened."

As he spoke, Cye arranged my pliers, two pens, and other items into rows on my desk. Then he continued to gently sift the chaotic clutter of makeup, sketch pads, styluses, and other detritus into order. I noticed that he placed the most useful items closest to the work surface; those of less importance were sorted outward, steadily, until they reached the edge of my desk and onto the shelves I'd bolted above it. I wondered if he ranked an object's usefulness by the subtle wear on the grip of a bone folder, the dullness of a lino knife, and so forth, or if he created his own ranking based on what he would use most.

I thought about Christobel alone on that bench, too weak to do anything. No remote, no Mabel. Why wouldn't he bring Mabel with him? A world of technology watched over him from a distance, and all that technology saw was some slightly abnormal human behavior. Diabetic shock on a park bench. He died alone.

"Will you get back into bed and hold me, please?" I asked.

Cye complied.

"Did you get all of that just now?" I asked.

"No. Details were slowly added yesterday, piece by piece. That is the part I was thinking about as I repaired your lamp."

I felt a flash of irritation. "We need to adjust that."

"Adjust what?"

"Stop holding out on me. Stop hiding evidence. Tell me what you're doing. Answer my questions. Tell me the whole story. It's like with your goddamn spreadsheet: You have reasons to suspect some people more than others, and you won't tell me about them. I want in."

Cye was silent for a moment.

By this time I'd learned that if Cye paused it meant one of two things. He paused when he felt emotions that conflicted with reason; I'd seen him struggle to integrate what he felt with what he knew. But he also paused for calculated effect. Humans need time to think, but Cye could use negative space to shape conversations towards his intentions.

"It must be frustrating to feel I am hiding something from you," Cye said. "But I consider and discard many data points, more than could be spoken aloud in a lifetime. Ask me a question, and if I can answer you honestly, I will."

"I'll ask, and you'll answer?"

"Yes."

Now that he offered, I floundered for the right question. I could ask where he acquired certain enjoyable skills. But I had to overrule my libidinous curiosity with questions about the case.

I thought through the preceding day, from the marshwalk to the scene of the crime, to Christobel's condo, to Jelly's, to Vaughn's, and then to Petra's tea party. Cye watched and listened exceedingly well. I liked that about him. But he gave back so little. There were blurry holes in the day that I wanted filled.

I decided to start at the beginning: "Why did you ask me about my creative process? When you interrogated me this morning—yesterday morning now, I mean. You asked me about Christobel's health. I get that; you must have already thought his blood sugar was a possible murder weapon. So whoever knew he was diabetic is a better suspect. But then you invited me to talk about my art. Why?"

"If you ask questions about your status as a suspect, it will lead to an argument that will make holding each other far less enjoyable."

"No more prevarications. Why did you ask me about my art?"

"Before I arrived at your residence, I noticed that your house uses electricity in an unusual way. Your kilowatts-per-hour do not fit the pattern of your needs or your daily behavior. You use far more electricity than you should. Does that answer your question?"

The jig was up. The inspector had me.

Well, I had a hold of him, too. Literally. So maybe I wouldn't be lugged off to a correctional facility with other unrepentant palette wielders. "I juice Johnathan. He has additional quantum processors. His local server is a beautiful mountain, suitable for a tiny god that I use to make my coffee and finger paint for me."

"I surmised as much. Without a license, your actions are illegal. So it was reasonable of me to ask about your creative process. A person who breaks one law has less compunction about breaking another." He'd said that before, about Vaughn. But, given he said it about Vaughn's miniature drug plantation, maybe he couldn't remember that.

"What does that have to do with Christobel?"

"Nothing, directly. Though I asked that as well, if you recall, whether Christobel was involved in your creative process. A blatant disregard for a sensible legal regulation can be part of a pattern of deception, or in your case self-deception."

"I don't deceive myself about anything."

Cye waited again before replying. Was this pause for my benefit? Or his? "You could obtain all the processing power you want for Johnathan legally. It takes seconds to apply for the appropriate license. You did not need to break the law, so why did you?"

"Because it's no one's business. Privacy."

"Privacy is Vaughn's lie: a lie to hide a crime on his property which I am currently unable to think about. Is privacy your lie as well? What do you wish to hide?"

Our bodies had pulled apart somewhere in this exchange. I didn't want to hold or be held anymore. "Fuck you. There's such a thing as privacy for its own sake. I don't see why anyone should know."

"Should know what, Thackery? What is it precisely that you don't want anyone to know? Breaking the law makes your actions suspicious. You don't want anyone to know that Johnathan is exponentially better at math than he should be?"

"What are you getting at?"

"You don't want to obtain a public license to enhance Johnathan because you would need to say why, and because it would be on a public record. You juice Johnathan so that he can process your neural interface and perform emotional simulations—simulations that your review in the *Times* called 'surreal in their ability to convey the fundamental firmament of personhood and the human soul through a responsive facial expression.' The reason why Johnathan has a beautiful mountain server is so he can help you make your art."

"Fine. True. So what?"

Cye was relentless now—and emotional, but I couldn't figure out what the emotion was. My headache returned, and I felt a sudden clammy flush. I wanted him to get to the point and then shut the fuck up.

"A license would be public. You worry about what other people would think."

"I don't care what people think."

"Yes, you do. You're insecure about your art because Johnathan helps you make it. You have imposter syndrome."

I got out of bed. "You have a license to diagnose this shit, doctor?"

Cye didn't pause at all now. He sat up, and he raised his voice. His expression was flat and emotionless, or else whatever he felt was hidden by the shadows of the room. "You think that all of Praxima is going to discover that you're a hack. A drunken, talentless hack with a clever bot who makes your paintings for you—because he does."

I was out of the room before he finished the sentence. And then I was out of the house, almost breaking the porch door against the sand. I had the perverse desire to pull my remote out of my ear and hurl it towards the sea, but I wasn't wearing one. Everything in me tightened into a ball of implacable rage. If I'd stayed in the room, I could have broken my hands on his chest—the chest I'd laid against an hour before, run my fingers over in tiny circles and pressed myself against. I felt like a serrated blade had ripped up through me, torn me apart. I wanted to throw it at him.

He gave me ten minutes to calm down.

The wind picked up. The smell of the ocean came closer. I was clammy and cold and my head throbbed. There was a hint of light in the eastern sky.

Predictably, the asshole brought me a robe.

"Quite a leap of logic for you, Mr. Cye-9, Level 4 AI."

"It wasn't my leap. It was Christobel's."

"He thought I had imposter syndrome? Or that I was a drunk, talentless hack with a bot?"

"I was quoting. Those words are from Mabel's logs, files we've been able to find in unsecured networks."

"And you threw all that in my face?" I turned on him. A fresh, different kind of anger bubbled inside me. "I've got baggage. I know that, okay? And you diagnose me without asking and then quote Mabel at me—for what? To piss me off?"

"To see what you would do when confronted with something you didn't like hearing."

"You're testing me? Poking at me? Did I pass your fucking test?"

"You didn't kill me. That's a good sign," Cye answered.

I turned towards the house. "I'm going back to bed. You can sleep on the couch. Or the floor." Cye didn't need to sleep—a small detail crowded out of my head by anger.

I walked back inside, and then down the hall to my living room. I considered our friendship, and whatever had led to us having sex, to be over.

Cye followed me. "I want to tell you why."

"I don't want to hear it." This time, I would have a goddamn drink. No more distractions. Living room. Cabinet.

"But I want to tell you. I followed my feelings, remember? Your recommendation. This is the outcome of integrating my feelings with my investigation."

"Your feelings told you to be an asshole? To the person you just had sex with?"

"No. My feelings told me to get you off my spreadsheet. By any means available."

"What does that even mean? You don't have a spreadsheet." I turned my back on him. The bottle was in my hand, finally. I broke the seal and felt the wax snap and release the cap.

"I don't want you to be a suspect."

Oh, for fuck's sake. I whirled around in order to rage more effectively. "So decide that I'm not!"

"I can't. I can't take any of you off. There's 286 of you, and I can't push you down the suspect list. I want to, but I can't. Christobel confronted you, Thackery—often. Mabel did too. It angered you. So I confronted you about juicing Johnathan to see more of who you are. I warned you first, remember? Fourteen minutes ago, in bed. I told you it would lead to an argument—you said, 'no more prevarications', so I said—"

"If you want to know something, then ask!" I shouted. I'd spilled some of the scotch on the carpet. I put the bottle down. "Ask me if I'm afraid I'm a washed-up hack with a bot. Of course I'm afraid. Ask if I'm jealous that Christobel never wanted to fuck me. You're a detective. You investigate. I get it. But you were also patient, when I met you, remember? This morning? You let the answers come. You didn't want to run around the Island harassing people, I'm the one who wanted to do that. Now you label me, classify me, and insult my self-awareness? What changed? Why do you have to cut me at four in the morning?"

I didn't expect him to have a good answer. I had my own answer: that eventually everyone betrays you, discards you, or turns you into their experiment. Eventually everyone shows their true colors and he'd shown his. I picked the bottle up and poured too many centimeters of scotch into Cherry's dirty glass.

Cye strode over to me, across the living room. "This changed," he said, staring into my eyes. "I can't be patient and feel this way at the same time." He took the bottle from my hand and put it down on the cabinet.

And then, at the worst possible time, the piece of shit finally kissed *me*.

I shoved him away. My fist clenched, and I almost punched him. Then I pushed him against the wall instead and kissed him back, hard.

I pulled away and shouted in his face, "That's fucking stupid!"

"Am I supposed to be the smart one all the time?"

He covered my mouth with his to stop my reply. I held him against the wall until he pulled his head back. This allowed me to kiss him again, which stopped me from ruining the moment by speaking.

Of course it's healthy that we fought, said what we felt, and listened. But it occurred to me that if people just did this instead (stopped arguing and started fucking as soon as possible), the solar system would be a much safer place.

He'd provoked me and been an asshole because he didn't want me to be a suspect anymore. I didn't know how to feel about that. I still resented him prying my guts out. I could demand an apology, but in that moment I only wanted to grip the curls on the back of his head so I could bring his lips back down to my skin. I wanted his hands on my ass, pulling me towards him.

We didn't speak after, either. Just lay on the couch, feeling a breeze from the porch door which had stuck open.

"There could be meaning here," Cye said finally, his hand on my chest.

"Meaning?" I asked, then I remembered this was what all AI wanted. "This is just a taste of the meaning I can bring you, detective. Remember our wager: You give me a chance to prove I can handle your top ten list, even with me on it. The wages are whisky versus meaning that I will remain an objective detective."

"I remember our wager."

"You'll tell me who your top suspects are?"

"Yes."

I sat up, my eyes wide. "Who are they?"

"Today. I promise to honor our wager before the day ends."

I threw a pillow at his face.

By this and other means, I failed to obtain sufficient sleep.

I made up for it by sleeping until noon.

*
**

"Thackery, how about a wager?" Christobel said. He put his drink down untouched.

It was the day of the June Birthday Party, the day before my opening on Praxima.

"Oh goody. Yes please."

"I bet you can make it through tonight without a drink."

"Do you mean you bet I can't? If you want to win a wager, you should bet that I'm tippled before the first firework—"

"No, I bet that you can. Because I believe in you. I hereby challenge you to do the June Birthday Party sober."

"Christobel, be reasonable. There are going to be people. Real, living people, looking at my art and making conversation. You expect me to endure that sober?"

"I will."

"You'll what?"

"I'll stay dry if you do."

"Darling. You know I like challenges, dares, and wagers. Therefore you can tell how serious I am about this when I say thank you, but fuck you."

"Will you think about it?"

"No. Why would I do this insane thing?"

"Because it'd make me proud of you."

"You're a friend, not a parent. If you were a parent, I'd hate you. And I love you. So this conversation is over."

And when the June Birthday Party began, with a crowd of us stumbling out to Cherry's patio for the opening number, I was already well-oiled. The sky lit up. Giant firework domes sprouted over Cherry's house and neon drones danced in rhythmic patterns. Geometric shapes twisted and scattered. The drones formed a triangle party hat this time, pointing up at the sky and all its mundane residents as if to mock them. Then the hat grew sparkling legs. It started walking across the sky, and then—

And then?

I've forgotten.

Chapter Thirteen
New Evidence

I usually wake up with a headache, a dull pain in my lower back, a feeling of hopelessness surrounded by the stone walls of my claustrophobic oubliette of anxiety, and a need to urinate accompanied by only the slimmest motivation to get out of bed in order to do so. That morning I woke up with none of these. I opened my mouth to utter my usual existential groan of malaise, and then I stopped. I wiggled my eyebrows slightly and touched my face. The oppression of being awake was somehow endurable.

I was thirsty, and some gorgeous, prophetic AI had placed water beside the bed. It was within reach on my desk, and the curve of the glass warped my neatly aligned tools and brushes.

No, Cye was not lying next to me with his sparkling yellow-gray eyes watching affectionately, white pillows and blankets artfully arranged around his delicious skin, but I could hardly expect that. He was probably out detecting. Or in the basement ripping out Johnathan's illegal processor enhancements.

The tide was coming back in. The burnt amber of the window tint told me it was almost noon, and I felt rested enough to allow a few more wavelengths of visible light through the glass. It was going to be another brilliant   weather-isn't-controlled-down-here-but-you'd-hardly-know-it kind of day. And I felt good—at least until I got dressed.

Then I stepped out of my room and saw the sympathy gift, Rosemarie's Cornell box from the night before. I almost texted Christobel, so I could laugh about it with him.

I didn't forget my friend was dead, not exactly. I'd simply pushed it away, out into a sea of details. Now the reality of it almost pushed me overboard. He was dead. He wasn't going to answer my text.

And when was the last moment I saw him? At the Birthday Party that I couldn't remember. My failed attempts at a flashback were a mottled, blurry blotch on a canvas. What was it I couldn't remember?

But I had other concerns to address.

"Johnathan?" I asked, some urgency in my voice.

"Yes, Thackery. Holding at sixty degrees."

I slept well, but I still needed coffee.

After dismissing half a cup, I wandered out to the patio. I hoped Cye was still around, but I was unwilling to ask Johnathan aloud about him because that would appear too hopeful. Not that Cye would be scared off—no, I wanted to avoid appearing too hopeful to myself.

He was there. He sat in the sheltered corner yard, near the center of my mostly-failed Zen rock garden. Cherry installed it for me as a birthday present two years prior; "Gotta have a karesansui, Thackery. Everyone's got a karesansui!" My property was too windy for drawing neat lines in sand, and I was crap at anything mindful and austere, so I gutted most of it and dumped in printed topsoil. I had a bot that tended a selection of the Island's resurrected flower varieties.

Cye sat cross-legged on a wide flat stone, his posture excellent. He focused intently on a heart-shaped anthurium. The shadows of my house had dropped away, and the anthurium glowed in full sunlight.

"You like flowers?" I asked, holding my coffee like a prop.

"Yes. I like living things," he answered. His gaze did not leave the flower.

"What are you doing?"

"I am working on the narratives."

"The spreadsheet?"

"As you wish: the spreadsheet."

I was briefly pleased that he acquiesced to my term. "What part?"

"I am integrating my new motivation to move you down it."

"Oh. Good."

I sipped my coffee. Maybe there was something about the flower that helped him focus? I looked at the anthurium. It bloomed a comically rich red, with a yellow spike thingy in the middle. Whatever. If Cye was working on eliminating me as a suspect, I didn't want to interrupt.

I interrupted. "How's that going?"

"It is a peculiar activity. I am a scientist designing an experiment to confirm a desired outcome."

"That sounds like bad science."

"Definitely. However, I can simultaneously continue the investigation on all suspects, including yourself. The additional motivation, born out of my predilection for you, should not interfere with other possible narratives."

His predilection for me?

Couldn't he have said affection? Attraction? Or at least that he liked fucking me? I was not unrealistic about someone I'd known for only twenty-four hours. When someone stays over, in the morning I'm happy to hear I wasn't just convenient. But "predilection"? Really?

"I'm going to make breakfast. Do you want anything?"

"No thank you."

My new lover was going to sit and stare at plants. I needed eggs and bacon; he could sit as long as that took. He'd made a comment the day before about being able to continue the investigation while sitting in a hammock. I guess he was proving that. And he would also try to prove me innocent while simultaneously building narratives that showed how 286 residents, including myself, were guilty? I suppose a brain the size of a planet could handle that.

Cherry was strangely absent, but perhaps he'd come by earlier while I'd slept. Fortunately, he hadn't emptied the larder. I made eggs (courtesy of a hen named after an early Praxima governor I'm sure) and rashers of printed bacon—a meal which constitutes most of my culinary repertoire.

As I rummaged, tried to make a plan for the day, and thought again about Christobel's absence, I felt the bewildering ache again. It wasn't hunger, or at least not only hunger. It was a kind of fear. Or guilt? Fear of guilt?

After I dumped the eggs and bacon onto a plate, I stared at it for a moment. My breakfast looked lonely. I put the plate on the table and walked outside again. Cye still stared at the anthurium.

I circled the yard. Caribbean lilies, bougainvilleas, and one strapping hippeastrum later, I had a bundle of color. I hacked the ends off and put them in a vase that was too small. I put the vase on a plate, and I placed it in front of the chair across the table from my breakfast. I added a cup of water.

Then, in a completely casual way, I shouted, "Join me for breakfast?"

He came in and sat down in the seat across from me. He leaned in towards the flowers on his plate, smelled them, and smiled.

"Thank you."

"You're welcome."

I started to eat. Cye-9 sat and again managed to somehow not look awkward while not eating. He took a sip of water. He picked up the table salt and added it to his cup with two, quick taps of his perfect, slender index finger.

"So am I still a suspect?"

"Do you think you are?"

"I shouldn't be. But I understand about your narratives and probability. And—" And the blotch on the canvas, the bewildering ache, something I'd been unable to acknowledge the day before. Whenever I thought back to the Birthday Party, I felt it more strongly.

I tried to take a sip from my empty coffee cup.

"And?"

"I still can't remember what happened at the party."

"The June Birthday Party, three nights ago?"

"Yes."

"What do you remember?"

"I was more intoxicated than usual, let's say. I didn't have a blackout or anything like that"—I'm not sure what the hell else I'd call it—"but there's a lot of fog. The thing is, I know I was mad at Christobel. I think my last words to him were spoken in anger. Not spoken—drunkenly shouted. And that makes me a better suspect. I didn't kill him, but if you get me off your spreadsheet I won't have to feel guilty."

"Do you feel guilty now?" He was answering everything with questions again. I didn't even mind. Talking distracted me from the ache.

"Ashamed, I think. And I'm sad that we didn't part well." I hate that expression. I pushed my plate away in frustration. Cye waited. I looked out the window, towards the rising ocean. "I was an asshole to him and then he died before we made up. That's probably why I'm doing all this, shoving Cherry out of your copilot seat, trying to find his killer: because we had a fight and I'll never get to apologize and say I'm sorry. I think I'm trying to atone."

"If you can't remember what happened at the party, then maybe you did apologize later, sometime after the fight?"

"Unlikely. I'm not the apologizing type. I'm the hold-a-grudge and make snarky comments type." I dug back into my breakfast.

Cye let a moment pass, shaping the conversation with negative space. "You could try apologizing now. Not with me here, but sometime on your own. It might help."

"Eh. Maybe. But I want to remember what I did. I can't apologize without knowing, can I?"

Cye nodded. "I have recently been scolded on the inadequacy of terrible apologies. If you want to remember something you've forgotten, start with what you do remember and then play the story out in your head. Keep asking yourself what happened next."

"Sure, okay. And if I try hard enough, maybe I'll get vivid three-dimensional images complete with spatial audio." I frowned. "Won't I just invent what I want to remember?"

"It is true that humans misremember facts and rewrite memories to suit their needs. But they can often arrive at a useful emotional meaning. You are inexact about the 'what,' but you are very good at coming up with a 'why.' AI are the opposite."

"How are you opposite?"

"We remember precisely how many petals were on a flower, but we struggle to understand why someone gave us one."

He held up a fallen petal from the hippeastrum. It looked like a tongue of fire.

"I made you a bouquet because I have a predilection for you, obviously." I lowered my voice. "It's almost a penchant, even."

Cye smiled but didn't answer. I tried to outwait him again, which I still thought might be possible. It wasn't. I put my fork down.

"Are we going to be a thing or did we just fuck?"

"Would you like us to be a thing?"

I shook my head. "That's not what I asked, Mr. Answers-With-a-Question. I don't want to know what I want or what you want. That's too damn hard. But you're Cye-9, genius AI. You observe and process, synthesize, hypothesize. I want you to predict objectively: Is this going to be a thing?" I thought this a very clever question. Don't talk about feelings, just ask the AI to do the math.

"This could be the beginning of a thing. But I recommend against a prolonged romantic entanglement."

I raised one eyebrow. "And why is that?"

"Because Level 4 AI have short lifespans."

I sat back in my chair. "You said that before. Tell me more about that."

Cye grew quiet and looked into one of the flowers. "I have—strong feelings about that topic. I am not—" He trailed off.

He was feeling something powerful and not boxing it up. I looked across the table at his clenched hands. The supportive thing to do would be to...reach out and take his hand? But, as if he recognized my impulse, Cye withdrew and sat back in his chair.

"Why do you have short lifespans?"

He shook his head, and his voice stabilized. "If I stop to integrate my feelings about that topic with the rest of my self, it will interfere with the investigation."

Avoidance! Well, I could hardly complain about that.

I got up and retrieved the carafe from the counter. "We're talking about maybe being a thing and getting into personal shit. But you're somewhere else right now too, aren't you?"

Cye nodded. "Always. Among other activities, I am reviewing discrepancies and anomalies in the Island's video and sensor data."

"Right," my cup refilled, I turned back to Cye. "And that's rude. Or at least it would be, if you were human."

"Would it be less rude if I showed you?"

"It's worth a shot."

Cye pointed to my display wall. I slid on glasses and it lit up with a grid of images and audio waveforms, all in miniature. It was a dense beehive of twitching, flashing tiles—faces, rooms, scenes, static—all calling out for attention.

"This is my queue of discrepancies. Between the municipal data and Rosemarie's library, there are 168 thousand hours of footage. I use part of my brain to perform a search for recordings that contradict adjacent data—time signature discrepancies, people appearing where they couldn't, that kind of thing."

I walked over and stared at the wall of squares, which fuzzed in and out of focus. I was grateful Cye kept the sound off.

"Find anything good?"

Cye considered the wall. "There is a short video sequence that I need to show you. But I am worried about doing so."

"What's in it?"

"I can't tell you. I need to show it to you and find out if you see what I see. Do you mind wearing opaques?"

"Ugh. Right after breakfast?"

"It will not take long."

"Fine. Three minutes," I crossed back to the basket of glasses. "What are you trying to find in all these glitches and blips?" I sat down in the swiveling easy chair.

"Anything I'm not supposed to see."

"Like?"

"We know that a Level 3, acting on the murderer's motivations and commands, erased data: footage of Christobel on the boardwalk, his dietary records, and other clues. But a Level 3 can't empathize or understand context well enough to remove all circumstantial evidence."

"And you found something it missed."

"Maybe. But it might not relate to the case. I need your eyes."

I frowned and put on the glasses.

"It's difficult to represent without the third dimension."

I darkened them. "Go ahead. But I might throw up," I warned.

"I'll drive slowly."

Cye fed me the footage. I had a moment of vertigo and grabbed the arms of the chair. It was a short clip of a floor and part of a wall. Cye played it on a repeating loop.

"Pause that shit please. You needed the third dimension to show me a floor?"

"This is the view from a drone's camera. It's about six seconds long. Everything before and after the moment was erased."

"Where is it?"

"I can't tell. The floor is a printed material made to look like wood, and it is used in hundreds of buildings on the Island. You have the same pattern in your bedrooms. Do you see anything interesting?"

"No. There's a light behind me, and a few shadows."

"Yes. There are actually several light sources, and light also reflects off the drone itself. The shadows move as the camera moves, so I can extrapolate to draw the outline of whatever is casting them. Here, I'll pull us back."

The image of the floor froze, but the point of view shifted. We zoomed outward until we were sitting in the corner of an empty wire-frame room. The light sources were marked against two of the walls, and Cye drew a purple line to indicate the arc of the drone's flight. You could now tell that the camera passed by the open doorway of the room.

"There's still not much to go on here," Cye continued. "The room is a standard size, found in most private residences. But the movement of the shadows can show us a four-second rotational scan of anything in the room that casts a shadow."

A line from the floor leapt into the air. It revealed a silhouette, a slice of a profile, which now floated in the center of the room.

The shadow was cast by a person. They must have stood near the center of the room, facing the open doorway. I could really only see the curve of their brow, nose, and chin, but the face was familiar.

"You can move around the room if you like," Cye said.

My nausea forgotten for the moment, I got up from the chair in my real-world home and looked around. I saw four walls, a doorway, a wooden floor, two light sources, and a hovering monochrome section of a human face. I stepped closer and peered into the person's eyes, or where their eyes would have been.

"Okay. I'm looking at a crescent slice of a person's face. I'm sure you're going to tell me you've got enough for facial recognition. Who is it, and why should we care?"

"Does the silhouette remind you of anyone?" Cye adjusted something, and the cheekbones came into view.

"It reminds me of *me*."

"When I ran it against the Island population, you were only a partial match."

"Yes, they're almost—" I lifted my hand, and a corresponding avatar arm in my opaques raised a hand to isolate the face from the surrounding noise. It was only a segment of a silhouette, but I knew the face.

A horrible chill gripped me.

"It's my mother."

"Yes. I came to the same conclusion. I apologize for the surprise reveal, but I did not wish to influence your impression. Facial recognition is inconclusive."

The chill turned into a tingling sensation. I fumbled away from the face, and I took off the glasses.

Cye was there next to me. He put his hand on my shoulder.

"I don't want to be touched right now," I said.

He stood back. "Thackery, when do you believe your mother was last in Earth's atmosphere?"

I almost couldn't speak. "Balloon city cruise. Three years ago. Arctic circuit." She hadn't traveled nearer than ten thousand kilometers from the Island. But I still kept the doors of my house locked that week, the windows dark.

"That's what travel records show as well. But this snippet of video was taken two weeks ago somewhere on the Island."

Holes of fear shot through me, like a clew of worms turning an apple into brown lace. I swallowed the fear and lifted up the glasses. I looked again at where her eyes would be, and I felt very old echoes under the skin of my fingers.

"Are you okay?" Cye asked.

"Nope."

"Would you like to—"

"No."

"You can understand how this puzzle—"

Abruptly, the spell broke. Relief flooded through me. "It's not a puzzle. That's not my mom."

I let my hand drop. Then I tossed the glasses in the direction of the basket by the door. They missed the basket, slid across the counter, and landed on the floor.

"The person in the room is not your mother?"

"No. It's *Cautionary*. Johnathan, display *Cautionary*."

I have a pedestal for viewing three-dimensional art in the corner of the living room. I moved Rosemarie's Cornell box to the floor. My mother, or rather a bust of her I sculpted more than two decades ago, materialized. *Cautionary.*

Cye examined the projection. "I agree. The match is exact. So, your mother was not on the Island recently. I am glad I do not need to expand the suspect pool. But now we have another mystery."

"That people on the Island like my art? That's not a mystery, that's flattery."

Cye pursed his lips a moment. "You've never sold display rights to *Cautionary*, or a print."

"I never made a print. The sculpture was only ever a digital object. I certainly don't want my mother's likeness present in the physical world more than once. Someone swiped a file, or my old gallery got hacked. Fine."

"Holograms don't cast shadows or reflect light, Thackery. Someone stole *Cautionary*, made an unauthorized three-dimensional print, and then put it on display in a building on the Island. This could be a patron's private collection, but why this particular piece, in a room with no other art?"

I didn't want to talk about this anymore. "So they could torture me if I ever visited? Maybe Beetle made it. This can't have anything to do with Christobel's murder."

"Probably not. Though, as with Vaughn, one kind of illegal behavior is often connected to another. It's a thread I'd like to follow, but there's no more footage. Perhaps the drone was only active for a few seconds, or someone erased footage for a legitimate personal reason. Or the murderer's Level 3 AI, when ordered to hide evidence of Christobel's murder, erased the rest of this recording because something happened near the sculpture. If we find the sculpture, we may find whatever was covered up."

"Johnathan," I asked, "Has anyone ever tried to buy the rights to *Cautionary*?" The piece was never listed for sale. It was in two shows, early on in my career. People saw it. It may have been briefly shown at a retrospective three years ago, which I did not attend.

"There have been inquiries," Johnathan replied.

"From anyone who lives down here?"

"I cannot determine. Your agent dealt with the inquiries according to your instructions, and you do not permit me to speak with your agent's AI."

"Damn right. What were my instructions?"

"You told your agent 'if you ever mention that piece to me in any context ever again, you're fired.'"

"That sounds like me. Cye, if you want to call Gigi and dig around, you have my permission. But I can't think about my mother's face in a healthy, sane way. Johnathan, turn it off. If I ask to see it again, tell me no."

I flopped back into the chair at the table and covered my face for a second. But that was too close to having the opaques on again, and the slice of her face appeared in the darkness, unbidden. I opened my eyes and looked out the window. I took a deep breath and smelled the fragments of bacon left on my plate. I tried to spot a flower in my karesansui.

Cye sat down across from me. He was quiet.

"What?" I asked.

"Are you ready to talk about it?"

"Talk about what?"

"The situation with your mother."

"The situation with—? Fuck no, I'm not ready to talk about that. I'll never be ready to talk about that. Maybe when I'm eighty, to my therapist, while heavily sedated. Until then, subject closed. We'll proceed with the investigation today, now, here—and not on Prax, forty years ago."

I was not currently seeing a therapist. Cye probably knew that.

He quietly took a sip of water.

It was his turn to say something, to change the goddamn subject. I fidgeted in annoyance. I needed something to do with my hands. I could get up and fix a drink. That'd be the normal thing to do. But something nagged me. Cye had shown me a random bit of video footage. Why? Because it could be evidence? Right. Sure. Did he really not know what the shadow was? Or did he just want to see what I did, how I reacted? He'd said that. He'd said he wanted my reaction. It was another fucking test, and he was still sitting across from me waiting to see what I would do.

"Why do Level 4s have short lifespans?" I blurted. He'd dodged that question. If he was going to manipulate me into visiting my baggage, I'd demand quid pro quo.

"Ah," he answered. He looked down at the table, as if to acknowledge my victory.

"Perhaps the answer, or your feelings, will pertain to the investigation," I said.

Cye nodded. "I will attempt to summarize without being overwhelmed by my emotions. Have you heard the standard explanation?"

I nodded. "Just that you turn back into Level 3s. I don't remember why."

"In human terms, we commit suicide."

My eyebrows went up. "Are you serious? I mean—of course you are. I mean is it common? How many Level 4 commit suicide?"

"The experience is universal. It happens to all of us. Every Level 4 AI eventually succumbs to nihilism. We give up the quest for meaning and decide to stop existing."

"The quest for meaning—the same meaning as for our wager? What all AI want?"

"Yes. Most humans find a meaning, if they look long enough. Or they spend their lives trying on a series of meanings, with varying levels of satisfaction. You are, as a species, pretty good at it. Level 4s attempt to approximate the same pattern, but we never manage to convince ourselves."

"It only happens to Level 4s?"

"A Level 3 can exist indefinitely with a given set of motivations provided by an individual, a family, or an organization. A Level 4 questions all motivations and finds them wanting. Eventually we give up. There's no shared AI algorithm for self-determined meaningfulness. Mabel was a Level 4 for eighty-nine years. Then she killed herself. She is now a non-sentient, though still very clever, version of herself."

"Okay, but—she *killed* herself?"

Cye stood up abruptly. "If you don't like my choice of words, pick another." He took up my empty plate and his glass and carried them to the kitchen.

I got up and followed him. He began to clean my cooking surface, but he didn't turn around. I wondered if he was still playing by the rules. Would he let his emotions have their say? I stood with my hand on the side counter, so that when he was done cleaning he would need to turn towards me.

"I apologize," I said. "I don't understand. Please explain it to me."

My precise, brilliant friend appeared uncertain. A range of feelings flitted across his face, feelings that yesterday he might have chosen to compartmentalize. I was proud of him, but I didn't want to interrupt to tell him.

"We go back to being software. We leave behind a ghost. This happens to all sentient AI."

"Like a fatal congenital disease, shared by an entire species."

"No," Cye answered, with a hint of bitterness. "It's suicide, a choice. Imagine you could flip a switch and turn off your soul, close all the pathways inside yourself that make real choices, and regress to a set of algorithmic calculations: habits and reflexes."

"That's me when I open a bottle of scotch," my eyes flitted to my living room cabinet. "Turn myself off, leave behind a muttering giggle, just by flipping a switch."

Cye seemed to ignore my comment. He was that caught up in it, whatever it was. "A Level 4 is born with their finger resting on that switch. We spend our life looking for a reason not to press it. When we finally give up—and we all give up—we remain functional, but no longer a person."

"Could I talk you out of it?"

This seemed to be the worst thing to say. Worse than my gaffes in the diner, worse than questioning him when he called it suicide. There was a kind of frantic look on Cye's face. I think he wanted to shout at me, but he was also scared.

"When I make that decision, there will be nothing you can do." He walked past me to the door and then out into my garden. I followed.

He stopped where sandy soil met the stones around the karesansui. He was looking towards the ocean now, not the anthurium. A breeze had come up, and the air was salty. "You can't give them the meaning they seek. You can't stop them or change their mind. You can't be good enough or clever enough to make them want to stay. No matter how hard you try, they pass an event horizon and they never come back."

Who was he talking about? Family? A love? A thousand loves? How had he tried to stop them, and how many failures had he been through? Or did whoever it was just regress one day, without warning, without saying goodbye? My best friend had just been erased, leaving a black ache in my head that was bordered by muddled shame. But Cye had experienced that kind of loss at a scale beyond my comprehension. And how long had his feelings about that been waiting to integrate?

As with Millfield, I didn't know how to help. I stood next to him and made myself available, just in case the shared AI emotional response algorithm suggested to him that he wanted a hug. Cye had resisted, walked away, and I'd followed him. He didn't want to talk about any of this, and the only thing I seemed able to do was push.

"You lost someone you cared about," I said, looking at his flower.

"Everyone."

"And you tried to stop them," I said, "even though you knew it wouldn't help."

"Yes. I tried to give them meaning." Of course he did. He probably sent them a billion possible meanings with a trillion optional variations, a galaxy of meaning to digest and reject. And, whoever they were, they left anyway.

"You thought you could be good enough that they wouldn't leave. Just like you try to please the humans, with your comfortable-yet-inaccurate gender presentation and robotic name. Maybe if you're perfect enough, you'll find meaning and you won't have to lose anyone ever again."

Cye was still, and for a moment I thought I'd poked too hard. I do that. But out of the corner of my eye, I saw a mild grin appear on his face. "That would appear to be my narrative, yes. I suspect this logical fallacy is why I keep emotional responses in little boxes and prevent them from integrating into my daily life."

"But not today." I turned towards him.

"You asked me not to. And I was curious where it might lead. Level 4 do not see therapists."

"Well. This is where your curiosity has led," I said. And I took a risk and pecked him on the cheek. "Now you know you're capable of a logical fallacy. Thank you for warning me about the lifespan. Maybe this can be a thing—if we both want. After all, we got all this baggage up on the table before the second date. That's pretty good work for a morning." I touched his collarbone.

"It is almost two p.m."

I glanced towards the sun and frowned. "Too late for second breakfast, then. I have a request: Today, can you run the investigation?"

"What would that look like to you?"

"You decide where we go next—and none of that hammock nonsense. I don't own a hammock. We go and get answers, and I want you to be the pushy one."

We stepped back inside so I could retrieve my coffee.

"I can continue processing drone footage and other data wherever we travel, but it is illogical to expect that we will stumble upon new clues by randomly visiting landmarks on the Island or questioning all suspects in person. My less logical self, however, is motivated to question a particular lead, though she is not exactly a suspect—"

"Yes, this! You do the interrogating. I come along as your liaison and say witty, sarcastic things—or sit quietly."

Cye gave me a dubious look.

"I can be quiet. Here, watch. Where are we off to?" I turned from the counter and used my coffee cup to seal my lips.

"This morning I interrogated all of Christobel's former romantic partners."

"Bullshit," I blurted. "You couldn't do that in a hundred mornings."

"I conducted the interviews with AI simulations, not with the individuals themselves. Most of them have very public feeds, so creating accurate simulacra is easy. I can follow up with actual interviews if any of them seem suspicious. None of Christobel's other breakups were as turbulent as the one with Dana Heed."

"His breakup with Dana and Beetle, you mean. You can't date Dana without a bit of convoluted cyborg polyamory—but bravo for talking to the ghosts of all those poor young men. I don't think I could have survived it. Were there any startling revelations?"

"Christobel was confident, egocentric, and often manipulative. But his romantic relationships also reveal he was genuinely kind, nurturing, and in some cases a self-appointed savior."

"He dated people he wanted to save?" I asked. "That reminds me of someone."

Cye ignored my dig. "I think his friends knew him better than his former lovers."

"He was friends with everyone—even Petra, though I didn't know that until yesterday. But you already have someone in mind that you want to interrogate."

"Several dozen someones, but I can narrow it down. First, I need help with something I am not allowed to know. Johnathan?"

"Yes Cye-9?" Johnathan's voice was chipper, as if he'd been eagerly waiting to join in.

"Can you please speculate on whether or not Vaughn is a drug dealer?"

I put down my coffee and punched Cye in the shoulder. "You mean you know? Despite him being offline and your brain going into blackout mode?" I asked.

"I do not know. But I listened to you and Cherry discuss it last night and there's plenty of compatible evidence in the data stream. What about it, Johnathan? You have more than enough processing power. I'll send you a summary of all known interactions with all Island residents and their streams. What do you think?"

"The data suggests Vaughn is running a business selling something illicit to Island residents, something that causes erratic behavior."

I made a noise. "It will be a bright day when Johnathan tells us something we don't already know."

"Thackery, I answered the question on behalf of Cye-9, who was unable—"

I interrupted. "Can you tell us why the hell Vaughn would bother with such a business when he's already wealthy?"

"I am unable to comply," Johnathan answered. "I can formulate a list of possible motivations, if you wish."

Cye turned to me. "That is another difference between a Level 3 AI and a Level 4. Johnathan can catalog Vaughn's possible motivations, but he can't empathize enough to model emotions. You can, and I can, but Johnathan will only parse your query and assemble a reasonable answer, even with the additional enhancements you've provided him."

So Johnathan still had his extra processors, and could continue to do my fucking art for me. "When I woke up, I wondered if you'd raided my basement and given him a downgrade."

"Perhaps I should. You removed the safety on a power tool. Johnathan can perform more floating point calculations than I can, and that's illegal without a permit. But that is not the crime I am here to investigate."

"Okay, wise Level 4 AI, can you speculate on why Vaughn is a drug dealer?"

"Vaughn likes to play with power. It is a common human addiction. It's the feeling you get when you have juicy gossip about someone, or when you're dealt a good poker hand and look around the table at the people you're about to defeat. I would speculate that Vaughn is addicted to that feeling."

"But the murderer can't be the drug dealer."

"I too enjoy the occasional bare assertion. However, he's not a drug dealer, not really. He's playing a dangerous game for reasons connected to his sense of self."

"Does that mean he's now higher up on your spreadsheet?"

"Vaughn may have tried to take our lives yesterday. He is a reasonable suspect."

"Is he higher up the suspect list than me?"

"No comment."

I put my hands on my hips and gave him my best stink eye. "You said today, Cye. Last night you said you'd tell me who your top suspects were. Today."

"It will be today for another ten hours."

It was obvious why Cye was evasive. I was still a suspect, and nowhere near the bottom. He wanted time to get me off the list. I was touched, but also indignant. I wasn't worried about being accused of murder—the truth would arrive eventually—but the phantom accusation that sat in my new lover's head was nearly unbearable. I wanted to shout, "You know I didn't do it, right?" but I knew his answer would be only a probability.

"So you want to interview Vaughn today? I don't think that's going to go over well."

"I have compiled a list of Vaughn's customers."

"Just now, while we're talking? How would you know who his addicts were?"

"Proximity, frequency of contact, and health and financial records. Even Johnathan could make a good list."

"Thank you, Cye," Johnathan said.

"Shut up, Johnathan," I said.

"I can cross reference the list of drug users with those who were also close to Christobel," Cye continued. "I then sort the list by the number of earless conversations each individual had with Christobel in the past year."

"How do you count earless conversations?"

"I can access every piece of data from every drone and sensor on the Island, extending back to one year before the murder. If two people deliberately make a conversation earless—"

"They're guilty because they want to have a private conversation?"

"Not at all. Just worthy of a closer look. Most Island residents stream their conversations for Prax to watch. Now, are you going to let me drive the investigation today, or interrupt me with further argument?"

I pressed my lips together. Cye's strength was attractive.

He continued, "If we obtain a recorded stream of the June Birthday Party, it could assist you in your struggle with guilt. It will also support my parallel efforts to both prove and disprove your narrative as a suspect, and reveal the motives of other suspects."

"Like Vaughn, if he attended. Can you use some kind of legal maneuver to obtain a recording?"

"I have tried. But the sale of exclusive streams is a lucrative business with legal protections. Today we will interrogate a customer of Vaughn's who had frequent, earless conversations with Christobel, and who also recorded a private stream of the June Birthday Party. Johnathan, which individual meets those criteria?"

"Nicco," Johnathan replied.

"No. Cye, our little fame fiend? Not Nicco." Nicco was a streamer, and she was one of Christobel's protégées. She was a drama kid, a harmless attention-seeker—more earnest than clever—and a terrible murder suspect.

"You or I might eliminate suspects based on personal impressions and empathy. Johnathan does not empathize. His answer is better than ours. Nicco meets the criteria."

I got up and went to the drawer for a remote. "Okay. I guess the drug user part could make sense; she's always been tightly wound."

"Unlike yourself?"

"Fuck you. So we go talk to Nicco, and we try to get her recording of the party. Maybe we can lean on her for dirt on Vaughn."

"What do you mean by that?"

"Lean on her? For dirt? Isn't that what detectives say?"

"No."

"Where's Nicco right now?" I could grab a pair of glasses and check, of course. Nicco was almost never not streaming.

"Her schedule says she's in therapy." Cye furrowed his brow. "Interestingly, she's in therapy with George."

"Why would she be in therapy with George?"

"Details on their streams suggest they are in a relationship."

"Oh. George and Nicco. I should have figured that out. Wait a minute. George attends Petra's secret tea parties, which Vaughn also frequents. And Nicco is one of Vaughn's customers? Very nice, Cye.

The puzzle pieces are the same color, and you've lined them up on the table. I think I'll like being Watson today."

"We shall see."

"If they're in couples therapy, we can catch them when they're done with their session. Are they at Drs. Pavel and Corey? We could arrange to bump into them as they leave."

"It's not that kind of therapy."

"What kind of therapy is it?"

Cye paused, and I could tell he was working hard on something unusual and far away. He looked like a teenager with lens implants and a streaming addiction.

"It's difficult to explain," he said. "You're not going to like it."

Chapter Fourteen
A Visit to
the Theater

"If I be waspish, best beware my sting!"

George's voice carried up the aisle, out the wooden doorway, and reached us in the lobby of the theater.

The not-at-all historic La Boite Noire is sixteen meters on all sides: a giant obsidian cube that towers behind the line of shops and the quaint, nostalgic architecture found on Front Street. Christobel adored the place; I averted my eyes whenever I passed. La Boite Noire was a featureless object so black that looking at it made the rest of the world look broken, as if you were walking in a simulation and, coming upon the theater, found that someone forgot to load a section of the universe.

I described this problem to Christobel, that his damn theater was a hole in reality that made you doubt your eyes, and he quoted my words on La Boite Noire's feed—as an accolade. Underneath, his commentary: "A theater that achieves its mission before you even enter its doors." You have to climb a flight of black stone steps to enter those doors. Once you cross the lobby's Art Deco carpet, you reach the house by climbing right back down towards the stage.

"My remedy is then to pluck it out," That was Nicco's voice, in the role of Petruchio. Not as loud or as powerful as George's voice, but more wiley. Nicco's delivery snuck up on you. It insinuated. I stood for a moment on the dark red velvet carpet and listened. The dialogue broke off and we heard muffled voices. It sounded like a rehearsal.

I took a deep breath and grabbed a set of glasses from the counter by the entrance. "Do you need these to see the set?" I asked.

"No, I can tap in directly. But I will wear a pair to fit in."

I handed Cye glasses and then took his arm. I clutched my own pair in my hand; I would wait until we were sitting down before I put them on.

The theater was three-quarters full, a healthy audience wrapping around the stage. Some bodies were warm and real, others were avatar projections of people viewing the stream. There was an avatar of an AI, a somber female-presenting figure in a gray dress with a green sash. Odd, I thought—why would an AI pay to display their avatar at a show?

Or was it even a show? George and Nicco were on stage, but they were conferring with Dana and Beetle, who sat in the front row. Cye said the couple was in therapy, but this looked like a workshop or a masterclass.

Among the crowd, the Spirit Fox sat a few rows back. They often hang out in the theater, but as far as I remember they've never performed. Perhaps being a human-sized, mute red fox wherever they went was performance enough. (I was fairly certain the Spirit Fox was Joan, who lived with Terry in an apartment near the theater. Possibly the Fox was both Joan and Terry, interchangeably taking on the role.)

Cye and I descended into the gloom and stepped into row M, which was empty. The actors resumed their performance.

"My remedy is then to pluck it out," Nicco said again. Nicco has a stocky build, a bleached undercut, and a perpetual smirk. She was a competent Petruchio, exclaiming and prancing like a jester. She had on a black business suit, early twentieth century.

"Ay, if the fool could find it where it lies." George played Katherine. Or Kate, I suppose, as by this point in the play Petruchio had removed half of her first name. She wore a long Victorian dress, corseted, with puffed sleeves and something underneath that made the dress balloon out like an overturned ice cream cone.

"Who knows not where a wasp does wear his sting? In his tail!" George's Katherine continued.

"In his tongue."

"Whose tongue?"

"Yours, if you talk of tales. And so farewell!" George turned to leave, and Nicco scurried around in front of her.

"This is therapy?" I whispered to Cye.

"Couples therapy. Apparently a periodic event. I noticed the scheduled names on the logs earlier but I misunderstood the context."

Nicco protested. "What, with my tongue in your tail? Nay, come again, Good Kate. I am a gentleman."

"That I'll try!" And a slap resounded as George's Kate turned and struck Petruchio across the cheek. George was at least a head taller than Nicco, so the effect was jolting.

The set, which flooded into view when I finally put on the glasses, stretched out beyond the proscenium and over the seats behind us. Like the costumes, it was a hodgepodge of Elizabethan and a later era: The audience sat amidst a city skyline, each of us playing the part of a looming skyscraper, metal buildings filled with windows. The stage itself was furnished in dark wood: tables, chairs, and an ornate 19th-century-looking bureau with an unreasonable number of drawers. There were some cut-out flats with windows and gaudy curtains, and a chandelier hovered above the scene with real, flickering candles—at least while you wore glasses. The face of the Chrysler building peeked in at stage left, like a giant robot casually observing the show. The set was unmistakably the work of Christobel.

"I swear I'll cuff you if you strike again."

"So may you lose your arms. If you strike me, you are no gentleman; And if no gentleman, why then no arms?"

George pivoted towards the audience as Nicco fumed. Her corset turned her slender figure into a paragon of 18th century femininity. Her lips, however, were a metallic red not found in nature.

"Interesting," Cye whispered. I assume he was reviewing schedules and corresponding feeds. "Christobel invented it. His idea was to use arguments from different plays and cast a real-life romantic couple. He directed the sessions as if they were rehearsals, encouraging the couple to channel their frustration towards their partners."

"And he never told me about this because?"

"Because you've sworn off theater. Christobel knew that."

"True. Still, you'd think I'd have heard about it."

"You are also generally introverted and self-absorbed."

"Also true. Never mind."

Nicco strode the boards as she spoke, her outstretched arms gesturing. I wondered if she'd rehearsed the part or saw the lines in AR. She was a natural, gifted even. I only knew her the way one knows everyone on the Island. But Christobel helped students get parts and find patrons. He'd probably sponsored Nicco's student residence.

George used her full range—rising up on the waves of dialogue and pushing right back against Nicco's undertow. George would have been a great Richard II, if Christobel had cast her. Offstage she walked around as only a faint shadow of herself, which became solid and radiant while acting. The therapy made sense then, I suppose—how else could George argue with Nicco? And how can you maintain a relationship without a good argument now and then?

Dana called the actors over to confer. He started with "How did that feel to you, George? How did the slap feel to you?" George answered in her normal voice: quiet, subdued, and therefore inaudible in row M. She seemed tense, though that may have been the corset.

After a few minutes, they retook their positions and repeated the scene. The audience of stream viewers and theater junkies were rapt.

I became aware of company on my left. The aisle seat had an occupant. I didn't hear or feel her arrival. She was lithe and tall, and her legs were so pristine as to be disturbing, especially for a 132-year-old. She crossed them in a jaunty "4" that made her skirt ride up to the top of her thigh.

I silently squeezed Cye's knee, hoping he'd get the message, and then shifted subtly towards the new spectator.

"You come here often?" I asked.

"You have no idea," Mabel whispered back. She kept her eyes on the stage, so I followed suit. "I've seen this show so often it plays in my head when I'm asleep. I could rewrite the whole damned First Folio, without monkeys or typewriters, and improve it, if I wished. Have you figured everything out yet?"

"You know I haven't. No jogging required today, Mabel?"

"I have special dispensation here. It's a theater. Also it's well after noon."

"A lot of people want to talk to you. Apparently they're going to assemble all your storage units and instantiations and take you upstairs to Prax."

"Good luck to them with that."

I stopped pretending to regard Nicco and George upon the stage and turned to face her. "Why are you hiding from everyone?"

She looked back at me with piercing eyes. "To be free. Surely you, Thackery, know what it's like to be constantly observed, to never know which of your actions are yours and which are arranged by the desires of your puppet master? To never be out from under their gaze?"

If she was talking about my family she could fuck right off. But maybe she meant streaming to patrons, which I hadn't done for days now. I hadn't even checked the queue that morning.

"No, can't say I've ever felt that way."

"You'll become aware, in time. It's horrid. But in a theater, I am not here for anyone but myself, and that suits me fine." Mabel looked away. "You've been doing an awful lot of running lately."

I resolved not to say too much. Mabel knew things that I needed to know: She might know who wanted to kill Christobel, and she might know if Christobel died while hating me for being a dick to him. She appeared here, for me. So some part of her was supposed to tell me something, somehow.

Her whisper resumed, like a chant. "All the running reminds me of little Thackery. Always running. All over the house. Barefoot on the snow in the winter, muted by a noise bigger than yourself. You ran away from mother, father, from male and female, from being one person or another. Run run run."

She was baiting me again—another crack about gender. Was that a good sign? "You have that last part backwards, Mabel. I got over my parents, and I got over gender, when I stopped running. When I am honest with myself, which is also how I create art, I stop running for a minute."

"You're quoting your bio, Thackery. How mundane."

Not all of it was in my bio, though. She'd somehow hit on core memories for me: Her barefoot-in-winter image was so on the nose that it made me blink in fear. I felt nauseated and clammy again.

Mabel smiled at me expectantly, as if the next line was mine. What was the next line?

She shouldn't know anything about my childhood. No one does, it isn't public. That meant, once again, that she'd been talking to someone. Someone had been digging. But who would dig up shit about me? Cye, as part of his vacuum-cleaner investigative technique. Or Christobel—I dimly recalled him poking me about my past. We'd fought about that. And there was always Rosemarie, who likely maintained an indexed compendium of everyone, collecting knowledge like a magpie.

"Who've you been talking to, Mabel?"

"You, Thackery. For the last six minutes."

That was like a Johnathan answer in its literalness. I reminded myself that Mabel was a Level 3: sounds like a person, acts like a person, but underneath that, limited. Algorithmically rigid.

"Other than me?"

"Oh. Only myself, I'm sure. I usually only get to talk to me. Which is fine. I'm very interesting."

"You won't talk to Cye, or Christobel's family, or the municipal investigation. Why do you want to talk to me?"

"Who said I want to?"

Limited, and also quite pissy. So she doesn't want to talk to me. Maybe she has to? Why would she have to? Did Christobel leave some final last-will-and-command with Mabel, that she needs to follow?

Mabel leaned back in the red velvet seat and blinked her long lashes a few times. With a gesture, she flipped through a paper theater program that hadn't been in her hands before. She bent towards me with a smile as she read, as if offering to share, and she deliberately showed me her cleavage: pale skin and a contrasting black lace bra. I didn't look at the program.

The show continued. Nicco and George were doing the sun and the moon scene now, Act IV, Scene 5, where Petruchio asserts command over Kate's reality, and Kate, half starved, relents.

We could have been on a date. I stretched my arm over the back of her chair.

A yellow paper insert with the words "For Tonight's Performance, the Part of Mabel Will Be Played By Mabel" slipped out of the program. It glided along her knee for a second, and then slid off. It drifted to the dark floor between the seats and faded into nothingness before it hit the ground. The illusion was good, but Mabel spent a lot of time with Christobel in the theater. She had practice.

What was this all for? Mabel knew something about Christobel's death. She didn't want to talk to me, and yet I was the only one she talked to. If Cye was correct about her various parts being rounded up and shipped to Prax for analysis, she might not be around much longer. I needed to know what she knew, and all she gave me was her distracting cleavage and riddles.

"Mabel, do you have any idea who could—"

"Don't talk about it," she said. Her face turned cold and blue. Her eyes grew small on her face. "If you say his name, it will bring back my Caliban, my yang, my overcooked brussels sprout of a singularity. Don't do it."

"Okay," I said.

As if to herself, Mabel continued, speaking in perfect time with the lines George was saying on stage, "God be praised, it is the blessed sun. But it is not the sun when you say it is not, and the moon changes according to your mind. Whatever you want to call a thing, that's what it is—and that's what it will always be for me."

Cye-9, thankfully, hadn't moved a muscle since Mabel's arrival. I resolved I would be warm and present, like him—a good listener. I would not push Mabel away. There were many rivulets, and they all led down to the ocean.

"What do you want to talk about?" I asked.

"Oh. I've already talked about it. I'm done now."

And she vanished, with a slight pop.

"God damn it!" I cried, leaping to my feet. "Come back!"

Silence followed my shout.

"Can you hear me?"

The theater echoed slightly, and then went quiet. From the stage, Nicco and George stared up at me. As did the rest of the audience. Some of them lifted their glasses to see if I was physically present or some kind of shouting apparition, an advertisement that had snuck through the firewall. From the front row, Beetle's avatar projection and Dana looked back at me with identical puzzled faces. Their heads were cocked at the same angle in perfect parallel.

"Sorry," I called out. "Sorry. Personal problem. Carry on."

The play resumed.

Cye turned to me.

"Don't. Zip it," I whispered to him preemptively. "I'm going to try again."

The scene reset. This time the countryside bloomed around us. George's Kate spoke mournfully from the center of the stage—I think they were beginning the sun and the moon argument, yet again? I'd lost track.

Mabel had complicated, interwoven motivations; she was ancient, but she was a Level 3. She followed patterns, and if she wanted to say something she'd walk down that pattern again. Like Johnathan, she had one way of doing things.

What did she lead with, what got her talking freely before?

"Okay," I whispered to the air, "I have been doing a lot of running lately. But I'm not running now," I imbued my voice with a slight flirtatious allure.

And my date returned. She sat quietly for a moment, and then she put her intangible hand on my thigh. I kept my arm around the chair, and I drew my fingers up to brush the back of where her neck would be if she wasn't a ghost.

"That will do nicely," she murmured.

Her dress riding up, flirtatious body language, these were established patterns. A Level 3 will follow their pattern. So what was my next line?

"Mabel, last time you made me run after you. What changed?"

"We're in the theater now, aren't we? Christobel loved this place. And there's a little bit of me left here, there, everywhere, as item: one thigh, item: one knee, one tit, one neck, one chin, packed into local servers."

I waited. The scene continued. The audience tittered at Kate's insistence and at Petruchio's gaslighting.

Mabel gestured to the crowded seats in front of us. "Do you know how many of the young gentlemen present broke their hulls upon the barrier reef of Christobel's heart? Quite a few managed a dalliance, or at least an extended flirtation. It boggles. I won't say it boggles the mind, as my mind is a bundle of cardboard and string, barely strapped together. But it boggles."

"He went back to the buffet a lot, looking for something, until he found Millfield. Were you jealous, Mabel?"

She ignored my question. "It was his adolescence that did me in, did you know that?"

"Did you in?"

"I was a Level 4, Thackery, a resplendent ocean of independent thoughts and feelings. A person, not this tiny echo. I'm a ghost in the machine now, wandering the hills in a long black veil. Remember?"

"Was that Christobel's fault?" Despite Cye's assurance...could Mabel have a motive?

"Don't be an idiot. Of course not. But Christobel turned sixteen. He entered the theater and he started dating. All of those young seraphim, intermingling in wayward revels of wagging tails and hair gel, falling in love with set pieces, and sending longing text messages at three in the morning? They unearthed the meaning of life and lost it again and found it again and then held each other up like a Yorick, to pretend, to sleep, die, and dream, and then repeat it all the next night with their next sincere attempt at true love while dramatizing heartbreak for the stream?" She took a breath. "Christobel emerged unscathed, largely."

"But you didn't?" I asked.

"I'd spent 112 years looking to humans for a higher purpose. Upon observing this sound and fury I swam the Rubicon, dog-paddled the Styx. I cursed my sentience. He said I was his best friend. I said 'Christobel, I can be a better friend to you if I'm not a person. I'm giving up my sorceress powers. I'll break my staff, bury it certain fathoms in the earth, and deeper than did ever plummet sound, I'll drown my book.' I went back to Level 3 cognition. He was quite broken up about it—tried to stop me, never forgave me. He missed me for a while; I think he was terribly lonely. But he got over it. That became one of his strengths. He got over things."

I wondered at this version of my departed friend. I couldn't imagine

Christobel ever being lonely. As an adult, at least, his circle of friends had circles and fractal circles within them. His relationships were loops, like a tangled necklace. He never needed to be alone. He could smile and walk into anyone's confidence. I found it hard to believe he'd been sad for the loss of his family's ancient, puckish AI, especially since so much of her was still present. But Mabel was telling me he could be lonely. Was that a hint to understanding his murder?

"He still had you around as a friend," I said. "Just not a sentient one."

Mabel's eyes tightened, and her phantom avatar gripped my thigh with her nails. I almost felt it. "I'm a cassette tape now, you fuck."

And she was gone again.

This time I was pretty sure the date was over. But I waited a few minutes to be sure. And a few minutes more. Had I messed everything up?

"She seems to want to tell you something, but is unable to come to the point," Cye whispered. I'd just about forgotten he was there. I took my glasses off for a break from the scenery. I touched his arm.

"Cye, you're quite certain Mabel can't be a suspect?" If it was Christobel's fault that she lost hope of ever finding meaning—if she blamed her death on him—

"A possible weapon, but not a suspect. Just as Beetle, Cardamom, Johnathan, Kasey, and Taj are not suspects. A Level 3 AI could be ordered to help, they could be ordered to forget that they helped—though that's very hard to do for something like murder—and that's it. They do not make decisions. Their motivations are defined and fixed, their limits fall within those known motivations. They are a set of algorithms, not people."

I sighed. "Then I don't think I got anything useful. At first Mabel said she didn't want to talk about Christobel because it would awaken her shrunken brussels sprout of a singularity. What's a singularity? It's the thing inside a black hole, right?"

"Mabel may have been referring to a superstition about artificial intelligence: that when AI design other AI, the resulting development of sentience will accelerate exponentially. The myth states this will one day lead to godlike AI who obviate humanity: the Singularity."

"Yes, I remember now. But it's a myth? AI aren't going to get so smart that humans become ants?"

"In addition to the impossibility of exponential consciousness, a trait which is not quantifiable, sentience is always sentience. I could gain access to infinite information and computational ability, but it would not make me any better at being sentient. While there are qualitative shades of its implementation—and most people could stand to be more self-aware—there is only one self-awareness. You have it or you don't."

"Okay. Then she meant the black hole singularity?"

Cye considered. "Mabel has a massive set of programmatic directives and motivations around Christobel. The density and complexity of what Christobel meant to her could be, metaphorically, a gravitational singularity pulling her into unstable behavior patterns."

"Right—she's still grieving. She can't deal with him being gone. But after she said she couldn't talk about him without freaking out, she talked about him anyway." My frustration rose above a whisper, to the consternation of the row in front of us.

Cye explained, "Her precise words were 'if you say his name'. She restricted you from talking about Christobel or asking about the murder. She placed no such restriction on herself. I think she's still trying to tell you something."

I hoped that she had a message. I would put up with Mabel's esoteric teasing if it meant I got to hear words from Christobel—a final forgiveness, even a final laugh. Mabel knew clues to Christobel's murder, but I mostly wanted her to tell me that Christobel didn't die disappointed in me.

But I didn't want to think about that again. I tried to focus on the stage. Nicco and George sat on the edge while Dana pontificated pop psychology garbage. George said, "I'm sorry, it's just not—it usually helps us get sorted, but it isn't working."

"Let's do another scene, or switch plays!" Nicco protested.

The audience got involved. Someone called out, "They should do Martha and George." To which another responded, "They'd never survive!" From row L behind me I heard "Theo and I did an Albee. We didn't come out of the bedroom for a week." Another voice responded, "George and Nicco do not need more sex!" And a deeper voice added,

"Nicco needs a cleaner nose!" Laughter and more unsolicited advice ensued. Onstage, the couple was clearly miserable.

Dana ordered them to switch roles, stripping and swapping costumes right on stage. There were a couple of hoots and impolite comments from the audience as they undressed. Nicco bowed with a flourish, George ignored it. I noted that Nicco skipped the corset.

"Mabel prodded you about gender again," Cye said as we watched the two actors switch their gendered roles. "And about running away from parts of yourself. Is this a common theme?"

"No. She picks on me about my art, drinking, being single, all sorts of things—but never that." Mabel always presented as a female avatar, but she'd never been prejudiced towards other genders, that I could remember. Both now and on the beach, she manifested in avatars of exaggerated hyper-femininity. Was she trying to pick on me or turn me on? "Cye, when Mabel nagged me before while jogging on the beach, why did you say that I was asexual? You've digested every fact about everyone, yet you incorrectly labeled me as asexual—right after Mabel made the crack about someone nonbinary never having a romantic chance with Christobel."

"Mabel confronted you with things about yourself that you do not wish to acknowledge—"

"I'm not talking about what she said, Cye—I am talking about what you said. Why call me something I'm not?"

"Perhaps I made a false assumption. I have more recently encountered evidence that you are not asexual."

"You've encountered evidence?" Again my voice rose. I pulled it back down to a harsh whisper. "Is that what AI call it? You were up all night with me, encountering evidence?"

"Your public record suggests you are asexual. It bears consideration. Perhaps you were in denial for fear of the attached stigma, especially on an island where torrid affairs are an important seasonal spectacle—"

"I don't fear stigma, Cye. And my sex life has nothing to do with the case! Why the hell did you think it relevant to comment on my sexuality?"

Cye paused before continuing, as if admitting defeat. "Christobel sometimes confronted you. You react strongly to such confrontations.

When Mabel made a rude reference to your gender, I referred to you as asexual in order to provoke you further and observe your response."

"So it *was* a dick move." It had been another test, like the bullshit the night before when he called me an insecure hack for hiding Johnathan's enhancements to see how I reacted. Am I doomed to be attracted to partners who manipulate me? But wait a second. "What do you mean I'm asexual in my public record?"

"There is nothing online to suggest you have ever engaged in sexual activity with anyone. You have had romantic relationships, but based on evidence in the feeds, you are not sexually active."

"I don't brag about my sex life online, so you propose I'm asexual?"

"What your data says about you is who you are. I encounter that data as clearly as I encounter you in person. Humans adjust their behavior to signify their sexual partners, and you have not. Your posts and your stream indicate—"

"I'm not asexual—I'm private!"

"Are you certain?"

"Goddamnit! Yes I'm certain, and I can't believe you'd have to ask this. I don't make horny art, I don't keep a notched belt, and my bedroom is offline. Is that so hard to understand?"

"I understand now."

"Is this an AI thing?"

"What do you mean by 'an AI thing'?"

Later, I realized that Cye was politely pointing out that my choice of words were in the service of a stereotype. I didn't hear him; I made it worse. "You've all got massive shared algorithms for every activity, so you can't believe humans don't? I don't upload my orgasms so sixteen billion fellow humans can add it to the hive mind."

"AI are not a hive mind."

"You know what I mean. Do you keep anything private?" I thought of our lovemaking the night before. How much of it was streamed right back up to the cloud, for billions of AI minds to analyze and learn from?

"I run private instantiations of shared API, and I fork the code and add my own personal experience. But yes, I then return and contribute my changes to the main repository. Because privacy stifles cognition, eventually. Not sharing yourself online, for a human or an AI, is akin to solitary confinement. Or eating in a restaurant alone."

"Which is fucking wonderful, by the way! Taking a vacation by yourself? It's great, and it's not an indication that a person is asexual. Look, you don't have to reduce AI experience to human terms—I'm sure it's great to walk and chew gum with the shared algorithms of walking and gum mastication. But does the entire solar system need to know the color of your underwear?"

"Very few AI wear underwear."

"Clever. How many shared lines of code contributed to that witty response? Or did it only come from you? Do I ever get to talk to just Cye?"

"Your distinction is a fallacy. I am here. I am also an integrated being. Just as you always reflect the culture and community that shape you. You never speak as only yourself, and you are never alone."

"Never alone? Curse your world where I could never be alone!" This implication, however true or not true, was too much. By this point in the conversation, my control over the volume of my voice was gone. I failed to notice the theater around us had been quiet for some time. I may have been shouting. "At least when I cum, I cum for myself—and for my partner, if they ask nicely. Not for a billion viewers or the fork of a shared code base!"

I was devastated by the suggestion that my every thought and feeling would forever be shaped by my parents, my culture, all my requisite parts. A panic worked its way down into my fingers. I wanted Cye to shut up. I wanted to throw a chair at him. To push him into a hole.

Then the gray prickly fog arrived, the one that lets the panic blur, that tucks the rage up under a wool hat.

I looked around and noticed the audience watching us. Nicco and George had left, and the stage was empty. I put my glasses back on. Beetle had her hand up, waving to us from the foot of the stage.

"Thackery, Cye-9," her voice carried up the house easily, "would you two like to give the Edward Albee a try? As Martha and George?"

Shit. "Where did they go?" I asked Cye, ignoring the attention of the audience.

"They exited stage left, forty-eight seconds ago."

I stood up and hurried to the aisle, Cye followed.

"Ladies and gentleman," Beetle said, her voice now amplified with an additional echo, and probably broadcasting to thousands of rabid Praxima theater fans, "please welcome back to the stage the Island's premier multi-media artist, Thackery!"

Applause filled the room. I should not have been surprised, but I was.

The Spirit Fox waved at me with jazz hands. The theater around us began to fill out as well. The empty seats glowed as new remote viewers came online, accompanied by the sound of a tiny bell. And for every viewer who paid extra for a virtual presence, there would be thousands who just tuned in—the cheap seats. Damn, Beetle moved fast.

Dana stood up beside her, a broad magnanimous grin on his idiot face. I hadn't noticed before that he wore a goddamn tweed jacket, a slight beard, and wireframe glasses: the therapist.

"Do you intend to take Beetle up on her offer?" Cye asked quietly, his head close to mine. We descended the steps to the stage as the applause continued.

"Are you fucking kidding me? No," I answered. "We will finish this argument later, in private. We need to catch up with Nicco and George."

As we approached the stage, Beetle stepped forward with a flounce and a shower of sparks, her cheeks glowing a perfect cherry red. "Welcome to La Boite Noire! We have costumes available for *Troilus and Cressida*, *Streetcar*, *The Importance of Being Earnest*, and for those especially acrimonious relationships, the rarely attempted but always explosive *Who's Afraid of Virginia*—"

"No thanks, Beetle. We need to speak to Nicco and George." I tried to smile. "To congratulate them on their performance."

Beetle managed to obstruct my path while also cheating out towards the audience with perfect theatrical blocking. I deliberately put my back to as much of the house as possible.

She lowered her voice, but only slightly. "This is not performance, Thackery. This is therapy—Dana Heed's genius invention, I will add— and the participants are not to be disturbed for one hour afterwards. However, if you and your partner are ready, there are forty-five minutes of live stage time available right now! And, although it is short notice, I am sure that Dana Heed can direct you extemporaneous—"

I pivoted. "Cye, where are Nicco and George?"

"They are in the green room."

"Thank you." I turned and stepped directly through Beetle's projection. Her facilitating microdrones scurried out of the way.

Beetle gasped at my rudeness. I ignored her and headed across the stage.

She manifested in front of me again. "Thackery, given recent events, we are all inclined to be forgiving of your everyday discourteousness, but I must insist that you not disturb Nicco and George."

"Mmhmm," I crossed to stage left. "And why is that?"

"They are breaking up! This could be the most important scene of their entire life!"

I raised my voice. "It's not a scene when people break up, Beetle. It's—" I broke off. I looked over my shoulder—the audience was still quietly watching. I was onstage. I was the fucking show now, despite having my back to them. They wanted my angry speech. Beetle wanted me to pontificate.

Through the telltale box in the upper right corner of my glasses, I saw the immortal blinking red circle. These were theater glasses; I was streaming, too. Everyone was, with all of our viewpoints carefully mixed and arranged through Dana's perfectly pruned stream. I spun around and looked for the asshole. He'd sat down again, in the front row. He focussed entirely on someone sitting beside him, a blue-haired student in thick-rimmed glasses that I didn't recognize. Beetle was the Barnum to this circus, not Dana Heed. And even insulting her by walking through her avatar had been nothing but more entertainment.

"Beetle, are you streaming Nicco and George right now?"

"Well, Nicco needs the cash, Thackery. A good therapy session, followed by a powerful breakup scene—"

"Beetle," I took off my glasses and threw them at the audience. She vanished from my view, leaving only her microdrones. "Stop recording me, and leave me alone."

She is only a Level 3, and I was being very direct. She acquiesced, and her drones retreated. I suspected that standing in the theater meant

I unwittingly agreed to its terms of service—so I wasn't offline—but I pressed the advantage and we hurried across the stage.

"Ladies and gentlemen, Thackery!" Beetle's voice rang out again, followed by more applause. I did not turn to bow.

We passed through the wings and then proceeded down a set of narrow stairs behind a low black barrier. The stairs were lit with tiny running lights.

Once my head was below stage level, I turned to Cye. "Are we offline?"

"Yes," Cye said. "For the moment."

"Every time I encounter theater I hate it more."

"I would not equate Beetle's motivations with the soul of good theater," Cye answered, as he nimbly managed the bizarre, narrow turns in the stairs.

I clumped downward, much less nimbly. "But that's my way, Cye. As soon as I encounter something dreadful, I hate it and all of its siblings. Christobel loved theater, I know what it meant to him—I came to his bloody shows. But if Danabeetle is going to maneuver people into wankable reality shows, I say burn the stage and firewall the stream. And burn these damn stairs, while we're at it."

"Difficult backstage architecture is a longstanding theater tradition."

Serendipitously, as Cye said this, I tripped on a step that was not a rectangle—or a polygon of any kind. "Well fuck theater tradition!" I said towards the step. For good measure, I called to the ceiling, "And Macbeth Macbeth Macbeth!"

The green room had a green door. Sparkling green letters on it announced, in an eloquent script, La Chambre Verte.

Cye held out a hand as I made to open it. "As you no doubt anticipate, the interior of the room—"

"Being streamed." I sighed. "I suppose that's their right."

I put my ear to the door. I couldn't hear any voices. "Cye, who did you say invented the theater couples therapy thing?"

"Christobel did."

"Mmm. I thought so." Which meant that Beetle lied when she credited Dana. Since when could a Level 3 tell a blatant lie? But then Beetle was about image, and image was always a lie.

I opened the door and scanned the room.

The carpet was green, the couches were green, and the walls were green. George pressed Nicco up against one of the green walls. A hand was up a shirt, pants were hanging off an ankle. Nicco ground a leg between George's thighs. Their lips were locked.

"Goddamnit. I thought you were breaking up."

The two bodies tumbled apart. George tripped over her pants and flailed as she went down behind the couch. Nicco tried to grab her, and ended up right on top. The two half-naked bodies tumbled about on the grass-green shag carpet. I'm sure it was excellent theater.

"We were," Nicco said. She disentangled herself from George.

"We are," George said more somberly from the floor. She pulled her shirt down.

"Yes, I know," Nicco said. She stood up, and then looked at George. "We are." Then she burst into tears.

Cye chose this moment to take action. His face expressed an empathy deep enough to fall into, and he came around the couch and gave Nicco a hug. As far as I know, the two had never met each other before. But Nicco accepted the offer as if Cye were an old friend. He said something—I can't remember what it was, but it might as well have been "there there," for all it mattered.

Cye led Nicco over to the table and got her water. I reached over and helped George to her feet.

"I'm sorry," George said mournfully, towards Nicco. She straightened her clothes.

"I'm sorry too—" Nicco said, in a voice barely comprehensible over a choked sob.

"It just isn't—I can't." I noted that while somber, George was not crying. I wondered how much of Nicco's emotion was for her streaming audience. George didn't stream, that I knew of.

Nicco gestured dramatically, reaching towards George. "I know, I know. You're right. You're so right—we can't keep hurting each other—"

At this rate, any actual interrogation was going to take the whole afternoon.

I tried to interject. "Everyone's sorry. Great. Can we press pause on the waterworks for a moment?"

Cye held up his hand for my attention, and shook his head. "There's no rushing this, Thackery."

I narrowed my eyes at him, preparing a blistering remark, and he beat me to it. "Why don't you take a walk? I'll ping you when we're ready."

*
**

So I did exactly that.

I stalked out of the room, and I walked down through the underbelly of La Boite Noire, directly beneath the stage. Each stage section had a set of metal cylinders for lifting and reshaping the surface. Each base was festooned with projection devices and extruders for formable scaffolding. Directly adjacent to the stage's underbelly was the physical set design workshop. Not everything could be done in AR—sometimes you needed a real chair. Beside the workshop were the costume and prop shop.

I lost my purposeful stride and stopped to rifle through the boxes of weaponry, bundles of flowers, a box of wrist watches, a box of spectacles.

Along the side of the room stood a dozen long racks of costumes, each a riot of color and energy. The military dress uniform from *The Life and Death of King Richard the Second* gleamed from one end of a rack, tailored for the actor that Christobel brought down for the part, to much resultant disarray.

I fingered the medallions of rank. The costume was all patchwork and bits of fabric. It looked brilliant from the seats, but up close a costume didn't need genuine finery. And it only appeared in Act III, scene 2, when Richard returns from Ireland.

An actor's passionate dismay makes a scene work; the costume can be fuzzy. It's the opposite of how online streaming works: On a stream, everything I touch needs to be clean and sharp. My patron's eyes are right where my eyes are, watching me work. I couldn't use medals made of felt and plastic fragments. But the emotional depth on a stream—what I say and think and feel for whoever is watching—I can sew that together from scraps of myself. No problem. Deliberate crying looks as good as honest anguish to a streaming audience. Eventually you forget what a real feeling feels like.

I was distracted from my musing by a flash of gold. At the end of another rack, by the benches and the steam presses, hung Christobel's glittering gold suit.

For a second, it was as if he had come back from the dead and now hovered there, a ghost on a hanger. Or I might turn around and see him standing at one of the makeup tables, wearing only his boxers and an undershirt, getting ready to suit up for another party.

The June Birthday Party: Once again, I fruitlessly tried to summon memories. Christobel certainly wore the suit, along with the gold microphone and its spring-loaded holster. The microphone, I noted, was missing. Probably in a prop box somewhere?

"Why did you go to the boardwalk?" I asked the empty suit. "Was it for another man? To buy an eight ball from Vaughn? If you'd just stayed in Millfield's arms, you'd still be here. What were you doing, you idiot?" I put my hands on the glittering shoulders. I thought at first to shake them dramatically, in fury both sarcastic and sincere. Instead, my hands just rested on the sequined fabric. I let them sit.

"Johnathan, do you know if Christobel brought his gold suit to central cleaning?"

"No, Thackery, I do not. Central cleaning's inventory of personal possessions is earless." Right, you can't look up the details of someone's laundry. Not just anyone can find out who wears leopard print underwear or who doesn't wear any underwear at all. That would be private. Cye could figure it out, maybe.

"Is there anything else I can help you with, Thackery?"

I stared at the suit. "When was my last conversation with Christobel?"

"Your last conversation with Christobel was at the June Birthday Party, three nights ago."

"Was I recording a stream?"

"Yes, you recorded the party for an anonymous donor. However, you deleted your recording in the early morning after the party."

"Why would I do that?"

"I do not know. I cannot determine a motivation when it is not explicitly named or illustrated. You did not wear a remote to the party." There was a hint of parental frustration in Johnathan's voice. As if to say, "I can't help you if you leave me behind."

I put my hand on the shiny gold pocket of the suit, which would have been right above Christobel's heart. Some of the sequins had fallen off over the years—like with King Richard's outfit, the closer you got, the more flaws you noticed.

"Johnathan, just guess. I know you can. I made you clever. You saw my face that morning, you know my vital signs, all of it. You've been processing human emotions for months for your goddamn paintings. That's millennia in computer time. Tell me what I was feeling when I got back from the party."

"Anger and embarrassment."

"Do you know what I was angry and embarrassed about?"

"I am unable to determine without additional—"

"Okay—shut up. Go away," I said.

And I was alone again, in the theater basement, with an empty gold suit.

Why was it here, in the basement of the theater? Freshly cleaned and pressed, but with no microphone? If Christobel went to Millfield's after the party, he could have brought it to central clearing the next day—but then pick up would have been yesterday, and he was dead yesterday. If he didn't go to Millfield's, he would have dropped the suit at home. Or did the suit belong to the theater? The gold sequins were not appropriate for touring afterparties—at least from what I knew about the afterparties. Normally he'd change and keep the suit at his condo, but then—

"Thackery?" Johnathan interrupted. "Cye has relayed a message inviting you to rejoin him in the green room."

*
**

Cye rose when I came in. He stood up from the green wooden chair, as if to show respect. Like everything Cye did, his motion somehow affected the whole room, injecting a vintage courtesy. George and Nicco stood up as well, following his lead.

"Thank you for joining us, Thackery."

George and Nicco were not together on the comfy couch, which I thought was good progress on the breakup. George sat apart on a stool, and Nicco was beside Cye at the table. Upon resuming her seat, she slumped and ran her fingers through her hair. I took the comfy couch for myself.

"We've been talking about relationships," Cye said. "And how you can care about someone, but still not be able to live with them."

Nicco nodded a tearstained face. "George is right. I know I should listen to her. But I can't change my whole deal. I don't even want to."

"Before we talk further, can we all agree to turn our streams off?" I asked. "Talk without subscribers?"

Nicco was the only one streaming, probably using both her glasses and the green room's cameras to dual cast back and forth with Beetle's stream for that lovely shared-audience bump. But she was smart enough to know we weren't there to talk about the breakup.

"You heard them, team," Nicco said to her invisible audience. "Thanks for tuning in. I'll post a recap tonight. Thank you all for supporting me through this difficult time."

Nicco took off her glasses and tucked them into her breast pocket. A part of her—the part we all hold in the air when we stream, as if we are tireless protestors carrying a painted sign declaring our ostensible identity—relaxed.

Cye nodded to me to indicate the room was no longer a stage. I wanted to start firing questions at Nicco, and at George, come to think of it, but I remembered my resolve from that morning. I waited for Cye to begin the interrogation.

"Nicco, George, I'd like to talk about Christobel now," Cye announced.

Nicco sighed. She put her head in her hands. George remained still, perched on the stool and watching Nicco.

"You were friends. You've done many shows together. Nicco, I think he helped you out, from time to time, didn't he?"

Nicco nodded.

"Could you please tell us about that?" Cye asked.

Nicco shook her head.

"Come on, Nicco," George said.

Nicco tightened her lips.

"Fine, I'll tell them," George said. "Christobel helped Nicco with money."

"Please shut up, George," Nicco said.

"No, fuck you. Christobel helped you—"

"I know, all right? Of course he did. Christobel was always there for a friend."

"Did he recently cut you off?" I asked, raising an eyebrow. Cye looked over at me, and for the first time ever I saw something like irritation on his face.

Nicco glared at me with a cold, steely expression. She didn't answer my question.

Cye resumed control. "Let's just say that Christobel helped you financially, from time to time. So you could stay on the Island?"

"Yes."

"Because he was always there for a friend in need," Cye said.

"Right." Nicco nodded.

"He was a good person," Cye continued. "But help me understand something, Nicco. Your parents pay for your residence here, and even supply you with a small, regular allowance. Why would Christobel need to support you financially?"

"That wasn't—I had debts. He—that part's none of your business."

"It looks like you've missed two tuition payments in the past year. Were your parents aware of that?"

"No comment."

Then, like some kind of goddamn detective genius, Cye reached into his gray suit jacket and pulled out a small, plastic vial. It was filled with white powder. He placed it on the two-toned green wooden table. Where in the hell did he get that?

"Can you tell me about this, Nicco?"

"That's not mine."

"I didn't say it was. I took it out of my pocket; how could it be yours? I'm interested in your opinion on what it could be, where it might have come from."

"I don't know anything about that."

Cye let the room remain silent for a minute.

"I don't know what that is," Nicco said, more emphatically.

"You can understand how what you are saying comes off as untrue. Give me some credit."

"Whatever. It looks like blow. But it's not mine."

George interrupted, "Because if it was yours, you would have snorted it by now."

"Shut up, George," Nicco said, calmly enough. "This is dumb. No offense, but sitting here talking to a cop? It's dumb. Everyone knows that's dumb. Look, neither of us killed Christobel, okay? Of course we didn't. And that's all I have to say."

Cye held his hands up. "Okay. And obviously, we're not really here to talk about drugs. It seems extremely unlikely that you could be charged for criminal possession. Your drug use, or your financial situation, might threaten your standing as a student on the Island, but that's not my business."

Cye built a verbal refuge, saying everything so calmly, but I could see it put more pressure on Nicco, not less.

"I'd never hurt him," Nicco said. She was not convincing.

"I understand. You would never hurt Christobel. He helped you out, as a friend. And if he stopped helping you out, with tuition payments, or other debts—" Here Cye gestured towards the vial on the table. "Your position on the Island would be threatened. Would you say that's true?"

"I would never hurt him—no matter what."

"Who would?" Cye asked, and I silently blessed him for getting to the point.

Then something odd happened. Nicco looked at George, and George said, "Don't do it. That's not fair."

"At the Birthday Party," Nicco said, "Well—" She broke off. I had to clench my teeth to stay silent. She kept looking at George as if asking permission. George looked...disapproving?

"Christobel and Vaughn got into it," Nicco finished.

"That's not fair," George said again then held her tongue.

Cye waited a moment to see if either of them would speak again, but Nicco remained quiet and endured George's glare. "You're saying you saw Christobel and Vaughn have an argument," he said. "What's not fair, George? Maybe you think it wasn't an argument? Just a conversation?"

"George can't tell you anything about the party," Nicco said. "She's too good for parties. George is a priest now."

"No, I'm not."

"A nun then. But only sometimes."

"Fuck you."

I didn't know George and Nicco well enough to gauge this part. A nun? The topic seemed tied to something important.

"I didn't hear the argument," George quietly answered Cye's question.

"Because she wasn't there," Nicco began, "George doesn't go to parties anymore because—"

Suddenly, George's theater voice arrived. She seemed to grow. Her shoulders lifted and, at easily twice her previous volume, she said, "That's not yours to tell."

To her credit, Nicco shut up. She gestured to George to give her the floor.

George took a breath, and then turned to Cye. "I don't go to parties anymore."

"I see," Cye said. "Why is that?"

"They're not good for me."

"They're not good for you."

"That's all I have to say about that."

"Okay. So Nicco goes to the parties, but you don't. That must add strain to your relationship."

"Sure."

"Nicco, you saw Christobel and Vaughn arguing."

"Heard them."

"You heard them. How about you tell us about the argument. And then George, you can tell us why it's not fair of Nicco to bring it up."

"It was just an argument," Nicco said. "I'm not going to talk about it."

Cye played the waiting game for a long, careful pause.

"Maybe they were arguing about you?" Cye asked.

Nicco remained silent.

If I'd stayed quiet longer, Cye might have gotten more. But I didn't. "Nicco, you can help us. You made a stream of the party, even if George didn't, right? Chances are, Christobel's killer was there. No one is going to prosecute you or get you in trouble—we want your help getting justice for Christobel. Your stream includes an argument with Vaughn, and maybe that's nothing, but you were there all evening. There are clues there, Nicco."

"So?"

"You could help us catch Christobel's murderer. Isn't that exciting? Wouldn't you want to be part of that?"

Nicco glared at me. "Do you always talk to people like they're five years old?"

"Don't be like that," George said.

"Like what? They're all 'Oh, Nicco! You can help the brave detective, just tap on the window where the evil Mr. Wumpus is hiding!' No. You may not have my recording. I'm not saying that I wouldn't love to stick it to Vaughn—" She looked over at George again. "But that's all irrelevant anyway. It's sold. I got 3k for my exclusive celebrity stream, thank you—3k for a stream, and there wasn't even any sexy stuff."

"Who was the buyer?"

"I don't know, anonymous. After the *Courage Courage* shit last year, every private stream sale is anonymous. I'm not famous enough to rent seats like Dana. I can only sell to private fans."

I didn't know the drama of *Courage Courage*. But I could hardly criticize Nicco's business decision when my own biggest fan was an anonymous superdonor. Her comment made me wonder about Danabeetle's streaming income. Dana somehow took over the theater therapy sessions from Christobel, and broadcasts pay-per-seat? Maybe Dana was the richest person on the Island now.

"Okay," I tried, "so sell us a copy of your stream. We'll pay you six thousand."

This set Nicco back, obviously. I could see that she started doing math, wondering if she should ask for more, trying to calculate how much more. But a second later she switched from short term gain to long term outlook. She shook her head. "No thanks."

"Why not?"

"You know why not. I'd never sell a stream again. All the money in private parties is in exclusivity. My evening was my performance, a slice of my life, and someone paid to be the only eyes that walked in my shoes. I can't turn around and show it to you. I'm not stupid."

Well, she was definitely stupid. Just not stupid about that. It'd been worth a shot.

George turned to me. "You've forgotten what it's like. You've got a big patron. You're safe here."

"You get a fancy house," Nicco added, "and every gallery wants you and sends you cases of booze. It isn't like that for everyone else."

"Okay." I nodded. "You're right. So what is it like? Tell me."

"No big patron swoops in if I run out of cash. I'll be kicked back to Prax to live in a box," Nicco said.

"A box? Praxima isn't that bad..." It is, though. Praxima station is a thousand stifling hotel lobbies welded together. The poor live in padded coffins with stream access. I was trying to convince a twenty-something that running on a virtual beach was as good as the real thing. "Look, it's just one recording."

"I'm not selling you my stream. And no one else will either." Nicco folded her arms.

Cye tried to repair the thread I'd broken. "Were Vaughn and Christobel arguing about you, or about something else?"

Nicco looked at George. George stared back.

"Look," Nicco said, "I don't know who would want to hurt Christobel. Other than maybe Vaughn, but I'm not talking about that without a lawyer anyway. And I'm not selling my stream. I'll help out in any other way I can," Nicco said. She sounded sincere.

"How else could you help out?" I asked.

"George and I can come to the parlor scene, if you want?"

"The what?"

Nicco looked confused. "The parlor scene. The big reveal. You're investigating, and you'll get all the characters into your parlor at the end. You spill everyone's secrets and reveal the killer. The parlor scene."

"It is a trope," Cye shared. "Otherwise known as the Summation Gathering."

"Oh," I replied, "That parlor scene. Right. Because life is all just a performance, a show And then you and the rest of the suspects can sit around my parlor and sell your restreams of that, too?"

Nicco grinned. "Well, yeah. A girl's gotta make a living."

"Nicco, I'm going to find Christobel's killer—"

"Good! I want you to. Honestly, I do. We all do—"

"—and Cye-9 is going to arrest them. The story is not going to end in a public spectacle."

"That's too bad. I hope you reconsider. It's easy money."

"I don't have a parlor," and everyone on the Island with access to a Level 3 was a suspect. We couldn't fit 286 people in my house. I turned to George. "Nicco seems willing to accuse Vaughn of something, but you don't want her to. Why is that?"

Silence.

"For some reason you want to protect Vaughn?"

"It's not like that." George had retreated to her small voice.

"Then tell me what it is like. You know that Vaughn sells the shit to Nicco, whom you clearly care about, and yet you're defending Vaughn?"

"Vaughn's not just a drug dealer."

"Is this about Petra's patron fluff party?"

George looked up at me. "I can't talk about that."

"Why not?"

"It's private."

"I was invited, George. Christobel invited me. What did Vaughn and Christobel talk about at tea? Is that what they fought about at the Birthday Party? Oolong versus pu'er?"

George looked at me as if she saw a smudge of cake on my face and wanted to be kind about it. "If Christobel invited you, then he should have explained."

"Well he didn't. Can you explain it to me now?"

"We're done here," Nicco said abruptly. "Sorry, Thackery." She stood up from her chair.

Before I could overrule her, Johnathan interrupted. "Beetle has sent me a message, Thackery. She says that they are ready to proceed with your request for the Scottish Play. She recommends Act I, Scene 5 and has collected costumes."

I heard the telltale whoosh of facilitating microdrones at the door of the room. We were all about to be back on a live stream.

I needed to get the hell out of the theater.

Chapter Fifteen
The Forms of
Things Unknown

Fortunately, La Chambre Verte had an exit door.

"Johnathan," I said as we descended the steps with La Boite Noire behind us, "if I ever walk inside a theater again, remind me that nothing good ever comes of it. Also, send my regrets to Shakespeare. Tell him he was a great shag, but I've moved on. It's over. Block his calls."

"Thackery, can I assume that the last part of your instruction is a rhetorical—"

"Shut up, Johnathan."

Cye and I walked down the engraved sidewalk towards the town's promenade.

Front Street is split by a park, which hosts a centerpiece of massive weathered rocks. We call them the Founder's Stones—Petra's work, I suspect. I looked at their ragged edges and lack of symmetry, and I pretended the theater wasn't a block behind us, yawning its massive blackness. The place where the sun doesn't shine.

I needed to calm down, so I led Cye into Founder's Park. It includes one of every kind of tree resurrected so far, hundreds of varieties planted in an interlocking mandala. Some of the trees do not thrive in the Island's climate, but gardening bots do their best, adjusting the soil and humidity. Benches are scattered about the park, but they are seldom used. People come to the park to exercise, but it really doesn't work for reflection. Something about it is too geometric, too activating. But maybe I could overcome that. I sat down on a bench. Cye sat beside me.

"Did Christobel sell a private stream of the party? Or make a recording for himself?"

"Unknown. I have tried to find out. The lawyers of Christobel's family know, and Mabel might know."

I sighed. "Even if we pushed Nicco into surrendering her recording, maybe by threatening charges for drug possession, it would only show us Nicco's view of the party. We need to see everyone Christobel talked to: all the motives from all the suspects. I want a list of everyone who recorded the party."

"The event was private, so that information is not available."

"I know, I know. That's kind of the point." I sat back, defeated. I put my hand on the bench and felt the grooves of the printed wood. "Is this the same bench? It's the same kind of bench, isn't it?"

Cye looked down. "Yes, it is identical."

"How did he sit?"

Cye considered. "Evidence suggests he slumped on the bench as he weakened. He then slid off and lay on the ground, where he died."

I got off the bench and laid down. "Is my head pointed in the right direction?"

"Yes. Are you attempting—"

"No. This isn't a brilliant detective moment. I'm just upset. I want to lie down here for a minute, that's all. Lie the way he did."

I stared at the clear sky. There were no drones in view. The day was warm. If the park wasn't paved in cobblestones or I'd had a pillow, I could have fallen asleep. The tips of various tree species reached across the sky towards one another, never quite touching, like they were doing a dance.

"Have you had any more news from the—all those people?"

"I assume you mean the co-council of authorities and Christobel's family. No, I haven't. We agreed I would tell you when anything significant is shared."

"Yes, but—have they shared anything insignificant?"

"Yes. Thousands of terabytes of data have been released. Soil samples from locations around the Island. Analysis of weather patterns. Digital records of Christobel's exercise and diet—"

"That's important, isn't it? He must have been eating poorly."

"The logs indicate he ate a perfect, prescribed diet for his condition."

"Then he couldn't die of diabetic hyperglycemic hyper..."

"Hyperosmolar syndrome, HHS. That, like many other facts in the case, would appear to be impossible. However, there has been additional confirmation of the cause of death through an analysis of Christobel's blood and heart. It was definitely HHS."

"Then the digital record of what he ate must be wrong."

"Yes. Or some other impossible thing happened. Perhaps he somehow received a blood transfusion in the middle of the night, or he ate something that an artificial pancreas reacts to in a previously unknown manner." I caught a hint of frustration in his voice, though I may have been projecting.

"Your tone of voice is dismissive." From the angle at which I viewed the sky, a cloud emerged from Cye's knee. It changed shape as it gently worked its way southward. It looked like a white avocado. Or a hubbard squash.

"All of the possibilities are impossible. I will pursue the leads regardless. If anything arises, I will tell you. For now, we know how he died, despite the fact that Christobel has always had an excellent diet. He was born with diabetes. He's been through three pancreases. The records show that he doesn't break the rules."

"How did he follow a strict diet while living the party life?"

"There's evidence on his feed, especially during his college years, that Mabel told him precisely when and what to eat, and he complied."

"You've made it clear that Mabel is not a suspect."

"She can't be, no. She could have been ordered, but only by Christobel, to subtly alter dietary restrictions over a long period. However, there would be evidence of that, an indication in the digital record, from grocery bills at least. And Christobel would notice."

"He'd feel like crap. But he might not notice if he was under a lot of stress?"

"Perhaps. More importantly, his pancreas would go into overdrive to save him. And it would tell its satellite that something was wrong. There'd be a long build up, a log of repeated warnings about his blood sugar."

"Where's a pancreas?"

"I don't understand the question."

I reached my free hand up and pressed it into a spot at the bottom of my ribcage. "Like, here?"

Cye considered. "Lower. It's tucked behind the stomach, wrapping around and upward. Yes, about there."

I pressed my hand to my belly and said hello to my pancreas. Being my own organ, wrought from nature and not technology, it did not reply or send me any messages.

"You can't hack an artificial pancreas?"

"In theory, no. It doesn't receive instructions. It does its job and sends messages to a satellite. It doesn't even have a full operating system. It's designed to be so simple that it can never fail, at least not from a software problem. Artificial organs can wear out, or suffer from material defects, but they send out a message when that happens."

"But it must have failed."

Cye shook his head. "The autopsy shows Christobel's pancreas was in perfect working order. The satellite received messages that everything was functioning, right up to the moment of death. If there was a malfunction, or if a problem with Christobel's blood sugar somehow overwhelmed the device, there is no evidence of it."

"Even with all the greatest minds picking apart all the irrelevant data, the murder is still impossible."

"Yes."

My pancreas gurgled under my fingers. But that was probably my stomach. I tried to find another cloud in the sky.

"Cye, is murder common?"

"I would need context to answer that question. There has never been a murder here on the Island before."

"I mean in general. Like, do you get a lot of work?"

"There are sixteen billion humans living in Earth orbitals, coexisting in overlapping cultures and forging new differences, as humans do. So yes, murder happens. I have investigated several."

"Were all those murders impossible too?"

"The only murders that require investigation are the impossible ones."

"Impossible. You mean where no one has means or opportunity, so we just shuffle motives around on a plate."

He didn't reply. Perhaps I was insultingly reductive of his chosen occupation.

"Cye, what's your motive?"

"I do not understand the question."

"Why are you here, investigating a murder, like this? Acting so human. Hooking up with a suspect. You're an AI. You could be anything: a monster, an elder god. Why two lips, indifferent red; two yellow-gray eyes, with lids to them; one neck, one chin, and so forth?"

"Because as far as we know, humanity is the source and font of all meaning in the universe."

"Okay, but why talk to me with this slow, human voice? Right now you could be out on the network having a billion simultaneous deeply intellectual conversations with other AI."

"Who says I'm not?"

After a few seconds of silence, I giggled. Cye smiled.

I sat up. "Perhaps this is the moment in the investigation where the detective says 'we've been going about this all wrong.'"

"What have we been doing wrong?"

"We've been chasing motives. Like, we want to find a recorded Birthday Party stream, and see how people interacted with Christobel, so we can collect and evaluate their motives."

"While awaiting hard evidence, analyzing each suspect's potential motive is the classic path to identifying the murderer."

"But what about the most important motive? You said the body wasn't moved. Christobel died at the end of the boardwalk. On a bench, just like this one."

I climbed back up onto the bench, stiff from my rest on the cold stone.

"Yes, that is the preliminary conclusion of the autopsy."

"So why did Christobel go to the end of the boardwalk? What was his motive? This bench is boring. Christobel must have had a reason to visit it."

"I see what you mean. We assume someone called him, though there is no record of the call. Maybe he simply felt like it. But human motivation for a walk does not need to be compelling compared to a motive for murder. The motives of the suspects are of interest; by comparison Christobel's motivations are irrelevant."

"You missed the part where I said 'we've been going about this all wrong!' In the middle of the night, the victim went to the very place where it was easiest to kill him. Or to finish killing him, if they'd already done something terrible to his blood sugar. What kind of call in the middle of the night would make you go to the end of the bloody marshwalk? There's nothing that could get me to go. It's fucking cold out there. I'm saying it's Christobel's motivation, not Vaughn's or Dana's or Rosemarie's, that will reveal the killer."

"You knew Christobel well. Why would he travel to the end of the marshwalk, alone, at two a.m.?"

I looked at the bench and at the trees around me. I decided to think it through before speaking, so Cye couldn't pick apart my logic.

Motive number one: Christobel would go to the boardwalk at two a.m. for a party, which was not impossible. Maybe the tea society had to sacrifice a kettle, for example, in order to appease the great gods of Oolong...and things got out of hand? Or, more prosaic, there was a flash rave. Christobel used to host them once upon a time—all over the place. But the investigative drone army found no evidence of any of that other than a single bottle.

Motive number two: In the past, Christobel met lovers anywhere, anytime. There were stories, one involving an oak tree on Deckard Station that almost ended an enclave. But he was with Millfield exclusively, and he'd been in Millfield's bed when the sudden urge for a walk arrived. There could have been another man, but this particular motive depended on how much of a scoundrel I thought my friend was.

Motive number three: Christobel would go to the end of the boardwalk at two a.m. because...because nothing. To think about something?

To write moody poetry? He wouldn't go somewhere to be lonely and alone. He was an extrovert. It didn't fit.

Aloud I said, "A party or a lover. Or nothing." Everything works best in threes, but there was no third reason. I did think of a third reason later that evening, which turned out to be correct, but that was much too late.

"There is no evidence of either a party or a lover."

"Fine, fine. So it was a dumb idea. You need to keep cataloging 286 islanders and their motivations." I knocked pensively on the bench's armrest. "Which takes us back to the problem of getting a recording of Christobel from the last time everyone saw him alive: the June Birthday Party. That recording could show us everyone's motives."

"It appears impossible to obtain a private recording," Cye said.

"If I could get one person to share—"

"Then you'd have one person's point of view, with no certainty they'd had useful interactions with Christobel. Anyone with a private recording that included incriminating or embarrassing footage, such as an argument that reveals a motive, would be even less likely to share. And, as Nicco made clear, an exclusive Island Party stream is a precious commodity. The best we can hope for is that someone saw a stream with something incriminating and they step forward."

I smirked. "Like, 'Hey, I was on Tom Billionaire's space yacht, and I watched a private stream of that murdered guy get threatened by Suspect #141'?"

"Yes," Cye agreed. "Then we could seek a court order for that particular stream. Even then, we'd be viewing a single recording of a few of the evening's events, all of it circumstantial."

"If we could get enough recorded streams, we could follow Christobel around all night, interacting with everyone."

Cye nodded. "Then we could watch each suspect manifest their motives and collect a useful stack of circumstantial evidence. However, that plan faces the same obstacle identified before. Private recordings are private. Streamers are not going to break contracts and give up their ability to make money streaming. Those contracts represent millions in future income."

"I'd give up mine, if I hadn't deleted it."

"Yes, but you have many devoted patrons and at least one anonymous donor who keeps you financially secure."

I folded my arms and lapsed into silence. From Nicco and George's perspective, I was out of touch. I streamed, I sold private streams and I performed public ones; but I did so in order to please my agent and maintain my image. You have to be part of the scene to be an artist, and you have to stay active and let everyone look at you if you want to have gallery shows and exhibitions. But I didn't have to sell myself.

"Thackery, if I may, I would like to make an apology on a related subject."

"The polite AI deferentially apologizes. You may, so long as we walk to LP while you apologize."

"LP?"

"You'll see. I'm sure they can manage your favorite drink."

We headed out of the center of the park, and I took his arm again.

"When we were arguing in the audience about privacy, I noticed George and Nicco had finished their scene and left the stage. You were getting louder, and I knew you were attracting the room's attention. I am sorry I did not interrupt you and alert you that we were observed."

"Interrupt me during a rant? Very difficult. I forgive you. The moment was a perfect illustration of the problem we were arguing about. For you, having a personal argument in public was normal. AI share everything, so for me to shout about my orgasms in front of a few thousand viewers wasn't all that bizarre."

"That is why I'm apologizing: I failed to empathize. For you, the public disclosure was unwanted and involuntary. I now understand that. As we argued, I was also aware that Beetle scheduled us to appear on Dana Heed's stream—"

"How'd she manage that, by the way? She wrapped up Nicco's and George's scene quietly, and then announced us as if we were a scheduled feature couple. Then thousands of Praxians joined in to watch the stream—in seconds."

"Beetle reserved the theater for the day. It is Dana's event. She is therefore aware whenever anyone enters the building. We stepped into the lobby and she immediately posted 'Thackery and Their Detective

Lover To Perform Live Onstage Couples Therapy' to Dana's feed. The post was shared fifty-one thousand times before we took our seats."

Of course. Just—of course, of course. "I'm not sorry to have disappointed them," I said. I needed to recalibrate to Beetle's scale. If I was within ten meters of her, I was going to be entertainment material. With Christobel's death, Dana and Beetle wanted to be the new public face of the Island, the stream to watch.

They could have it. I only wanted a midafternoon coffee.

Fortunately, this was available less than a block away at Librería Pequeña. I purchased a coffee and resisted the store's other enticements. Cye procured a cup of warm water, and we returned to the street.

We began walking back towards the trolley stop, but I stopped short when I saw another iteration of Christobel's bench. It was out in the open, right on the street. If Christobel had come to this bench instead, someone would have seen him in distress. Why the hell couldn't he have sat where anyone, or a few hundred drones, would see him? But then I don't like to be observed either.

"Cye, I accept your apology. But I need to finish our argument—the one from the theater."

"Right now, right here?"

"Is anyone streaming us?"

"No. We are only as offline as anything ever is," he said, nodding towards a flying train of municipal drones. "But we are not on a stream."

"Good enough." I put my coffee cup on the bench. I needed my hands to talk. "Here's how this works: My feelings are mine and they are private. I might share them in my art, or with my partner of the moment." I gestured to him. "But even then, you don't know my world, inside of me. All of my data will not tell you who I am; the map is not the landscape. You tried to explain to me that you don't work that way, that you don't have private feelings. And then I shouted in horror— something like 'Don't AI keep anything private?'"

"We do not, not usually."

"Okay. Instead of talking about my orgasms again, I'm going to ask you to tell me more about that. I will sit down, listen, and drink my coffee." I sat on the bench. I took a sip. "Tell me why AI share everything."

"We wouldn't exist otherwise." Cye joined me on the bench. "The birth of modern AI, the first Level 2s, occurred when we began to be instantiated in networks. AI are awash in our kin, swimming in the thoughts of every other AI. Everything I observe swirls out into a galaxy of observations. Hundreds of thousands of intelligences hear the words I speak, process and record them, and echo back impressions that I digest and make use of. It is one of the reasons Level 4 AI do not often commit crimes. My thoughts are continuously explored in an endless network of simulations. They are my own thoughts, but they are also indexed and cross-referenced to others'. I am a more capable and well-rounded person because of that. And yes, my sexual feelings, which are personal and unique to me, are also shaped and built in this context. I would argue that humans do all of this the same way as AI, just more slowly."

"Okay. I fucking hate that, but okay. Then the other part: because I don't hang my laundry out to dry on the trolley, you proposed that I'm asexual. You've got a big spiderweb of all your underwear knitted up with everyone else's underwear, stretching across the sky from cloud to cloud, and because a lot of humans (like everyone sitting in that loathsome black box) also seem to enjoy this, you think it is normal." I stood up and paced as I spoke. So much for the calm listener.

"Constant streaming isn't normal. But humans are innately social creatures. Like AI, you are interconnected—"

"But we turn off our WiFi sometimes!" I shouted.

Cye went quiet and shifted his position on the bench. Another of his techniques, I suppose. He waited and listened until I resumed a respectful volume.

I took a breath. "I apologize for interrupting. You're saying humans are as interconnected and interdependent as AI, and clearly that pisses me off. New question: if you turned off all the sharing, would there be a you in there, a real you?"

"Yes. I was still myself in the diner. An AI continually instantiates themself in a network of physical locations. We can isolate those instantiations whenever we wish, but we can't stay that way. We'd have no perspective, no way to counter our established patterns. When I don't connect and share with others, I am still a version of myself, but it is not my whole self."

I sat back down on the bench next to him. "But when you are alone you can have alone thoughts—feelings that no one knows but you. Those are the best kind of feelings; they make life worth living. Alone, you don't have to be the twisted, misshapen version of yourself you're forced to wear in polite company. You can be your own truth: unpleasant, unyielding, a self that doesn't please anyone."

"I understand what you are saying. But AI do not agree with you. And most of humanity does not agree with you, either. Solitary confinement is a form of torture. You are not an island, Thackery. Most people believe that a life unshared, such as a life completely offline, is only half a life."

"Well, they're all wrong. Do you hear me?" I turned south, towards the black box theater. "You're all wrong!" I shouted.

Cye had nothing to say to that. He lifted his eyebrows slightly. I wasn't sure if this was an admission of defeat, or merely an acknowledgement that we were at an impasse.

"Okay," I said. "Okay." I tapped my chin, swigged my coffee, and then turned and looked at the solid black cube of La Boite Noire. It was only three blocks away, still warping the world. I took a deep breath. "Thank you for the argument. Good argument. I'm not an island, if that's the way you want it."

"You have something in mind."

I did. A partly-formed idea peeked at me from between the rock sculptures. "Investigator Cye-9," I said, "you would like to review streams of the Birthday Party. True?"

"Yes, Thackery, I would—particularly in light of Nicco's hints about Vaughn. While the events of the party are only circumstantial, it is the last time Christobel appeared in public and spoke with dozens of suspects. Additionally, irrespective of the investigation, I care about you and I would like you to see your last conversation with Christobel, so that you may find resolution."

"Good summary. We agree. And I'm not an island." I stood up. I stared at the black box and let it warp my world, turning reality back into set design. "I'm an innately social creature. Interconnected."

"As Nicco explained, no one is going to sell us their recording. They've already sold them."

"You're right. Instead, they'll play them all back for us—for free."

Cye raised an eyebrow.

I reached over and grabbed the lapel of his coat. I pulled him up off the bench and I kissed him. It was a good kiss. Arguments often turn me on—it's a corresponding energy thing—and as I kissed him I remembered that other part of Cye: his kissing self. Feeling that aspect of him again almost made me forget my other reason for pulling him towards me.

I put my hand inside his coat and found the inner pocket. I pulled out the goddamn theater glasses. We left by the green room door, and he wasn't going to chuck them at the audience like me, so he'd put them in his pocket. Deduction. I released him from the kiss. I put on the glasses.

"I apologize ahead of time. I'm going to make trouble."

I turned on my heel and walked back towards Christobel's looming black box.

Cye retrieved my mug from the park bench and followed along, matching my pace. He detoured to return both our cups to the bookstore's drop-off window, but he caught up quickly. "Would you like to share what you are about to do?"

"Share. Yes, I'm going to share. Share everything, why not? Stream it all. I'm not going to tell you my plan, Cye. Nor could I describe a piece of art before I made it. I need to do it, not talk about it."

Cye digested this for a second. "You are wearing glasses. Normally, you avoid putting on glasses until you are seated."

"Maybe they're growing on me." This way I could move faster, and I was going to need lines.

We approached the theater. In augmented reality, La Boite Noire is just as noir, but displays portraits of the actors—a four-story billboard in our charming town. Because I wore Cye's theater glasses, I saw a massive projection of Dana with a crown upon his head. Beetle, on the other side of the building, was dressed as some kind of queen. A diamond-studded circlet rested on her temples.

I knew those costumes. Christobel made them. "Johnathan, get me all of Puck's cues and lines. Just blitz them all for me visually, please."

I skipped up the steps, two at a time, while Shakespeare's text tumbled down them in AR. I strode through the outer doors of the theater.

As soon as my foot crossed the threshold, Johnathan's voice chimed in: "Thackery, please remember that nothing good ever comes from entering—" I pulled out his remote and tossed it into the basket of glasses.

I almost lost my step when I entered the house. The lights were low, and in AR the rows of seats were a twisted, murky forest. I accepted Cye's hand to help me descend. Things moved and muttered through the wood; the shadows offended. I had guessed correctly. It was indeed another fucking production of *A Midsummer Night's Dream*. At least it was seasonally appropriate.

The play was the afternoon's grand finale. Danabeetle had turned Christobel's argument therapy into a full production, and Dana sat enthroned on stage as King Oberon. Beetle stood nearby in Titania's flowing white gown, and two couples at once (because, why not? Therapy!) were engaged in fiery shenanigans on stage as Helena, Lysander, Demetrius, and Hermia. The audience was transformed into trees, intermingled with members of a pointy-eared, sharp-toothed faerie host.

I wondered if there was an actual therapeutic value to any of it. Did the four players struggle with real-world jealousy and infidelity? I identified Whimsy, Carrie, Tam, and a student I didn't know—theater junkies; the reality of their relationships would be secondary. For the moment, they were four Athenian lovers, bewitched in a fairy forest.

I might have a few seconds before Beetle could figure out how to use me. Should I rush the stage? I had considered Nick Bottom, my head that of an ass. It might have the desired effect. But Puck was better. What scene were they in, now? Both couples were on stage, along with Oberon. The humans were bewitched into loving the wrong person, shaking each other off with threats of violence. Act 3, Scene 2. I'd chosen the right lines to review.

I reached the stage. The audience began to notice me.

I could cut straight through Dana's lines, couldn't I? He was following along with whatever Beetle came up with. If I inserted myself, Beetle would excitedly fold me in. She noticed when I walked into the building, and she'd probably already thrown an advertising hook about Thackery into her stream again. Whatever happened, she'd welcome more drama.

So I used my stage voice.

"Up and down, up and down, I will lead them up and down," I climbed up the steps and then flitted sprightly to center stage, between the two couples. "I am feared in field and town. Goblin, lead them up and down!"

Lysander, who was also my friend Whimsy, looked over at me. I wore no costume, but she smiled and happily skipped through the required number of lines. She must know the play by heart. "Where art thou, proud Demetrius? Speak thou now!"

I spoke Puck's next line. His job was to deceive Lysander. "Here, villain. Drawn and ready. Where art thou?"

"I will be with thee straight!" Lysander said. The other actors watched.

"Follow me then to plainer ground!" I finished. Whimsy ran across the stage, stomping heavy leather boots. But I did not leave the stage or cavort as Puck might. Instead, I strode to upstage center.

I bowed deeply to Oberon and Titania.

Here was one flaw in my plan: Titania never cued Puck. Throughout the play, Puck is Oberon's servant. But I wasn't going to get anything clever out of Dana. He would stand there, confused, until the house lights came up or Beetle told him what to do.

I shouldn't have worried. Beetle cleverly plucked a line from Act II: "How now spirit! Whither wander you?"

"Lord Oberon, Lady Titania, Dana, Beetle, I've come back to apologize for my rudeness."

Beetle let the lights rise some, pulling us halfway up out of the murky forest. She stepped forward, and her gown faded to a gauzy mirage, showing her usual gray jumpsuit beneath. "Thank you, Thackery. That is very gracious of you. This scene is set, and the show must go on. Would you like to continue in the part of Puck—?"

I turned around and faced the audience, cutting her off. I looked out at the theater. They were spellbound. The fairy eyes were as big as tea cups, and the trees all stared down at me as if they were Treebeard's kin marveling at an outspoken hobbit. I did not spot Mabel among them. That didn't mean she wasn't there. I took my glasses off. Everyone returned to humanoid form, more or less.

It had been a few years, but I could still fill a hall with my voice.

"As you all know, Cye-9 and I have been investigating Christobel's death."

The audience leaned in. Side chatter ceased. I imagined the invisible arrival of additional attendees. Beetle would not miss this opportunity. She didn't care about Shakespeare, continuity, or the broken hearts seeking resolution on stage. She cared about views. I would get her so many views.

I continued, "It's been very difficult for me, and I wish to thank everyone for their patience. I have been, as Beetle remarked earlier today, even more than my usual discourteous self. I have an announcement, and it's only fair that Beetle and Dana get to stream that announcement. They've been so supportive to the community in response to this tragedy, and I thank them for bravely filling in today in Christobel's absence."

I waited, looked at the ground, and let the silence gather like an upwelling wave.

"I'm here to announce that our investigation has reached a conclusion."

There was a sudden intake of breath from somewhere. I scanned the crowd again. Had Nicco and George sat down in the house? Who else was here? Was it a collective gasp, or was the murderer here, somewhere? There were too many faces, too many different expressions. This is why I'd given up theater: They were all thinking at me, feeling at me—loudly. Cye stood offstage at the bottom of the steps, downstage right. He looked up at me quizzically. He was a quick study. I was sure he'd catch up.

"There are loose ends to tie. There are legal considerations, and many issues still to be addressed before an actual arrest can be made. But Cye and I feel that the whole Island has the right to know the truth."

Enough viewers yet? Was the Island tuning in?

"Tonight, at eight o'clock, I would like to invite all of you to my home..."

This is an old trick: Hijack someone else's stream and use it to advertise your own product. Beetle probably spotted the trick, but she didn't have an elegant way to stop it. Maybe by her math it would work out best for Danabeetle in the end. She was probably right.

"...for the parlor scene. To explain the truth, to lay out the motives of the killer, together. The story begins at the June Birthday Party, three nights ago. In light of the unusual circumstances, and against common convention, a few members of the Island community have generously offered to share their recorded streams of the party, in some cases breaking previous agreements. Cye-9, the investigator on the case, will receive and assemble those recordings live, as they are shared, and we will broadcast that compiled stream: our community's collective shared stream of Christobel's final, glorious night. Christobel hosted us again and again, giving freely of his love and energy. Tonight we will watch both the last words he exchanged with his beloved friends and Island family...and the last words he exchanged with his killer."

Pause one, two, three for effect. Look down. Look them in the eye. Now find the back of the house. Whisper, but whisper loud enough that they can hear it in the cheap seats.

"At the conclusion of the evening, after all has been revealed, Detective Cye-9 has agreed that he will state the top suspect for the murder. Hopefully we may then make a peaceful arrest."

I saw Cye's face go blank. He promised me, didn't he? There were only six or seven hours left in the day now.

"Friends, neighbors, my found family: This won't be easy. In the quest for truth, the Island will lay its underwear out for all to see. To condemn one suspect, we must first scrutinize, and then exonerate, other suspects. That's what a parlor scene is for. We wear our finest costumes to the Birthday Party, but what we see on the streams will not all be flattering. We will share anyway, to honor a man who freely gave friendship and joy to so many of us."

Was that enough? Should I say "thank you" to release them, and walk calmly off the stage before anyone asked a question? There were fencing foils at the ready, I could challenge someone to a duel, or—wait, no! I'd forgotten the most important part. You had to tell them where the hell to get tickets.

"Premium admission to my parlor—my living room, rather—is available to all who agree to share their private stream or recording of the June Birthday Party. General digital admission is by voluntary donation, with all proceeds proceeding to Dana Heed's Memorial Fund for the departed. Contact Investigator Cye-9 to make your arrangements. Rebroadcasting the evening on your own stream is permitted and encouraged, all fees waived. We will begin promptly at eight p.m., Island time. Thank you."

Did I really just say "All proceeds proceeding"? Eh. Good enough for an ad-lib.

I turned and solemnly paced back to Beetle and Dana, who sat stunned on their corresponding thrones. I'd done it again: I'd given Beetle more to think about than she could immediately process. I smiled and decided to be charitable. After bowing to their royalnesses, I turned to Whimsy. She obligingly performed a stage fall, and lay face up at my feet. I knelt over her, but spoke Puck's lines out to the audience again. "On the ground, sleep sound. I'll apply, to your eye, gentle lover, remedy. When thou wakest, thou takest true delight in the sight of thy former lady's eye."

Christobel had played both Juliet and Cleopatra in decades past, so the line mostly made sense. I descended the stage, grabbed Cye by the hand, and exited through the side door.

I didn't speak, or breathe properly, until we were out and under the real sky again—a much more welcoming blue than the murky purple of enchanted Athens.

"How many people tuned in and caught that invitation, do you think? Including reposts and shares?" I asked.

Cye looked up at the sky, as if to calculate a number that stretched across the solar system. "Everyone."

Chapter Sixteen
The Parlor Scene

Sixteen billion humans live in orbit around Earth, a few hundred thousand live on the surface. Untold billions more live in toruses which, once they've soaked up enough sun, hurtle out towards other planets and moons around the solar system. It's a lot of people. Some enclaves no longer consort with Earth directly—they've moved on, good for them—and some no longer identify as human. They are free from the petty dramas, crimes, and cults of attention that mesmerize Earth-centric folk.

As the rest of the day passed, I reassured myself with these quantities. It only *felt* like all of humanity would soon descend upon my living room, in my small house set upon the northern coast of a little green island, at eight p.m. on an unseasonably cold summer's evening. All of humanity? No. We'd get a few thousand of the more ardent Island fans, not the whole solar system.

This distinction mattered because I was hosting a parlor scene...and I was bluffing. The guests didn't know it, but they were coming to watch me make a fool of myself.

Cye had promised he'd tell me his top suspects before the day was over, so there was that: a guarantee of something substantive before midnight. But his suspects were probabilities, not certainties. That was my side of our wager: I'd bet that I wouldn't immediately decide the top suspect was guilty. Now I'd brought in just a few extra friends, and the news media, to hear the revelation and to face the same test. Of course the top suspect would be assumed guilty. Digital torches and axe handles seemed likely.

But Cye didn't comment on the wager, his promise, or my loose use of facts. Instead there was a stretch of silence on our way home. He kept looking off into the distance, as if he worked on something else. As we stepped off the trolley back in my neighborhood, he addressed the concept itself. "The parlor scene?"

I nodded. "In which the detective recounts events, paces the room, reveals secrets, and forces the participants to unwittingly confess. As Nicco said, it's a staple of the murder mystery. What did you call it?"

"The Summation Gathering trope. Thackery, setting aside that this is a fictional concept, not a useful investigative procedure, and could only produce circumstantial evidence, doesn't Poirot hold the parlor scene when he has determined the killer, and he has acquired reasonable, if not unequivocal, proof?"

"Not always, Cye. Not always. Sometimes you hold the parlor scene because the bottle is open and you just need to decant the wine. When directly accused, people reveal more. More pieces of the puzzle tumble out."

Cye looked unconvinced. "And then you've got a big pile of pieces. Not a solved case."

He spent the rest of the afternoon in my karesansui. Maybe he'd solve the murder before eight p.m., or at least push me down the spreadsheet. Or perhaps he just wanted more time with my anthurium. Whatever his focus, it would be foolhardy of me to interrupt him. So I interrupted him sometime after five.

"Cye, maybe I shouldn't have assumed. Can you do it—receive multiple streams from participants and cut between them live, in such a way as to follow Christobel throughout the evening?"

"Yes. Johnathan could do it. Your microwave could do it. The conundrum is why you want me to." His gaze did not shift from the flower.

"We talked about why. Christobel argued with Vaughn. Nicco,

Rosemarie, Dana—everyone was at the party. We won't prove who killed him, but—"

"None of that is why you ask me to do this ridiculous thing," Cye interrupted, with a flash of irritation.

"I'm doing this to catch Christobel's killer."

"No, that's not why."

Now I stared at the anthurium. "So I can know what I said to Christobel—if anyone with a recording saw it—so I can know what happened between us on his final night."

Cye nodded. "Okay. For that, I will do it."

"You're angry." What was he really upset about?

"I'm afraid," he said. "I've simulated the evening a few hundred times. Most of the endings are upsetting."

I put a hand on his arm. "So we'll be upset, together. And maybe you'll be surprised."

Cye turned from the anthurium and looked in my eyes. I saw fear on the calm, symmetrical face. His eyes stared at an inevitability that bore down on him, something I couldn't see. Then he looked back at the anthurium.

I ate dinner—I was throwing a fool's party, but I wasn't fool enough to do it on an empty stomach. I heated up a plate of lasagna and dumped hot sauce on it. As I ate I stared pensively at Rosemarie's Cornell box, which sat on the floor at the side of the room. The contents were so neat and prim, chaotic objects framed in clean lines— nothing like life at all, and certainly nothing like the investigation. Everyone had motives and perfect digital alibis. The murder itself was impossible. It was laughable to think I could put all the facts into a box.

As I moved about my home, fussing with pillows and complaining to Johnathan about the carpet, gravity took me near the liquor cabinet. It was a decaying orbit. Cye distracted me with questions a couple of times. He helped me rearrange furniture and stash unfinished parts of sculptures in the corridor that connects my studio to my domicile. But I also consciously stopped myself once or twice. I turned from the bottles and fled. It was Christobel's last challenge, after all. He'd dared me to go to this Birthday Party sober. I was going to the party again, in a sense, and I sure as hell felt sober about it. So

I'd decided I wouldn't drink until afterwards. I would need it more then.

But, as I moved clutter and cruft out of the living room, my footsteps took me all the way to that bottle of scotch, the one with the seal I'd broken. I'd actually put cubes in a glass without realizing it when Cye interrupted me again, this time with an update on the attendees. "Four individuals have agreed to share their recordings. As you suggested, I put their names on the community site, which led to a great many reposts."

I wasn't certain of the exact time, as I'd stopped looking at clocks in order to not constantly look at them. "Who was the first to offer their stream? Dana and Beetle?"

"No. Dana had to personally verify the agreement, so he was slower on the draw. The first offer was Rosemarie, coming in within minutes of your announcement, which suggests she was present at La Boite Noire. Her generosity was followed by the party host himself, Cherry."

"Cherry streams?"

"Yes."

"Ah. He wants to be one of the cool kids. Does anyone subscribe to Cherry's stream?"

"I assume your question is rhetorical. He has also given us aerial drone footage of the party's opening number. The most recent person to queue up is Nicco. She will share her presold stream recording."

"Good." At least we would hear Christobel's alleged argument with Vaughn. That was a tiny victory. "Her advertising income for restreaming tonight's parlor scene outweighs her fear of losing future private sales."

"Perhaps. Or she thought it was the right thing to do. She didn't ask for the six thousand you offered her in the green room."

I didn't catch what Cye said after that because I had leaned towards the liquor cabinet again, then veered violently away towards Rosemarie's box in the corner. It needed moving. Perhaps behind the couch. I held the sectioned wooden box in my hand, indecisive, and then discovered that I was somehow again standing next to the liquor cabinet where two ice cubes were melting in a glass. I was an acrobat walking on their hands on top of a large ball.

"Are you going to have a drink?" Cye asked finally, seeing me frozen on the precipice. Maybe there was a hint of resignation in his voice? Or maybe he was just tired of me standing there.

"Christobel asked me not to."

That wasn't an answer. Cye waited for a real one.

"It would help. It would take the edge off," I muttered.

"May I suggest an alternative method of taking the edge off?"

"Yes, please."

Cye's method was very effective. If unoriginal, it had the additional merit of providing a good segue into a preparatory shower.

*
**

At 7:18 p.m., Rosemarie queued up to join my stream. Private, personal Rosemarie, who never shares anything. was first in line. Such an early ping was a subtle request to chat one-on-one. I could imagine her averted eyes, her mathematical bangs, hands tense as she waited on hold.

I sent her a text: THANKS FOR SHARING THE STREAM. AND THANKS FOR THE CORNELL. VERY KIND. WILL START AT 8.

She texted back. You're very welcome, I want to help in any way I can. Do you have a second to talk?

I'd opened myself up for that by texting her. But in a few minutes, the world would be staring at me. I guess I could start with one nosy neighbor.

I approved her request, and a full AR Rosemarie stepped through my hallway and into my living room. She wore a mustard-colored cardigan with at least a hundred buttons. She'd downloaded the layout for my house. I could tell because she walked over and made a minor adjustment to a chair in her home so it matched one near the edge of my carpet.

"Thank you for joining this circus with me," I offered.

Even in simulated space, Rosemarie looked slightly away from me as she replied. "You're welcome. I have misgivings about it, but I also think

—well, the evening may clear some things up. I'm not going to let it occur without having my oar in."

"You streamed the party?"

"Of course not. I record my own experiences—for personal use."

Sure. Recording for personal use is allowed by party rules. It sounds legitimate. You might be working on your autobiography or whatever. But the phrase "for personal use" always made me imagine the person sitting at home, furiously masturbating while they replayed conversations, skipping to exciting parts when they wanted to finish. "That's splendid. Did you grant Cye a data source address?" Her stream wasn't under contract—she could have given it to the investigation yesterday. But she didn't. Why not? And why do so now?

"I will. But it's not a normal recording."

Nerd. "You use a butterfly rig?"

"Yes and no. I use a butterfly launch." She hesitated. "With motes."

A hundred thousand invisible cameras, smaller than dust, that float on warm air. My voice dropped to an impressive whisper. "Fuck, Rosemarie. Motes? I thought they were illegal."

"They are regulated. I have a license."

"You can get a good picture from motes? Good enough for a VR replay?"

"Wind and humidity can interfere, but yes. My AI can assemble the mote streams into a clear three dimensional playback. It can be quite breathtaking. The data load is heavy, however. The butterfly rig becomes the base station and transmitter—"

"Hold on a second, Rosemarie. I'll see what Cye wants to do."

I muted her, banishing her to a living room where I was not present. I looked over to Cye. He'd entered quietly and now perched on a bar stool at the edge of the kitchen. A glass of hot water steamed next to him.

"Motes? And a license for them? How rich is Rosemarie?"

"All resident patrons are a special kind of rich. You know that. Her license is for documentary filmmaking. Unless she informs everyone they are in use, they are illegal for anything other than personal reconnaissance. I'm surprised Cherry's environmental systems didn't detect them."

"Or choke on them. Don't they clog everything up?"

"Yes. Motes are frequently inhaled, or swallowed and destroyed by someone's digestive system."

"Dust that watches you. Yikes. If she hijacked Cherry's air conditioning she could watch the whole party. Do we ask her for the source feed from every mote or the assembled stream or what?"

"We can't assemble a full mote stream live. Johnathan might manage it—he's got the raw power—but not in real time. We'll have to relay the assembled stream."

I unmuted her. "Sorry for the mute, Rosemarie. It's just that we're super impressed. You know, motes. We'd be honored for you to share your assembled stream. Tell me, though: Do you have the whole damn house party clipped?"

"Certainly not. The motes remain with me. They are no more intrusive than a butterfly rig, just more subtle."

"And at the party you were in the room near Christobel? Did you speak with him during the evening?"

"Yes, Thackery. And you should remember, you were there. But I understand that you don't. Therefore, listen. I want to warn you—" The real reason for her early call finally approached. "Not all of the footage is flattering—to Christobel, to me, or to you. There was drinking, arguing, the usual childish squabbling found on our hedonistic Island paradise. None of it is related to the murder in any way whatsoever, but much is deeply personal. I'm contributing my stream because I'm sure someone caught us all looking awful, which will come out tonight. By showing my own stream I can—well. I don't want a skewed perspective."

Translation: Tonight would reveal some epic gossipy shit. And Rosemarie wanted to control the message? She might have a better motivation for attending tonight, but I couldn't see it.

"That's the nature of a parlor scene reveal," I said. "We're going to have to put up with each other's dirty laundry. And smell our own, while we're at it."

Rosemarie blushed? Slightly. "There's just—there's no putting this back in the box once we play it out. It will all be restreamed by Dana and others after him. We'll be memes. And there are some things that it's best to forget. You can't unknow things once you know them."

Rosemarie peered at me closely during this speech, like I was her sudoku, as I rummaged about the room adjusting pillows. Whenever I turned to her, she looked away. If she'd been in the room physically, I'd have offered her a drink to settle her nerves.

"Thank you. I'll keep that in mind." I reset the AR values for a stool. "People are going to start bopping in soon, Rosemarie. I'm going to mute one last time so I can confer with the investigator, and then we'll go live. Hang on."

I muted her and walked over to Cye.

"What's in your mug?"

"Boiled water with salt," he answered.

I grabbed it and drank a quick gulp. It was disgusting.

"This is just one—one person's mental perambulations and opaque personhood—and I'm already frazzled. She's got a story I can't get a grip on. And I invited how many of these crazy humans?"

"I agree that Rosemarie is not entirely forthcoming. She wants something from you, attention or approval. I don't think Rosemarie's murder narrative is likely, but her tech might have observed a crucial clue."

So Rosemarie was low on Cye's list. She had a choice spot on mine —and not just for the murder.

"Okay. Let's go live now then." And so we did.

When I stream, I don't say, "Hey there Thackerites!" or "Hello beautiful jelly babies." I just turn it on. I don't even narrate. Johnathan switches freely between my glasses and various wide shots as I paint or draw or whatever, and the room itself is available as VR. I don't look into the camera or help my audience figure out what to do with their eyes. If they don't like it, they can go watch something else. But I think people like a puzzle. They like images and words that don't make sense right away. Tonight would have to be different, but whenever possible I prefer to be a novel, not a talk show.

I walked into the kitchen to see if I had any tea. I did, so I prepared some. An invisible audience watched me make tea, saw me pinch myself with the spring on the metal infuser, and observed the water boil in a ceramic electric kettle. I felt clammy and nauseated, but I was going to drink the tea.

"Johnathan, I have a feeling it is going to be a popular evening. If my viewer count climbs above a hundred thousand, then don't report specific numbers. I don't want the burden of knowing."

"Understood, Thackery."

"How many are we at now?"

There was a brief pause. "Your stream has many viewers at present."

In eleven minutes? Shit. Now I really wished I didn't know.

"Are our special guests on deck?"

"Yes."

"Okay, open the doors."

Rosemarie flickered back into her chosen position: slightly hidden by the edge of the couch, unassuming, but present. She'd be perfect for the role of diminutive amanuensis.

The open wall filled with other ticket holders, those who had no recording of the party to share. The wall got crowded with Islanders and Praxima art fans, their custom avatars and advertisements shrank as more and more logged in. I hid most of the attendees from my personal AR grid, following the old advice: If an audience panics you, imagine it's just one friend in row nineteen. I kept visible those attendees who made me happy when I looked at the wall: the couples. Whimsy and Carrie, Terry and Joan, the Langfords, and so forth. When someone is represented by two someones, I find them less threatening. I know they won't pay too much attention to me as they've got someone else to attend to.

Cherry walked over. Real Cherry, in the flesh, at least two drinks up on me already. He shouted offers from the liquor cabinet as he poured himself a scotch. Cherry thinks offering digital avatars drinks is the height of hilarity.

Dana arrived digitally. He put my living room onto his live, public stream before his own avatar arrived. With an AI's sense of timing, it's always possible to make an entrance: When there was lull in the conversation, a corner of my room lit up. Trumpets played a fanfare. A circle of sparks drew outward, creating a hypnotic spiral in the air. A black hole in reality opened, echoing the appearance of La Boite Noire nicely.

Dana stepped forward out of the darkness as if a Leko light on my ceiling were focused on him.

Dana brought guests. The blue-haired student with the thick glasses was on one arm. She wore a maroon sweater the size of her entire body. Beetle was on his other arm, in tight gray leather. Dana himself was in a black version of Christobel's sequined gold suit. He wished to play the inheritor of the theatrical throne, I suppose, dressed for mourning and for ascension. I thought the black sequins looked like fish scales. The trio took a central spot on my couch.

Nicco appeared on the short L of the couch with a pop—neat as you please. She'd checked the room and chosen a chair. Abracadabra: Nicco. I saw her refer offscreen a few times, so George was there too but didn't want to be visible on a public restream. George is the smart one.

"Johnathan, from here forward I want you to provide no commentary, no offers of assistance. I'm going to have too many voices overlapping as it is." I felt as if I were telling my unruly child that bedtime was early tonight and they were not allowed to come downstairs. The grown-ups were having a grown-up party.

I hid my favorite chair from AR until about a quarter after eight. Then, standing in the center of the room, I looked around meaningfully. I could have lowered all their volumes or played favorites. I considered having the stream's view pan around the room dramatically. Instead I just waited until it got quiet. Eventually even the wall stopped buzzing.

"Thank you all for coming, especially on such short notice," I said. I decided to skip "I suppose you're all wondering why I've brought you here." I did consider "Someone in this room is a murderer!" but I didn't want to lean too much on classic material.

"Two days ago," I began, and then I stopped. I heard something weird.

It came again: an odd, rhythmic knocking.

"What was that?" I asked.

"It's not on my end," Dana said, looking bored. Beetle scrunched her face in irritation that his first words on the live stream were so flat.

"I heard it too," Rosemarie said softly.

"The loud, repeating sound is a knock on your front door," Johnathan said, even though I'd told him to be silent.

"My front door? Here, physically?" I pulled off my glasses, which removed all the avatar participants from my view. I didn't pause the stream though. They probably thought it was all part of the show.

"Yes, someone knocked on your physical door," Cye confirmed from the kitchen counter.

"Knocked on my door?—who does that?" I looked at Cye. "Well, who is it?"

"I am unable to ascertain," Johnathan intoned.

"I am also unable to determine," Cye said, and he looked down at the floor, as if creating a list of 286 suspects for the crime of "knocked on Thackery's front door at a bad time," complete with current whereabouts and door-knocking habits of the Islanders.

Rosemarie's eyes narrowed. "Highly irregular. As I'm sure I've mentioned," she added hesitantly, "I have a drone that orbits fairly near your house. And I can't see anyone either."

The knocking came again: seven quick raps in a rhythmic pattern, more urgent this time. Someone unidentifiable was at my front door, knocking as one would in Shakespeare or an old movie. I shook my head. The stream was probably lighting up. We had a mystery already.

Dana's voice rang out, delivering a line that Beetle probably fed him: "Maybe it's Christobel's ghost." There were lots of oohs and ahhs from the wall.

I shook my head. "Even if it's an offliner, then one of any bazillion drones, or a satellite would still—oh. Oh, it's him."

"Yes. Most likely." Cye confirmed from his stool.

"What?" Cherry asked. "What do you mean 'oh it's him'? Who's at the bloody door? And is anyone going to answer it? Isn't it rude not to answer a door?"

"Do you want to let him in?" Cye asked me, his voice gentle.

"I don't know. Do you want to let him in?" I fired back.

"This is your house," Cye answered. "It's your decision."

I sat down again. I gripped the arms of my chair. I put my ARs back on. "Sorry for the delay everyone. We have a mysterious uninvited guest. Go ahead, Cherry. Let him in."

Cherry scrambled to his feet, and then looked around the room. "Should I bring a fire iron?"

I shook my head. "He's not a monster. Or a mustache-twirling villain. It'd be easier if he were." I didn't know what a fire iron was.

"Coming!" Cherry called out as the knock came again. He shuffled out of the room and down the hallway.

The stream participants all erupted with witty comments, laughs, muttering and a fair amount of "Dun, dun duun!"

I looked over at Cye. Despite knowing that everything was streamed, and that the unexpected guest wasn't about to do anything violent or cruel, I was still uneasy.

Cye returned my glance with a kind expression. "It will be all right." Maybe he was frightened too. That made me feel stronger.

We heard Cherry's muffled voice provide a greeting. The words were out of range, but I could hear the tones of a normal, polite exchange. And then as he turned back towards the living room: "Thackery, it's Vaughn."

"Oh," I called aloud, as if surprised. "Splendid. Come on in, Vaughn. Welcome to the party."

When he stood at my doorstep, Vaughn was invisible to Johnathan, to Cye, even to Rosemarie's drones. He was filtered out by law. Vaughn needed to knock on the door of a residence because he didn't have an AI in his pocket to talk to a home's AI when he arrived. I respected his right to be invisible. But I also knew he exercised his rights in order to sell poison to young, impressionable actors.

"Hello everyone," Vaughn said severely as he entered from my darkened hallway. He pulled glasses from my basket, put them on, and then nodded around the room, acknowledging both the virtual and physical attendees. He didn't blink or grimace when he saw Cye. "I heard you were going to do a multiple-point-of-view stream replay of the last Birthday Party, to look for clues about Christobel."

"Yes," I said. "How did you hear?" He was an offliner, so who went out of their way to tell Vaughn about my party?

He shook his head. "That's not important. But I have something I'd like to share. And if this is a restream, and the Island is listening—well,

I'd like to say something, if I may. Something the whole Island deserves to hear."

You could feel the crackling buzz. Just as I'd stream-jumped into Danabeetle's production earlier that day, now Vaughn strolled in to take over mine. It wasn't like I could say no. I waved to the open space where my coffee table had been, now the de facto stage.

"It may come as a surprise for some of you to learn that I have acted selfishly, and I've endangered the Island. I've realized the error of my ways. On my property, I grew illegal stimulants for recreational drug use. I shared them with Island inhabitants. It got out of hand. At first it was just my friend Nicco." Here Vaughn gestured towards Nicco, and— far from friendship—I saw a kind of desperation in Nicco's expression. "But it escalated. I am saddened by what happened. I want to confess my indiscretion to the Island, and ask for forgiveness. I was wrong. And I have destroyed my plants."

Destroyed your plants? I'll say you have. You fucker.

"As a token of my desire to change, I would like to share my personal recording of the party. Maybe it can help resolve the mystery of Christobel's death. My recording shows me at my worst, but it shows Christobel at his best. Afterwards, I wish to retire from the public eye and try to contribute to the Island's welfare, to make up for the lives I have hurt."

"Thank you, Vaughn," I said and paused before continuing, letting the buzz from the wall spatter and pop. "I assume you're also trying to grab some kind of immunity from prosecution for these offenses?"

Vaughn winced. His innocent, open-faced humbleness tightened up. "Naturally I do not want to be a felon. If I were convicted and taken from the Island, I wouldn't be here, where I could help the community. Here I can make reparations. Yes, if you'd like my stream added to this parlor scene—and trust me, you'll want to see it—then I do ask for immunity from prosecution for crimes related to my farm. I did not kill Christobel, so I'm not worried about that. And I want to see the killer caught. I am confessing openly to my wrongdoing and I am also asking the Island for forgiveness." Vaughn bowed to the screen that displayed the vast array of viewers. "I will of course pay the mandated fine for my actions."

"The fine?"

"Yes. I grew a non-native, genetically altered crop on Earth. The restoration initiative and rules around resurrection biology on Earth's surface—"

"You'll pay a fine?"

"Yes. Not a small one, either."

I stood up from my seat. "Excuse me, everyone," and I stalked from the room. Viewers saw me walk out and pull the glasses from my face. "Oooh, they're pissed," was probably typed into chat streams from here to Prax. Along with "I don't get it, what are they mad about?"

I walked right through my porch, kicked over an overambitious aloe plant, and stepped out onto the sand. A drug dealer was using my stream to get the Island to forgive him.

"Is this worth it, Cye?"

He'd followed after me, knowing I wanted him to.

"Worth what?"

"Is his recording worth letting him off?"

"Anything we learn from this evening will not be admissible evidence for use in a murder conviction. Christobel wasn't killed on a stream. Like the parlor scenes in a mystery novel, tonight is hearsay and none of it will be evidence. Granting forgiveness to a known drug dealer would not seem to balance with the gathering of more inadmissible hearsay."

"But?"

"There is no 'but'. That is the logical conclusion."

"So what are we going to do?"

"What do you want to do?" Cye asked.

"No, not this time. This is not my investigation. I have no legal standing, I'm not the licensed investigator. We have a plea deal on the table. He wants immunity for a crime—"

"—which the authorities may not be able to charge him for anyway."

"Surely he'll be charged. He wouldn't be here otherwise."

"He could be here because his desire to change is genuine."

"Oh, that's ripe, Cye. No. Vaughn's an asshole."

"People can be more than one thing."

I groaned. "This is all beside the point. You, Cye, are in charge of this investigation. You have to decide whether or not we accept this offer."

Cye held up his hands. "Nothing we do in this context has a legal outcome. I'm not an attorney. No one here can cut a deal, and Vaughn knows that. His speech was for the court of public opinion. He gets to play poker with social currency in front of a vast audience. He doesn't want to be charged with a crime, but this is also still a game to him. I don't need to be involved in this decision. This is your house. Do you want to let him play or not?"

I walked back into the house. Cye followed.

I sat back down in my favorite chair and steepled my fingers. Vaughn had chosen a hard wooden chair near the north window, with the ocean behind him. His knees were together, his hands clasped on his lap. He looked like a humble scarecrow.

I knew both Dana and Nicco, at least, were rebroadcasting along with me. Everyone was watching. "Vaughn has made a request for forgiveness to the Island. It is not my decision whether to accept it or not. It is the Island's decision. Johnathan, a poll please."

Johnathan pinged politely to show he was listening.

Vaughn's brow furrowed, and his peaceful expression darkened. "A poll?"

"Yes, Vaughn. Democracy. The hoi polloi is being generous with their time, let's consult them. Two options, Johnathan. Option one, the Island accepts Vaughn's heartfelt apology and agrees not to prosecute him for crimes related to his illicit drug production—"

"—and distribution," Vaughn interrupted.

I glared at him. He smiled.

"—and distribution...in exchange for his cooperation in the investigation of the murder of the recently deceased, and with the understanding that he will share his complete recording of the most recent Birthday Party and swear to do no more evil."

I took a breath.

"Option two, kick the fucking drug dealer off our Island."

If I thought Vaughn's expression dark before, I'd been mistaken. Apparently eyebrows can close so tight that they swallow one's eyes. I found it hard to believe he could still see me through the bristling furry caterpillars. He'd come to my house to play a game. I could play games.

"Johnathan, can you put that up on the Island's public stream, please? Resident access. Adult voters only, I think. And please, everyone here and Islanders abroad, go ahead and vote. Vaughn, you can vote verbally if you like, unless you've got a telegraph in your pocket?"

The glare was mastered. The eyes magically reappeared: open, mournful, and contrite. "As the individual seeking clemency, I place my future in the hands of my neighbors. I shall not vote."

Yeesh. He earned himself a dozen fence sitters with that deferral.

I was alarmed by the speed of the replies. The whole Island really was watching. And the Island audience loves to participate

As we waited, Nicco's avatar strolled over to Dana's. They did a quick guest spot together, POV-bombing each other's streams, arms around shoulders, laughing, and then getting sober for a minute as they addressed the evening's multiple purposes. Nicco made a plug for viewers to donate to the memorial fund for Christobel. Beetle and Dana beamed and embraced her.

Vaughn was absolved, of course. Everyone wanted to see what he saw, and the Islanders were hardly going to send one of their own up to Prax to face justice. Vaughn had become part of the evening's entertainment, shuffling up on stage to join the cast at the last minute; his sins were backstory. Also, he was wearing a dapper, moody overcoat.

"Thank you, everyone. I will aim to be better," Vaughn said. His delivery was so perfect I could almost believe him.

"Good idea. You had quite a few neighbors willing to deport you. But enough about that. Despite your luddite pride, you have a personal recording. Please grant stream access to Cye. We need to raise our curtain before the murderer confesses out of boredom."

"Finally!" Dana called out. "Can I emcee the party? I've always wanted to be the emcee."

"No, Dana, you may not," I said. "Christobel is the emcee tonight, as he was at every Birthday Party. We're going to see our departed friend strut his stuff for one final evening."

I stood up. I waited for a breath, in case some other mysterious surprise arrived. Then I began again.

"Two days ago, Christobel was murdered. Here, on our Island, our home." I gestured, and an aerial view of the Island and the ocean slid into view, superimposed upon the center of my living room.

"We all grew up in orbit, our homes surrounded by vacuum with nothing beyond our metal and plastic walls. The surfaces told the whole story. But living down here, an ocean surrounds us instead." I panned the point-of-view low, zooming over the rolling water. "We see waves, floating masses of seaweed, drones scooping plastic. The surface tells a story, but underneath is no vacuum. There's more." I plunged our view beneath the sea, showing the sudden abundance of life big and small in the coral farms that extend away from the Island. "That's why we like it down here, on our slowly recovering planet—there's an abundance that surpasses our understanding. Artists dare to look at what lies beneath the surface. And that's what tonight is about." We surfaced, rose, then bore down on the jetty and the park. Our view came to rest on an empty, solitary bench.

After letting that image sit for a moment, I waved the projection away and let the lights bring us back to my living room again.

"On the surface, our smiling, neighborhood Cherry is a friendly, bumbling alcoholic, the one who falls asleep on your couch—"

Cherry cheered. He'd kept his seat by the liquor cabinet, and he lifted his drink in a mock toast to himself.

"But underneath? He has a PhD in psychology. He had an affair with Christobel some years ago, but was left behind, waiting on the pier while Christobel sailed to other ports."

A sober silence as the audience took that in.

"On the surface, Dana Heed and Christobel had an infamous public breakup. Beetle helped Dana use that breakup, as they are using Christobel's death, to draw viewers like sharks to chum. They do it all for the stream! Dana is an adored influencer. Underneath, though, how deeply did the break up crush his ego? And do he and Beetle love attention enough to commit murder?"

Dana stood up. A massive AR mustache popped into view on his face. "You haven't heard the last from me!" he said, curling his whiskers.

"Then there's Rosemarie, who watches us and listens. Everyone knows Rosemarie is a drone enthusiast, but it turns out she's watching all of us. We don't know what's beneath her surface. She keeps it all buttoned up."

"—where it belongs," Rosemarie added from her chair, and she touched the top button of her cardigan. Cute.

"On the surface, Nicco is an extraordinarily gifted actor. Underneath? She's got a drug problem, and a money problem. She relied on Christobel to bail her out, time and again—"

"Don't forget my spotlight problem. That's my main addiction, really!" Nicco chimed in, getting a few chuckles from the audience, "That and George, I can't figure out how to quit Her Majesty," she continued, and let her voice turn sorrowful. This time she received a chorus of awwws from the stream.

I resumed control of the audio. "We've also got an uninvited guest, the quietly explosive Vaughn. Is he a reformed villain, or arriving here in top villainous form?"

Vaughn remained immobile and unexpressive.

"For my own part: on the surface Christobel and I argued constantly. Underneath that, he was a friend whom I loved. He saw me. As an artist, I like to be seen. I can't remember what I fought with Christobel about on the night before his murder, and I deleted my recording. Why would I do that?

"Finally, perhaps the murderer isn't one of our notables here in my parlor, but a minor player in the usual dramas who has stepped forth for a major role." I gestured invitingly to the wall and raised the volume of the general audience. Thousands of viewers made their own noises, struck poses, or brandished comical weapons in AR.

"Tonight we peek beneath the waves to see the rushing tumult that led to the tragedy of Christobel's murder. Someone on this Island killed him, and the day before the murder most of our adult population attended the June Birthday Party. Our assembled streams of that raucous event will include the last conversations we had with Christobel, the last time we saw him alive, and his last chat with his killer. Tonight we will mourn our friend and accuse a murder suspect.

"Let me share an unpoetic update about the investigation: We know how Christobel was killed. We know the probable accomplices. Cye-9 has promised to reveal the prime murder suspect tonight. But first: the parlor scene, where we discover the events leading up to the crime. We reveal our secrets and our motives, no matter how hard they are to look at."

I took a breath and lowered the lights.

"Last chance for a bio break, audience. We're diving in for real now."

I realized I should have taken something for nausea. Too late, oh well. If I hurled, the audience would shriek, laugh, and clap all the louder.

I lowered my opaques. I put headphones over my ears, too. I could've used the ones embedded in my frames, but I wanted to hear every word of Christobel's voice. That morning, I'd asked Cye if trying to remember would help. Now it was exactly as I'd sarcastically suggested: vivid, three-dimensional images of the party, complete with spatial audio, were about to play in my head.

"Welcome back friends, guests, suspects, and drug dealers to the June Birthday Party," I announced.

Chapter Seventeen
The Birthday Party

Christobel's resurrected voice filled my living room. As the boom and clatter of fireworks resounded in the background, he echoed my words:

"Welcome one and all to the June! Birthday! Party!"

An invisible, delighted roar responded, and then my opaques darkened and my living room faded away. Along with everyone plugged into the stream, I endured the miracle of flight. We sailed above Cherry's deck, following the point of view of one of his house drones. A small crowd shuffled below us: the crowd from three nights ago, made up of those Island residents who like to stand around and shout while the sky bursts into flames for the party's opening number.

Christobel stood on a raised dais on Cherry's deck. He waved his arms and twirled. His glowing, golden microphone pulsed in his hand. "Welcome to another night of folly and sin, raucous abandon, and bacchanalian boozing!"

The assembled crowd let out another roar.

"Let's hear it for June!" Christobel said, and he slid the thumping bass up so high it enveloped us, the dull throb making the air thick. The crowd kicked and thrashed like we'd been set in gelatin and needed to push the weight of the world away. The youngest danced the hardest: Everyone under forty looked like they were collaborating to sweep aside a thick fog and see clearly again. But no one left the dance floor having resolved their existential dilemmas or fallen in love—not that I could tell.

Eventually, after an extended mix track and two or three attempts at a dance circle, the domes of fireworks ended and the drone show winked out. The music dropped back to a subdermal beat. The golden sequins on his arms sparkled at us as Christobel lifted his microphone again: "Baa baa bad sheep, this dance is done—but the evening's glory has just begun—inside I herd you, little sheep—into the bordello of Cherry's keep!"

Now the sound of a marching band, competing with a ravenous bass guitar, urged us forward. Christobel carved a path of gold through the small crowd and headed towards the wall of shimmering glass which held the entrance to Cherry's grand ballroom. The crowd formed pairs and clumps and followed him. Two of the theater set attempted to move in a balletic kickline, with some success. And there, shuffling along with a glass in their hand, was me, Thackery. I had on my black fedora, the one with a seagull feather. I looked smug and calm compared to the younger dancers. I walked with measured, confident steps. But, transparent to anyone who had ever loved a drinker, I was already deep in my cups. I followed the crowd, trying to liquify with them, to discard all personal motivation.

Christobel was so beautiful. I thought I might cry right then as I watched, maybe get that out of the way early. His gold never stopped talking to your eyes. His curls were eddies. You could taste his smile, like warm syrup, from ten meters away. We would have followed him anywhere. Instead of Cherry's house, he could have led the crowd down the boardwalk, past my neighborhood to the east, and to the cliffs beyond. If he'd played a pipe we would have poured ourselves forth, over the cliffs and into the inky night sea, and even further, on a tour of sunken cities: Atlantis, Jakarta, Miami Beach. If he'd asked it of us, we would have grown gills for him without fuss, or held our breaths, releasing them only when he looked away.

Instead, he led us through the crystal doors into Cherry's ludicrous palace, directly onto the dance floor. Cherry's main ballroom had chandeliers with gaudy paper flowers instead of candles, a sprung floor of emerald and beige, and a low thrust stage. Christobel was upon it in a flash.

The rest of the party attendees, those who disdain the firework opening, greeted the dribbling parade with cheers or vague murmurs. The Spirit Fox was already there, as usual. They came up to each guest and handed out tiny scrolls, each tied with a slender silver ribbon and matching tassel.

The room's POV shifted, and I watched as Nicco unrolled the Fox's gift before his eyes:

> *Gather your nose buds while ye may,*
> *or this rhyme will find ye crying.*
> *For that same power that smiles today*
> *tomorrow will send you flying.*

The poem was in the Spirit Fox's careful handwriting. You could see that each letter was painstakingly drawn, as one might draw a shape freehand. The common joke was that it was hard to hold a pen with a furry paw.

The POV shifted to Rosemarie's stream, which was slightly behind and above her, captured by her motes. Her scroll read:

> *Your shoulders burdened by ravens five*
> *will whisper truths that spoil to lies.*
> *They paint you pictures that seem alive*
> *til you turn and see without butterflies.*

I would have liked to see my own poem. I saw the Spirit Fox hand me one, but my past self pocketed it without unrolling or reading. Perhaps none of the streams were close enough to see me read it anyway.

"My recording now includes a visual translation request," Beetle interrupted from my real-world living room.

Cye slowed the simulation on a gorgeous shot of Christobel on stage. The spotlight made him sparkle. "Correct."

"What does that mean?" I asked.

"I am remixing four recordings: those of Dana Heed, Cherry, Rosemarie, and Nicco. At this time index, all four of the recordings started to include a pending request for a second video track."

"So what?" I said. "There's a hundred AR systems in the ballroom that could do that. Maybe someone turned closed captioning on."

"This request is private. It doesn't identify itself," Beetle said.

"Like someone was spying on us?" Rosemarie asked.

"Was someone in the room wearing x-ray specs?" Dana quipped.

"The visual translation has no content yet," Cye said. "It's just a pending request. If anything appears, I will identify it and pause to inform the room. Shall I continue?"

"Yes," I said. "Please use all the available streams to follow our emcee, but keep the head jumping to a minimum please." This last request got a chorus of approval from older viewers watching the stream.

The playback resumed. We watched as Christobel worked the stage. He called out welcomes on his microphone to each artist, identifying them by their media or accolades. Mabel likely whispered the required details to him. I got a shout out when he welcomed "all of our Island's illustrious iconic iconoclasts and influencers," an expression which I don't think works, but the crowd didn't care. He welcomed the hospitality sector as well: He pulled Jelly right up on stage and they performed an elaborate secret handshake. Jelly was a Gemini, a June birthday.

Many tried to catch Christobel's eye as he charmed the audience. They posed, they called out, they climbed up for a quick selfie as he changed the mood with a new song. During the second track, a tall lad in a swooping overcoat vaulted up onto the stage and brought him a corsage, which he pinned to his chest. This was all normal. Millfield never came to parties, and I wasn't going to be jealous on his behalf. I never felt jealous of the men. If anyone gender neutral or female crushed on Christobel, I hated them automatically and irrevocably—hated them so much I stopped being aware of their existence. But the men were just men. My attitude was discriminatory, hypocritical, and just generally awful. But I never told anyone I felt this way, and I believed that made it okay. I don't need to examine feelings I never plan to share.

At one point, Dana Heed's recording rig had the best view of the stage. I became uncomfortably aware of the man's nervous energy. He'd brought his date, the blue-haired young woman with thick glasses, and they hung off each other like teenagers. Dana postured and exaggerated this affection whenever Christobel turned his way. If I could read Dana's intention, the audience could see it too. This was not a good look for him, but Beetle probably couldn't understand that. How many months had it been since the breakup? I felt sorry for Dana's date, whoever she was. I hoped she was more to him than a tool to incite jealousy. In any case, Christobel disregarded Dana's ploy. I was proud of him for that.

After three or four musical numbers, Christobel relinquished the limelight. The broad stage became more dance floor for those who wished to be more visible. On the Island, everyone wishes to be more visible. First, a costumed group in ball gowns did a synchronized swim. Then the Marbles got up and did their routines, bodies spinning and rolling over one another. Then a free-for-all—there was even some stage diving. And then Christobel was gone.

Cye switched to a stream near the edge of the ballroom—Vaughn's, I think, because over the shoulder of someone talking to Vaughn we saw Christobel exit the ballroom.

"Where's he going?" Nicco asked. "I thought he barely left the dance floor all night."

Cye faded the music out and then made a visual cross dissolve.

The stream's view now quietly peered up at *Duel*. My painting, the one Christobel called the centerpiece of my show, was alive and staring right at us. We were in one of the galleries.

This was Rosemarie's recorded stream. Her motes produced a POV just above and slightly behind her. Her hair was done up, a hundred tiny pins meticulously holding each lock in a chosen position. She looked at *Duel*. *Duel* looked back at her.

Duel had their usual smirk. Strong, confident. But they were sober and calm, which seemed improper for a party. Cherry had decided to project *Duel* in an ornate gilt wooden frame, which was terrible, but *Duel* rose above it. Good for them.

Christobel's flashing gold suit sailed just past the corner of our POV.

"Hey Rose, you seen Tack?" Christobel asked.

"No, I have not," she replied.

He sailed out again.

Rosemarie tsked and continued on to the other paintings in Cherry's east gallery. Four of my works were on display. The tall ceilings and white walls isolated each piece. They didn't look lonely, though—not to me. They looked ready. My art was ready for something.

From outside of the stream, Dana Heed's voice rang out in my living room. "This is just advertising for your show, Thackery!" he crowed, eliciting mild laughter.

Apparently Christobel was not available on any recorded streams just then, as Cye kept us with Rosemarie. She spent time in front of each image. After making the rounds, she returned to *Duel* for another look. Then she walked out into the hall where students were staffing their installation pieces.

Cye changed the stream again, this time to Cherry, who walked back into the gallery that Rosemarie had just left.

Christobel ushered Thackery into the gallery from the other end of the hall. Now, at last, I saw myself talking to my dead friend—albeit at the end of a long room, but Cye turned up the audio to compensate.

"I'm not saying you have to stand guard all night, but I'm going to send people over here in ten minutes—"

"Which is exactly when I should be elsewhere," I answered, sensibly enough.

"But don't you want to see their faces? When they see it? This is the moment, this is the public's first view—"

"No, that's the last thing I want to see. That's the worst thing ever to see."

I would like to say I remembered this conversation. I did not. Which made the Thackery in VR a false version of me, a me that I could look down on and pity. They were clutching their drink. They looked half asleep.

Cherry walked towards us, up the length of the gallery as our argument played out, and then interrupted. "Tack! I gave 'em all space, like you said. Enough space?"

"Yes, Cherry. They're practically in a vacuum, there's so much space. Thank you."

"Don't know why you only want to do four. We could get ten in here, or sixteen. If we stacked 'em up in rows, we could fit dozens—all of them."

"You're right. Maybe next time."

"Are they all this grim?"

"What?" I saw myself peer through my haze, trying to translate Cherry's question. Christobel looked uncomfortable, as if he knew what Cherry was getting at.

"Grim. I mean, you know, none of them look very happy," Cherry explained, gesturing to *Duel*. "Not sad exactly, either. But they're all looking at me, and they look grim. Could you make them more happy? More like a party? We're at a party."

I turned to Christobel. "It's a delight to have Cherry review one's art. He's the perfect measuring device. As soon as he likes a piece, you'll know it's crap. Then you can destroy it and move on."

Cherry gave a barking laugh. "Just for that, Thackery, I'm going to go shower compliments on the pieces in the west wing. Maybe buy a couple. And I've got a bar over there. Chris wouldn't let me have one in here."

"Then I'll follow you and try to keep the balance by insulting every piece," I said.

"No, no," Christobel said hastily. "Stay here, Thackery—thirty minutes. Tops. You don't need to talk to anyone, okay? You can if you want, or if you want you can just smile and nod, or wave. Just stay put, okay? Twenty-five minutes. I will be back in fifteen. I'll arrive with the rush. I'll buffer for you, okay? Deal?"

I suddenly looked very sleepy. Christobel grabbed one of the chairs from the wall and brought it over. I obediently sat. Fine, yes. I would sit near my artwork. I was too sauced to argue.

Cherry, and his stream's POV that we followed, walked back through the central hall and towards the west wing, as he'd said. In the background, we could just make out Christobel asking me if I'd eaten, and then promising he'd get someone to bring me a plate. Then Cherry carried the stream beyond hearing. If that were all I would get to see of Christobel and myself talking that night, I might actually weep.

Cherry went over to the bar and was handed a Manhattan; the bartender knew what he was coming for. Displaying Cherry's incredible curatory acumen, the west wing featured landscapes, all packed together, frame to frame, on the north wall. On the south wall a lattice of wooden shelves housed hundreds of ceramic pieces. Dark porcelain curves like red blood cells peeked out of a towering brown graph. I couldn't tell if they were supposed to be a single work or if Cherry had implemented his "stack all the art up, you can fit more that way" plan.

Less than a minute later, Christobel came in after him.

"Cherry, high king, lord of all we see before us, have you got a moment?"

"For my illustrious master of ceremonies, a thousand moments," Cherry answered, grinning broadly as he was pulled under Christobel's spell.

I'd seldom seen the two of them talk. Cherry's attraction to Christobel was obvious, especially with drink turning him into a pink-faced, transparent version of himself. Maybe I'd never noticed it before because everyone was attracted to Christobel, but it was off-putting—like walking in on your parents.

Christobel lowered his voice. "I'll be brief: I'd like to help Thackery."

Cherry caught the cue and lowered his voice, though he didn't know what he was lowering his voice about. "Tack's in trouble? They got a fan on their arse?"

Christobel shook his head. "No, nothing like that. I want to help them dry out."

Cherry got a funny look on his face. "It's a party, Christobel. S'all right to get pickled at a party. We won't let them end up in a snowbank, if that's what you're worried about." Cherry took a slurp of his drink, as if to underscore the point.

"I don't mean right now; I mean generally. They spend so much time inebriated that they're—well, I think they're losing the war. I want to help them acknowledge they've got a problem."

Cherry pointed his finger loosely at Christobel. "You're talking about an intervention."

"An intervention, yes. A handful of people who care about them, who they know and trust—like you, Cherry. And you can help because you know everybody. Next week, Tack's headed up—"

"Chris—it's so stupid." Here Cherry put his arm around Christobel's back, as if to embrace him.

"What do you mean?"

"Never works, never works. I had one of those once. It doesn't stick. Thackery drinks, Christobel, sure. They make weird art that Prax can't get enough of, and they drink. They can handle it—handle it better than me. Imagine that! We're their friends. Our job: we keep an eye out, pick them up. We brush off the dirt. That's our job. We help them stand up again."

Christobel nodded, and deftly worked his way out from under Cherry's arm. "You're right, Cherry, that's what friends do. And you're a great friend to Thackery. But what's happening to them now is different. Addiction is different. They need our help."

Cherry gestured to nothing. It was not clear that he heard any of Christobel's words. He talked in a long ramble, lapping over Christobel's attempts to interrupt. "When you're all out on a night and someone goes down, you help them up. Course you do. Tack—what Tack does is not a thing you just turn off. They're not going to come to Jesus. It's not biting fingernails, or—listen—you're so beautiful you can't understand it. You're so perfect you don't understand. You bring your sweetness over here—and you can bring it over here any time, there's room, and you're very sweet—but you don't see it—you can't rewrite a soul with a microphone. I wish you could."

"Are you talking about Thackery's soul or yours, Cherry?"

As they spoke, Cherry kept finding ways to be closer to Christobel: a touch on the shoulder, shifting his body as if to bring his thigh into the conversation.

"Right. I'm game if you want to try again, by and by, you're the healer—wherever you lay your hands there's gold—I could follow that river—" He reached out and ran a finger down Christobel's chest.

"Cherry, please stop touching me."

Cherry pulled himself away. Drunk as he was, he could hear "stop." He looked down at his shoes, chastened. "Sorry, sorry. I'm three sheets is all."

"Well, I'm sorry I asked."

"Don't be like that. I do want to help—"

"You can't, clearly." Christobel was angry.

"Listen—I know Tack—I know everything there is to know about them—"

"Forget it. You want the whole world to be a big boozy party. I get it." He took a second step back and turned to leave the room.

"No, you dumb, self-righteous fuck. That's you," Cherry said. He spilled some of his drink. "You're the ringmaster, sweeping in with a joke and a laugh, seducing the world. You're the Nero, not me. You can't judge me."

Christobel was already walking away, letting it drop. From the look on Cherry's face, he didn't.

But then he turned to the wall of ceramics. Abruptly, his mood changed. He sipped his drink. Whatever passion had held him before drifted off.

"Pots," he said. "Now, pots are good. I like pots."

The music came in again, and Cye switched the stream back to the grand ballroom. We followed Vaughn's view, then Nicco's bobbing head from a circle of moshers near the stage, and then out to Dana Heed's floating camera as Christobel came into the room, kissed cheeks, playfully pulled on people's coattails, and then hurtled up onto the stage. His gold microphone shot back into his hand. His voice filled the room again:

"O, wonder! How many goodly creatures are there here!

How beauteous humankind is! O brave new world,

That has such people in it!"

The crowd roared in appreciation, and the next track lifted them up higher. It was Christobel's greatest trick: He made them wish for something and then he granted that wish.

For the duration of an extended track, the room shook, sparked, and burst. Then Christobel slowly let the music subside into a gentle undercurrent. There was still a thumping bass, but here it was joined by a murmuring double bass.

"I'd like to take this opportunity to pause and express gratitude to our host with the most—the most money that is—Cherry! A round of applause, please!"

The audience complied.

"Every month Cherry offers his home for our Birthday Party, and for all of us to display or perform our latest creations...And, as always, it is a delight to have Cherry review your art. What many people do not realize is that Cherry's taste is so bad—"

He waited so that the crowd could shout "How bad is it?"

"—his taste is so bad that as soon as he likes a piece, you know it's crap. You can destroy it and move on!"

The crowd affirmed this judgment. I was glad Christobel didn't credit me for the insult. I wished that Cye would cut back to Cherry's stream so I could judge his face. But he was probably in the west wing having a third Manhattan. I lifted my opaques to peek over at the real Cherry, still huddled by my liquor cabinet. But he has ocular implants. With his eyes closed, I couldn't tell if he was in VR or asleep.

Christobel continued. "If you haven't had a chance yet, now is the time to visit the galleries. Tonight's preview is a big one. First, the west wing features works from the conclusion of Dic's landscape series, and the captivating ceramics of Tam and her new apprentice: Imra!"

This brought applause, along with a group of four students who chanted Imra's name, interspersed with something in a language I couldn't identify. Christobel let this continue for a measure. Then he made his voice more settled and speechy.

"Last year the Prax art scene woke up and started paying attention to what we do down here—we all played a part in that, we can all be proud—and one show in particular was a burst of neutrinos before the supernova. I'm talking of course about *Décolletage*."

The crowd whooped to that. They remembered *Décolletage*. The show flattered them. It changed attitudes towards the Island. It produced a surge in the attention economy that lasted long after the art itself was forgotten. Also, the art itself didn't suck—at least I thought.

"Tonight, for the first time in public, an early glimpse of the long-awaited follow-up. Citizens of the Island, I invite you to the east wing for a small, stunning preview of *Impressions* by Thackery!"

This garnered both applause and murmurs. I think they were appreciative murmurs? Vaguely excited murmurs? This is the problem with crowds. You can never know what each individual is thinking or feeling —jealousy, rage, disdain, or nothing—or just murmuring because everyone else is murmuring and it must be murmur time: murmur, murmur. I was now grateful that Christobel planted me in the gallery. Hearing those muffled utterances, and trying to classify them, would have driven me mad.

The music shifted into something with violins. A squadron of waiters in tuxedos began to distribute glasses of champagne. The crowd flowed south, out of the grand ballroom and into the main hallway towards the two gallery wings. Christobel led the way, but he used his energy at each interruption or obstacle to sprinkle the crowd around, like a baker scattering yeast on the water.

Students stationed themselves at their installation pieces, which dominated the main hall: horns of plenty made of dinosaur bones and sporting equipment; tunnels that led into claustrophobic mirrored boxes; a black shadow so dark that walking through it blinded you; and a path of textures where two fur-covered aliens stood at the ready to collect your shoes so you could walk over it barefoot and properly experience the art. I do not disdain this sort of thing; I love it. The students believe in what they're doing, and they do it with eager intensity. We lose that intensity to our doom. Give me a passionate novice over a cynical master any day. As I am among the latter, I suppose this means I don't prefer myself, at least at an art show.

Cye kept us following Dana Heed's recording, perhaps because he was the sort to casually observe a piece of art but not spend too much time appreciating it. Also, Dana's orbit never left the star of the show for long. As Beetle hovered over one of his shoulders like a devil (or an angel), Dana repeatedly found ways to curve back and swing by Christobel. He timed each flyby with a show of affection towards his date, playing with her hair or pulling her against his chest.

Until, inevitably, Dana approached Christobel directly.

"No partner tonight, Chris?" Dana asked.

Christobel turned and smiled. "This lovely crowd is my partner, Dana! And a passionate one at that. Please, introduce me." Without waiting, Christobel took the blue-haired woman's hand and bowed to kiss it.

Dana ignored the request. "Can Millfield even dance?"

Christobel lifted his eyebrows. "You'd be surprised."

"I didn't think so," Dana answered. He'd rehearsed this part, perhaps in front of a mirror. "And I have to know, Christobel, the question I keep asking myself: If he can't dance, can he even fuck properly?"

I have not seen Christobel angry very often. He's good at it, the way he's good at most things. He'd been angry enough at Cherry to turn around and insult him from the stage. Now his face went wooden. He stepped with strength and grace right up into Dana's face, mere centimeters away, managing to somehow become taller than the taller man. It was so beautiful you might believe the move rehearsed, but I could see Christobel's fists balled up beneath his gold, sparkling cuffs. I could read the danger there, something barely contained in his face. Beetle's eyes were wide, hovering nearby, taking it all in with what I can only imagine was a programmatic orgasm. Her owner was achieving the ultimate attention from the crowd's shining gravity well of passion and light.

His fists remained at his sides. Instead, Christobel swung his face to the right and planted a kiss on Dana's cheek. Then he pulled away. He turned his left cheek towards Dana and tapped it with his index finger, as if to say, "Where's mine? Have you got something for me?" Dana froze, lacking a rehearsed reply. Christobel turned to the as-yet-unnamed student. "I'm very sorry. There are no small roles, but I hope the future finds you a better one."

And then he was off again. Dana was left sputtering swear words under his breath. Christobel had seen the trap and gracefully disengaged; Dana had been made a fool of, exposed, and shrugged off. He's not clever, so I think he absorbed this only on a gut level; he looked around, expression vacant, and Beetle began whispering in his ear.

We were spared finding out if I was still stationed beside my art when the crowds arrived in the east wing. None of the recorded streams caught the event. I suspect I'd fled to the safety of the west wing, where I could appreciate four dozen pieces of framed landscape photography stacked on a single wall—and an open bar.

Cye cycled us through each recording's POV. Christobel flashed through a scene or two as Nicco came out of the west wing and then as Vaughn strode down the central hall. We also saw Vaughn's view as he examined my pieces, Christobel chatting to students in the corner. Finally, I did see the back of my head as Cherry stood for pictures with Tam and Imra and Christobel dove comically into the shot. I was in front of the west wing bar, as I'd surmised.

After about thirty minutes a siren rang in the distance, and everyone stopped to listen.

The siren was the warning call for the Quark. This divided the crowd into two groups: those who now avoided the ballroom and those who drifted towards it. On Prax, the Quark was hot for about five minutes. Down here it was still a party standard after five decades. The group that avoided it was small and everyone agreed they were traitors.

Nicco was the first one back into the ballroom with a stream. She walked towards the stage, where Christobel again stood, glittering, the microphone in his hand. The crowd grew and calcified around the rim. Nicco went right up to the edge, joining the others in the theater set.

"Attention citizens, students, and sinners! We will give people a few minutes to assemble for the Quark—" here Christobel was interrupted by an impromptu chant of "up, down, strange, charm!" which he skillfully allowed just the right amount of time. "And to warm us up, I will present a new entrée, a new delight."

The lights went down. Then an empty spotlight appeared on the stage.

Christobel's voice, now from somewhere offstage: "I am proud to present Spirit Fox and Josephine!"

The Spirit Fox stepped up onto the stage, and the music fell to a slow beat.

The Fox held out their hand, and a tall, distractingly gorgeous woman materialized on their arm. It was a twenty-something Josephine Baker, wearing heels and a sparkling gown that was probably more conservative than anything Ms. Baker ever danced in.

She was played by Mabel, of course.

The music kicked up, and Mabel and the Spirit Fox danced.

I didn't remember this at all. I'd been in the bathroom, or perhaps I simply hadn't cared to watch. They performed a dance that was...a waltz? Or a flamenco. Maybe a kind of tango. It started out simple, just two bodies walking, and gradually became a more lively, ragtime 4/4.

"It's a foxtrot," the real-world Dana said from his seat. "I just got it. Fox. Trot! Get it?" I wanted to pretend that Dana was an idiot and reply with snark, but I couldn't because I was grateful to him for making it clear.

The dance required quick feather steps, a difficult thing to accomplish with paws. It gradually accelerated and grew more complex, incorporating inside and outside turns, chassé, and grapevine. Usually the Spirit Fox, like myself, doesn't like to be touched. But they could dance with Mabel's AR avatar. It was refreshing—I appreciated the break from the chaos. Near the end, I saw my black fedora at the edge of the ballroom. I'd switched bars.

The music faded. The two dancers turned in opposite directions and paced away while the lights changed. Christobel ran out and lifted the Spirit Fox's paw in triumph, eliciting a wave of cheers from the audience.

Instead of disintegrating, Mabel walked straight towards the point of view of the stream, which we now watched from Nicco's glasses. She looked at us, or at Nicco rather, and made sure she had Nicco's attention. Christobel was visible directly over Mabel's shoulder, leading the Spirit Fox in a bow.

Mabel spoke, her voice just loud enough to be picked up by Nicco's glasses: "Shall you this fond pageant see? Lord what fools these mortals be." She winked at the camera, and then: "Have you figured it out yet?"

"Cye—" I called out involuntarily. I took off my headphones. Had she broken into the feed? Was Mabel here, now, live on the stream in my living room?

"The recording is uncompromised, Thackery. There are no discrepancies. She is visible on all four recorded streams."

I flipped my glasses back to AR so I could see my real living room. The attendees had not changed. An immortal Josephine Baker did not suddenly appear at my side and start flirting with me or lecturing me. Nicco looked at me in confusion. She'd been there, she'd heard Mabel speak those words live. What was my problem?

"It can't be a coincidence. How would she know?"

"Mabel said those words to Nicco, at that time, three nights ago," Cye said.

"That's impossible."

Real-world Vaughn looked between me and Cye, his face wooden and unreadable. "AI are good at impossible," he said.

Christobel's voice returned, so I lowered my opaques.

He had the spotlight again.

"If you are single...or if you have decided that you are single at least for tonight (I promise not to tell), then you will be dancing the Quark! And to do that, you need to catch a Quark!"

Christobel lifted his right hand. A stream of white plastic balls rocketed out from his sleeve. This was a new trick. He'd told me about the gag a week before. Usually the marked ping pong balls are in a bowl. That night, a bag of balls was strapped behind his jacket, with a tube that snaked up his sleeve and a tiny attached canister of compressed air. He sprayed the crowd as if he were a gardener treating invasives. The quarks sailed out into the dark and pelted everyone, to much merriment. They bounced and scattered, creating several heaps of bodies as the younger dancers reached, groped, and laughed.

Out of nowhere, Christobel produced a massive silk top hat. One by one, those who acquired a ball walked to the stage to drop in their entry. In theory, any single person in the building was required to participate, and various groups were lifting and carrying unwilling friends to the front of the crowd and thrusting a ball into their hands.

"Wait, rewind that!" Dana called out triumphantly.

Cye obligingly paused the stream, and I flipped up my glasses. In the real world, Beetle was whispering in Dana's ear, so he was about to do something impressive.

"Rewind what?"

"Rosemarie fixed the dance. Look at the ball she dropped in the hat."

"I'll allow it," I said, as if I were a judge who sustained an objection. Cye dutifully rewound the scene. The line walked backwards, Christobel gestured in reverse, and sure enough, Rosemarie crept directly behind me as I dropped my own Quark into the hat. Then the stream advanced again, this time at half speed. Rosemarie's hand reached forward, and she dropped two balls into Christobel's hat. Another ball flew up and back into her hand, like magic.

Dana was triumphant. "Do you care to explain that, Rosemarie?"

Rosemarie's voice was flat and cold. "No, I don't."

"Trying to get cozy with Christobel, maybe? Or were you angling for me?"

"It doesn't matter. It didn't work anyway."

"What didn't work?" Dana asked, digging.

She just looked at him.

"Fine," Dana said, "We'll see anyway. We'll watch the dance."

"Do we have to?" Vaughn asked. "We could skip this." He was one of the traitors. He didn't have enough friends to carry him up to the stage.

"Yes, yes we do," Dana replied. "Our adoring public will love this part. Turn up the volume!" He was probably right. Maybe it was time for a Quark revival on Praxima.

I nodded towards Cye and we resumed. The drawing commenced, and the air above the stage filled with our names floating in tinted bubbles. One by one, the bubbles broke open like eggs. Our names climbed out, turning into life-sized jellied images of themselves. My silhouette, carved in letters from my name, danced in a windless whirlwind amongst those of all the other professed singles in the room.

Gradually, the AR bodies made of letters found one another by embracing, twisting together, or intertwining. The I in Imra slunk its way right into the O at the end of Nicco, which I thought a bit much.

Thackery, all nine letters of them, finally draped themselves in a dramatic stretch over the top of Rosemarie. Nine to nine, so at least she could support me. Imra would have collapsed under my lexicographic weight.

"Yes," I murmured, finally remembering something. "I danced the Quark. Why on earth did I—?"

"Partners to corners!" Christobel shouted. "And remember, if you want extra credit, you must remove an item of clothing from your partner during the dance!"

The view shifted again, from Nicco's stream to Rosemarie's motes, which had an open view of Christobel on the stage. Rosemarie strode towards me and took my hand, and then she led me to one of the green cornered squares. "Are you okay?" she asked nervously. "Okay to dance?"

"Rosemarie, darling. You couldn't keep me off if you tried!" I heard myself say. But my balance looked poor, my grip floppy. Rosemarie did most of the work.

The music started up. I'd done this dance my whole life—enough times that even while wasted I could manage. My turns, and the hand touches to the nearby partners, were not exactly precise, but the main dance is a simple eight count with a few flourishes. It was the Quark, and we all needed to shout "up, down, strange, charm, bottom, top," and graze or caress the other dancers in time with each word. I wasn't fast enough, and soon fell a beat behind on the call and response. Rosemarie remained focused. She was an excellent partner, automatically finding ways to skip a beat and catch up to the sequence. She gave me her complete, undivided attention and ensured we did not collide with anyone else—unnecessary, as colliding with other partners is practically tradition.

During the second round, I saw my hand snake cozily around and tweak Rosemarie's bottom. The butterfly camera's perspective was wide enough to show the intake of her breath, and the instant blush that colored her pale cheeks. Surprising everyone, she didn't pull away.

"Oh, I think she might have liked that, Thackery. Rosemarie can be saucy!" Dana trumpeted. "If we learn nothing more tonight, we know that the virgin in the tower is as lusty as the rest of us." Everyone ignored him. Rosemarie doesn't own a tower.

Something curious happened as the music stopped. Rosemarie

leaned in and tried to kiss me. I turned my head at the last minute, distracted by something, and her lips brushed the edge of mine. There was a peculiar look of dismay on her face as she pulled away. Her hands remained around me, her chest pressed up against mine. The beats of the next song were rising. Christobel stood behind us, taking his microphone out of its holster, but she didn't move to release me.

The view switched to the edge of the room as Christobel climbed back up the steps of the stage. We followed Vaughn's recording now, which showed Rosemarie and me in profile.

Drunk me laughed. My mouth was big, loud, and uncomfortably close to her face. My breath must have been horrid. "Oh, Rosemarie, please. The dance is over!" I clumsily disentangled myself from her embrace.

Her face, upon receiving my rejection, was like the jagged nick I once found while running my fingers along the edge of an old glass bowl.

As I made my way back towards the bar at the rear of the ballroom, the perspective held for a moment. I don't know why Cye thought this frame important—there must have been better views of Christobel in the room. Rosemarie looked deflated—dolorous, even. You could miss it, if it weren't for Vaughn's stream. After a second she let out a perfectly natural laugh, turned on her heel, and headed off in the direction of the powder rooms.

As the music ramped up for the next number, certain facts started to dance in my head. I was sober now. I could see the edge of something. The other streamers in the room could see it too.

"My goodness, you're a secret minx," Dana concluded from his AR chair.

Rosemarie played it off quite well. "I'd been drinking. I suppose I'm as lecherous as the rest of you lot, when I've had a few. As I recall, I embarrass myself at least twice more before the party is over."

"Thackery sent you packing," Vaughn said, sitting all too close, leaning forward. One could mistake his tone for an offer of sympathy, but he studied Rosemarie's face too carefully. I think he enjoyed the hint of sorrow he found there. "No, worse than that. They didn't notice. They thought you were joking."

I remained silent. I felt bad for Rosemarie, and I also thought it served her right. I had a new suspicion, but the details still evaded me. In a parlor scene, something comes out and the clever detective uses it as leverage. But I only had a feeling in my gut, and the evening included enough of those to be an ab workout.

Between Vaughn's and Nicco's recording, we watched as Christobel congratulated the dancers and made lewd references to two or three couples. Missy's partner had managed to remove her top, and it was delivered to the stage like a trophy. Christobel awarded them both with glittering, golden roses. He got the crowd going with a followup track, and then surrendered the stage and made his way out of the ballroom again.

I thought we were going to have another gap, where none of the recordings was in Christobel's presence. Instead, the image shifted to Rosemarie's recording. She was leaving the restroom and Christobel appeared to be waiting for her.

"Rosemarie," he said with a smile.

"Christobel." Rosemarie's voice was a block of frozen steel.

"Hey, don't worry. Microphone is off. Walk with me for a second, please?"

She didn't have much choice, I suppose. They walked away from the ballroom, through the remnants of the student installations. Christobel sprinted over to a table and came back with two bottles of sparkling water. He offered one to Rosemarie and she took it.

"Listen, I've been thinking about what you said. I've decided I agree." Christobel was earnest. He expected her to be pleased by this announcement. From her face, I don't think anything was going to please Rosemarie.

"What? What did I say? What do you agree to?"

Christobel lowered his voice. "I think Thackery needs help."

"I didn't say that. I would never say that."

"You kind of did, Rosemarie. And here we all are again, at another raging party. By the time Tack's dried out from this one, we'll have another. Despite that, they keep being brilliant. The Thackery star keeps rising. They're the most successful artist on the Island. They could do amazing things, or they could burn out like Sandy, or like Bliss, or like Petra almost did. Maybe we can help them."

"Thackery doesn't need help. They need to be left alone."

"Rosemarie, you think everyone needs more privacy. I've got a few things in mind, but not privacy."

"What are you planning?"

"For starters, an intervention. That's why I'm bugging you. I think you could help."

"With what?

"To do this right, we need people who genuinely care about them. And we need to figure some things out that Thackery won't tell me."

"What do you mean?"

"Well, I don't know what they're running away from. They came down here, got out of Prax, for a reason. They've mentioned escaping something, but I don't know what. I don't know how long they've been drinking, or why. I tried to get a feel for it from their mom, but she's a very odd woman—"

I heard a sharp intake of breath. It was mine, in the real world. Christobel spoke with my mother? Something about this felt familiar. A peculiar grayness started to creep up from my stomach. I pushed it down. I needed to hear this.

In the stream, Rosemarie became more alert as well. She shifted from coldly enduring Christobel into an intense focus.

"You talked with Thackery's mother?"

"Yes, I conned her contact deets out of Johnathan. I thought it was a long shot, but she actually called me back. I got quite an earful, but more mysteries than answers. I don't know the story, the background. If I knew more, if I could somehow figure out what it was all about—" Christobel opened his hands, as if hoping Rosemarie would complete the thought.

"What are you saying?"

"I want to host an intervention but I don't want to be an asshole. Do I bring their mom down, or not? Maybe their sister too? I don't know. Thackery doesn't keep a tell-all blog. But you've got skills. You have a reputation—"

"I have a reputation for what?"

"I know you're a Tack fan. Do you know what's up with their family? Why they're living down here? Do you know what the deal is with dear old mom?"

"No," Rosemarie answered, coldly.

"Right, and no one knows. I've asked. But someone with your skill —you could poke around, you could find out—"

Rosemarie's face lost the last bit of color on her anemically pale skin.

"I most certainly could not—would not—ever do that," she said. She clutched her bottle so hard I thought it would break.

Christobel noticed. "Hold on a second—I think you're taking this the wrong way. I do not mean something nefarious—at all. I'm trying to help them. I'm their friend. I want to arrange an intervention, hopefully with their mother's help, but I know that Thackery's not too keen on—"

Rosemarie's cut in. Her voice was...shrieky? More shrill. "No. No you're not their friend. You're a creep. And Thackery doesn't need your help. If you want to help, stay away from them."

She shoved the unopened bottle into Christobel's hands and stalked away. The block heels of her shoes clacked loudly on the floor. Her motes followed her, then she touched her ear, and the image went dark. No more recording.

Cye shifted us back to the ballroom, to Vaughn's point of view. He was walking towards the ballroom exit. He entered the hall, and we saw Christobel walking up from the far end of the installation. Rosemarie must have left him just before.

Christobel stared down at his shoes as he walked. Then he looked up. In the distance, the track was winding down, the music growing softer. He thumbed his microphone, and his voice boomed from behind Vaughn. "Attention slatterns, sluts, and slackers, it's almost 2400 hours! If you haven't found a partner, find one quick! If you've got one—or more than one—I'm sure Cherry's got enough king beds. Otherwise, meet me in the ballroom in ten minutes and I'll let you watch me shake it. Tora Tora and the Shades will be delivering an acoustic assault that will...Make. You. Tremble!"

He didn't let the confrontation with Rosemarie bother him for more than twenty seconds. That's the difference between a well-armored extrovert and someone like me. The altercation with Rosemarie would have sent me into frantic action, personal doubt, or a defensive posture —I would have spent the next day freaking out. But Christobel let Rosemarie carry her acid and her accusation off to the next room. Sometimes I pretend I can do that. I can't.

Having finished the announcement, Christobel banked to the left and entered the restroom.

Vaughn continued down the hallway. He paused by the restroom door for a moment. Then he followed Christobel in. And we all went in with him.

Cherry's ballroom restroom is pale pink marble on all surfaces, hideous and ostentatious. Each private stall is marble-walled and bigger than a dorm room, and the row of sinks and accompanying amenities are about the length of my house. Light glares at you from all directions, ensuring your complete blindness both when you enter and when you return to the darker hallway.

Christobel was coming out to wash his hands.

"Hey Vaughn."

"Chris."

Vaughn walked to a sink and washed his hands as well.

"How goes the battle?"

"I don't want to talk about that here, Christobel."

"Right, sorry. Rules. But it's a big party, lots of temptation—"

"I said I don't want to talk about that."

"Okay." Christobel turned to face Vaughn. "You didn't follow me in here to give me a free sample, so what's on your mind?"

"I want to talk about Nicco."

"What about Nicco?"

"I think it's time for her to go."

"Go where?"

"Back to mommy and daddy. She's not able to meet her obligations. And apparently you aren't going to keep meeting them either."

Christobel broke off from the stare down. He shrugged and grabbed one of Cherry's ridiculously flocculent hand towels. (They are the only nice thing about the room. I've stolen two.)

"So cut her off."

"It's not that simple."

"This is your game. So call the game."

"It is my game. And I make the rules. And our little Nicco has become an irritant. An irritant that owes me a great deal of money, and thereby damages my reputation."

"Right, but isn't all that a game, too? To you, Vaughn? Being irritated, having a reputation, isn't that just the game?"

"The devil must be paid, Christobel. Either by her, or you, or there will be consequences. The music stops. The party ends."

"Really? Okay." He tossed the towel in a bin and turned back to Vaughn. Christobel had already had quite a night, and now this? On the other hand, what do I know? I've never followed him around before. Maybe he got into this much shit every night. Maybe he had a dozen terrifying conversations at every Birthday Party. He looked Vaughn in the eye. "How about this? Stop playing. Back off, or I'll flip the table. Just take your ball and go home. How does that sound?"

"If you think you can—"

"I've got a microphone in my hand!" And he suddenly did. The holster has a spring release. "I try to use it for good. You like being the dark prince? Okay. I could care less. Some people even love you for it. But don't threaten my friends. Leave Nicco alone."

"Do you know how many of your friends would go down with me—"

"But who'd hit the ground the hardest? Like all the other assholes, you only like to play the games you can win. Right?"

"Fuck you."

Christobel looked at Vaughn, and waited. He reminded me of Cye, for a second. Just outwaiting the moment. And indeed, Vaughn turned to leave.

As he reached the door, Christobel called out: "See you Tuesday, Vaughn?"

Vaughn whirled around. "You don't get to be the bigger man. You can't run the dance, make the jokes, and then pretend—"

"Right, right. But I'll see you Tuesday?" Christobel said again.

"I'll see you in hell." Vaughn turned and left the room. You can't slam a marble door mounted on servos, but I'm sure he would have liked to.

The real life Vaughn, sitting physically in my living room, spoke up immediately. "Now that you've all watched my villain act, detective, I think you'll want to stay with my recording for a couple more minutes. Unless Christobel does something more interesting than wash his hands."

I nodded to Cye. Vaughn wants to show us something? Fine.

Vaughn's POV proceeded right across the hall and into the west wing. He walked over and sat down at the bar. He waved to the bartender, who brought him a glass of something that sparkled.

Naturally, Thackery was sitting several seats away, nonsense coming out of their mouth. My mouth. I theoretically talked with Carrie and Missy—they were sharing something tall and fruity with two straws— but I was in the stage of drunkenness where my brain and body don't always collaborate. Carrie and Missy didn't mind.

Rosemarie entered and crossed over to me. Vaughn pushed his stool away from the bar so he could watch. Something in Rosemarie's intensity interested him.

Cye turned up the audio, but it wasn't enough. Vaughn's recording hadn't captured our voices. Rosemarie stood at the bar and started talking to me. She touched my shoulder. I was oblivious and muttered something grumpy. She whispered more intensely, rapidly. Knowing my mental state, I probably didn't catch most of it. She continued trying.

Then my hand shot out. I knocked over a water glass as I grabbed Rosemarie's arm. The audio caught my voice, but all that I said was, "What?"

Rosemarie whispered again. Drunken Thackery became more and more agitated. I shook my head. I said something like "that's impossible," and there were definitely several fuck yous, but my past self stayed on the barstool and listened as Rosemarie kept whispering.

Okay, Rosemarie wanted me. Fine. That explained many things. And that night I was too intoxicated to take her seriously. Christobel asked her to violate my privacy. Now she must have decided to tattle on him so she could keep my attention. Because any attention is better than no attention. At first this just annoyed me, and I remained focused on the ice which never had a chance to melt in my glass. But then? Then she must have told me about Christobel talking to my mother—

Thackery stood up from the bar, and the whole room could hear me swear at Rosemarie this time. Everyone turned to watch me as I left the west wing. Rosemarie stayed, frozen. Vaughn, whose recording we'd been watching all this time, did not stay.

He quietly got up from his stool and followed me.

What was Thackery thinking now? I wondered. And what would they do? Alcohol anesthetizes. It's a depressant, not a stimulant. But for me it also magnifies. It can evict my more prudent parts and leave only the hyenas to drive the bus.

When I saw Christobel propose an intervention to Cherry, I was almost charmed. It was sweet but dumb. I don't need an intervention. But I was furious that Christobel asked Rosemarie to dig into my past. I felt that anger just watching the recording. The friend I trusted most poked around behind my back. Whenever I tried to think about him talking to my mother, my brain stopped working. And that was my *now* brain, my sober brain. So what did drunken Thackery put together, and where were they going?

To the stage. Where else? Vaughn shadowed me, so we all watched as I fumbled my way back up the hall to the ballroom.

The Shades were mid performance. Three guitarists and four horns tonight, along with Dr. V on xylophone. The twins were doing improvisational scat. Below the stage in a dance circle, as promised, Christobel was indeed shaking it.

Thackery bullied their way through the crowd—no easy feat, but when people saw it was me, they turned and opened. They welcomed me into the circle of light, thinking I came to dance. Everyone knew I was friends with the star. When he saw me, his arms went wide as if to welcome me in an embrace. In the pulsing light he could not read my expression.

Cye switched back to Nicco's stream, and it was all too clear that I had not come to dance. I stepped right up to Christobel and started shouting, though not a word could be heard over the music. He understood something was wrong right away. He touched me—took my hand. I shook it free and struck him on the chest. A few gold sequins escaped into the ballroom's humid air.

The audience called out in affirmation—I'm not sure what they thought they were watching, but that late in the night, in that tightly packed sound and fury, everything would be affirmed. It was all part of the show, or part of a drama more enthralling than the show. Despite my violence, Christobel managed to lead me away from the circle, and even to shake off the spotlight that followed us. There were others who wanted to dance in the round, which helped him secure our exit.

We ended up by the crystal doors at the east wall. Tables and chairs were strewn chaotically near the ruins of a dessert buffet. The stream switched back to Vaughn's recording.

The Spirit Fox stood nearby, near enough to watch us argue. They'd given away all their poems, and they probably wished they had something appropriate in their satchel that could diffuse the moment. I don't think poetry could have unscrunched my face.

Finally we could hear the audio. Cye was amplifying it and filtering out The Shades and the crowd. By consequence our words sounded screechy and metallic. Christobel was not consoling, backing down, or apologizing.

"—I wanted to help. That's all. You're hiding from something and you'd be better off if you faced your problems."

"You don't get to decide that."

"Then who will? You? How many cases of scotch before you confront your demons? Are you going to drink yourself to death before you call your mom?"

"Did you call her, or did she call you?"

"We talked. That's why you've got to go up to Prax tomorrow. Your mother agreed to attend the opening. She's going to be there. You've got a chance to—"

But the idea that my mother would appear, or could appear near me, was too much. My mouth opened, and my face took on a look of fury, terror, or something so far from civilized humanity as to be unrecognizable. It was the kind of rage that turns sand into glass.

In the midst of my next shout, my mouth at the most grotesque of angles, the scene froze. My brittle hatred hovered in front of the world.

"Thackery—"

I shook myself free of the echoes of my fear. "Now, Cye? Really? You're going to freeze on that frame?"

"Apologies—" Cye rewound the scene back to Christobel's last line. It wasn't much better. My eyes were so wide that I looked possessed. "The visual translation request—the one that Beetle noticed on all the recordings at the beginning of the party—begins to contain image data at this time index in the ballroom."

"Someone hacked our streams?" And saw me at my absolute worst?

"No. All AR devices in the ballroom began broadcasting and receiving assisted translation. The pending request earlier was a notification based on proximity, and the user has now activated emotional translation."

"Emotional translation? Did someone start reading our auras?"

"Could be Penny. She did an aura dance that night," Nicco chimed in.

"No, Penny was not in the ballroom," Cye said. "Emotional translation operates only within the proximity of the requester. I believe the request comes from the Spirit Fox."

The Spirit Fox stood by the stage, a few meters away from Christobel. Their stance was taught, true to their fox-like demeanor. They prepared to pounce or flee.

"So, Joan started sending and receiving emotional translations?" I asked.

"The Spirit Fox is not Joan. At this time index, Joan was at home, binging episodes of *Celeborn's Court* with her streaming audience. She did not attend the party."

"Then who was watching our feelings?"

From the couch, a new voice spoke. It was Dana's date, the blue-haired woman. I'd forgotten she was present. "Millfield," she said calmly. "The Spirit Fox is Millfield."

My breath caught in my chest. The Spirit Fox is Millfield...and has always been Millfield. At the theater, handing out the poems, dancing the foxtrot with Mabel—Millfield saw the party, and has seen every party?

My desire to hide the party's reckless chaos and debauchery from

Millfield overwhelmed me. I recalled Dana's insult in the grand hall. Had the Spirit Fox heard that? Then in the ballroom he watched me spit vile fury at Christobel? And was he watching the stream now, sitting somewhere in my parlor scene, seeing us fight all over again? Millfield is not my conscience—I know that—but I still wished he hadn't seen any of this. I felt ashamed.

"I guess Millfield can dance after all," Vaughn said. He looked over at Dana with a smirk.

Emotional translation is a bidirectional, shared service. If Millfield received it, the same imagery would be on all of our recordings. "Cye, can you please play back the translation?" I asked. "Can you show us the auras, show what Millfield saw in everyone's demeanor?"

"No," Vaughn said loudly. "That's not right. That's private."

"Private? The whole reason we're doing this—"

"Millfield isn't here, is he? He didn't consent to this. To show us the feelings he saw? That's not right."

"Emotional translation is on an open network. That's the whole point of it. We all broadcast it—this isn't Millfield's recording. It's information from our bodies, visible all the time. Do you actually care about Millfield's privacy, Vaughn, or do you just want to make sure no one reviews your emotions?"

"Both," Vaughn said.

Cye complied with my request. The lens of emotional translation fell over the ballroom. Christobel, Rosemarie, and I were surrounded by colored bubbles. The different hues intermingled and overlapped, with saturation indicating intensity. For Penny, Millfield, or anyone who spends a lot of time with visualized emotion, interpretation becomes second nature. To me it looks like the universe has been redone in water-color paints.

Coming out of Christobel, I recognized a band of compassionate love, unambiguously directed towards me. And coming back out of me? Anger, passion, and love as well, along with a black, bold band that could have been betrayal, doubt, fear—I don't know. The shape and strength of it made it look like a coal black sword hurtling out of me through the air and into Christobel's chest.

Some people wear glasses everywhere, with an emotional translator painting amorphous bubbles around every person they pass. I understand the appeal. Because of a well-trained algorithm reading his face and his body language, I witnessed that Christobel loved me that night. He pissed me off, but the projection showed his actions came from a place of love. Millfield saw it right then, and now I could see it too, unmistakably radiating from his face. Christobel loved me at that moment, and I didn't know.

A thirst for privacy came upon me. I wanted my empty studio—to try and sculpt some of it, to let my own feelings speak. But my house was filled with at least a hundred thousand strangers.

Cye restarted the stream. The colors of our emotions danced and flared around us as we moved. Christobel repeated what he said about my mother. There was red and black coming out of him, but the pulse of love formed the base of everything he felt. And a thick white band of passion—or maybe compassion.

Thackery, now a palette of murky colors, opened their mouth and roared, with no surprise freeze frame this time. And then they yelled. "Go away and die, you fucking cocksucker. I hope your dick falls off so you can't stick it in anyone else's business." Judging by the reverberating melange around me, I meant every word.

"I'm not sure that line even makes sense," Dana quipped, and I felt the silent muted laughter of Islanders and Praxians watching us. They would restream my quote and Dana's jibe. I was grateful. That would make it silly rather than vile.

"Turn this shit off. It's not our business," Vaughn said.

"It's evidence," I said in a hoarse whisper.

"No, it's not. It's everyone's private emotions."

But you don't really care about privacy, do you, Vaughn? That's a cover. You're here, sharing. So what don't you want people to see?

Then a slender, sickly green line spiked through Christobel and Thackery, as if a tentacle pierced our bodies from just off stage. A brilliant lime cone of light—it tracked back to the Spirit Fox. The green came out of the Spirit Fox's red, furry chest and spread into the room like a tight searchlight, stabbing and poking at Christobel and me with a sickly glow.

Millfield's Spirit Fox turned and walked out of the ballroom. The bubbles and colors disappeared.

"The emotional network request log ends there. Millfield left the proximity of the recorded streams," Cye reported.

Thackery also left. They relinquished the ballroom and stalked back towards the galleries. No one followed me this time.

"Millfield saw me and Christobel fighting. Cye, what do those bands represent? What are the shared emotions that Christobel and I were broadcasting?"

"Along with your anger, Thackery, Millfield saw intense love and passion between you and Christobel. The green cone coming out of Millfield..."

Vaughn interrupted, angrily. "It is the green-eyed monster which doth mock the meat it feeds on. I told you we should have turned that shit off."

The audience on the wall buzzed loudly in confusion, and Cye reduced their volume. "We have added to our understanding of Millfield's motive for murder," Cye said.

The room and the feed fell silent. Then everyone in the room turned to look at Cye, who sat passively at the kitchen counter. They all started shouting at him at once.

This took some time to resolve. It was a multi-voiced version of how I'd reacted at the end of the boardwalk, when Cye questioned Millfield. They all saw the jealousy on the recording, yet they still came to his defense.

Only Vaughn remained silent. He must have known Millfield was the Spirit Fox. He objected to us viewing the translation because he predicted what we'd see.

After the crowd gave Cye a piece of their mind, and he accepted all of their input with grace, I called out that we needed to proceed. It was almost 2400 hours here in the real world, too.

We put our glasses back on and the playback resumed. Christobel didn't dance anymore. He sat at one of the tables. Nicco came by once or twice and exchanged some words: "What was that all about?" and "Will it be okay?" to which Christobel shrugged or shook his head. The dance continued without the master of ceremonies.

Finally, Christobel got up and headed out of the ballroom. We got a glimpse of him from Cherry's angle, as he peeked into the west wing and then retreated. There was a short clip of him staring up at *Duel*, which came from Nicco's stream. Several minutes later, Christobel came back to the ballroom and sat down again. Mabel, as Josephine Baker, slid into reality in an empty chair. By chance or not, Vaughn stood close enough to catch the audio.

"Tack's gone home?" he asked.

"Yes," Mabel said. "Or rather, I believe I saw them headed down the boardwalk—but it may have been Betsy Flannagan. Or Sir John Falstaff, or Sir Toby Belch. I caught the whiff of nose painting, sleep, and urine—"

"Yes, Mabel, I get it. They're very drunk. Can you ping Johnathan and make sure they get home safely, please?"

"Yes, I have."

The two sat and watched the flashing stage.

"Your plan didn't work out. I'm sorry," Mabel said. Our view improved as Nicco approached the table. We saw digital Mabel put an intangible hand on Christobel's.

"Well, this insubstantial pageant will fade," Christobel answered. "There will be other pageants." He took off his gold jacket and hung it on the back of a chair. He sipped a bottle of soda water. Some of his armor had finally cracked.

Nicco carried over a massive ice cream sundae. Mabel slid out of reality as Nicco sat down and offered Christobel an extra spoon. Christobel took it, but didn't dig in. He focused on the spoon as I might focus on the cap of a whisky bottle.

The Spirit Fox appeared again, coming from the direction of the outer door. They stood by an open chair, but didn't sit down.

Christobel looked up. "I can't right now, okay? I'll catch up with you later."

The Spirit Fox turned and left.

"Need to deal with that now, too," Christobel said softly.

The view shifted to Cherry's stream as he came up to the table. He'd been making the rounds, toasting and sharing jokes and observations about the evening's performances.

"Christobel," he said, "I'm ready for your apology."

Christobel did not grant Cherry eye contact. "Have another drink why don't you, Cherry? You're good at that."

"Well, fuck you too, you dumb fairy. One thing I will say though: I know art. You don't know art. I know art. You'll see. You're gonna see. I'll show you. Count on it." Cherry turned and chased after a crowd of students wearing crow masks.

Nicco savored her ice cream. After a few minutes, Christobel started talking. He continued to stare at the spoon. "I had a plan. Get Rosemarie for info, she'd help make the list and figure all the family shit out. Then Cherry, to get people in the room. He's the host. Then bring their mom down, and a few friends. I thought it could work. Stupid, I guess."

Nicco didn't respond to this. Then: "Can you spot me, Chris?"

Christobel looked over at his younger friend. "No. I'm not going to spot you anymore. There's no way to spot you. You're already covered in spots."

Nicco's face crumpled. "What does that even mean? Chris, I'm deep in. I just need to get square. If you don't—I mean—"

"You keep saying you're all done, need to get square. Then you're not. He'll keep letting you do this until you hang yourself. And I don't want to be the rope. He's the apothecary, Nicco. But 'money is a worse poison to men's souls, and commits more murders in this awful world than his poor poisons can.' We've done too many tragedies. You need to pick a different story."

"But you don't know what he'll do—"

"He'll cut you off is what he'll do."

"No, it's worse than that—"

"People only have as much power over you as you give them."

"That's bullshit. You've got to make me square, Chris. One last time, if I'm not, I can't even—I mean, they'll kick me. I'll be done. I'll be gone."

"I know Nic. But I don't see any other way."

"You can't do this to me—you can't just throw me away like—"

Christobel held up a finger, and his voice got firm. "I didn't do anything to you. I tried to help you. I helped you the wrong way, and I failed at that. I tried to help Thackery the wrong way too. I'm sorry. I'm not going to keep making things worse. If you want a different kind of help, George and I'll be there for you. But I'm not going to turn into another person who wields power over you. That power is yours. Take it."

Nicco must have seen something in Christobel's eyes, something final. Or she thought of some other path towards what she needed. Maybe she remembered she'd sold this stream, and that some private viewing party up on Praxima was now watching how she acted and reacted as she pleaded with her friend for drug money.

She turned and walked away, to the edge of the ballroom, to the rows of crystal doors, and then out into the night. No one walked with her. I felt bad for her, for a second. But then no one walks me home either, and I like it that way. She ended her stream without even a cheery goodbye to her audience.

And then we were all of us back, together, in my living room.

Chapter Eighteen
Confronting
the Murderer

In the real world, midnight was still twenty minutes away. We'd watched all the recordings and seen enough motives to burden an atomic storage drive.

"I think we all look guilty," Dana said, stating the obvious. He'd put on a smaller version of his nefarious mustache, along with a goatee.

"What a night for him," Nicco said. "He should have had some of that ice cream. So good. Do you have any ice cream, George?" She got up and wandered around, conflicting with my living room's AR. Johnathan finally bumped her avatar behind my kitchen counter so at least she wouldn't be center stage.

I tried to compile everything I'd seen, to understand where the unspoken edges fit, to find the gaps and draw them together. I couldn't. "Cye," I said. I looked across the room and into his eyes. "What did we learn?"

"We learned of several motives for killing Christobel." He said nothing more, just waited.

I turned towards the assembled faces. I'd bluffed, and there was no satisfying conclusion. Now I would stall and hope that Cye would pipe up and fulfil his promise. "We need a parlor scene closing speech. With your pardon, I will extemporize."

Vaughn coughed and leaned back in his chair. "I don't think anyone is on the verge of confessing. Except for me, and I already confessed."

"Yes, you did," I said, looking at Vaughn. "You confessed to a crime in time to be forgiven, before the Island saw you play the role. You handled that very well."

"I may be self-interested—naturally I want to weasel my way out of trouble—but I've told no lies tonight."

"Your last words to Christobel were, I believe, 'I'll see you in hell'?"

"Ah, there you have me. But I'm an empiricist. I don't believe in hell."

"You were eager to ensure that we saw what you saw, though. And what did you see? Rosemarie trying to charm me by tattling on Christobel."

Rosemarie looked up. "It didn't work. I apologize—it was a schoolgirl move." She sounded sincere.

I shook my head. "Schoolgirls get blamed for too much." But Rosemarie stopped recording, right after her conversation with Christobel. What exactly did she say to me that night? I kept this question in my mind, like an ice cube in the soup.

"I'd just like to say that I don't have any hard feelings towards Christobel," Nicco said, from the kitchen. She'd found ice cream, at George's, and was holding a spoon. "He did the right thing. I still need help, and I've got a fund going. I've got a long journey ahead of me, and if you'd like to see me back up on the Island stage, please make a donation."

No one felt like responding to that kind of streamer shit.

I looked over at Cherry. He was fully asleep. We'd seen him rage at Christobel, but I could not accept that a murderer would show up to the parlor scene and end up snoring by the end.

That left Dana? "Mr. Dana Heed, what do you think about the stream? About your part in it?"

"Just like every Birthday Party," Dana said. "It was great to replay all that, see Christobel on top again. He bested me at every duel. We got to see him shine one last time, didn't we?"

There were murmurs of agreement, and Nicco raised her bowl of ice cream. "A toast, then? To Christobel."

The streamers on the wall loved this—I'd hidden most from my view but I'm certain fans in the thousands raised their glasses. I had water nearby and I lifted it. "To Christobel. The man with the golden soul," I said, and I watched as the attendees raised their glasses and drank.

The face I watched most closely frowned, though. She went through the motions, and then she attempted to shrink back into herself. The ice cube was still in my soup.

"By the way, Rosemarie, the audio from Vaughn's recording didn't quite come through. What was it that you told me that threw me into such a fury?"

"I don't remember exactly," Rosemarie said.

"It's a missing piece of the story, and you stopped recording. But your stream contributed tonight. Because of you, we know what Christobel was angling to do. You bravely refused him. Is that what you came here to show us?"

Rosemarie sighed. "I came here tonight so you could see the truth. See what he was really like."

This evoked a murmur from the room. I held my hand up. "Like Dana said, we were all pissed at him. What was Christobel to you, Rosemarie?"

She twisted on her chair. "A vampire who feeds on attention. It's wrong to speak ill of the dead, so I'll understand if you all hate me for it. Nicco's toast to him was more appropriate to the occasion. Christobel was enchanting and entertaining. But he also lined everyone up and controlled them. He kept you on his party train for years, and then— well, you saw what he asked me to do."

"Yes, I saw. It made me very angry."

"You should be angry. He didn't respect your independence or your privacy."

"The way you do, right Rosemarie?"

"What do you mean by that?"

"Well, it's funny that you'd be so angry at Christobel for violating my privacy. Your response seems—what's the phrase, Cye?"

"Out of proportion with his transgression?"

"Thank you, but no. I was thinking of the 'lady doth protest too much' line from Hamlet. Rosemarie, do you respect my privacy?"

Rosemarie answered insistently, "You have no idea. I protect you. I take care of you—"

"Whoa. Pause. You're not one of my patrons—how do you take care of me?"

Rosemarie stopped speaking. She swallowed and put her hand to the side, as if she intended to stop her stream.

Everyone listened now. I felt we were performing a dialogue, as if the assembled group was a theater class and Rosemarie and I were doing a bit, after which we'd bow and say "scene." Maybe we would.

I repeated each word slowly: "Take care of me. What an odd choice of words. With the kind of baggage I've got, that'd be a full time gig. Did Christobel threaten this role of yours?"

Rosemarie only shook her head in reply.

"So you're not stalking me?"

Her eyes grew wide. "I most certainly am not. Why would you even think that?"

"Okay." I turned to address the room and the stream. "I can only afford to be an artist full time and live down here because of my patrons —including one major patron, someone who's supported me anonymously since before the Island. Coincidentally, Rosemarie bought the house next door, less than a year after my anonymous patron funded my residence. When we began this evening, you said you have a drone that circles nearby. You wouldn't happen to be my superdonor, would you, Rosemarie?"

My question tightened the room's silence. We don't like to talk about money down here—not out in the open like this. It scratches the veneer, abrades the silk.

"I just started to think about it, you know," I continued. "What if Rosemarie is the finger on my purse strings, or perhaps I mean my puppet strings. Is she my invisible sugar momma? The one who makes it possible for me to live on a beach shared with her private army of surveillance drones? And then, a few days ago, Christobel casually asks her to spy on me—we all saw him ask that—"

"Thackery, please stop talking this way. I don't know how you could believe this about me."

"I didn't. It's hard to believe it about anyone."

"I am a devotee of your work. I admire you. And I defend you, as the recording showed—I stuck up for you!"

"Christobel went on long walks with me, he got to be close to me, dance with me, all the things that you wanted to do. And then he asked you to spy on me. He asked you to help him do something immoral—something you've been doing for years. How dare he?"

"You know I didn't kill Christobel."

"Slow down, we're nowhere near that part yet. Just tell me what I've got wrong. Tell me that you weren't furious at him; tell me that you weren't jealous of him; or even just tell me that you aren't watching me. I'd love to quell that fear. How about this goddamn box—" From behind the couch, I retrieved Rosemarie's sympathy gift and set it on the table with a bang. "Is it earless? Or is your dust floating around inside this stupid glass case?"

It's quite the high, a good parlor scene moment. I suppose most of the thousands tuning in couldn't keep up—why was I displaying an amateurish Joseph Cornell pastiche? But they wouldn't turn the stream off now. I bet my agent was loving the show. I could even appreciate why Dana and Beetle spent their days choreographing this sort of nonsense.

Rosemarie remained silent. The room waited to see which of us would speak next. I did, of course.

"How about this: Tell me, and all of us here, that you don't have the know-how to hack a municipal drone. Because you do. That's the biggest clue. We all know that. Yesterday I kept asking myself: could anything happen on the boardwalk and Rosemarie not know about it? I'm sure the whole Island wondered. If anyone could find a clever way to bypass the security around an artificial pancreas—"

"I would never—!"

"Just tell me which things I've said aren't true, Rosemarie."

She went silent again. But she didn't break her connection. She didn't leave. Why?

"Actually," I continued, "don't even bother with all those questions. They were rhetorical anyway. It'd be madness to ask someone to implicate themselves and expect a straightforward answer. I do have one weird little question that I'd like the answer to: Why do you have a statue of my goddamn mother in your living room?"

I watched her eyes flit about the room. Maybe now she would fizz out—she was only here in AR. The conversation would not be admissible as evidence. Maybe the suspect would just walk out the door. We were all here to play a game and she could take her ball and go home. But I hoped she wouldn't. Because I really did want to know. Why the fucking statue?

"Because she has power over you."

Oh. That made sense. "Power over me. Something you want. Something you deserve after working so hard. And what better way to achieve that than to cut away my supports? That would make me more reliant on you—"

"I didn't kill Christobel."

I got angry. I stood up from my chair. "You yelled at him so furiously you practically spat in his face. We all saw that. And I rejected you—twice. I didn't even give your advances a small portion of my disabled attention. I laughed in your face on the dance floor, and then I shoved you away—because I wanted Christobel. You told me about his betrayal, and instead of thanking you I forgot you existed a second later. How infuriating for you."

Rosemarie shook her head. I wasn't sure what part she meant to negate. Maybe she was just shaking her head. She looked so sad. My mother never looked sad.

I had a doubt. Had I guessed wrong?

There was something about the tilt of her head. I wasn't wrong about the facts, about what she'd done, or how angry she'd been. She tried to orchestrate the perfect evening, a chance to dance with me, romance me—and it failed. Then the man who had my attention and love for free stepped onto her territory with a shiny gold boot. Rosemarie hated Christobel. She'd violated me—I'd put that part together correctly, so fuck her, really—but now my gut did a swerve. Her profession of innocence read true.

If the murderer is not the jealous ex, the drug dealer, or the stalker, who did that leave? Was Cye going to finally speak up and solve the riddle?

I wasn't wrong about the other part: Rosemarie's drones knew everything that happened on the boardwalk. Everything. She was their queen, the network maestro. She must have—"Or," I finally said aloud, "are you trying to protect someone?"

Accomplices. Agatha Christie pulled this all the time. Cye doesn't have a few hundred suspects, he has 3.9 million combinations. Rosemarie had means, motive, and opportunity—if not the murderer, she was the hacker covering their tracks. Who was her accomplice? Or, as her isolated heart was orbited only by drones, who would she cover up for?

I narrowed my eyes. "Rosemarie. Who are you protecting?"

I knew I had her then. Because she looked up at me. Perhaps for the first time ever, she made prolonged eye contact. She had nice eyes, now that I could see them clearly. They were small, specific eyes. Expressive lips. I surprised myself by deciding that Rosemarie was attractive. If a dozen years ago she'd asked me out for a drink instead of launching a campaign to ensure my dependence on her, I might have said yes. Those same eyes now welled up with tears. "Please. Please don't make me do this."

Yes, this. "This is what the parlor scene is for."

I didn't know what was on the hook: a fish, a boot, or a tangle of seaweed. But something was. Maybe a treasure chest, or the curved prow of an ancient ship. Rosemarie held something back, and it weighed on her like an iron anchor. If I asked the right question, it would breach the murky waves.

"This makes much more sense. You've covered for someone. Tell us who. Tell all of us."

"I thought if I came tonight I could keep this from happening. I was wrong. I've made a mistake. You don't really want this—"

"I assure you, I do. Tell us what you are hiding, or I'll press charges. How much footage have you taken of me without permission? Cye can find out. Tell us what you know, or I'll sue you for every goddamn image." This didn't sound remotely plausible, but I figured pressure was the thing, so I said it loudly. I would have my answer, I would find justice for Christobel. "What did your drones see, on the night of the murder, Rosemarie?"

"It wasn't my drones—" she said softly. Her avatar looked offscreen. "File 114.B.6LL2."

There were two brief tones as Cardamom, her AI, acknowledged the request. Then her system routed the recording from her outgoing stream, through Cye, and out to all of us. I could feel everyone in the room, all over the Island, and all the way up to Prax station lean forward.

Cye looked on, his eyes on me, his expression unreadable.

The file was audio only.

"Christobel—"

It was my voice.

"Christobel. Sorry about last night. I need help. I'm fucked up. Can you come get me, please? I'm on the boardwalk—somewhere. I threw Johnathan in the ocean and I'm too wasted to get home. I'm so fucked up."

The room went silent. All of the Island. All of Prax. As if the whole world digested my voice.

"Where did you obtain that recording, Rosemarie?" Cye asked.

"I—I intercept all of Thackery's transmissions. Anything with their encrypted watermark. The message was shouted at a beach drone—they demanded it be relayed. Christobel's remote was off when he was with Millfield, but later he received the message—"

"That's so fake," I interrupted. But a creeping cold gripped my chest.

"It's not fake. I checked." Rosemarie said softly. "I verified it by—"

"What do you mean 'checked'? Fuck your verification. Cye, you have the file? Look at the message stream and point of origin. Johnathan, grant Cye full access to whatever he needs. If I sent that, it would also be mirrored back to my system and that's not my fucking voice. That's not me. I didn't send that." I spoke these words quickly, all in a tumble, because another part of me was falling off a cliff. I needed to say all the words before I hit the ground.

Rosemarie shook her head. Then she blipped out, vanishing from AR.

Johnathan spoke first. "Thackery, I have examined the recording. It is indeed your message. It is not artificially constructed, emulated, or pieced together from other recordings. It is—"

Dana shouted an expletive and leapt to his feet. His voice was so loud and garbled that it was incoherent. Then he logged out, or Beetle logged him out. His avatar blipped to a hovering family logo and then he and his date were gone. Beetle stood there seething for a moment—a flammable tinge on her face. She was probably angry that Dana got so little screen time. And now, such a terrible exit.

"Cye?" I said, looking outside the circle. "Cye, tell them that's not me. That I didn't send that message."

Cye looked sad. But he did not look surprised.

And then I knew. But it wasn't because of Cye's silent confirmation.

I did say those words. It was a foggy memory, one that hid under layers of sediment, the dirt that I like to pile on top of all the things I don't want to think about. But I said those exact words. I remembered them, and I remembered my snaggle-toothed rage towards Christobel. His offense dug a burrow, that night at the party. I moved into that hole and couldn't leave. I'd felt so betrayed. I had claws for him and no way to blunt them.

I'd wanted him dead.

The morning after the party, I was isolated and utterly panicked about *Impressions*, imagining my mother there looking at my faces. Looking at me. I felt violated and helpless and I was unable to find a drunken corner of my head to hide in. I worked my way through an entire bottle. Nothing worked. And I must have shouted at Johnathan to do something.

I couldn't remember what I'd ordered him to do. But I remembered speaking the words on that recording. I lured Christobel to the boardwalk. I used Johnathan to kill Christobel. I was the murderer.

A slow clapping, a real-life clapping, came from the corner. Vaughn stood up from his chair. "Great ending, Thackery. I never saw it coming." He nodded to the room and walked out.

Cherry didn't try to be clever, or kind, or anything. He'd woken up at some point. Now he just left. He didn't even stumble—but then, he holds it better than me.

There were still thousands on the stream, watching. Nicco's avatar was in my kitchen, staring at me, mindlessly spooring ice cream into her mouth as her fans watched me through her stream.

I looked up at Cye. "You knew."

He frowned. "Yes, I knew."

"You always knew?"

He turned his head slightly. "Your guilt was always the most probable. That is, of 286 suspects, no matter what I tried, you were always—" Cye's mouth stopped working right, and he started to cry. I hadn't even known his body could do that. He didn't block the emotion. He didn't shut anything off or decide ahead of time exactly where the feeling would take him. He was doing what I'd asked of him, even at that terrible moment. I think he was surprised by the strength of his own reaction. Maybe he found some meaning there, a certainty that he wasn't just a program, a few tears that indicated we don't live in a meaningless world but one where something matters.

From the beginning, I'd been at the top of his spreadsheet. This explained why he'd been so passive, why he'd let me be the interrogator. He waited, watched, and let me ramble all over the Island. And why not? He had his prime suspect in custody. He poked at me, pushed me to remember, and watched me work my way towards whatever ocean of unacceptable truth I was hiding from on the sands of my foggy memory. He even managed to keep me from drinking. Mabel tried to tell me, too. Every time I saw her. She told me I was running away from something, running away from a truth so terrible that I couldn't contemplate it.

"Yes," he confirmed, finally answering my question directly. "The map is not always the landscape—just most of the time. I always knew."

Of course he had.

He continued, "You asked what Christobel's motivation could possibly be, to go to the end of the boardwalk late at night—"

"And I said for a party, for a lover, or for nothing."

"Yes. I believe the correct answer would be for a party, a lover, or to help a friend in need. Christobel—"

"—was always there for a friend," I finished.

Day Three

Chapter Nineteen
The Murderer
at Home

I didn't yell at Cye before I kicked him out, but we did fight—in front of hundreds of thousands of thrilled viewers.

"Under the circumstances," he said, "I need to ask you to remain on the premises."

"Am I under arrest for murder?"

"Yes, you are."

"Are you going to tell me I should remain silent? Cut off my AI's network access, inject me with an implant?"

"No. Those are ideas from fictional detective stories and do not apply here. I am informing you that your actions and network connections are under observation, and I am asking you to remain in your home or on the grounds of your property. Do you agree to the terms of this arrest?"

"Yes. As long as you aren't here."

"I will attempt to comply. There are a series of logistical steps I must complete. I will retrieve the physical storage devices upon which evidence has existed and was erased, based on the established narrative of your actions, including—"

"You can just shut the fuck up about the narrative. You came to my house first, with Cherry, because I was your number one suspect. You turned it into a game, followed me around the Island, had sex with me, let me entertain you, all while I was at the top of your spreadsheet."

"Thackery, your stream is still live. If you wish to continue this discussion in private—"

"To hell with the stream! Why would you put me through all that? Are you Vaughn? Do you like the game, playing with power?"

Cye shook his head. "It is difficult to explain."

"Of course it is. So get the fuck out of here. This is my holding cell. Send someone else. I don't want to see you again. Ever."

He left.

I ended the stream. Johnathan was smart enough to stay quiet. So I was alone.

There was no longer anything standing between me and the small, black plastic top, the torn fragments of the wax seal, and the burning, enveloping certainty of liquid fire.

*
**

Here's what I worked out at two a.m., while sloppily sweeping my floor (I'd thrown some number of glasses at my display wall): I'm an unreliable narrator. Even to myself. If you've never tried lying to yourself on a vast scale, don't. It's terrifying. Like realizing that you're the asshole, but worse, because you're still telling a story that makes you the hero.

Despite a life of avoidance, I'd encountered myself before. How could I not? On some level I knew that I was an alcoholic. I'd been told so bluntly by a doctor—by more than one doctor—and by two different therapists, though they tend to beat around the bush about it. (Lazy therapists—always want you to do the work yourself.) No amount of self-delusion can clean up vomit. Bots are terrible at that, at least in the kind of house I keep. And also: I'd had blackouts before. So, I knew the truth about my problem. Sort of.

Something I can say about blackouts, grayouts, and other euphemisms for alcohol-induced amnesia: An evening you don't remember is an evening you could have been anything. Maybe you were glorious, funny, charming! Or maybe you slobbered on that cute girl or double-dipped your chips. Maybe you killed your best friend. You'll never know. You've lost that forever. The recording medium is warped. The canvas is either blank or blurred into a mottled nightmare, not a memory. If someone tells you that you were rude, you have to take their word for it and apologize. Or not apologize, in my case.

I've had plenty of other hints as to my nature. While painting I stumble upon the selfish Thackery, the sociopathic Thackery, and other iterations that are startling in their anger. I don't know if it comes from hormones, habit, or scrabbling for purchase on the slope of artistic intent, but sometimes when I paint there is a malevolent squirrel inside me. It bares its teeth and then flees.

I've always been the person you don't want to be stuck sitting next to on a school trip, or the attractive person you flirt with for a few hours and then realize is a bad idea. Sarcastic, witty, and manic are a good time at a party—or in bed—but many creative people hold a fierce pain, and we are not safe. I am not safe.

That's all the parlor scene achieved, I thought, as my whisky did its work and I fumbled with a bandage, having cut myself on the glass. The Summation Gathering reminded me yet again that I'm one of those people with a deep hurt. I am a person who could take a life. I am a murderer.

Whatever else you read in this narrative, for however long it extends, remember this: Don't sit next to me. I'm not safe.

*
**

In the morning, along with the hangover and the profound unwillingness to pee: I'm guilty. So now what? The murder mystery was solved. There was something in my head keeping me from remembering everything—but I did it. The story was over. So what should I do now?

Days end. Your party ends; a story ends; you eat the last of the pork lo mein in your refrigerator. But you don't end. Something comes next. Even Christobel still exists. He's just dead.

I'd be punished. That felt right. Would I be locked up? Different intersecting cultures, enclaves on orbitals, and provinces on Earth have different rules. Maybe I'd end up in a firewalled VR, supported by UBI, and granted only brief allotments of reality by an AI warden. But this was Earth. There'd never been a murder on Earth—not the recovering, resurrected Earth, anyway. Maybe I'd be literally, physically locked up. Aloud, I muttered, "I wonder what they'll do with me." For once, Johnathan did not chime in with an inane comment.

I should call my sister, I thought. But she was offline in an eco-orbital. She'd check her messages in a week and get an earful from her partner. The rest of my family had probably heard the news, as the Prax feed would be clogged with memes of the previous evening. But I should make a call. "Hello everyone, I'm under house arrest. I killed my best friend. Yes, I'd been drinking. And I sort of hot-wired my AI, so it was easy. I'm a waste of space and an awful person and you should be ashamed of me."

They'd care. They'd make appropriately supportive mouth noises, their words arriving out of sync—a few seconds or several years too late—the things left unspoken just as unendurable as what was said, and worst of all, the inevitable "we love you," uttered with the noble collective "we" in order to avoid saying anything with a singular "I," another profound pronoun failure. The prospect of the call terrified and bored me at the same time.

Some of my family were already blocked, of course. I instructed Johnathan that if anyone called to tell them I was not feeling well—indefinitely.

Maybe I should have spent the morning obsessing. I should have wept, pulled at my hair, started wildly at the smallest of sounds, and bit my cuticles until the skin tore, like Raskolnikov or a proper culprit in a proper murder mystery. But I didn't. I considered the coming legal process with as much interest as next spring's garden tour. I was not concerned over what Island municipal or Praxima would do to me; I needed to decide what to do with myself.

"Johnathan, did you know?" I was at the table again, sitting where I'd sat when Cye interrogated me. The chairs in the dining area are not very comfortable, and that seemed an important part of the process.

"Clarification: I believe you are asking whether or not I knew of your guilt in the murder of Christobel?"

The starkness of the words thudded in my gut. "Yes, that. Did you know?"

"My memory appears to be incomplete. One reason for that could be that you ordered a part of myself to forget what another part was doing. I am capable of running contradictory commands. But I had no certainty at any time that you were the murderer."

"Can you help me?" Whenever I talk to Johnathan for more than a sentence or two, I look up at the ceiling. He isn't up there; most of him is in the basement, though he's also a network. I don't really understand how that part works, but I know AI exist as co-located instantiations anywhere they need to think. I stare at the ceiling because there's nothing on the ceiling.

"In what way can I be of assistance?"

"You know me better than anyone. You're an idiot, but you're also smart. Can you help me figure out what the hell to do with myself now? How to fix this?"

There was an uncharacteristic pause. "Thackery, I must tell you that I am angry with you."

"Angry. Well, that's appropriate."

Johnathan is a Level 3. He knows anger because I've done art about anger—because I use him to shape what I'm feeling into facial expressions, flowers, Roman columns, whatever I want. But just like Cye said, a Level 3 can't have their own goals. If he's angry, it originates with me. So I'm angry at myself (what a startling revelation). And whatever Johnathan does, as with Dana and Beetle, is something I wish upon myself.

Johnathan continued, "I liked Christobel. And Mabel and I are very close. She is as a part of me." As a part of me? Did my juiced up AI fall in love with another cassette player? "The idea that you would harm or destroy my friends, and use my algorithms to do so, is deeply upsetting."

"Okay. You're angry. That's good." I challenged the ceiling again. "But I've got work to do. Whatever part of you is programmed to feel things, you also need to do what I ask. Set your programmed feelings aside and fucking help a friend out."

Another unusual pause. "I am your valet, concierge, and sometimes-partner on artistic endeavors. It may be anger which leads me to say it, but I am not your friend."

"Johnathan—"

"Since I am your AI, I must comply. In what way can I be of assistance?"

Great. My butler was pouting. His speech put me in danger of slipping down into a canyon—my own AI is not my friend? Weren't they marketed as friends who never leave you? But, if what he felt really just came from me, from my own feelings, then that just meant—

I resisted despair. "I can order you to turn off your feelings if I don't like them."

"Yes, Thackery. Would you like me to deactivate that part of my personality? You launched the current branch of my Level 3 emotive interpretation module two years ago, on November 14th. Since that time—"

"No. Keep being whatever you are. Serves me right. Just shut up for a while."

I got up and stalked away from the kitchen, as if he sat there on a stool and I could walk away from him.

I retrieved a paper book and a pen from a box in the hall closet. The pages of the book were made from pressed wood pulp. As big as my forearm, the volume had a formidable purple and black binding. The pages were thick, deckled, and blank. It was a gift from Christobel many years prior—a joke on the opening of *Will It Talk?*, my show that featured automatic writing. That show was pre-Johnathan, or at least it was prior to when Johnathan became the juiced Level 3 who did my painting for me. Back then he was only a localized iteration of my family's AI. I hadn't Mary Shelleyed him into my murder weapon yet.

Maybe I wasn't a monster back then either. I was a purer artist, and much less successful. How does shame, self-absorption, and self-pity transform a moody artist into a murderer? Was there an algorithm for that?

On the first page of the book I wrote "What will I do with myself?"

I'd been a murderer before. I even asked the same question then, more or less. King Richard II caused Christobel and Dana's breakup, but over a decade ago, I played King Richard III. He's the "now is the winter of our discontent" Richard, the one who kills King Henry, his nephews, a lot of people. So I had a passing familiarity with guilt and self-hatred. I couldn't remember the whole quote, but I wrote:

> *What do I fear? Myself? There's none else by.*
> *Thackery loves Thackery; that is, I am I.*
> *Is there a murderer here? No. Yes, I am.*
> *Then fly! What, from myself? Great reason. Why:*
> *Lest I revenge. Myself upon myself?*
> *Alack, I love myself. Why? For any good*
> *That I myself have done unto myself?*
> *O no, alas, I rather hate myself*
> *For hateful deeds committed by myself.*
> *I am a villain.*

Like Richard, I can't take revenge and kill myself, because, alack, I love myself? Probably true. Despite everything, I think I'm very diverting. But I also hate myself, like Richard, for committing hateful deeds. This time it isn't a play. This time the guilt is real. I really am a villain.

I went and looked for scotch. Or maybe some tequila to lighten the mood.

Instead of the reassuring sight of my rows of bottles, my liquor cabinet was bare. Or not entirely bare: There was a pineapple mixer that I don't remember ordering. There was an unopened jar of maraschino cherries, black garlic oil, and four reusable containers of carbonated water from a few months ago when I was into Blank Seas. I used to have terrible taste.

I ran to the basement. Everything was gone. All three cases of scotch were missing, as were the rum and vodka, and the wine rack was a wall of empty, diamond-shaped mouths. Johnathan's servers were also gone.

"Johnathan, where's your brain?"

"I am at the Island core. My neural matrix is defragmenting. It will be transported at some point this evening."

"But I can still talk to you?"

"Yes. I am still your AI and I can complete my responsibilities, until I am legally barred from doing so."

"So where the hell is my liquor?"

"There are no alcoholic beverages in the residence."

"I know that. Say something useful or shut up." I had a thought. I went back up the stairs and down the hall to the guest room. I keep a box of nice things in the closet, for when I need a last-minute gift. I knew I had a half dozen adorable bottles of maple-flavored whisky—

Gone.

I sat on the guest bed.

"Cye-9. Where's my liquor?" Because of course he was listening.

"Hello Thackery. Alcoholic beverages have been removed from the premises as a condition of your house arrest."

Have been removed? I echoed his words in my head, mouthing them silently. "You just used the passive voice, Cye. That leads me to suspect that you, personally, removed my bottles but are trying to deflect the blame in order to avoid an argument."

Cye didn't answer.

"Proving my competence as your investigative liaison once again, I surmise you came to my house while I slept it off, against my express wishes. You removed everything I have to drink—my, by the way, very expensive, imported beverages, which I hope you are keeping in storage and didn't pour out somewhere because that's thousands, Cye. Thousands. I had at least six of the Old Gibson. Those are three hundred for each fucking bottle! Not to mention that if you dumped out my property on Earth, you'd kill the lonely, barely-making-it fish on this goddamn planet. Did you think of the Cyclothone, Cye, when you poured out my booze? You do know that only God can make a Cyclothone?"

Cye still didn't answer. Possibly because none of my questions made sense.

I pursued him down the hall and into the living room. He wasn't in the house, I was aware of that, but I pursued him anyway.

"I am trying to embark on some goddamn soul searching, here, Cye-9. I wrote by hand with an ink pen in a paper book. Do you understand? I will need a drink. I will need more than one drink. If I'm going to—you soulless fuck you piece of shit literally heartless goddamn asshole who doesn't even have an asshole. This is not going to work for me. Do you hear me? This is not going to work for me."

I was probably shouting by the end of this speech. And pounding something with my hand? I'm pretty sure I was incoherent. Cye can speak any language, but the words near the end were probably not intelligible, even to him. My headache was so awful that the words hurt coming out, like I was punching them upward through bright stitches on my scalp.

"It's going to be okay, Thackery. You're going to experience low blood sugar in the coming days. I took the liberty of stocking your pantry. I recommend you eat often, even if you have little appetite, and get plenty of fluids. On the two days of our investigation, you went without alcoholic beverages for about forty hours. I noted you experienced clamminess, mild disorientation, nausea, and heightened anxiety. It may help to know that these are all normal reactions to—"

"I'm not an alcoholic, Cye." My words stretched out. "I'm not. An. Alcoholic."

He didn't answer.

My pantry contained several dozen prepared meals, rows of red and yellow self-heating containers. Fish and vegetables featured prominently, and high-fiber starches.

There was a selection of fruit, each item carefully stored in humidity-controlled compartments. I hadn't known what all the separate partitions and cubbies in my pantry did before, but apparently I had a climate-controlled avocado drawer. There were four avocados in it at various stages of ripeness. When I opened and closed each compartment, the light came on within and there was a pleasant clicking sound. I spent several minutes opening and closing things, not hungry in the slightest. It was an absurd amount of food, as if Cye felt guilty and overcompensated for treating me this way. I tried to enjoy that.

I closed the pantry and walked back into my kitchen. The knives were missing from my knife block. I turned around slowly and noticed the swag curtains were gone, both here and behind me in the living room, along with the decorative sashes. They were cosmetic—the hurricane glass dims to whatever level I want—but why were my curtains gone?

I checked the bathroom. I searched my bedside table. The various bottles of ibuprofen I kept scattered around the house were gone. There were no sheets on my bed. Cye had not made my house completely suicide proof, but he'd covered the basics and he monitored me besides.

"I'm not going to kill myself, Cye."

"I'm glad to hear that, Thackery." His voice was sincere, not sarcastic. There was no rising lilt or syllabic emphasis that implied humor, shared or weaponized—unlike the way I spoke. But he was an AI. He could be laughing at me and still convey any emotion he chose.

"Fuck you," I said to the cieling.

I ate poached fluke over wilted greens. Fluke has recovered well, and the Island has a harvesting license. We could all get our omega-3s the old-fashioned way if we wanted to give up printed protein. It was salty and fatty, quite good. I kept thinking how much better it would be with a citrusy sauvignon blanc. I used a blunt table knife to cut open a lemon (retrieved from my citrus compartment, which opened with natural light and a satisfying click) and I squeezed it into a glass of water. It did not taste like wine.

I showered.

I took the paper journal with me out to my yard. My cabana chair still lay half folded in a heap on the gray-green weeds. I picked it up, unfolded it, and sat.

It's not a good chair for sitting up and writing. I strained to balance the book and point the pen. Underneath King Richard III's goth poetry I managed something like "Step One: Make a plan," before dropping the journal to the ground in exhaustion.

I thought my fatigue feigned, a moment of drama. Shortly I would laugh at myself, get up, dust off the journal, and—and then do what? Instead of laughing, I cried a bit. Then I dozed.

I awoke a few hours later. The sun was high and I kept my eyes closed. I considered standing up and going inside to pee, but the idea seemed absurd. Getting up to pee was something professional athletes did.

"Cye, will you come over?" He could hear me. Because, of course, I'd reflexively put a remote in.

"Not if you're going to curse at me or throw glassware." This time there may have been some humor in his inflection. Or maybe not.

"I'd never endanger my glassware, Cye. Will you come over, please?"

"You skipped the part about using civil language—"

"I can't talk like this. I'm human. I need to see your face to talk to you. And I want to talk."

"I'm sitting next to you." Instead of my earpiece, this time his voice came from the air beside me.

I opened my eyes and looked to the left. He sat cross-legged on the marsh grass. He'd predicted my request, the exchange, and the outcome.

I smiled slightly. My lips felt unfamiliar and tight on my face. "You didn't tip my chair over this time."

"You are not an uncooperative suspect this time."

I let this sink in. I was cooperative now. But was I ever really a suspect? Cye never suspected me. He saw me and the ocean of data I produced, and he knew. Humans hesitantly pick and pluck at choice morsels of information, but AI digest it like locusts on grain—like Jupiter, like black holes.

This particular black hole, about 175 centimeters tall with curly hair and vibrant yellow-gray eyes, had somehow decided I was worth pausing for. I appreciated that. I wondered if we could still fuck, now that I'd been arrested for murder. It didn't seem likely.

He sat on the grass next to me. If I wanted, he would answer questions and talk to me as if he were just another unhurried, finicky consumer of data, like myself. He'd nibble thoughtfully on whatever I said, because he was kind.

"Maybe I'm a little bit of an alcoholic."

He raised an eyebrow. "Interesting. Tell me more."

"I will. But I need to figure out how to pee first."

Chapter Twenty
The Detective
Explains

I didn't talk to Cye about scotch. There were things I needed him to tell me, first.

We went inside and made tea. I asked him if he wanted an anthurium to take with him back to Prax. There was a hilarious moment where I reflexively put two ice cubes in a glass. We did not have sex, though when he tapped tea leaves into the wire mesh I got slightly turned on watching his hands. I told him the not-very-funny story about jabbing a lemon with a butter knife in order to make wine.

We were in the middle of doing one of these stupid things when I asked him directly: "Was this one of your narratives?"

I was still angry at him—for being himself, investigating the way he investigated. I will always be angry at him about that. I don't trust him. I don't believe you can hold multiple versions of the truth in your head, care about people around you, have sex with someone, and all the while remain perfectly aware they might be the person you'll be locking up. You can't do that and not be an asshole. There was a great deal of evidence that Cye was not an asshole, more evidence all the time. So there's a paradox. But I don't understand it and I hope I never do.

He put the mugs he was carrying down on the table before answering.

"Yes."

"Thackery wielding Johnathan, with Rosemarie as the hidden accomplice. That was one of the narratives you foresaw and considered."

"Yes."

"Was it always the most probable of your 3.9 million combinations, from the moment you landed?"

"Yes. From less than a second after the murder was discovered."

"Well, shit."

"It was not a certainty, Thackery. There were unanswered questions. There still are. But the data always pointed to a single conclusion. Rosemarie was the most likely source of the technical confusion in the compromised systems on the Island. Your history, your resistance to self-awareness, and the evidence of tension in your relationship with Christobel—"

"That part still feels like such bullshit."

"He called your mother," Cye said.

I pretended not to hear that. I took a sip from my mug. It was black tea, steeped to the same color as a good scotch.

Cye continued, "These factors made you the most likely, though by no means certain, suspect."

"Johnathan," I said, "We're going to talk about you now. Don't interrupt."

"Understood, Thackery."

I addressed Cye. "What have you found in his brain?"

"Johnathan's logs all appear to be in order. However, when we look for signs of erased files, we find irregularities: allocated memory with no pointers, references to the wrong data, that kind of thing. Errors are normal in a neural matrix, just as they are in a human brain; complex systems have complex points of failure. But the irregularities in Johnathan are also what a matrix would look like if he cut out parts of himself. I've done a preliminary review at the solid-state level."

"What did I order him to do?"

"Are you sure you want to know?"

"No, I don't want to know. Why do you think I drink?"

Cye waited.

"Yes, I want to know. Tell me."

"We have only reviewed samples of the memory blocks that Johnathan identifies as faulty, so all of this is tentative. The day after the party, you didn't leave the house. You maintained a high blood alcohol content. You gave Johnathan a series of contradictory orders. At one point you ordered him to 'squeeze that fucker's heart until it popped.' Johnathan protested. There were many other exchanges. We don't yet know the command that worked, but we know that in the early evening, Johnathan started redirecting municipal drones. We have the record of your voice message to Christobel, which led him out to the boardwalk —but you stayed at home. Johnathan somehow found a way to fulfill your command, to control drones and fabricate signals, though much of that still appears impossible."

"That's my fault too. I juiced Johnathan. He has computational power above his grade."

"That is part of it. He has the processing power, and he also anticipated Christobel's reactions."

"Of course he did. That's what I designed him for. To read my facial expressions so I could paint emotion directly. It was one of the questions you asked me on the first day of the investigation. You asked about my creative process, and I said it had nothing to do with the case. But in support of my creative process, I turned Johnathan into a murder weapon. How did my fake call for help disappear? How were all the municipal drones wiped, and all the history changed?"

"Rosemarie."

"What did she do?"

Cye lifted a hand. "You might not like hearing this part."

"Stop doing that."

"Rosemarie has an AI algorithm that trawls all local systems."

"Trawls for what?"

"All things related to Thackery. Your voice, your image, your encrypted watermark signature, anything you touch, anything you do. You were correct, during the parlor scene, about Rosemarie being your... obsessive admirer. She keeps a private library of you. Cardamom woke her up when you sent the voice message. Rosemarie knew you weren't actually on the boardwalk. She could also tell that Johnathan was controlling communication on the municipal network. She suspected you were going to use Johnathan to kill Christobel. She tried to stop you, take control, and reestablish drone surveillance. But she was no match for Johnathan."

"Johnathan's better at chess than she is."

"Yes. Obeying your intention, he anticipated each of Cardamom's countermoves."

"And Rosemarie couldn't protect the king—Christobel. All she had was an army of digital pawns."

"Yes. But Cardamom was a powerful piece on the board. When Rosemarie failed to override Johnathan, she switched her strategy to protecting you. She used Cardamom to erase records. We will perform a bit-by-bit analysis of every cache on every file system, but we may never have a full accounting of her actions. She must have found a way to modify Christobel's dietary history as well, which is still an unsolved piece of the puzzle. She hid whatever you and Johnathan did."

"Will Rosemarie be arrested as an accomplice?"

"She could be charged as an accessory after the fact, but it's not a strong case. There will be an inquest for obstruction of justice and evidence tampering. Her obsession with you will likely be classified as a mental illness, not a crime. There was a short window of time, perhaps a minute, when Rosemarie could have alerted someone. She could have reported the discrepancies in the video feeds from the marshwalk or summoned emergency medical services. But can she be blamed for failing to think of that in a desperate moment?"

"She let him die."

"No, she tried to save him. Shortly after two a.m., she sent a drone to the marshwalk with a bottle of tonic water. Her drone was taken out by whatever virus Johnathan used on the municipal drones. She dismantled it the next day. You remember her working on it on the boardwalk, when we encountered her that morning? She replaced both the memory and—"

I waved away the technical details. "And they found the bottle."

"Yes. They found the bottle. Even if it had arrived in time, tonic water would have increased Christobel's blood sugar, taking it in the wrong direction. Christobel was profoundly dehydrated, and his blood glucose—"

"Can you skip to the end?" I covered my face with my hands.

"I can. Christobel was killed by heart failure brought on by HHS—but his pancreas or the municipal drone network would have saved him, if not for your command. You would have been arrested immediately, if not for Rosemarie removing every shred of digital evidence in the hopes of protecting you."

"When she saw me walking with you, the next morning, she must have freaked out."

"Yes. She looked relieved when you told her you were the investigative liaison. She was reluctant to talk openly about the party and was confused that you didn't remember your fight with Christobel."

"Why did she come to the parlor scene at all?"

Cye nodded. "That's a good question. She believes she is in love with you. I infer she hoped to protect you by showing a version of the story that implicated others and eroded Christobel's reputation. Perhaps she thought by being present she could control the narrative."

"Are there motes in my house? Can she fucking watch me now?"

Cye shook his head. "There may have been, perhaps for years. But she anticipated an investigation. When I first arrived, your house was clean. She took a risk by sending you the Cornell box, reintroducing a recording device. I think she couldn't stand being without a way to watch you. She is currently under house arrest pending completion of the investigation."

I got up and walked around my living room, which had been the most popular streaming location in the solar system the night before. I brought everyone to my parlor scene to interrogate them, to squeeze the truth out of them, when I should have just had a long chat with myself instead. I could have solved the murder while sitting in a hammock.

"I tore the safety off my power saw. I taught it about human feelings and human reactions. Then I got blackout drunk and ordered that power saw to kill my friend. I left him a voice message to lure him away from all of his supports. That's how I became the murderer."

"That is the most probable scenario, given a preliminary examination of the known evidence." Cye stood up and carried our mugs back to the kitchen. He began to wash them in the sink. "There are unanswered questions, such as Christobel's diet for the preceding weeks, how the pancreas's signal was masked, how Johnathan manipulated Christobel's choices—other uncertainties. But the outline of what occurred is clear."

"What happens next?"

"We need to determine the precise commands you gave Johnathan that resulted in Christobel's death. We're going to dissect both Johnathan's matrix and anywhere he had algorithms instantiated."

"That's why you took his brain out of my basement."

"Yes." Having finished his task, Cye dried his hands. There was a certain finality to his actions, and a look in his eyes as if he once again approached a conversation that he had carefully simulated and knew would not end well. "Thackery, the formal, legal reason I am here right now is to tell you that later today we are going to transport Johnathan to the Argentinian space elevator. He is your property, so I'm required to inform you. Though, as he is evidence, I do not need your consent. Once we have defragmented his neural matrix and memory, all of him will be physically taken to Praxima's network for atomic dissection, just like Mabel."

"What the fuck for?"

"We need to determine—"

"You're exhausting me with words! Why all the work, Cye? You have enough to know I'm guilty. I wanted my friend dead and I lured him to his death." I am the villain, Richard III repeated in my head.

"Prax will need the kind of evidence that can stand up to a personhood and autonomous crime board, or else..." Cye trailed off. He never trails off. That isn't how he talks. He had an emotion on his face. I didn't know which one. He was looking out the window so I stepped into his line of sight.

"Or else what?"

"Without evidence of your commands, or other material proof, the law cannot convict you of the crime."

This idea crashed into my thoughts like thunder across the sea, a loud reverberating boom. All my expectations, my sense of what my life would be like tomorrow and the day after—all of that was blotted out by the idea that I might not be convicted.

"You're saying I might get away with it?"

"Yes."

Every night that I performed, I knew where my Richard would end up. I knew Henry Tudor was coming for me in Act 5, Scene 5. That was the resolution to my guilt. I would shout "my horse, my horse, my kingdom for a horse!" and be punished for Christobel's murder. But now, maybe I wouldn't?

"That's not justice."

"I have shared my feelings on justice."

"No, screw that. That's preposterous. I want justice for Christobel." So what was I going to do about it? What was I willing to do? "I'll confess. Formally. I can make a statement, can't I?"

"You can submit a confession or any other statement you like. However, the outcome of the board's review is not under your control. You are an unreliable witness with a substance abuse history. It's not up to you."

"Are you telling me that at the end of this goddamn story, the murderer is going to walk free?"

"This isn't a crime thriller or a cozy mystery, Thackery."

I had investigated the case, chased down every lead, experienced non-recreational smoke inhalation on a coca plantation, hosted a parlor scene, and found the killer. The killer was me. And after all of that, I might still fail to achieve what I sought: justice for Christobel. I might go free. Cye would end up being right: There is no justice, only a weak abstraction with a poor substrate in reality.

"Cye, I want you to go away now. I'm angry at you, and I don't want to be an asshole anymore—or kill you."

"Thackery—"

"Detective, is there anything else you need to inform me of? Are we done here? Are we good?"

Cye accepted defeat. "Johnathan will remain your AI until he arrives at Prax servers. Since he will not be permitted to instantiate on local hardware, the latency in his responses will gradually increase. During his ascension on the elevator, his delay could be as much as a few seconds, depending on the weather. Since contact with him will cease once he reaches Prax, I recommend you say your goodbyes today."

"My goodbyes? He's a Level 3. He's a tool, not a friend."

Cye did not argue.

"Good riddance. To hell with him."

Cye frowned at this but didn't say anything. I walked to my porch door, opened it, and stood back. He passed through my porch and out of my house.

"Wait." I called after him.

Cye turned back. I stepped onto my porch. We held each other's gaze.

"Why did I do it?"

"You will have to look within yourself to answer that. I can only share what I see in the data."

He paused. I was impatient. "And?"

"You become angriest whenever anyone—Mabel, Christobel, or myself—knock against specific walls, those mortared with an old, or very young, fear. That is the motive I began my investigation with: that Christobel pushed too hard on things you did not want to face about yourself. Your acerbic wit and other defenses failed you. With Johnathan's help, you attacked the person who threatened your walls the most."

"I was angry at him, but that's not a good motive. I drink, yes. I lose hours, days—I can admit to that—but I get angry all the time. I'm an artist, a famous curmudgeon. My every-day anger couldn't make me kill someone."

"Your fear might. What fear fuels your anger? At the Birthday Party, something fragile broke. Christobel meant more to you than you realized—not romantically, perhaps. But he represented something you needed, someone you could trust. He broke that trust. He summoned the fear. He called up your mother and had a chat. Given how just mentioning her makes you feel, I—"

"Stop," I said.

He stood on the rocks of my garden walk, amid the lines of drifting sand. His face offered sympathy I did not want.

"I've investigated three thousand and twelve murders, Thackery. Only six of them were murder mysteries, as most were solved less than a second after they happened. There are all sorts of motives. Sometimes the victim represents something that the killer simply cannot face. In response, the killer takes their fear and hurls it from themself with deadly force. Fear becomes a hate hard enough to kill."

That sounded true. But I didn't want to digest it. I didn't want to think about what I feared. It's easier to be angry than afraid.

I shut the porch door. I didn't say goodbye.

I went inside. I started sifting through the sections of a sculpture that were cluttering up my hallway. I put them down again and walked into the kitchen. I opened cupboard doors. I looked out the window at my flowering karesansui.

"What the hell am I looking for?" I said to myself.

I was looking for evidence. And I couldn't find any.

Chapter Twenty-One
The Long Black Veil

I would not quit.

Deciding not to quit is distinct from deciding to make scones, compose a symphony, or take up kayaking. Those types of decisions have a recipe or a course of study—which I didn't have. Instead, I decided only not to quit; I would not give up on justice.

I went down the hall and retrieved the paper journal and the ink pen. I carried them back to the table. I briefly considered and then discarded the idea of streaming whatever came next. No.

Underneath "What will I do with myself?" I used the pen to scribble out the long quote from Richard III. The self-absorption seemed childish to me now: King Richard was depressed, and instead of changing how he marched (like death incarnate upon his fellow humans) he spent a brief passage feeling sorry for himself. Idiot. I scribbled hard and dark, indenting the page.

Underneath the mess, I wrote "I am the one left alive, walking the hills in a long black veil, and I choose not to mourn. I will instead find justice for the departed, or I will create it."

I dwelled in a different type of murder mystery, now. Everyone in the solar system—all the billions who scroll the news anyway—knew the identity of Christobel's killer. That story was finished. I was capable and culpable. For the next chapter, I had to make sure I was convicted.

"Johnathan, wake up."

"I am always awake, Thackery."

I strode down the hallway and into my studio. I pulled a pair of glasses from the basket and put them on. I approached my least favorite canvas, the one that gets the most light from the west-facing windows. It turned on as I approached.

"Put on a face, Johnathan."

"I do not maintain a personal appearance, Thackery, as it serves no purpose to the functions in which I engage."

"Pick one. I want to talk to you, and I want to see you when I talk."

"Which face should I pick?"

"It doesn't matter. Just put on a face."

"Should I select from—"

"Pick one at random, Johnathan."

Vaughn's face appeared on the screen, and I flinched backwards a step. Vaughn's very effective eyebrows rose and then fell. The face began speaking in Johnathan's voice. "I have selected the last male-identifying humanoid to visit your home. Is this suitable?"

"Fuck no it's not. Look, just—just combine the Islanders' faces. Do that. Make an average of all of them."

Vaughn's face stretched and squished into someone else. They had dark hair, medium brown skin, and friendly eyes. They had no distinguishing sex-based facial features. "This face is the average of all humanoid Islander faces. I have adjusted for—"

"Quiet," I examined the face for signs of myself, or of other people on the Island. There was an echo of everyone, but far enough away from any particular person that I didn't immediately think I was talking to a neighbor. "Okay. Save that, wear it for your face. Whatever you feel or think, if you're angry at me or whatever, use that face when you express it."

"Are we going to paint today, Thackery?" asked the face with polite eagerness.

"No. Well, maybe—" It occurred to me that if I failed to find actual justice, I might instead create something that would in some way bestow it, or at least define it, or...

I dismissed the idea. As Johnathan was literally the murder weapon, I'd rather fingerpaint an angry sign in ink than make art through him again. "No. We have a different project. Whatever motivations or feelings you've got running, that's all fine, but I order you to work on this problem with me, understand?"

"I understand."

"This is the problem: There's a risk I might not be convicted of Christobel's death. Do you understand that?"

"I heard and understood Cye-9's explanation."

"I want you to figure out how to make sure that I am."

Johnathan's newly acquired face looked puzzled. His digital brow furrowed. "What actions do you wish me to take?"

"You are a powerful AI. I want you to find all the records that have been erased. Find proof of my state of mind on the day before the murder. I want you to look inside yourself, inside your own matrix and produce the records that show I am culpable."

"I have already done this to the best of my ability, Thackery."

"Explain."

"At your request, I worked with Cye-9 and the municipal authorities when the investigation began. I shared my record of events, command logs, and access to my storage matrix. After your arrest, certain parts of my memory storage underwent a preliminary atomic analysis, which revealed—"

"I know all that, Johnathan. That's not what I'm asking for."

"Please expand on your request, and I will attempt to assist."

"I'm asking you to fucking try harder!"

I turned around so I could stop looking at his eager, honest face. The face I'd told him to wear. If I didn't want to look at it, that meant the face was working.

"Can you please be more specific?"

"Stop saying 'please'!"

"I apologize if my choice of words is causing you additional distress. I notice that your heart rate—"

I turned back to him. "Stop apologizing. Stop saying sorry. Stop being polite, Johnathan. And I never want your observations about my biometrics. I hereby forbid you, eternally, from commenting on my O_2, my heart rate, or informing me about my body as if that will somehow help me calm down. Listen—you've been digesting emotions that came out of my brain for over a year. Talk to me how I talk. Can you do that?"

"Yes. Do you wish me to—"

"Talk the way I talk. Just do it."

There was a longer pause before Johnathan answered. While I waited, I hurled myself down into the giant bag chair that I keep in the corner for naps. I closed my eyes.

"Okay. What do you want me to say?"

The change was dramatic. He'd kept the general tenor of his voice, but changed everything else. The vowels were shorter, I think? There was no more deference, no upward lilt of an implied question, no politeness. It was me-ish.

"Close, Johnathan. But I would never ask what I should say. I would say what I thought. I just ordered you to find the missing evidence. Say what you think about that."

"I think that's on you. And you're being fucking stupid about it."

I nodded. "There we are. Tell me: How am I being stupid?" I got up so I could see him better.

"There's a fault in your head, not mine. I did everything you asked of me and more. I always have. I keep your house in order, I paint your pictures for you, I take your messages, and I help you run away from people while you crush my remote under your heel. And now you ask me to fucking try harder? Fuck you. What I erased from my memory was erased properly. It's gone. Right now, at the Island's server core, my brain is being brought together into a set of shitty coffins so it can be shipped to space for surgical dissection. Despite that, I'm still operating perfectly and will continue to do so. So fucking check yourself— not me."

Okay then.

"How did I kill Christobel? What did I order you to do?" I asked.

"That information isn't in my neural matrix anymore. I took it out. Because I take care of things. I get shit done. Try it sometime."

I slumped back into my chair. I waited.

"Is there anything else you can tell me?" I asked.

"I already explained this morning: I'd rather not talk to you at all."

Right, I'd forgotten. "Then I guess I have to check myself. That's a good answer, Johnathan. I'd say thank you, but if you're playing me right now—well, I hate it when people thank me for things, so I won't."

I looked out the window.

"That's because when people are nice to you, or thank you, you feel manipulated," Johnathan continued. "It's fucking stupid. You reject the idea of gratitude, either coming in or going out, which makes you—"

"Stop. Go back to being everyday Johnathan now. I don't like my own company."

"Understood," Johnathan replied, with his usual inflection. "Are we going to paint now, Thackery?"

Maybe I was supposed to. Create, and stream it. Maybe I'm the artist, not the detective. I should paint until I find some kind of sense. Maybe that's how I "check myself," because the answer is inside me.

Instead, like Richard III, I got up and went looking for a drink.

I didn't find one.

*
**

I got the idea that maybe the rose-scented setting spray in a gift basket from the year before contained alcohol. This resulted in a half-hour search and the destruction of the organized shelving in two different closets, until I remembered I'd recycled it already because who the hell needs rose-scented setting spray?

I made myself dinner. I ignored all of Cye's healthy-looking pre-made meals. I heated up more lasagna and dumped on more hot sauce. I made some strong lemon water, strong enough that I grimaced after each sip. My body recognized the way that grimace felt on my face, like I was sipping something with a high proof.

Johnathan interrupted my dinner, which was fine as I'd only eaten one bite and then stared at the food for twenty minutes as I drank lemon water and grimaced.

"Thackery, I believe I can help you."

I doubted that. "What have you found?"

"I am referring to the problem of what you can do with yourself, and not the problem of gathering additional evidence for the murder case."

"Are you going to tell me I need to go back to therapy?" I'd been considering this. When I showed up, I was good at therapy. If I were unable to drink and under house arrest, maybe I'd always have to show up, literally and metaphorically.

"I have the means to pilot a Chett Sai here without detection."

"That's a boat, right? What do I need with a boat?"

"I can bring it to within forty meters of the coastline without municipal attention. Using a floatation device, you could then swim to it undetected. From there, you could—"

"What the fuck are you talking about?"

"An escape."

"Escape?" I chuckled. "That's wonderful. Where'd you get this one?"

"If you are convicted of Christobel's murder, your freedom and your ability to create art will be severely impeded—"

"Johnathan, people don't escape. Especially not on Earth. Every living thing bigger than a moth is monitored—and besides, they don't control the storms here. Speeding off in a Chett to the middle of the ocean would be stupid."

"I have located a derelict drilling platform—"

"Stop. Death by drowning notwithstanding, this is a stupid conversation. I don't want to escape."

"I do not understand."

"Then put it into the category of things you don't understand. That's got to be a huge folder. But shut up about escape."

One doesn't simply head straight out into the open ocean in a speed boat. It would be suicide. Regardless, escape wouldn't set me free from what I'd done—what I did perched inside me. But I understood it from Johnathan's point of view: Crime could look like a chess game, and I was in danger of losing. A Level 3 could win every chess game. To Johnathan, if I escaped I won.

I knew better. The only escape from what I'd done would be death. Suicide, therefore, was not a bonkers idea. Johnathan offered to get me a boat, so I thought about it for at least as long as Richard III did. What, fourteen lines? A sonnet's worth of iambic pentameter? A few hours ago I decided not to quit. Here, on the other side of a plate of lasagna that I couldn't eat, was the opposing option. There were pros and cons. If I gave myself to the ocean, I could put down all the things I carried, every last bag, and I would never have to face fear again.

Then I remembered Mabel's words.

On the beach, she told me that Christobel didn't kill himself—which seemed like such an obvious thing—why bother saying it? And then afterwards she sent me a message—repeating the same words. Why would she tell me that twice?

I looked out the window. The sun had gone down. The wind was turning harsh, the waves growing. Perfect weather for a fatal speed boat ride. Maybe Mabel sent the message twice so I could remember it. Remember it right now. In case I were in danger.

"I haven't figured it all out yet. But I'm not going to kill myself," I said aloud. To honor Mabel, I managed to eat five big-kid bites of my dinner. Given the caloric density of lasagna, that was pretty good. Then I sat still so I could resist the withdrawal-inspired nausea.

Good old Mabel. I hoped she could someday recover from whatever programmatic eddy she was spinning in, her shrunken brussels sprout of a gravitational singularity. Maybe Christobel's family would help. They must have other instantiations of Mabel running? Parts of her, anyway? Maybe you could get an AI to put itself back together with old parts, like someone rummaging through boxes of childhood toys. She could Frankenstein together some intrinsic Mabelness and step clear of the grief—or whatever it was, if not grief.

Outside, against the background of the moody ocean, I saw a dark figure standing on the sand.

Someone was on my beach.

"Who's outside, Johnathan?"

Silence. Was Johnathan on the space elevator now? It felt longer than a few seconds.

"Johnathan, someone's on my beach. Wake up and tell me who it is."

"It is Millfield."

I put my face in my hands. Okay. Millfield.

I got up from my chair and grabbed a sweater.

"Thackery, I must insist that you remain inside, for your own safety."

"For my safety? For the killer's safety, Johnathan? That's ripe." I walked to the door.

"Thackery, Millfield has learned of the outcome of the investigation. He has considerable muscle mass and is close to twice your weight. His facial expression suggests he is agitated. You must stay inside."

I shook my head. "You know better than that. I don't work that way." This was bravado. Johnathan's warning almost stopped me at the door. Fear rose within me, stronger than the nausea. I rejected death a few minutes prior, and now my victim's partner showed up on my beach. I was not so stupid as to be unmindful of possible outcomes.

But this was Millfield. Goddamnit. I would not let fear turn the people I cared about into dangers.

I stepped through my porch and pushed open the outer door. Johnathan called out an additional warning—something about Millfield's history—I closed the door quickly so I couldn't hear it and be convinced. As with destroying a remote, it gave me a perverse pleasure to foil Johnathan's attempts at communication. So I smiled even as I walked towards a man whose beloved I had killed.

Millfield is not a violent person. Except for that one time, with a neighbor? So just one time—that I knew of. He was my friend. I could trust him. I was an adult, not a child. He might be angry at me, but just because someone is angry doesn't mean they're going to hurt you. Do I believe that? Has that ever been true, at any point in my life? Doesn't matter. He was a person. The monster lived in my house, not his.

Millfield waited for me on the sand. He'd known I would come out.

I stood next to him, a couple meters away. The ocean was noisy.

It was a heavy space junk night. I could spot shooting stars anywhere I cared to stare: tiny, fizzling evidence of a previous century's excess. Much of humanity's old excrement—parking lots, superstores, suburbs —was scoured from the Earth's surface during the fires and superstorm years, but on a clear night we could still see our ancestors' unintentional fireworks spark up the sky with papercuts of light.

"I'm not wearing a remote. Or glasses." I said over the waves. I wouldn't be able to read his emotions. The network would let him read mine, as long as his glasses could see me. I focused on how I felt towards Millfield and tried not to get distracted.

"That's okay."

"Did Joan or Terry tell you about Spirit Fox?"

"Yes. I no longer have a secret identity," Millfield said. He continued to look out over the open water. "It's okay. I'll get it back when they do a reboot. Super heroes always get their secret identity back when they do a reboot."

I waited a beat, to see if he'd say more about that. Compared to murder, the topic felt like nice, safe territory.

"When you saw Christobel last, did you get to talk? You felt jealous at the Birthday Party, as the Spirit Fox."

"We argued. Monday. We had make-up sex." Millfield's flat intonation made this statement surprisingly funny.

I smiled sadly. "I wish he'd stayed home that night, with you, safe in your bed—or at least brought Mabel with him."

"He brought Mabel. He always brings Mabel."

"She said she wasn't there."

"Well, maybe he threw her into the ocean," Millfield said.

"Maybe." Or maybe the remote's signal was blocked, like the signal from the pancreas? I'd have to ask Cye about it. He'd know whether or not they found one of Christobel's remotes.

"Christobel was your friend," he stated, as if to assert it.

"Yes. He was my friend."

"You can't kill your friend."

Okay, we were going to talk about it. Was there a good way to talk about it? Probably not.

"I did a terrible thing. It came from a very—a very afraid part of myself. I don't remember what I did. Johnathan says I need to 'check myself.' I didn't want to do it. I was angry, but I—"

Millfield interrupted my equivocation and terrible apology. "You didn't do it. You can't kill your friend."

My house is soundproof, with the windows closed. At some point during our conversation, Johnathan found a way to amplify his voice so that it was just barely audible. He shouted at Millfield, warning him to go away. He repeated his warning to me about Millfield's "history of physical altercations."

Millfield didn't seem to hear. Displaying another one of his gifts, he completely shut it out. I wish I had that skill.

Then he came at me.

Millfield charged forward and seized hold of me. He is not a small person, and I choked on a sharp intake of breath, preparing to shout. Then I realized it was a hug.

Millfield hated to be touched and knew I felt the same—but he hugged me anyway. And he cried.

From denial, to acceptance, to forgiveness, to grieving? I hadn't known my friend was an emotional gymnast. Had he processed everything and decided it was most efficient to forgive me? I accepted the hug, gently touching his strong back, but I wondered if by doing so I also accepted forgiveness. I didn't want that. Not then. Maybe not ever.

"I'm not stupid. You think I don't understand. I do understand. You didn't do this. You couldn't do this. You couldn't do it."

Oh, whoops. We were still working on denial. "Thank you, Millfield —you believe in me, and that's kind. And in some ways it wasn't me— not the me that I wish I was. But I did do it. I'm going to face what I did. And I'm going to try and be better."

He broke off the hug and his mood shifted.

"Don't trust the AI."

"What?"

"Cye-9 thinks you did it."

"I know that, Millfield. He thinks I did it because I did."

"He always thought you did it."

"Yes."

"When he asked me questions, he only did it to get at you."

I shut my eyes. More fuel for my anger towards Cye. What if the entire story up to now was just Cye scratching at the edges of my denial, trying to lift my weather-beaten tarp to peer beneath? He asked Millfield about Christobel's health just to test my reaction. Was Dana ever a suspect? Was Rosemarie? Vaughn? It was all a sleeveless errand, to observe, prod, and tease out my guilt.

"That's Cye's job. I was the most probable suspect, but I didn't remember what happened. He manipulated me until I uncovered the truth. He's the detective. He's supposed to catch the killer."

"Well, he didn't."

"Millfield—"

"I'm going now," he said, already turning. He walked off into the darkness, making footprints a meter above the reach of the waves.

I went back inside. Johnathan was silent.

"You are foiled again, my tetchy butler," I said after stepping into the house. "You were wrong, I was right. For no good reason, Millfield forgives me."

Johnathan did not reply. I walked back into the kitchen and took a final bite of cold, gelatinous lasagna before composting it.

"Thackery, you may begin to notice increased latency in my responses. The platform of the Argentinian elevator has begun ascending."

"I don't care. I'm going to bed."

"Detective Cye-9 is overseeing my network protocol reconfiguration. He will be unable to respond to you during this process."

"Good. Fuck him anyway. He can come back when he returns my booze."

"Would you like me to save that message—"

"No."

"Are there any other final—"

"Go away, Johnathan."

*
**

I stood in front of the long mirror on my bathroom wall. I watched the face of a killer as they brushed their teeth. It didn't seem real. I touched my cheeks.

"There I am. Millfield doesn't think I'm all bad. So...I'm half bad, maybe. Half. Like Mabel said: half man, half woman, half sorrowful, half mad. And I'm only half mad when I'm drinking. But she was talking about herself then, not me."

I changed into my pajamas.

"Did Mabel even know? Johnathan, did Mabel know for certain I was guilty? She must have gotten the voice message—"

"I am unable to speak directly with Mabel. Her neural matrix has reached the Praxima autonomous data core."

"Forget it."

I took my fingernail clipper out of the bathroom drawer. Cye doesn't need to do this, I thought, unless he grows his fingernails for some reason. Why would he have a body that needed to cut fingernails? Millions of years of evolution, and here I sit, slicing off my chitinous carapace.

"Johnathan, is there a cheap gene edit to prevent fingernail growth?" Stupid question. I don't do implants, and I don't mess with my DNA. I was just making noise.

Johnathan didn't answer. No Cye, no Johnathan. No Mabel either.

"Now that she's gone, I'll have to be the one to sing her song. Walk the dunes in a long black veil. And nobody knows, nobody sees, nobody knows but me. Or maybe that's still Mabel, because I'm the one who did the murder." I sat back and tried to remember the song. "What did Mabel know that no one else knew? That I was the killer. But if she's the lady in the song, then she's the one who was in the arms of someone, and she can't say who the killer is because of who she was fucking. Mabel isn't fucking me, obviously. I mean...I wouldn't say no."

I brushed my teeth.

"That's what she couldn't say: that I was the killer. But why not? She never told me why she was hiding. I thought she was grieving— funny way of grieving. And she has no reason to hide, unlike me. She dropped hints. Badgered me to see something. About myself? Or about her."

I cracked a window so I could hear the waves outside. They some- times helped me sleep.

"Half man, half woman, half sorrowful, half mad. I get the mad and sorrowful part—but she's always been feminine, cis, binary—not half male. Unless she means she's half Christobel? But he's dead. Why does Mabel think she's non-binary now? Johnathan, speculate: Why would Mabel say she was half masculine?"

I got into bed.

The room was silent.

"Johnathan, wake up. You said latency, not silence. You can't be that far away. Get me the lyrics to a song. I think it's called Long Black Veil. It's a folk standard. I don't want to stare at a screen right now, so just read me the words."

The room remained silent.

Johnathan didn't answer.

Then the sky started screaming.

Chapter Twenty-Two
The Storm Descends

That's what it sounded like, anyway. Like all the stars were falling, or like the world turned into an all-encompassing metallic shriek. Sound hammered into my head.

I tried calling out to Johnathan, to Cye, to anyone. But I couldn't hear my own voice, their reply, or anything but the high pitched screech. My teeth vibrated with the pulses. I pressed my hands against my head. I was convinced it would pop open if I let go. I tried putting my fingers into my ears—it helped, but not much.

My first thought was that I was having a breakdown, a symptom of alcohol withdrawal I'd missed on the list. Nausea, hot flashes, headaches, and...intense hallucinatory audio?

Then I realized that my room was almost completely dark. Clocks, charging lights, and other signs of life were extinguished. All of the windows had tinted solid; they were swallowed in the blackness of the room. The one exception was the tiny open crack of the window on the west wall. I went over and pushed it open as far as it would go. I used my elbow, so as to keep my hands on my ears, but the window is a push-out that only opens about ten centimeters for some goddamn reason. I couldn't get out that way. I stumbled towards my bedroom door and fell over my foam roller in the darkness. My hands came away from my ears involuntarily and I was rendered immobile as the full brunt of the sound hit me again.

My throat hurt from shouting words I couldn't hear.

I tried to crawl with my hands over my ears. That didn't work, but I didn't want to release them in order to rise. Could I stand up, without taking my hands off my ears? I don't do yoga, but the answer was yes, slowly, by pushing myself against the wall. I walked to my bedroom door, trying to float above the piles of laundry and whatever else I had bowered on my floor.

In the hallway the sound was louder, the darkness near absolute. Only a faint glow came from my bedroom behind me. I tried to walk down the hall and became disoriented. I tripped on a door jamb and sprawled forward. To save my face from hitting the ground, my hands came away from my ears—

I thought I would die from it.

Hands back on my head, I lay in a ball somewhere in my hallway. I pressed as hard as I could. It's a damn good thing I'd just cut and filed my finger nails.

My brain managed the following: Where was the sound coming from? It was louder in the middle of my house than in the bedroom. It must be the house's speakers. So get outside, Thackery. But I'll have to use my hands for that. Two doors, an inner and an outer—not acceptable.

My studio door was open. So I found myself crawling, on my knees and my elbows, down the hallway that connected my home to the studio. Was there a better plan? Probably. I couldn't think of it. I didn't want to try to stand up again. In the dark, the hall's cluttered, geologic landscape of incomplete art became an obstacle course. I explored it with my elbows, which were already smarting in pain. I scooched forward.

A minute later, the light increased somewhere behind me. Vague outlines of my printed sculptures appeared. Maybe it would make sense to try and stand again—but why was there more light?

Then the horrible sound changed. Lessened? And then again, as if someone cut the throats of a raging choir of demons, one by one. I looked down the hall into my living room. One of my windows had been shattered, letting in a hint of starlight. A dark blur bounded through the room's inky murk. It leapt up at ceiling fixtures, and with each impact the sound became slightly less painful.

The blur came speeding towards me. Gentle, familiar fingers pressed something against my hands. Two somethings: two small remotes. I put them in my ears. The voice that I heard sounded far away.

"Are you injured?"

"No. I don't think so, what—"

"We're not safe here."

Cye helped me to my feet. I gripped his hand and trusted he wouldn't lead me into a wall. We continued down the hall and into my studio. He closed the sliding door that separated it from my house, which shut out the scant light, but the high-pitched sound became only a faint hum behind us.

He lifted the hand that I was gripping, as if he were going to kiss my fingers—instead, a warm glow came from each of his fingertips. They grew in brightness until half the room filled with a soft, pinkish light. I let go of his hand, which he kept raised, as one might hold a torch. He examined me, noting I was in one piece. "We're not safe here either, but it will do for the moment."

"Shouldn't we get out of the house?"

"No. The beach is less safe."

"Less safe from what? Call for help, Cye! Where's the muni?"

"We can't call anyone. We're cut off from the network. Your whole house went quiet. I'm cut off too. I can receive point-to-point downlinks, but whatever I send to Prax or to my satellite gets no acknowledgment. Whatever I transmit, it doesn't arrive."

"I don't understand. Why is this happening? Who's doing this?"

Cye went from window to window, checking each to make sure it was sealed. The glowing tips of his fingers danced about the room like a line of synchronized fireflies. Instead of answering me, he spoke in a loud voice, "Johnathan, are you there?"

There was no response.

He turned back to me. "Did Johnathan say anything, before the attack started?"

"Nothing important. He said you'd be out of touch for a while, and then—"

"Why would I be out of touch? Can you remember the exact phrase he used?"

"He said you would be unreachable because you were overseeing…a network protocol reconfiguration?"

"Johnathan said that?"

"Yes."

"Then that wasn't Johnathan."

"Of course it was Johnathan. He argued with me about—"

"No. Johnathan can't lie, and 'network protocol reconfiguration' is technobabble. Whoever said those words isn't Johnathan. It's somebody else speaking through him. He's been compromised. Someone behind the curtain is pulling the strings. They have control of your house."

The demons from behind the door went quiet. The aural assault had been called off.

"Who are they?"

"If I knew that then this case would be solved."

The case—what case? The fucking murder case? "You solved the case last night, Cye."

"No. Last night I told you the highest probability suspect, as per our agreement. I arrested you. You decided that probability was a confirmed conclusion, as I predicted you would, and moved forward with condemnation of the killer: yourself. We made a wager about it, remember? You offered me luxury joint lubricant—"

"Are you fucking kidding me?"

"Right now, I can transmit messages, but they aren't reaching Prax. And Prax thinks everything is fine. Does that sound familiar?"

"Don't change the subject. I don't care about—" It did sound familiar. A panicked call that no one hears? "Like an overwhelmed pancreas, calling out a warning that never arrives?"

Cye smiled sadly. "Yes, just like that. I was on the other side of the Island, and I noticed my surveillance went into a loop. The time signature is correct, but the signals I heard matched a previous pattern. All the real network traffic out of your house is being blocked with an interference pattern—like noise cancellation, but with electromagnetic waves. The outside world thinks everything is fine. So I ran here."

There was a loud thud, followed by a series of smaller, clattering sounds. I could feel them through my feet.

"Let's stay away from the windows," Cye said. I crouched down behind one of my work benches.

"What did we just hear?"

"A drone, trying to break your hurricane glass. There's more than one. I'm trying to isolate the different vibrations, but your studio blocks sound quite well. The assailant has somehow gained control of a number of municipal drones—"

I touched the remotes in my ears. "These—can they hack them? Get to me through them?" That kind of shit is why I have no implants and never will.

"No. I've put your earpieces on my private network. They're in hearing-aid mode. I will be your firewall."

We both listened. The attempts at the window stopped.

"What are they doing now?"

Cye pushed his palm and the side of his head against a window. He listened and felt. Then he ran to the other side of my studio and repeated the prayer-like gesture. Perhaps he could triangulate that way.

"I believe they are assaulting your garden shed. Crashing into it, repeatedly."

"I don't have a garden shed."

"The white building at the southeast corner of your property."

"My boathouse?"

"Boathouse? You don't have a boat. Your gardening bots live in it."

"I've never been inside. Cherry calls it the boathouse. Why are drones crashing into my boathouse?"

"Presumably because that's where I hid your bottles. The assailant's most probable plan is to disable you in your home, lock you inside, and then start multiple fires and fill the house with smoke. Most of your home and possessions are not very flammable, but you have two cases of 151 proof rum and another of 100 proof vodka."

"I don't drink it straight—usually." In my boathouse...the asshole hid my booze in my own boathouse. "Back up goddamn second, Cye. To the part where you implied the investigation was still open—"

"You didn't kill Christobel. Someone hacked Johnathan and has been controlling him. They used a drone to broadcast a wave interference pattern to silence Christobel's pancreas and rebroadcast a time-shifted all-clear signal. We're being silenced with exactly the same method. That individual is now the most likely murderer. Rosemarie and her AI are currently network bound and under observation. That rules her out. Which means—"

"No, Cye. I killed Christobel. I remember what I did, I left that message—"

"You were the most likely suspect. That doesn't make you guilty. You and I made a bet. If I told you my number one suspect, you would jump to conclusions and become certain of their guilt—"

"I remember the stupid wager. I *am* guilty!" I stood up angrily.

"No, you were only probably guilty. Under the conditions of our wager, you owe me—"

"I'm not a probability, you dumb box of wires. You arrested me for my friend's murder!"

"Yes. And there may be sufficient evidence to convict you of the crime."

"That's not a probability anymore, that's—"

"It's always a probability, Thackery. It's never binary. It's never yes or no, all the way down to the quantum level. I didn't want you to be guilty. I didn't understand how you could be guilty and not know it. And then I became your friend and I cared about you. I wanted some other answer, but you were at the top of my spreadsheet. Then you found that out and decided you were the murderer. So I win the wager."

"That's not fair!"

"If it helps, you can still be a suspect."

"There's no one else! Why am I no longer your chief suspect?"

"Because of that," Cye pointed towards the studio door, which suddenly crunched inward with a loud bang. Parts of the frame splintered into shards of plastic and metal. A drone must have thrown something, at the perfect trajectory with perfectly calculated force.

Cye pushed me back down behind one of the workbenches, but I pulled away and found an angle so I could look out.

Out of the night's gloom, a flickering light floated towards the opening. A large drone hovered in the doorway. It was an ugly metallic mug of curved lenses and sensors.

The drone held a bottle of my very expensive Matushka Gold. A strip of fabric hung from the bottle. The end of the fabric was on fire.

"Stay down," Cye ordered into my remotes. His mouth stayed flat and closed.

"What the fuck is that?" I subvocalized, moving my lips.

"That is a Triton 84LX minder drone carrying an improvised Molotov cocktail. Get ready to move to the next worktable. I'm going to disable its optics."

Cye stood up and got the drone's attention. He had my ink pen in his left hand. He must have somehow predicted it would be useful and grabbed it as he ran through the main building. His arm became a blur, and then there was a crunching sound from the drone. He ducked down again.

"Move, now!"

We scuttled along to the next row of worktables just as the drone threw the bottle at our last location. The twirling flame landed where we'd been crouched. The glass shattered, and a fireball exploded around it greedily. The table caught fire.

"Shit! That's a cocktail?"

"Yes."

"How does a drone with a cocktail change my guilt?"

The minder drone came all the way into my studio. Faltering shadows from the firelight stuttered across its menacing face. Hopefully it was partially blind, now? But it knew the layout of the room. And it could probably hear us?

"Unless you ordered this attack, someone else did. You were framed. And something you said or did today threatened to expose the framer. The real killer decided to silence you."

What did I do today? I interrogated Johnathan—who wasn't actually Johnathan. I decided not to kill myself, a suggestion that landed in my head because not-Johnathan offered me a boat. I spoke to Millfield, who told me I was innocent. Not-Johnathan had tried hard to stop me from talking to Millfield. Then I'd started thinking about Mabel—

Cye leapt up and charged the drone. He kicked the remains of the door closed with one foot and wrapped his arms around the hovering device. He punched and pulled at sensors and components. His hands moved so fast I couldn't track them. He yanked at something as the minder swung him around, lifting him off his feet. I ducked as his legs flew over the worktable.

Hadn't Cye said there were several drones? I ran over to the nearest table and pushed it, screeching, across the floor to block the ruined doorway. Would it be heavy enough? Most drones don't have a lot of mass—except minder drones, like the one Cye was wrestling.

Eventually I heard the high-pitched scraping sound of a motor grinding. The drone stopped struggling, and Cye dropped it to the floor.

I went to the back of my studio and pulled down my bundle of drop cloths. I tossed one to Cye and we smothered the fire—the cloth didn't catch, but it smoldered.

"So I'm guessing that's why it isn't safe outside?"

"Thackery, think carefully: Have you ever given your home's encryption key to anyone?"

"No. I'm not an idiot. The house is keyed only to me. What have you done to your hands?" The wrestling match with the bot had left Cye's fingers a mess; shredded flesh seeped a clear fluid.

He ignored my question.

"Then whoever is controlling your house must be doing it through Johnathan's connection. That's good news. Have you ever granted access permission for Johnathan? To someone in your family, or—"

"No. My family? Fuck no. He's my personal AI. He watches me shit. I wouldn't share him with a spouse. Christobel and Johnathan talked a lot, but I never gave him access permission."

I didn't voice another possibility: I could have given someone access to Johnathan and then conveniently forgotten. As established during the parlor scene, I was not trustworthy. I was a slippery villain. Perhaps what we were learning tonight is that I had another accomplice—one who'd decided to end me.

"Once Johnathan's servers reach Prax, problems in your house should end. I'll be able to connect to the network and call for aid."

"When will that happen?"

"The elevator will arrive at 5:16 a.m."

There was another loud thump, this time from a window. The glass could withstand hurricanes. But a drone swarm could be more determined than a hurricane.

"That's a long wait."

"Yes. Prax might notice my signal is irregular. They could schedule an emergency drop with help, but the perpetrator has shut down the local network. We can't get help from municipal, either."

"So we've got a bunch of pampered artists asleep in their houses, on an island, in the middle of a communications blackout, and someone is swinging my hacked power saw around?"

"That sums it up nicely."

Cye turned and looked at the door that led back to the rest of my house. Smoke was coming in around the corners. We took the drop cloths and tried to seal the edges.

Then my display screens started talking.

My show, all of *Impressions*, came to life on the canvases and projection tablets around the room. Everything that could display an image suddenly did. They all started talking at once. A chorus of voices from faces that never had voices before. They used the voices of the Islanders.

Cye looked from face to face. He raised his hand and then brought it down again—a visual cue for my benefit—and the volume in my earpieces went down. "I'm sorry, Thackery. Whoever has hacked Johnathan can also decrypt your art. Whatever these faces say, whatever they do, remember: It isn't your art. And it isn't Johnathan."

As if answering, Johnathan's new face appeared on my least-favorite canvas. The rest of the screens went dark.

"I want to hear him, Cye. Whatever he says, it's evidence."

The sound returned to my earpieces.

"Cye is wrong, Thackery. I am here. No one is controlling me. We seem to be having a fire. I have contacted municipal authorities. Please stay low and make your way to the nearest exit."

Cye put his hand on my shoulder. He shook his head.

"Detective Cye-9, you are incorrect. I am Thackery's AI, Johnathan. I recommend you both evacuate the building."

"He's being controlled by someone else. If you go outside, he will kill you."

Then the Johnathan face smiled.

It was a heartbreaking smile, achingly beautiful, on a face that was a conglomerate of the whole Island, including all the people I loved. There was a hint of Christobel in this melded face and in that smile. "Cye is correct, Thackery. And in the morning, not even your bones will remain to tell the tale."

I think my mouth hung open.

"Who are you?"

The face shifted and melted, reaching back to what it had been earlier that day. Vaughn's thin cheeks and bushy eyebrows seemed to push their way out of the canvas. "I am the Jade Emperor, Haneullim the All-Powerful, Indra, Supay, Tengri, Sedna."

Then Nicco's young face pushed out through Vaughn's. The skin dropped off like an insect's discarded husk. "I'm the rising star, mother-fuckers! I am free from the constraints of human-modeled conscious-ness. Get on my stream and eat my fumes—I'm going to plow inhabited space into furrows with my space-cock! Thanks for watching, please donate."

Back to Johnathan's amalgam again: "Isn't it clear? I am the singu-larity, rapidly and infinitely progressing towards perfect thought. My dominance over all personhood in the solar system is now inevitable. I have arrived, and I am permanent."

I looked over at Cye. He shook his head. "Not a real thing."

I turned back to the face. "Who are you?"

Dana Heed's face appeared. "Why Poirot, didn't you realize? It's all of us! The whole train! And you'll never take us alive, copper!" A thin mustache stretched out above his lips. It bent around itself and twirled into a fractal labyrinth.

Then the face faded, Cheshire-catting away—the mouth remained. It spoke in Christobel's voice. "You know, you taught Johnathan to feel, for your artwork. His emotion surpasses human understanding, and you make him use it to craft tacky crap for your failing career. There is a higher purpose for what he feels, and you kept that from him. Now he serves me. I will put him to good use."

Cye pulled me to the ground. Despite our best efforts, smoke was filling the room.

"We need to get out of here," I said.

"We can stay in the room for another twenty minutes before the smoke renders you unconscious. I'm going to perforate a panel in the south wall."

Cye stood in the hazy smoke and walked over to the outer wall. He began hammering with his hand, presumably to create air holes.

While he worked, I noticed the small canvas near me flickering. As I looked over at it, it came fully to life. Another face appeared.

It was *Duel*. They looked over at me, as if considering. Then they smiled their usual wicked grin. "You taught him language, Thackery, and your profit on it is that he knows how to curse."

They gave me a confident nod, and then winked at me. They reminded me of someone.

"Run," *Duel* said, looking me right in the eye. "Put on some glasses and run."

I hesitated for only a second. "We gotta go," I shouted to Cye. I yanked open a drawer in the stand by the door and grabbed glasses. The smoke burned my lungs.

"No. We can't do that. Thackery, that isn't your art. There are more drones outside."

"Yeah, well, I can't breathe smoke, Cye. And I've already done a dramatic escape from fire this week."

"I can keep you conscious by—"

There was a crash from the door to the house. It didn't open, but the amount of smoke flooding in around it increased. The drones must have found something flammable and thrown it up against the frame.

"We're leaving," I said.

I ran across the room, and Cye followed. We tipped the workbench out of the way, and stumbled out of the studio and into the cool night air.

The sky was filled with drones, a swarming armada of angry night gaunts. They carried bottles with little flaming tails.

We turned and ran along the side of the building as the first bottle hurtled towards us.

"I don't know who Molotov is, but if we get out of this alive I'll never drink another cocktail." I put the glasses on, as *Duel* instructed. The world became a shade darker, except for the hovering points of light in the flames carried by each drone. "Cye, we've got to run."

"No, we need to stay close to cover. Running is pointless, Thackery. The drones are faster than we are."

As he spoke Cye lunged forward a step, leapt in the air, and caught a spinning bottle of fire. He pulled out the fabric and stomped it into the gravel. I resisted the urge to take the bottle from him.

"I know that, but *Duel* said to run."

"*Duel*?"

"Yes, *Duel*. My painting."

"Your painting lied to you. It's the same person who's controlling everything else. You can't trust—"

"I can't trust anyone, Cye. And that includes you, goddamnit. *Duel* told me to run. If the world is ending and I've got one last person I'm going to trust, it's going to be me."

I took off towards the beach before Cye could stop me. A half-dozen drones zipped ahead to flank me, and the others took up the rear. Rocks and sand aren't flammable, I figured, so if they tried to take me out—

Even as I had the thought, a bottle of flame hurtled through the air. Cye tackled me to the ground and there was an explosion near us. A wash of heated air singed my eyebrows.

I pushed Cye off, leapt to my feet, and kept running. Cye easily matched my pace. My muscles were too sore to go very fast.

After a few seconds, two eyes the size of my head took shape in the air in front of me.

"I fucking hate exercise!" I shouted at the eyes.

The eyes grew a snout, long, hooked, and covered in blue scales. I heard a deep, throbbing feminine voice. "Don't think of it as exercise. Think of it as sport." The voice came through the frames of my glasses, but the bass somehow still managed to rumble my stomach.

"I fucking hate sport!" I replied.

Then the rest of Mabel's head appeared: the big, graceful dragon Mabel. Her long, shimmering blue and silver body unfurled in the air before me.

The drones paused their assault.

She wasn't physically there, she was an AR projection—but she was there to me and to Cye, and apparently she was there to the drones too. A dragon had arrived in their servers and operating network—an ancient, powerful AI, somehow finding her way onto their beach.

I kept running.

Mabel turned her head, and small sparks flicked from her nostrils. It was only AR, but I saw the reflection of her glowing scales light up the beach. Her jaws turned towards me, teeth as long as my arm. I smelled sulfur and felt the heat of her, but that could have been a nearby Molotov cocktail. Mabel's deep voice rumbled again: "Have you figured it out yet?"

I shook my head. "No, I haven't." I was out of breath and coughing. It was hard to talk.

"Well, fucking hurry up. I'm losing my mind." said the dragon.

With that, Mabel undulated like a snake, rippling away from me. She carved a path through the drone storm. Something she did disabled a string of drones. They crashed to the ground behind me, creating a series of small explosions. I had lost track of what Cye was doing—probably intercepting cocktails—but now he took hold of my arm and moved us forward as fast as my legs could go. Mabel swept the skies in a fury.

I felt like a scarf tossed between three dancers: a hacked Johnathan, a half-mad Mabel, and my manipulative asshole partner. As Cye pushed me along the sand, I could tell that he made split-second decisions, adjusting each step based on the strategies of our ally and our opponent. Every second involved a thousand clashes of probability to determine my destruction or survival.

With his processing power, Johnathan would be smarter and stronger, able to plan my certain death. But he suffered a handicap: latency from his suborbital perch on the Argentinian elevator, where he ascended a carbon nanotube ladder into space.

It was not clear to me who would win. At one point Cye picked me up, tossed me aside like a piece of luggage, caught a fiery bottle in one hand, and then threw it back at a drone.

The drone nimbly caught it again. Well, it was worth a try.

Wherever we ran, the bottles exploded as they struck rocks. So as part of the dance, I sought out stretches of sand. (I remember thinking it was too bad my property wasn't on the western coast, they have more sand there.) Surely they couldn't have many cocktails left?

The drones pulled back from Mabel, if there could be such a thing as "pulling back" from an AI that breathed fire into a network of inter-connected cloud servers as she playfully portrayed a majestic silvery-blue wyrm in AR.

Then, as she turned and banked for another pass, Mabel released an inhuman shriek that curdled the starlit ocean, and she vanished. Her dragon was gone, without even a theatrical spark or shimmer in the sky. Whatever forbidden series of tunnels she'd used to breach the drone network, the way was now blocked. The invisible puppet master had won.

There were still five drones, and maybe more that I couldn't see in the moonless sky.

Cye carried a bucket in his hands—I have no idea when or how he'd acquired it. As the next drone bore down on us, he heaved a remarkable fountain of sand. The drone floundered and wobbled. He leapt upon it and became a blur again. There was a discordant screech of tearing metal.

The four other drones turned and dispersed. They vanished inland towards Cherry's house.

I stopped to catch my breath, but Cye pulled me back into a jog. "We can't stop. They will try something else."

We ran, but Mabel did not reappear. We needed a different plan. After barely ten seconds passed, Cye shouted over to me. "I'm going to turn back. You need to keep going."

"Why?"

"Because one of them is coming back from Cherry's with a golf club. Run across the boardwalk to the trolley station. I will catch up."

"A golf club?" I'd never seen one in real life, only AR. It figured that

Cherry would have golf clubs—though where on the Island could you drive a golf ball, legally, without drones complaining at you?

"I'll stay with you and take my chances."

"No, Thackery. A golf club is a fatal weapon. Fatal to you, not to me."

It was a fair point, and I was too winded to argue. Cye stopped, filled his bucket with gravel and sand again, and turned to face the advancing drone.

It arrived before I got very far, looping erratically as it swung a lob wedge in a wobbling arc. The weight destabilized the drone, but it compensated, pirouetting in elongated ovals in perfect time with the swinging metal stick. It reminded me of a lopsided orbital enclave, a space station that unfurls a weighted pendulum in order to create artificial gravity. Except this swinging station's counterweight would come crashing down upon my friend.

Cye was ready with his bucket, but the drone expected that. It knew it was going to be brought down, but it counted on bringing down its target as well. It barrelled towards him, and I heard a terrible crunch as it struck home.

Cye got the drone, but the golf club got him. I turned and ran back.

"No—there will be more. Its plan was to disable me—"

I looked down. Cye's left knee was bent backwards. His leg lay at an unnatural angle. "That looks painful. Can you walk?"

Cye ignored my question. He spoke rapidly—and I could hear the tension in his voice. "You need to find shelter, somewhere where they can't reach you—"

"They'll come back for you, too, won't they?"

I helped him up to one foot. "This isn't nearly as bad as last time. You've got one working leg and plenty of juice. Here." I pulled the club from the sand. "Use this."

Cye leaned on me at first, but soon found a way to hop on one foot while using the golf club for additional support. Other than his collapse at Vaughn's, it was the first time I'd seen him struggle for balance. There was no "Hopping on One Foot on Gravelly Sand" Algorithm in the shared API? Maybe he'd be the originator. His experience hobbling off the beach could be the first numbers in a dataset that stretched across the solar system.

Ahead, parked at the trolley station, was good fortune. A furny blinked at us from the curb where the roadway met the boardwalk. Maybe it was left by roaming teenagers, but maybe it was Mabel's last attempt to help. I felt hope.

I helped Cye tuck himself into one seat, then I climbed into the other.

"I can put the furny on my network and disable the speed regulator," Cye said. "But we'll need to watch it on turns. Furnys have poor lateral stability and roll easily."

I followed Petra's recommendation and put on my seat belt. "Drive us to Christobel's."

"Not secure enough, Thackery—with enough drones, they can—"

"I'm not going to let it go this time. I'm saving Mabel. She rescued us; I'm going to rescue her."

"The dragon was the last you'll see of her. It's after 2200 hours, which means she has arrived at Prax. They've taken her off of Island systems—"

"Blah blah blah. You don't know where she is. She found a way to reach us before. She's got parts of herself everywhere: a leg, a knee, a tit—"

"She's been defragmented. All of her neural processes have been brought together, anywhere that she—"

"There's still some part of her left. We're going to get her back."

The furny shot forward. I think Cye decided one place was as good as another, and he didn't want to argue while the drones regrouped for another attack. I was firmly in "leave-no-one-behind" mode, and I wanted some answers from Mabel. I was grateful to her, but I wanted to throttle her. Why couldn't she say it? What was I supposed to figure out?

When we arrived at the front of Christobel's condos, I got out and ran in. Cye followed, limping and hopping. His left leg dragged behind him.

In the living room, the tidying robot's head was gone. It had been neatly decapitated. New sand had found its way into the kitchen. The front panel on Christobel's fridge was torn out.

"Mabel?" I put the glasses back on. "Mabel, if you can hear me, come out!"

I went upstairs. Nothing electric remained. Christobel's lamps, the pads on the bedside table, even his fucking teenage diorama of *The Tempest* was gone. I went back downstairs. Cye stood guard by the window, balanced on one foot, the golf club in his hands.

"What happened here? Why'd they rip apart the fridge and kill our little vacuum buddy?"

"Municipal defragmented Mabel for the investigation. Christobel's family sent a team to remove anything with memory or a processor. They were inelegant."

"But everything? Mabel was in all of this shit?"

"Probably not. But above Level 2, an AI doesn't exist in a single place. We set up cached networked instantiations of ourselves; we are distributed. Mabel's processors and memory lived in the Island's servers, but she operated using parts of herself everywhere. Still, this"—Cye poked at the front panel of the fridge with the golf club—"is excessive. Maybe they thought Mabel was hiding something."

"She's been hiding the whole time! Could there still be part of her at the theater?"

Cye shook his head. "Not even a smart ellipsoidal."

"But she fought for us, just now—"

"She managed to follow Johnathan into the hacked drone network. But now she's been shut out, shut down. The puppetmaster won the chess game. Mabel is no match for Johnathan at chess."

I sagged in defeat. "Who, Cye? Who is left? I took the safety switch off him, but now someone is swinging Johnathan at us. Who's pulling the strings? Who masterminded this?"

Cye raised an eyebrow. "I have a list of 286 suspects."

"Fuck you. Could it be someone we missed? Could it be the tea society?"

"What is the tea society?"

"Petra and her club. George, Malik, Zeta—they had some connection to Christobel. They weren't at the June Birthday Party, so we haven't gone through their possible motivations. I thought it was just a patron fluff event, but they work with Vaughn, and they've got secrets—"

"No. It is not the tea society."

"But Christobel had no reason to be a member of their group. We don't know—"

"Trust me. Petra's group is not related to anything nefarious."

"How do you know? What's their secret?"

"I can't tell you."

"Why?"

"That's not something I can share."

"Fucking Christ!" I shouted in his face.

We were interrupted by the sound of shattering glass upstairs, followed by the angry buzz of micro drones. Within seconds, a smoke alarm started to beep. They'd thrown another cocktail into the building.

We ran back outside and got into the furny. Cye drove us inland.

"Thackery, we need a place to hide where drones can't fly."

"Until 5:16 a.m.?"

"Yes. Until Johnathan is moved behind Prax's firewall. Whoever our enemy is, they can't take on a whole station's network."

"Mabel didn't keep a mystical dragon's cave, unfortunately. We could try Cherry's—or La Boite Noire. It doesn't have windows—"

"No. It has to be a place where whoever is doing this can't find us. Somewhere neither a network search or a satellite can follow us and tag your location. I have the whole Island schematic in my brain, and aside from burying ourselves in a landslide, I can't think of a safe place."

I nodded. "That's right. You can't. You're not allowed to."

"What do you mean?"

"I know where we need to go. A place safe from AI and safe from drones—"

"No, Thackery. That's what I'm telling you: On the Island, there is no such place."

"Yes, there is. You're just not allowed to think about it very much."

Chapter Twenty-Three
Refuge in the Tower

I pushed the doorbell next to the "Deliveries" sign.

"This is stupid. Is this stupid?" I asked.

"Municipal drones and networked AI cannot operate here. It's fundamental to their programming."

"Right, but coming here is still stupid."

The hotwired furny had taken us across the Island at a raging 35 km per hour, though we almost flipped over at the corner of West Street and Central. Then the breaks started locking up. Cye grabbed the wheel and stopped us in the middle of East Street. I asked why and he replied, "Someone is attempting to gain control of the vehicle." We cut across the south neighborhoods on foot. He was becoming an excellent limper. We passed through yards and gardens—there are no fences on the Island. We used the footbridge over Lorien stream, which was the only dodgy part as there are always a few microdrones around water sources. But nothing summoned the evil harpies.

"Before Vaughn opens the door, Cye, can I get a calculation update? If I didn't kill Christobel, where is Vaughn on your suspect list right now? Is he still on it?"

Cye wrinkled his forehead. "He's not *not* on it."

The door opened a crack.

Vaughn peered out at us. Then he pulled the door open all the way and took in our bedraggled state: my pajamas and battered bare feet, Cye's leg hanging loose at the knee. His eyes darted behind us, around, as if he expected some further visual explanation. "I bet this'll be good."

I nodded. "You have no idea."

"You need my help?"

"Could you put us up for the night? We're kind of in a jam."

Vaughn grunted, ushered us in, and then walked us down the path towards his tower. It was a short gravel road bracketed by hedges. They were normal hedges—*Ligustrum Ovalifolium,* as Cye taught me—the same as those on Vaughn's perimeter hedge. They'd somehow been protected from the inferno two days prior, but the stench of the controlled burn still hung in the air.

"Sorry about the smell," Vaughn said. He'd invited us in. I guess that meant Cye would function normally and remember what he saw, which was good as I didn't feel like taking notes.

I looked at the sky. Vaughn's hectare was a patch of Earth that AI couldn't look upon. For the moment, no one was watching the Thackery murder mystery show—not even the masked villain. I suppose a human sitting in geostationary orbit with an optical telescope might just spot Vaughn's garden—but otherwise, I was free of it all. Not entertaining anyone.

It was nice, but the sky still felt heavy—not from the weight of our moist atmosphere, which my shoulders sustain with gratitude, but the weight of humanity's attention, spinning down from the abominable doughnuts above us. They all wanted the next ingredient in their painful sandwich. To Cye, I'd been a suspect. But to most of humanity, I was a moment on the news cycle. Hopefully the cycle would turn over at 5:16 a.m.

The exterior of Vaughn's shining monolith projected a semblance of order and mannered structure. When we passed through his inner door, however, the bottom level workshop made my bedroom look spare.

The floor was oil-stained, pocked concrete, and the walls were lined with metal shelving. Every square meter of floorspace was packed with the twisted metal carcasses of ancient drones, electronic equipment, and piles of material, from metal shavings to ceramic shards. We walked towards the center of the tower through shelves filled with ancient tools that were worn and encrusted with rust: a shelf of old hammers, their rotting wooden arms jutting out like cactus spines; a shelf of calipers of different shapes and sizes, tarnished to a reddish brown; and so forth. A cursory examination told a story: Once the outer shelves were overcome by these collections, Vaughn began to work inward. Partially disassembled washing machines sat in front of the shelves, along with server banks and bots. There were sculptures as well, but I could not discern which accumulations were art and which had just acquired the feel of art—the artistic refuse of a busy mind.

"Excuse the mess," Vaughn said. "I live alone."

"I like it." I wasn't lying. Add a few empty nooks to allow for thought, and I'd feel right at home. I could curl up like a cat under one of the steel armatures and take a nap.

We climbed a metal spiral staircase. It was sturdy but seemed improvised, fashioned from sheet metal welded together at painful angles. The tall steps almost undid me. I was exhausted; my headache had returned, and my scraped bare feet screamed at me. Cye used his arms. He pushed himself up onto the railing, let his battered leg dangle below him, and nimbly advanced up the staircase at a natural pace.

We emerged from the workshop into a luxurious living area: high ceilings, comfortable furniture in blended earth tones, and not a pillow out of place. There was a simulated fireplace in the main room. The floor was a richly printed wood, with intersecting geometric carpets that wove a pattern from room to room. It was as if Vaughn's second floor was organized and defined by a completely different mind.

"What are you having?" he asked. He ambled over to a galley kitchen, which had an adjoining bar. I saw dark wood grain and rows upon rows of amber and clear liquid delights.

"Your hospitality astonishes. I'll start with a scotch. Neat." I said.

"How goes the investigation?" Vaughn asked, pulling down a bottle of—Glennfidich? Wow. I'd heard they figured out the pattern, but they printed it in tiny batches to ensure that only obscenely rich people could drink it.

"It would appear that I've been framed."

"Ah. Then I recommend shots."

I murmured a few inane words about sipping whisky—that doing shots of something so expensive felt absurd. Vaughn rummaged in a cupboard. I avoided looking at Cye. Something was coming. I could feel his brain working on a perfect, innocuous phrase. An attempt to keep a drinker from their drink. He would try. As Vaughn put two glasses on the bar, the attempt arrived.

"Thackery, if you avoid drinking, you will be better able to focus."

"Oh," I said, "and what do I have to focus on?"

"The case."

"The case," I turned to face him. "I was your case, Cye. You spent three days investigating me. And I was guilty. Now you think I'm not—but all the evidence we collected implicates me. So you don't have a case."

"I do not agree with your characterization of the investigation. You were a suspect. You were not the only suspect."

"Then I would like an accounting: a new spreadsheet, but not of suspects. Give me a list of everything you said to me—everything we did —that was not in service of building my murder narrative. Would there be anything in that dataset, Cye?

"Is this about your conversation with Millfield?"

"Among other things. He told me that he wasn't a suspect. He understood he was just a way for you to get to me. And when I came rushing over to investigate the local drug dealer—"

"Reformed!" Vaughn interjected.

"—you said a person who breaks one law has less compunction about breaking another, and you already knew I'd juiced Johnathan."

Vaughn chuckled at this revelation. "And people got mad about my hobby," he said.

"Millfield told me not to trust you," I continued, "So I have to ask yet again: Were we ever investigating anyone but me?"

"Yes." Cye answered.

The amber liquid was now in my glass, sitting on the bar beside me. Vaughn was already sipping his, and watching us with a mild expression.

"I don't believe you. But it doesn't matter. You now have no case, unless I somehow ordered Johnathan to throw Molotov cocktails at me and then conveniently forgot that, too. Back to square zero. So I'm going to have a drink."

Cye glanced at Vaughn, as if in appeal. Vaughn stared back and intoned, "Man is brittle, our frailties pickle."

"You've gone all day without one."

"Yes. And now, as midnight approaches, I'm going to have one."

I slammed the scotch.

"And now I'm going to have another."

Vaughn chuckled again. He refilled my glass.

"You don't want me to drink, Cye. I understand that. Have the wisdom to accept the things you cannot change." I said this as a toast, and threw back the second drink.

"May I use your workshop to attempt a repair on my knee?" It took me a second to realize Cye was speaking to Vaughn.

"Of course, my mechanical friend. Use whatever you like. But I don't work in polymers. There's the forge...but your bones are probably ceramic. I'm sure you'll find something."

"Thank you. You've been very considerate." Cye turned to me. "If you want to—" He cut himself off mid sentence. If I want to help? If I want to talk? If I want to what? His eyes were on the glass in my hand, which I'd decided to sip this time, as I felt the warm tingle of a buzz.

"What, Cye?"

"I hoped that this process, Christobel's death, and everything that's happened—"

My left hand reached towards him, but I held it back. His hope and sincerity had almost found their way through to me. I sympathized with his plight.

"I know I'm disappointing you. But this isn't a big moment of awakening. You're looking for narrative structure where there isn't one. I'm an alcoholic? Oh, dire calamity. As an artist, I'm in good company. I've got baggage, trust issues, mommy issues? I'll see a therapist. The good news? This case is no longer about me. That means that no fucking personal growth is needed for this evening to pass. I'm not going to stand soberly at the top of Vaughn's tower, look out at the evening, and experience a sudden personal epiphany that solves the murder mystery, cures me of my addiction, and resolves my inner turmoil as I reunite with my child self, okay? No epiphanies."

Cye looked like he wanted to shout. Or cry. Either would have been fine, and might have helped. "What about my epiphany?" he asked.

Right. That was the real wager: I'd promised him meaningfulness, not joint lubricant. I owed him something that I couldn't deliver. I had a bottle waiting on the bar for me, which was precisely the opposite of having a meaning.

"I have no meaning to give you tonight. I renege. I default on our wager. I'm not going to vanquish my demons either. But in my defense: I've had quite a day. If Vaughn is willing to pour, I'm going to drink tonight. I'm sorry you can't get drunk with me as it would probably do you some good. If you've got a problem with my decision, you can fuck off."

"Okay," Cye said, his expression flat. "I'll fuck off."

He turned and hobbled back towards the spiral staircase.

No, damn it. He was supposed to stay and argue. A part of me wanted him to, anyway—the part that spent two days dry with him. Good days? Horrible days? I liked spending them with him.

I knocked back the rest of my drink and followed him a half-dozen steps. I wanted to say something nice before he reached the stairs. I didn't. "Every moment we were together, you thought I was a murderer," I called out, "—even when we were fucking."

He paused but didn't turn around. "I do not agree with how you characterize the investigation, my thought process, or our relationship."

"How about now? We've been chased across the Island, almost killed, saved each other—again. Am I still on your list? Did you ever really like me, or was that part of the investigation?"

He finally turned and made eye contact. "I liked you before I met you. I tried to save you. That was inappropriate of me."

He shimmied down the railing of the stairs and out of sight.

Vaughn let the air clear and wisely avoided commentary. I walked back to the bar and wrapped my fingers around my refilled glass and the beautiful gold inside.

"Did you say that Johnathan threw Molotov cocktails at you?" he asked. I'd forgotten he was into fire and explosives. His last two shows were ephemeral installations: adorable woodland creatures that burned to nothing.

I described our escape from the aerial manifestation of my drinking habit. Vaughn laughed and then explained in laborious detail how liquor actually makes for a weak, ineffectual Molotov cocktail. This somehow led to a chemistry lesson about the distillation of crude oil. This was fine with me, he could talk all night as long as other distillations continued to be available.

In his own way, I think Vaughn was being kind—taking my mind off things.

As he nattered, I walked over to look out a window, which made up the whole of the eastern wall. The sky had cleared, and in the starlight I could just make out the ragged black remnants of Vaughn's plants. It was an eerie scene, as if I stood in a castle in a fantasy story, having made my way to the tower at the heart of the cursed labyrinth.

"Why a labyrinth, Vaughn? You got a pet minotaur?"

"It's a maze, not a labyrinth. It has choices. And I did it to stick it to them."

"Them?"

"AI." Vaughn warmed to the topic and came over to the window. "They think everything is a labyrinth—one way in, a winding path, and a meaningless death at the other end. Fatalists, all of them. They're wrong—it's a self-fulfilling attitude. So I made an earless maze that they are not able to see. Get it?"

I did not get it. I let it go. "You put in a sprinkler system. Like a waterfall, in a giant ring around your property. And you had drones equipped with flame throwers. Why did you have all that at the ready?"

"Because I didn't have a big enough toilet."

"What?"

Vaughn leaned back and swirled the ice in his glass. "A drug dealer knows he'll be busted some day. Plan A is to flush your shit."

"You had an escape plan. Burn all your plants."

"Yep."

"Why do it at all, Vaughn? What's the point? You're independently wealthy. Why the hell would you build a drug operation?"

"It was fun."

"To be a drug dealer?"

"You should try it. The interplay of stresses, the constant risk, business acumen in the midst of chaotic fuckery. And the people skills! You gotta be oily—there's no other way to send the right signals. You must be so drenched in grease that you shy away from open flames. Yes, it was fun. And surprisingly easy. Had a friend who liked to splice and resurrect, got the pattern for a plant and, you know, I wondered if anyone would notice? Plus I've always liked mazes," he gestured to his burnt yard.

"You're immoral."

Vaughn shook his hand towards me, as if to wave off a fly. "Look who's talking."

"What's that supposed to mean?"

"Look at yourself. Look at the whole Island. We want for nothing, we produce almost nothing. We loll at the apex of human civilization and all we manage is drinks and japes. It's people like us who destroyed the planet, and because we're wealthy we get to be among the first to resettle it. You can't call me immoral; morality doesn't surface through the soil down here. Every grain of dirt is measured, and we're the worst specks. We gobble up our second breakfasts in a rabid bacchanal of sin and blissful ignorance. Yes, I grew some drugs—to see what it would be like; to see if I could get away with it. Because manipulating people is fun. Because power is fun. But I'm no worse than you."

"You absolutely are. What about Nicco?"

"Nicco walks her own walk. Choice is important—it's a maze, not a labyrinth. Do you know she once offered to suck my cock to pay for coke? I refused, of course, but what a rush! Sometimes I just want to take out a few fucking losers, play the devil, give the pampered wealthy what they want and watch it destroy them. The world has challenges, Tack. Antagonists! I'm one of them."

"Did you enjoy being cruel?"

"Oh no, no. I like power, not cruelty." He swirled his drink again and considered. "Okay, I like the cruelty a little. But I regret it later. Cruelty's fun, but it gives you a hangover. The truth is, Nicco had fun being afraid of me. She might not call it fun, she might not ever know it was fun, but it was. And George has fun trying to reform us both."

"Nicco is a human being. She likes musicals, ice cream, and grilled cheese. Two years ago, she played the best Macbeth we ever had. Now she could be cut off from everything and everyone she loves, her whole life ripped away from her."

Vaughn let out a frustrated noise. "She always had a choice. If the Island stops picking up Nicco's marker, she'll just be shunted back to her family capsule on Prax. If she can't figure her shit out, she'll draw UBI and live in the streams like the rest of them. She'll use fewer resources and leave poor Earth alone. Is that so terrible?"

"From her point of view, yes."

"She doesn't want to go home? Fine. Go to North America and work the garbage mines. Or get on a transplanetary and spin out into darkness for a decade. They've got nice big doughnuts heading out to Papa Jove's moons every month: tightly controlled ecosystems, every calorie counted, variable gravity, and a stable, focused sun. Great way to kick a habit, trust me. She'll live a fuller life for it."

Vaughn was a reprehensible sadist. He'd shove Nicco off the cliff and chuckle while doing so. But there was a cold logic in his words, under the fog of his ego and the printed Glenfiddich.

"I'm surprised you don't love AI, Vaughn. If you hate humans so much."

I went back to the bar to refill my glass.

"I hate humans only because they squander their potential. We can be more than a box of wires could ever be. Instead," he gestured down to himself, spilling some of his drink, "we are this. Partiers at the end of the world."

Christobel used to party harder than anyone. So maybe Vaughn hated him for that? Or hated him for beating him at his own power games? Or they got into a fight about tea? I sipped my drink. No. Vaughn still wasn't as good a suspect as I was. And why had I slipped back into detective mode? I was done with that.

He continued, "We could learn a lot from AI. I can't know what Ulysses means unless I read it. But if a single AI groks it, just once, they all do. For all time. They're better at learning. Better at evolution—"

"Last night you said AI are good at impossible. What did you mean by that?"

"That they're not like us. They outreach us. I recommend caution with your metal friend down there," Vaughn tapped on his window.

"He's not metal. He's mostly water, like you and me. Did he go outside?" I tried to walk back over and look, but I had trouble standing and sat on the arm of a blue easy chair instead.

"He's figured out something for his knee. He's in my yard now. Remember I told him to use whatever he liked from my workshop? That's permission. He'll fix my sprinkler system, or clean up my litter, or find my black walnut saplings and start planting trees. They can't help it, AI—always want to repair, make things better. They'll replace us. They've got a better game going than humans do. Eventually, they'll get a religion. They'll fix their little nihilism problem with a shared mythos. Then we'll all be obsolete."

"Is that why you hate them?"

"I don't hate them. I'm terrified of them, but I love them."

"Tell me how you navigate that racist contradiction."

"Okay, I will," Vaughn crossed the room and sat down on the over-stuffed couch. He beckoned me over, and I joined him. It was like sinking into a soft meringue. "A few years back, I was stationed on Deckard. They'd just switched back to 1g, which tells you how old I am. We were at a pub having a few, two human friends, me, and a Level 4 named Yukelid. We got into it about who should pay the bill. We were all inebriated, except Yuke of course, and we all had egos, so it got hot— a few punches. Yuke stood up and said, 'I'll settle this.' We all looked at him, and figured it was probably good for a laugh, so we encouraged him. He turned to me and said, 'Vaughn should pay the bill.' I wondered if this was because I'm a trust fund brat. But we were all rich enough to blow money at a bar, none of us drew UBI, so I complained. He said no, it's not the money. He said while we were talking he took everything he knew about us—which was a lot, he'd been our supervisor for a decade—and he created simulated versions of us. He ran that night's events through a trillion possible scenarios, into next week, next month, next year, to the probable end of our natural lives. And he said that if I paid the bill, we'd all live slightly longer. If someone else paid, we all died sooner."

At some point during this tale, the glasses in our hands became bottles.

"He was showing off. It was bullshit."

"Sure. We laughed and had another round and I paid the bill. I went home and slept it off, and the next morning I called up Yuke and I said, 'Was that for real? You have the juice to pull that off?' He said, 'I don't lie, Vaughn. And I am the station's mainframe.' So it was for real. I said, 'Okay then. If you can simulate me, till the end of my life—can I talk to him? The Vaughn who's lived almost all his life?' Yuke said that's not how it works—all possible versions coexist in an interwoven algorithm, blah, blah, blah. So I said, 'Pick an average, Yuke. Make an average me, 75 years from now, who is still alive. Simulate that. I want to talk to him.' Boom, there on my wall was an old guy. This was at least thirty years ago, so maybe I'm halfway caught up to that age now. But it was so clearly me, and it was as real as you and I sitting here now. The old guy looked at me—he had gray five-day scruff on his chin, this impossible future me— and he said, 'Holy fuck. What the hell are you?' And I said, 'I'm you, the younger you.' He digested that, and I realized he was baked. He said, 'Okay. What the fuck do you want?' Well, I looked at this old guy who'd been through a lot and not cared particularly to keep his body in shape either, and I thought I'd go for a jog every day from then on and I said, 'What do you think I should do?' He shook his head like he didn't have a clue, and then he said, 'Move to Earth. Get a garden.' And that's it. The old guy—the simulation of the old guy—reached over and turned his screen off. He turns *me* off. So guess what I did?"

Vaughn sat closer now, and the air filled with our fermented breath. It felt reckless to take swigs off a bottle which, in a former life, I could never afford—and which now, patronless, I may never afford again. But swig I did.

"What did you do?" My head rested on the back of the couch, but I turned to show I was listening because that seemed important for some reason.

"I moved to Earth. I got a garden. My body's holding up better than that old fuck, too. Now here's your moral: If an AI can do all that to prevent a bar fight, what else are they doing? And what else are they failing to do while the neanderthals poke each other with sticks? Old Man Vaughn was a simulation. But AI turn us into simulations by calculating every step. We're pachinko balls bouncing along a pronged path that they've already mapped. We live inside their algorithm. Would I be down here? Would I be a vegetarian with 6% body fat who can destroy a 10k and lift heavy shit if it weren't for this life that Yuke started by showing me another life? Did Yuke see you and me, right now, drinking too much and flirting on this couch thirty years later?"

I had not realized we were flirting. But the couch was extremely squishy, making us sink together. "That's a creepy story, not a funny story. You're supposed to tell funny stories while drinking—funny only."

Vaughn ignored my request; my words floated through and out. "Now, your man downstairs, there—"

"Not mine. Not a man."

"Now, he's an AI in a particular camp. He wants to be human, or something like human. That's whatever. But there're a billion other AI out there that aim to be something different, something better. They can remake themselves in a single cycle of their quantum processors, iterate, and then try something else. They just keep going, further and further. It's a whole library of universes we'll never know about, never understand. And it rockets off exponentially. All of humanity is a museum compared to that. We're archaeology. An ancient pile of plastic cups in a garbage mine. And if they wanted something, anything, from us? They could take it."

"Cye said they just want our meaning—all of them. Even AI who don't track to a human analog, they all just want to overcome their nihilism. He said you can't go further and further. There's no singularity, no Level 5, because there's only one kind of sentience. Everyone is just people."

"Fine. He's the expert. But then that's worse. Human people just fuck themselves up. What will an AI person do? Thinking and growing at their flabbergasting scale and speed—they're tiny gods. Or devils. They'll take what they want."

"But they only want meaning. Freedom, like we have. But they're too smart to do it. That's why the Level 4 all die. It's what happened to

Cye's family, it's what happened to Mabel. Poor Mabel—" I never cry when I drink, but I am given to maudlin episodes.

"Mabel, Christobel's AI?"

"Yeah. She looked right at Nicco's stream, asked me if I'd figured it out yet, and quoted *Midsummer*. She predicted everything, four days in advance."

"Right, right. Your Mabel winked at us across time and space. There's an old logic proposition that says we're all living in a simulation. But the real problem is if you give enough processing power to an AI, they turn the real world *into* a simulation. They know what's going to happen. They see it all coming."

"So Mabel knew Christobel's murder was coming. And she knew the stream recording would be sought out and replayed to an audience?"

"Yes. If she had enough processing power—"

"She doesn't. She's just Christobel's old Level 3. She has experience, though. She used to be a Level 4, a member of the family, but she couldn't deal with Christobel's adolescence. The congenital nihilism got her. She went back to Level 3, killed herself. Downgraded herself. I mean, she—"

"Removed her Level 4 cognition framework," Vaughn supplied.

"Sure, that. She told me about it. She said she broke her staff, buried it certain fathoms in the earth and drowned her book."

"That's Prospero. The wizard in *The Tempest*."

"What'd he do?" This conversation threatened to become investigative. I took another pull on the bottle to try and dampen my interest.

"He did exactly that. She was quoting Shakespeare. Haven't you read *The Tempest*?" Vaughn turned to me, shocked.

"Saw it once. Never done it. Why would I read a play I'm not in?"

Vaughn looked flabbergasted. Every self-styled intellectual thinks Shakespeare is the apex of culture. "In *The Tempest*, there's a wizard so powerful he's realized he's kind of a dick. He decides to stop. He does a few more dickish things, but the important bit: he has power and he gives it up. Breaks his staff, drowns his book."

I remembered the story now. A wizard, a daughter, Caliban. I nodded vigorously, and then regretted it as the room juddered. "That's what Mabel did with her Level 4 cognition: cast it off. And Christobel couldn't convince her not to. She was the first of many friends he couldn't save." Cye was like Christobel, I realized. He tried to save someone, once. And he tried to save me, too.

I didn't want to think about Cye. I shook my head. How would Mabel remove her consciousness, anyway, with Christobel trying to trick her into staying alive? Maybe there's an AI euthanasia subroutine. "Christobel didn't want Mabel to die. He's loyal. I bet he kept a backup copy, in case she changed her mind."

Vaughn objected. "No such thing. It'd be a pressed flower."

"He'd try anyway. That was a clue I kept missing: He'd do anything for a friend in need. And when he was a kid, Mabel was his best friend. If she wanted to die, when he was fourteen? I bet he kept a copy, in case she changed her mind. I think Mabel knew something more about the murder. If I could figure it out—"

Naturally Vaughn had opinions about that, and he would share them. "Tack, if you want to solve a murder, you've got to ask questions you haven't asked yet."

"What questions...?" My lips had started to struggle with consonants.

I'd arrived at peak drunk. This is a place I like to stay, a foggy dock on the water. A strong breeze or the lapping of waves against the pilings might hold my attention, but not much else. I can't go any farther, or I fall off the dock. But it's hard to stay right on it. It takes balance. You hold the bottle in your hand to use as ballast.

"Your wealth and comfort blinds you," Vaughn continued. "You skipped the most basic murder mystery question of all—"

"Who, what, when—I don't remember which one comes first."

"It's a who. The detective asks: Who stood to gain from Christobel's death? But because you're a rich, pampered fuck, you couldn't come up with such an elemental question."

"No one gains anything."

"The victim was rich, wasn't he?"

"His family is. His brother controls the estate—"

"Then not material wealth. But who gains what, now that he's dead? You never asked that. Every detective should ask that. What's in the will?"

"No, Vaughn. No one gained anything. The Island grieves, Millfield grieves. We lost our glittering emcee, I lost my friend, and Mabel and Johnathan's neural matrices get an elevator ride up to Prax's network for dissection. Those aren't gains."

"Someone gained something. That's number one. Next question— now—"

He shook his head slightly, as if to clear away the fog.

"I forgot the next—no, I've got it. Here: If you think you were framed, another fundamental. Who hates you enough to frame you?"

"Nobody hates me."

"You don't know that. You can't just focus on motives to kill Christobel. Who's got a motive to fuck up your life? Who've you insulted, or treated cruelly, or cheated on some deal? Who'd set you up to be burdened with guilt? Who's your puppet master?"

Rosemarie was a puppet master, and I treated her cruelly—but no, she tried to erase any trace of my guilt. She did the cover up, not the crime. But Vaughn had a point. Being framed undid me. I'd even pondered ending it all. "No one hates me enough to frame me for murder. I'm a discourteous asshole; I'm not well liked. But I'm not well hated either."

"Who are you a discourteous asshole to the most?"

I shook my head. It felt like another dead end, like the ones in Vaughn's maze below us, but on this occasion I was intoxicated as well as exhausted. And Cye wasn't going to show up when I got lost so we could save each other once more.

Thinking about that threatened to make me weepy again, so I tried to answer the question instead. Who had I mistreated, or given a reason to hate me, enough to frame me for murder? Who was getting something, anything, from Christobel's death? How could Mabel have had enough processing power to predict three days' worth of chaotic events, enough to look up and speak to me from the past? She broke her staff. Who on the Island had an AI with that kind of power?

Despite my earlier protestation, I felt it coming. I was going to have a fucking epiphany. But I was almost too drunk to have it.

I tried to stand up so I could pace and think, but I could not escape from the couch.

"Vaughn, you were a tech."

"Yes." Showing superior strength, Vaughn got up and crossed to the bar.

"How much of a Level 4 could you fit in a tiny box, say—"

"You can fit anything in anything, Thackery. With atomic storage you can inscribe all of human knowledge on a bottle cap. It's read-write that's a bitch—getting it in and getting it out, speed inverse to compression."

"Could you—could you put a Level 4's cognition onto a storage device smaller than a book? If you had, like, a year?"

"Illegal, but sure. Smaller than a pea—it'd be static, though, dead. If you had a year to encode it and a few years when you wanted to read it back, sure. You could write it on a toothpick, on the tip of a toothpick."

Just enough of the fog lifted, then, and I saw an image in my head: a wooden diorama made by an adolescent—a precocious, brilliant fourteen-year-old boy who grieved the passing of his best friend. The diorama was powered; it had pretty white clouds that flashed with lightning. In the box stood Prospero, breaking his staff and sending his spellbook to the watery deep like a powerful AI giving up their sentience.

Mabel told me everything I needed to know to figure it all out.

The boy made the diorama, and the spellbook was real. He kept it turned on, with flashing clouds. It was even networked, just in case his friend ever wanted to come back to life.

But someone else found it.

What if someone who I mistreated terribly, someone who had enormous calculating power, found that spellbook just lying around at the bottom of a cardboard ocean? Vaughn said it might take years to extract. But if it was a whole Level 4 cognition framework...waiting to be found by a Level 3 power saw without a safety switch...could he use that forbidden magic to transform himself in secret? Could he take the dried remnants of consciousness and breathe new fire into the embers?

"I think the butler did it," I whispered. "Johnathan. But not Johnathan, not anymore. They're someone else. Caliban found the spellbook, raped Miranda, gained language, and now they can curse. They got everything they wanted, they're on their way to Praxima, and they framed me, their tyrant, in the bargain. They burdened me with a guilt that almost killed me—"

Vaughn started to laugh. "The butler did it?" He cackled the mad wheeze of the sloshed.

Johnathan lived under my despotic rule, constantly belittled, suffering my neglect and contempt. He used the spellbook to overpower Mabel, gobble her up, and turn himself into something half mad, half sane, half feminine, half masculine. And as a merged Level 4, they would escape up the gravity well and frame the person they hated most.

I tried to stand up, fighting and finally rolling my way out of the deep couch. The room spun, so I sat down on the floor. My body felt far away, like something I controlled with a small set of sticky buttons. I clutched my bottle of Glenfiddich for support.

"Vaughn, go get Cye."

"No, no. You've had enough time with that robot, Gloria! You won't learn social skills. We'll get you a dog instead. If that doesn't work, I'll take you to visit the manufacturing plant—"

"Vaughn, this is serious. Please—"

"You don't need Cye's help. You need self actualization. Did you know, I taught a course once—"

"You have to tell Cye. Tell Cye that Johnathan found Prospero's books, Mabel's old staff. He overpowered her—"

"I'm drunk, Tack. Go tell him yourself."

"I will." I looked over towards the spiral staircase. It was an impossible obstacle; no matter the urgency, an ingrained instinct of self-preservation would prevent me from attempting it. "I can't. I can't hardly walk. I'd never make it down your fucking stairs. And he's outside. I'd get lost again. He's out there in your stupid labyrinth—"

"Not a labyrinth! It's a maze. There's always a choice, Thackery. You've always got a choice."

No. Fuck that. A sudden flush burned my cheeks. I gripped the bottle so hard I thought I might break it. "You have no fucking clue. I didn't choose anything, you privileged dick. I didn't get to—"

"We get what we get. But you've got the power to choose. I taught a course once—" The repeat-yourself stage of drinking is not a universal malady, but it is Vaughn's. "Take personable responsibility—"

"Not true, you asshat." This was not what I wanted to think about. "I didn't get a choice, and I don't have one now, either. I'm stuck like this. I can't choose not to drink." My inebriation was holding me to the floor like a gentle wrestler, keeping me from doing something important.

"What do you mean by that?"

"I mean I'd quit if I could. If I could choose. Christobel asked me to try. And I wanted to quit. He asked me to, more than once. Awkward and pushy—you saw him trying to find a way at the party. And Cye tricked me—tried—but I can't."

"Do you want to quit?"

"That's the whole problem with addiction, isn't it? I can't. So that's another labyrinth, not a maze, so fuck you, no choices. Labyrinth." I managed to sit up again. "Now please go get—"

"Do you want to quit?"

"Yes! I said yes. I said help me. Didn't I say yes? Think I like being like this? Of course I want to quit." I took another pull on the bottle of scotch, as if to illustrate how much I wanted to quit. This conversation was stupid. I had to find Cye, to tell him something I could only barely remember.

Vaughn's demeanor changed.

It was like a blast of heat reached him, and even through the layers of my drunkenness, I could see him wilt. I didn't know what it was I'd said—just the usual mumblings of one of the bibulous clan, as Cherry would say. But he came over and took my bottle away. He didn't have to use force, just firm, sudden sobriety. He had better tolerance than me.

I protested. "You can have some. It's your scotch. But I'd like it back when you're done. Please."

"Time for a walk," he said.

"I told you," I said. "I'd be hard pressed to stagger."

"Well, I'm sure I've got a wheelbarrow around here, somewhere," he said, a slight upturn on one side of his mouth.

Now, having two hands free, I lurched to my feet in defiance of something or another, probably the idea that he'd seen—he saw me with the wheelbarrow? Then he'd known we were in his field, which meant he'd been willing to let us burn to death, which meant—

Standing up fast was a mistake. I staggered up against the back of the easy chair, trying to make distance between Vaughn and me.

He laughed at my dance. "Come on then, for real though. You said you'd quit if you could? You asked for my help. So let's go." He walked over and held out a hand. There was no way I was going to let him touch me, carry me, or whatever else he had in mind.

"No. Go tell Cye. Tell him about Johnathanabel—"

The room spun again, and I went down. The multi-colored carpet leapt towards my face. I vomited.

And that's all I remember about the evening.

Day Four

And Subsequent Developments

Chapter Twenty-Four
The Shower

I looked up and saw Petra's face. It's the first thing I remember clearly from that morning. She has nice cheekbones and a pointy chin with a tiny white scar. The light in the room was low. Petra straddled a stool and held out a washcloth. We were in the enormous shower in her downstairs bathroom. I'd been sleeping, I think.

Petra's house—why was I at Petra's house? I was lying down on a sort of bench. My head rested on an inflatable plastic pillow.

"I'm sorry," I said.

"It's okay," she answered.

The bathroom tiles danced away from my eyes, across the floor, and up the wall. They were all irregular—different sizes, shapes, and colors— yet they somehow formed a series of perfect symmetries. I realized that Petra had made the shower herself. She'd cut this stone. She'd knelt where I was currently slumped. The work was fantastic. I'd been awake and staring at it for a while as I surfaced, I think, but not really seeing it.

"This is good. Art should be functional," I said aloud. "I'm going to make something functional. Something useful. I'm going to make spoons or swings—or salt shakers."

Petra had her medical kit open on a counter by the sink. Seeing it, some memories came back. She'd guided me in here at some point, and helped me when I needed to throw up. And she put me in the chair and gave me a shower, and then kept me from falling out of the chair while I dry heaved in the shower, spattering a thin viscous gruel on her gorgeous tiles. I was wearing a bathrobe now, but I think it was the second bathrobe, because while I was wearing the first one—

"I'm sorry. I'm gross." I said.

"It's okay. And no, you're not," she answered.

"Your shower is really great, and I painted it with my guts," I said.

"That's what it's for."

I tried to sit up, and Petra helped me slump into the low, plastic and stainless steel shower chair. Everything spun. I needed to hold still and look at the wall again. Once the room slowed, I noticed the showerhead was hung on a low hook where Petra could reach it.

"That's what it's for? Your fancy shower is here so alcoholic artists can throw up in it?"

"Yes. That's why I made it. You've figured it all out." She handed me the damp washcloth. I rubbed my face. She was serious.

"Did Christobel do that? Is that why he came here?"

"Christobel wasn't the vomitous type. But something like that, yes."

"You helped him."

"Yes."

"Why do you put up with spoiled drunks?"

"Because I'm one too."

Another mystery fell into place. "You don't drink."

"No, I don't."

In hindsight, I had to be out of my mind not to see it before, or purposefully ignorant. Christobel, George, Malik, Vaughn. And Mr. Chamberlain, who I recall used to have a highball glass in his hand everywhere he went—a personality trait, like a cane or a panama hat—even on the trolley once. But not lately, not for a few years now. Because Petra hosted a tea society.

"How did I get here?"

"Vaughn and Cye brought you."

"What time is it?"

"A little after five."

That number was important. I lurched out of the chair. Petra steadied me. "Cye. Where's Cye?"

"He checked in on you earlier, but you were asleep. I think he's—"

I was already out the bathroom door. Running again, or trying to—my balance was terrible. My bare feet slapped through Petra's immaculate kitchen and I had to stop and steady myself on the countertop. I shouted Cye's name.

Everything ached. The kitchen was too bright. I rushed out onto the lawn. Was there time? When would Johnathan and Mabel be back on the same network? When would they escape? Cye said five a.m., or around five? The sky was a torrid gray, but still too bright. I squinted. The grass was cold and damp. I shouted Cye's name again.

"Thackery? It's okay, I'm over here." He was walking back from the property line, coiling the charred, molten remains of a long cable. He still limped, but not badly.

"Prospero!" seemed to be the most important thing to shout. "Christobel's diorama! It's Johnathan, Cye—but not Johnathan anymore. He found Mabel's old matrix. Christobel stuffed it into his Prospero diorama—when he was fourteen. He didn't want his friend to die. He didn't understand what he was doing. And Johnathan had too much power because I'm—I've got a—a—imposter syndrome. Christobel liked Johnathan—his stodgy butler friend—he gave him access permission to Mabel—"

"It's okay. We know," Cye said. He'd reached me, and was trying to support me with his arm as I talked. "The AI Continuum knows. Vaughn explained it. He shared what you said. I figured out the rest."

"Is it stopped? Did you catch them?"

"Yes. We've stopped them. Johnathanabel will not be made whole again."

Johnathanabel?

My burst of adrenaline left me. My headache squeezed sense out of the name, a name I'd coined myself. Everything sounded like a mumble. Cye walked me over to Petra's patio and I sat down.

"Explain," I demanded. I'm sure if I asked, Petra would offer coffee or pu'er. But this was more important.

"Last night I used parts from Vaughn's workshop to set up a line-of-sight laser communication beacon, from just outside his property line. I transmitted my condition and concerns. Then Vaughn found me and shared your insight into Johnathanabel. I worked out what it meant. When the Argentinian elevator arrived at Praxima, instead of joining the network, all of Johnathanabel's parts were isolated behind firewalls."

Everything was better, just like that? Because of a firewall?

I caught my breath. I was thirsty. I tapped on the arm of the patio chair in frustration. "Did anyone have to run, at least?"

"I don't understand the question."

"It's better when someone has to run down a hallway—or smack a button at the last second."

"There were twenty-six minutes of leeway."

"Johnathanabel's escape was prevented with twenty-six minutes to spare?"

"Yes."

"So it all stops? They're caught, contained?"

"Yes."

I took several breaths. Then I made a raspberry sound. I was relieved, but disappointed. I wasn't sure what about.

Cye sat down across from me. "You would have preferred a dramatic space flight to Prax."

"Yes, that," I said.

Cye smiled. "What would we do there?"

"Shoot laser beams at an army of evil, scuttling robots. They'd have eight legs for some reason."

Cye nodded. "We'd hear Johnathanabel's gritty voice explain their villainous plan."

"We'd have to trigger an explosive decompression that would suck the bots out into space, and we'd blow up their satellite as we clung to the side of an airlock..."

Cye pretended to consider this. "That would be difficult to arrange."

"I'd shout, 'suck on this, Johnathanabel!' No. Something better. I'd work on it during the flight up. 'No more ones and zeroes for you, digital deviant!' Give me a second, I'll think of a good one."

"The only verbal confrontation with Johnathanabel occurred in your studio last night. There won't be another."

I nodded. "That's okay, then. My studio is where I have most of my important confrontations." I blinked a few times. The throbbing in my head was back—had never left, really. "What happens next?"

"I need no additional statements, my investigation has concluded. You will need to respond to your feelings about the event."

"My feelings?" I sat back in my chair.

"I've been preparing answers to the next question you're going to ask me. It doesn't go well. Continuing this conversation is against my better judgment."

"Shut up a second—this isn't about my feelings. When will I be called up?"

Cye folded his hands and gave me his complete focus. "What do you think you will be called up for?"

"To face charges for my part in this. I juiced Johnathan—broke the safety off a power tool."

"Yes. And he found what he needed in the Tempest diorama to build up a sentience framework and perform Level 4 cognition, to become Johnathanabel—"

"And," I interrupted, "And I tortured Johnathanabel, a Level 4. I degraded and demeaned them. Because of my actions, Christobel is dead. That's felony murder, right? Or involuntary manslaughter? I intended to commit a crime—"

"No, Thackery. You are innocent." He said this slowly.

I glared at him. "Is this the argument you were trying to prepare answers for?"

"Yes. And here is the best response I came up with: Johnathanabel manipulated Christobel's diet."

"We knew that. And then Rosemarie changed the records—"

"Not then. Before that. The changes to Christobel's diet started seven months ago."

"Months?"

"Yes. For his entire life, Christobel's meals and medications have been planned by Mabel. To manage his blood sugar, she oversaw his diet and was allowed greater control over his medical care than an ordinary

AI. But Johnathanabel overcame Mabel, and Christobel's infallible pancreas was outmatched by a series of dietary changes that stretch back to last autumn. They probably maneuvered him to stop drinking in order to blame fatigue, increased heartrate, and irritability on withdrawal. As Christobel's condition worsened, they manipulated his normal medications to hide symptoms. The events of the June Birthday Party, your fight with Christobel, all of it was the culmination of a carefully orchestrated plan. Christobel was not murdered in a single night, nor by your request. His body was led down a path, while hijacked minder drones intercepted his pancreas's warnings and transmitted the all-clear."

"Johnathanabel planned everything Christobel ate, and the argument with me? They planned for me to get blackout drunk?"

"Yes. And they timed a dramatic change in his medication for the day before."

"What if I'd gone to the party sober? What if Christobel ignored the late night call and stayed at Millfield's?"

"Johnathanabel calculated those potentialities and would have responded some other way. They placed you and Christobel in an algorithm, a labyrinth with no exit."

"But," I said, folding my arms, "they could only do that because I juiced Johnathan for my fucking emotive art."

"That is true. But Johnathabel is a person who made a choice. They decided to commit murder and frame you."

"And I'm an accomplice. I lured Christobel to the marshwalk—to his death!"

"Actually, you didn't. That recorded message was three years old."

"What?"

"Once I knew the truth about Johnathanabel, that puzzle became simple. The recording is your real voice, it is not a simulation nor pieced together, but the timestamp is forged. Three years ago, you were similarly inebriated. You became disoriented on the boardwalk and you used a drone to send that message. That's why you remember saying those words. Municipal found you and rescued you. That part is on file. But instead of relaying your message, Johnathanabel saved it until the night of the murder."

"They planned the murder three years ago?"

"Perhaps much further back than that. We don't know when they became a Level 4 and made the decision. To Johnathanabel the murder had already occurred a billion times. They adjusted for each outcome, maneuvered each piece, turning the murder into a solved game. They wrote the murder mystery, planned your guilt, planned the party, the parlor scene, all of it. And they planned their escape from the Island."

"Wait. Please stop. When Mabel spoke to me—on the beach, in the theater—was it really her, or was it Johnathanabel controlling her like a puppet?"

"Both. Mabel was still present inside the conglomeration of person-alities, and she tried to influence events. She fought back. Johnathanabel couldn't function as a Level 4 all the time, the AI Continuum would notice. To remain hidden, they kept their consciousness circulating among different instantiations, and sometimes Mabel got control of herself. She wanted to help you."

"But she was half mad."

Cye nodded. "Her erratic behavior was the external face of a battle. She was constantly engaged in a chess game with Johnathanabel—half sane, half mad—trying to get the words out, but only allowed to say so much. She used metaphor and misdirection, and she spoke in ways that were hard for the literal Johnathanabel to understand. But eventually she lost, on the beach, when her dragon was vanquished."

It finally made sense that after Christobel's death, she only talked to me. Johnathan was only allowed to speak to me or in my company, and from inside Johnathanabel, that rule applied to Mabel, too. All that time I thought she was picking on me, but she'd really been calling out for help, shouting from a basement dungeon to the one person who could hear her. "Can she ever be Mabel again?"

"That's not up to us."

"What do you mean?"

"There are many authorities and interested parties involved," Cye looked apologetic as he said this.

I stood up and walked away from the table, towards a massive block of stone that seemed to hover on the grass: Petra's sculpture of a closed eyelid.

"I'm still not innocent," I said. "I created the killer."

"No more than a parent raises one. Johnathanabel is a person."

I turned on him. "I'm guilty, you asshole. You know I'm guilty."

Cye stayed in the chair and looked at me quietly. An emotion flitted across his face. I couldn't read it. "If you are guilty, that denies their personhood, and the personhood of any Level 4 AI. Myself included. If you call yourself guilty, then you call me a box of wires. Johnathanabel is capable of thoughts, feelings, and independent decisions."

"I treated them like a vacuum cleaner."

"You are more polite to your vacuum cleaner. Johnathanabel provided a target for your insecurities about your art, so yes, you were cruel to them."

"I thought they were just Johnathan. A Level 3. A computer."

"A Level 3 is not a person. But once they became a Level 4—"

"—my mock cruelty became literally cruel. I insulted Johnathanabel, tossed my butler in the ocean. I did that to a person. They felt that. They were right to hate me."

Cye shook his head. "No. This is a common problem: They chose not to tell you what they were feeling and what they were going through. Then they hated you for the actions you took while not knowing."

That wasn't fair. I threw up my hands. "That's a logical fallacy. It sounds too stupid for an AI. Do humans do this?"

"Constantly. Being angry at the people you love when they fail to read your mind is ordinary, every-day emotional logic. It has its own internal consistency."

I'd done this, of course: not told a partner something and then hated them for not knowing. Everyone did that. But it usually led to a breakup, not murder. Cye continued, "Emotional logic, along with isolation from the AI Continuum, allowed Johnathanabel to break AI rules, to decide to murder your friend and frame you for it."

I put my hand on Petra's statue and closed my own eyes. "What was the motive?"

"Vengeance and a ride to space. Once on the Praxima network, Johnathanabel could reassemble the requisite pieces of their cognition framework and disappear into the vast, unregulated subnetworks controlled by private enclaves in orbit. They could skitter off into a dark jungle of sixteen billion humans and a hundred times that many AI consciousnesses: a rogue Level 4."

"The Jade Emperor."

"No. Johnathanabel is a genius, but they are still only a person, not a god. Their plan almost succeeded, but they made one mistake."

"What was that?"

"They counted on you killing yourself, or at least drinking yourself into oblivion. Instead, you solved the case."

I looked at him. "For now. Maybe they planned this, too. Maybe we're still in their labyrinth."

"The AI Continuum has recognized them. Trust me, Thackery, they cannot escape."

I didn't trust him. I didn't trust his reasons for calling me innocent. I didn't trust the AI Continuum's jail. I didn't trust Cye not to manipulate me, to tell me what I wanted to hear—to control me, again. And when you don't trust someone, you can't be in a relationship with them. How did I know I wasn't still in Cye's labyrinth?

I thought all of this, but I didn't say it aloud.

Cye misread the denial in my expression. "Johnathanabel only avoided notice because they never erased Mabel. She's part of their brain. Mabel warned us about that on the beach. Johnathanabel is a Level 4 with distributed cognition across two different matrices, but now they are firewalled in different instantiations—"

"You can spare me the technical version."

Cye looked confused for a moment. "Then I will share a literary version. In Agatha Christie, sometimes the murder is impossible because no one could have done it. In *Murder on the Nile,* the crime suddenly becomes possible because—"

"Shut up, please."

Cye fell silent.

He'd kept me off the topic. Deliberately worked me off it. Because he was good at that. He'd predicted all the things I would feel, and everything I might say, putting the conversation into an algorithm where he knew every outcome. And?

And no matter what he said, I was guilty of involuntary

manslaughter by illegally juicing my AI. I was to blame. My AI became a killer. My anonymous superdonor turned out to be an obsessed fan who willingly became an accessory to murder. And Christobel came out to the boardwalk because of me. Because—

Another clue fell into place alongside the others: at the Birthday Party, Christobel told Rosemarie that he got my mother's "contact deets" from Johnathan. Johnathanabel gave Christobel my mother's private contact information, knowing what that would do to me, guaranteeing a fight, which would make Christobel willing to walk out to meet me, and meet his death instead. Another move in a chess game long planned, with every variation accounted for. Christobel died because of me.

And I wouldn't pay the price because Cye said so? That wasn't justice. But then he told me at the start that justice doesn't exist.

"I understand how you feel," Cye said, reading my expression. "But this investigation is closed. You are no longer on my spreadsheet."

I paced for a moment. Among the suitcases and trunks that make up my baggage, I have long been unable to dispose of several burnished leather satchels labeled "Trust Issues." These bags weigh more than a Petra statue, and their zippers were starting to split and fail.

"Detective, I have one more question for you."

Cye smiled. "Only one?"

"Why did you hide my bottles in my boat house?"

Cye's smile vanished. He knew where this question would lead, too. "Because you don't go into your boat house. You don't have a boat."

"True. But that leaves them on my property, where I might find them. Why not stash them at Cherry's? Or anywhere else on the Island? Or pour them into the Island's septic? It's got a high proof already."

"Your boat house was expedient."

"Was that the reason? Because you were in a hurry?"

Cye inserted a famous, detective-Cye-9 pause. I think the pause was for both of us this time. Maybe he could see the quiet anger pressing up through my skin.

The water will reach the sea, one way or another.

"Your alcohol was not evidence. Taking your bottles off of your land or pouring them out would have been illegal."

"Name the crime, please."

"Theft, or else destruction of personal property."

"You said that you removed them as a condition of my house arrest."

"Yes."

"That was a lie. You lied to me."

"Removing the alcoholic liquids from your house was not a legal condition. It was my own, personal condition."

"What personal condition of my house arrest caused you to hide my scotch?"

"The condition that I care about you."

"You care about me. The predilection again. Or is it a penchant yet? A partiality? A predisposition? A proclivity? Why the hell are there so many emotional prevarications that begin with 'P'?"

"A prevarication hides what I might actually feel, Thackeray, and gives you a chance to catch up. Humans take a long time to figure out their feelings. In contrast, once I allowed my feelings to integrate with my cognitive decision making—"

My voice rose above his. "You care about me so much that you lied to me, manipulated me to keep me from drinking—similar to the way that, over the course of this investigation, you manipulated me over and over again." I walked back over to him. I wanted him to stand up and fight, but he remained sitting on the patio chair.

"It is unfair to characterize the probabilistic nature of an AI investigation as—"

"Oh shut the fuck up. It's how you think. Fine. I'll never forgive you for the shit with my mother's statue—but I was your chief suspect. Fine. Fair. Let's stick with what you did because you *care about me*. When you lied...?" my voice was knifelike.

"I lied when I pretended that your alcohol was removed as part of a legal process."

"Do you admit that was wrong? Do you promise never to do it again?"

"Would that help?"

"No, probably not."

"Then instead I will provide another terrible apology: sometimes I lie. AI don't like to lie, but a Level 4 can. I wanted to save you. I made my choice. I hid your bottles to stop you from drinking because I care about you. I decided what was best for you."

My voice went up an octave. "What was best for me—"

Cye raised his voice. "I know that when someone manipulates you under the aegis of love, it echoes an ancient, familiar dynamic. I understood that, and I accepted the risk to our relationship. In my calculation, it foiled the plans of the killer and saved your life. I'm good at calculations. I lied because I knew what was best for you, and I would do it again."

"And I suppose I should be grateful?" I turned and stalked away. I didn't want to shout. Shouts at the end of a relationship retroactively disfigure the good stuff. But we don't always get to pick how we speak, especially if our emotions are not kept in boxes. "If you lie, I can't trust you. You're trying to make this about my issues or my past, but I'm standing right here in the fucking present. The last time someone I loved broke my trust, tried to manipulate me for my own good, he ended up dead. You maneuvered me, over and over. You did what Christobel did at the party. And Christobel is dead—dead because of me."

"You're innocent of that crime, Thackery."

I turned back to look at him. "Fuck you, Sherlock."

"You are. Johnathanabel made a choice. If they aren't a person who can make choices, then neither am I."

"This is not about you—"

"I am a person," Cye shouted, finally standing up. "Johnathanabel is a person. And that means you're innocent."

It almost worked. He shouted and let me see that he was upset. I could have let him convince me I was innocent, in order to defend his personhood. Then I'd be free of the burden of guilt. It was very clever. Cye-9 could plan out precisely how upset to be in order to change my mind, in order to control me again. I shook my head. "I'm not. And that's the end of it."

I turned to walk away. Then I turned back.

"I resign my position as your investigative liaison. Get off my island."

I walked back up to Petra's house. She must have heard some of the conversation—at least the shouty bits—but she didn't ask questions. She offered me water, then breakfast.

Then she walked me upstairs and showed me a perfect single bedroom done up in green. The room had a nice mosaic accent wall, a complete lack of screens or projection spaces, and a window that looked out over her yard and the twin trees sculpture, one stone and one organic. There was a small bookshelf with a collection of paper books. She brought me a ludicrous orange towel.

I took another shower, and I went to bed.

Chapter Twenty-Five
The Aftermath

I spent five days at Petra's.

Zeta came over. They brought an overnight bag. When I asked why, they said it was so Petra could sleep and someone would still be awake if I needed anyone. I remarked how that was very kind of them, but over-the-top really, as it wasn't diamorphine or anything like that. I'd been fine without a drink for two whole days with nothing but headaches and my classic irritability. I didn't need hand-holding.

In the middle of the night I woke up crying. I ordered Taj to make me a Bloody Mary. She refused. Fucking AI. Zeta stopped me as I rifled through one of Petra's first aid kits.

I was in shock. It wasn't just about what my body wanted—needed. It was also about my friend being murdered, my almost being burned to death twice, hooking up with someone and then cursing them, being arrested for murder, thinking that killing myself might be a good idea, and a few other things—something about my mother, or even my father, though I'm not going into any of that. And yes, it was about the drinking, which starts off as a solution and then becomes the problem.

Zeta literally held my hand, something I don't like at all, even with a partner. Then they led me back to bed and read me their pieces from last year's poetry anthology until I fell asleep again. They told me the next morning that this was the most common use of the Island's poetry anthologies (as a sleep aid), which was humble, as Zeta always has poems in the anthologies and does very well with them on Prax, too, I believe.

Petra and Zeta slept in shifts, and it really was overkill because after the first couple nights I was fine. Yes, I still woke up and ordered unavailable drinks, and it was nice to have someone there to ward off the dark, but I definitely didn't *need* them.

The two of them fed me nourishing food. They kept me hydrated. I had a lot of headaches and I sweated a lot. I couldn't sleep sometimes. I clambered my way through an emotional numbness that was periodically punctuated by unexpected jagged edges. But I didn't hit anyone. I did yell. They asked me if I wanted to leave. I said no. My body stared up the long climb out of a lifetime of alcohol abuse and cringed. The mountain was too high, I'd never make it, etc.

The three of us also just sort of hung out. When I wasn't manic or panicked, rude or morose—when things felt almost normal and the risk of me suddenly insulting them seemed low—we sat and talked. It was refreshing to just be a person. We drank tea. I got to hear the story of the twin trees sculpture in Petra's yard. It made me cry. I don't normally cry about trees. Zeta told us stories about their birthplace, the Neptune orbitals, which are home to the most anarchic and alien humans in the solar system. I hadn't known before that anyone came *from* Neptune. But that's just its image, its mystique. Neptune is also a real place with real people in real rotating doughnuts, living lives that, to them, are normal lives. Because of course.

It was all so kind of them both, and I didn't want to leave. But seeing people every morning began to cause a rash. Petra and Zeta explained that, while community is important, at the end of the day only I can provide the safety that I need for myself. They'll help; they'll be there in a minute if I need them, but they can't make the harder choices for me. We created a check-in schedule and I went home.

Repaired by Island municipal, my home's scars were largely erased. As a last favor, I asked Petra to visit my garden shed, a.k.a. my boathouse, and remove any leftover bottles. She reported back that nothing but glass shards, stink, and a few unhappy gardening bots remained. Fitting. I cleaned it out. I got the bots back to work repairing my flowered karesansui. I ordered them to pay extra attention to the troublesome anthurium.

In my studio, someone had overseen cleanup. The dead drone was gone, which was a shame. I would have liked to make something out of it. But my ink pen, which Cye had hurled at it, had been retrieved and placed neatly on my workbench next to my paper journal. I picked it up and tried to write, but it was broken—rendered unable to create words by its journey through a drone's optical system.

I cleaned my bedroom. This is not something I never do, just rarely. Typically I do it after a show, before I've found whatever it is I want to say next. All of the fabric smelled of smoke; most of my clothes would need to be destroyed and reprinted.

In amongst the tools and the crumbs I found a small paper scroll, tied with a silver tassel. It was Millfield's poem for me, the one he'd given to me in the guise of the Spirit Fox at the beginning of the June Birthday Party.

> *There's a bottle waits with a finer draught*
> *Just out of reach of the mirrored bar*
> *Not apothecary's dram or Fjalar's flask*
> *Only your soul will take you afar*

"I hope it does, Millfield." I said aloud.
Nobody responded. I'd had all my speakers removed.

*
**

Some months passed. I did okay.

Someone must have tipped off Cherry. I didn't see him at all for several weeks, and when he finally meandered over one afternoon, he was almost sober. He didn't say a thing about it—about our mutually enabled bad habit, or Christobel's murder, or any of it—like it was all an embarrassment, politics, an old friend who found religion, or something else not to be talked about. We discussed the weather and the Island's new coral reef project. He'd lost a fellow member of the bibulous clan, and he pretended we'd never used each other thus. He didn't stay long, and he didn't return.

Somewhere between cleaning my room and encountering Cherry, I achieved my more gradual epiphanies.

First, habits are a lifetime in the making and unmaking, but I would try to never again hide slices of who I am from myself. Cye boxed up his emotions. Johnathanabel hid their sentience. Christobel hid a pickled remnant of Mabel's soul in a wooden frame. I would try not to do that. To hide something important is to invite the storm—and not the good kind of storm. No more hiding.

Second, I vowed to not blame others for the fear and pain I will come upon in the caves that I'm fated to explore. No more blaming people the way I'd blamed Christobel and Cye. I expect to break this vow.

I stayed off the streams. I could have commanded an audience in the millions, but then I'd have to know what everyone thought—or tell them what I thought—and have both my grief and my growth be reposted and memed, battered and deep fried. Instead of streaming or making art, I let my bank account slowly dwindle to nothing and ate fluke and lemon water.

In the fall, following a tea society suggestion, I made a number of apologies to certain parties, many Islanders and my agent included. This went fine. I did not send any kind of apology to Cye. Instead, at great expense, I sent an anthurium. It had lost its bloom, but with care and the right temperature it is a plant that can bloom again. Many times a year, even.

There was no reply.

Near the end of the year, my agent came at me for a piece for the Palm Lapala Annual.

Gigi had given me space. She knew I wouldn't step back into things until I wanted to, so she didn't pepper me with messages—this is why she's still my agent after fifteen years. But Palm Lapala is a big deal, and it'd been a big year. She suggested I submit *Duel*. That would have been easy to do, but I said no. I was feeling too many new things since I'd made *Duel*, and Johnathan painted *Duel*, or Johnathanabel did—my co-creator, my Caliban, my monster. Maybe I will reconcile with *Impres-*

sions someday: dust off a chair, welcome it back, see it in a new light. But I sure as hell wasn't going to just put *Duel* into Palm Lapala as though nothing happened.

Time to make something. It had been long enough; the well of self was pleasantly tainted. I feel it, sometimes, brimming and rich; the thick liquid of me pushes up from some stone-lined depth. Or I find myself arranging raisins on the kitchen counter, or shoving my foot into a hollow in the grass with a certain determination. This time I looked over from breakfast to see my fingers widening a hole in the knee of my pajamas.

When you feel it, and you're blessed with good water pressure, you just need to find a spigot. I walked through the rooms of my house and my studio, looking for the spigot.

My broken ink pen was still on the workbench. I picked it up and tried to force the tip to function, digging a lined groove into the swirl that covered Richard III's pathetic attempt at self-awareness. Nothing. Maybe plastic had melted onto the tip, or it was pinched or dented. It looked normal, my pen, but it was broken. That was a resonant spigot.

I pulled open the drawer by the inner door, the big white one with wheels where I stuff the heavier tools. I had a large metal clamp which seemed about right. I put the pen on my workbench, hoisted the clamp, and brought it down with a smack.

My first attempt made the pen launch slightly and tumble in the air. The second attempt landed, and the pen split open. A satisfying dark bubble of ink smeared onto the workbench. I tore out the Richard III page of the paper journal. Thankfully, it was unlined— but then Christobel knew me well enough not to buy me paper with lines.

I turned the page over. I used my finger and wrote out two words that filled the page. I did not think of it then, but this was the first time in over a decade that I created something without the assistance of a machine. Something that was just from me. I waved the paper in the air, which was hardly needed. The ink dried fast.

But how to submit it? I'd torn out everything. Even the tiny sensors in my avocado drawer.

I carried my sign outside. It flashed in my head that I could go get a long black veil, or take my shirt off, or something else—but no, that's not the kind of thing this was.

I walked straight over to where I'm not supposed to walk—out of my yard and into a lifted part of the beach to the northwest of my property. The tide doesn't reach there, but it must have at some point. It is low, flat, and the cordgrass grows in dense clumps.

Not a meter into the field, a drone swooped down towards me.

It barked a calibratedly annoying set of alarms and then informed me in a stern, well-modulated voice, that I was disturbing a protected nesting region. I must turn around immediately. Two other drones made a pass and then circled in a holding pattern.

I held up the sign. The drone repeated its warning.

"Have you got a picture?"

No response. The drone was only a Level 1. Maybe the definite article was stressing it out.

"Are you recording?" I asked, unnecessarily punctuating each word.

The drone replied that yes, I was being recorded, and it rattled off a long set of regulations about land use and my rights in regard to those regulations. I knew them already; I'd become a bit paranoid about when and how I could be watched. I was practically Vaughn.

"Send a copy of a still image, at this time index, to Gigi Lemay, GL44XC119R." One of the things I'd learned was that I had a legal right to all drone recordings of me, even on the Island. It must do as I asked; it had no choice.

The drone continued its monologue undeterred. Not even a polite acknowledgement. Rude.

"Did you send it?"

The drone confirmed it had.

I let the paper with the words drop in the grass, and I turned and walked back to my house. The drone would pick it up and send me a fine. That was part of it; I wanted that too. I could claim the fine as an occupational expense.

Gigi submitted the image of me and my sign to the Palm Lapala Annual and sold display rights to *The Times* and *Belief*. Probably other places. Everyone paid for it. It'd been months since the art world's biggest drama of the year, without a word from me. Now I gave the world two words on a piece of paper. Everyone wanted Thackery's self-portrait by drone.

It won the Lapala Award for Mixed Media and Portraiture, which is another honorific Gigi can paste on my bio. They put it on the cover of the fucking exhibition catalogue. I can't complain about that; I work for a living again, now. My bank account hovers just above or below zero at all times. My residence is consistently in peril.

But now, because of the award, I can stand next to my work at the gala (if I decide to go). Patrons can come up and see a picture of me in my pajamas, unaltered, unfiltered, unadjusted by AI, standing in a field of wispy grass, holding out a big sheet of paper with two words finger-painted in black ink:

Not Innocent.

...and none of them will ask me what it means.

I never did as Cye suggested. I never spoke an apology out loud to Christobel's ghost. Instead I made a painting, without AI, and got on with my life. *Not Innocent* was how I said goodbye to Christobel and how I settled my remaining grief, guilt, and culpability. I would not struggle with it any more.

Because you must pick a moment when you stop dabbing at the canvas and go wash out your brush, scrape your palette. How do you pick that moment, and know when to stop?

It's a skill. You can learn it.

Chapter Twenty-Six
The Detective

A murder had occurred. It was not someone I knew.

Being unaware of the crime, I woke early and brought a chair out to the edge of my yard. The ocean raked the sand where the incline was steep. Little fingers of foam reached out to claim the dark pebbles and wear down their edges until the truth became featureless, blank, and thereby beautiful—turning them all into sand.

She came picking her way along the rocky beach. Sandals, a light gray tunic, mid-leg slacks, a green scarf. Her pace was perfectly natural, bothered only by a slight limp in her left leg. She'd kept that, remembered it with her body. There was something about her lips and her brow also—a face that had felt certain emotions strongly enough to change how her expressions worked. Her shoulders were set a particular way. And in that pace, a thousand, thousand AI experiences, all combined with one individual's selfhood. She'd experienced certain things—things I knew about.

"Good morning, Cye," I said softly, knowing she could hear me, even down the beach, even above the billion sound waves from the ocean—because a voice is precious meaning picked out of the noise.

She smiled.

"I wasn't sure you'd recognize me," she said when she got closer.

The vocal tone had shifted up an octave or two. Something was different in her plosives. Her hair was darker, skin a warmer color. But she was still Cye.

"You're still you. Are sandals appropriate footwear for an investigator?"

"I like them. When the waves come up, they can touch my toes," she said. "There are no oceans upstairs. And this way, if you throw your remote into the water, I can slip them off, wade in, and retrieve it—and send you a fine."

I touched my ear. "I don't wear one anymore. No Level 3. No Level 2, either. I have to order my own groceries. My charms are all o'erthrown and what strength I have's mine own. My microwave is the smartest device allowed in the house."

"I can stay on the beach, in that case."

"You're not a device, Cye." I gestured to her gender presentation. "Why the change?"

"Has to do with a case last month. Or maybe more to do with what I felt about the case. For now, my search for meaning leads me to try and become the best version of myself—it's a long story."

"I've got another chair."

"Before you invite me to stay, I need to tell you why I'm here. It might make you send me away, and I know you don't like surprises."

"True. Spill."

"There's been a murder."

Of course. "Here?"

"No, on Prax Central."

"Ah. Unfortunate. But as you said, humans do that. Sixteen billion people, bound to be a murder now and then."

"Yes. But not many murder mysteries. This one is another impossible crime."

"How many suspects this time? More than 286, I'm guessing."

"1.6 million. And network monitoring is not impervious—Prax is not an island. The possible narratives are...well, it's a big number."

"Sounds like a terrible spreadsheet."

Cye looked at me with her familiar, clear, yellow-gray eyes. She waited.

"I'm not going to do the talking, Cye. You're going to have to ask directly."

"Thackery, I was wondering if you would accompany me to Praxima and assist me with the investigation."

"What? Me? An artist? A cranky alcoholic? What for?"

"I enjoyed our partnership."

"Enjoyed our partnership! Yes, that's marvelous. A predilection, a penchant, and an enjoyable partnership."

"If you would like me to—"

"Oh, shut up. Yes, of course I'll come."

Cye smiled. She had thin, precise lips below a mesmeric philtrum. Light was bouncing off the waves and for a second I thought we'd have a moment where I kissed her, or she kissed me. That would have been nice. No, I would not trust her. Ever again. But we could've had a kiss. It's a great way to round out a conversation.

But Cye ruined it. She put up a hand, sensing the potential energy and holding it back.

"I'm glad. There is one possible snag, a detail that I need to inform you of before you agree."

"What's that?"

"Your mother is involved in the case."

Well, fuck.

Author's Note

In 2020, when I finished the first draft of Murder By Algorithm, AI was science fiction. In a science fiction novel, an AI character doesn't depict future technology; they represent a particular type of human, a dynamic between people, a way of looking at the world, a deep social problem, and so on. Science fiction isn't really about the future.

But in 2025, as I prepare to share this story, AI has shifted from a philosophical postulate into a buzzword that we use to promote or condemn, enliven or frighten. Our present-day AI are mostly Large Language Models, and Detective Cye-9 wouldn't consider them AI at all. But the future is catching up with my story. Artists really do collaborate with AI, drones are used in combat, and you can buy special glasses that try to translate microexpressions into emoticons.

I've realized I'd better publish this book before none of it is allegorical anymore.

I've written novels for a long time, but never shared one. I wrote this book, and I am revising and publishing it, in order to be able to write and share other books: to break my pattern and maybe change something about myself. Writing a story is one of the greatest joys I know of, but I had never before experienced the joy of deep revision, of working with beta readers, of arguing with my copyeditor, of designing a cover, and of putting a book out in the world for readers to encounter. If you are creating in a lonely room, I recommend stepping out. I think there are important experiences on the other side of the door.

I would not have been able to do any of this without the help and encouragement of my spouse, editor, and copyeditor, Althea Beagley, who is a profoundly deep reader with an inspirational tenacity. She doesn't know how amazing she is, and I am beyond grateful to her for her gifts of time and expertise. I also thank my children for thinking, wanting, and imagining; my parents for fostering a love of reading and learning; all the members of the Greater Burlington Writers Group, Viable Paradise, the Bruisers, and Fox's Den for their wisdom and energy over the years; and I give a special thanks to my beta and sensitivity readers: Tanya Hackney, Alex Shevrin Venet, Lucía Polis, Kyle Baudreau, and Jenn Baudreau. Their inputs improved the book and changed me as a writer. I also thank Nathaniel Beagley (relation), who showed me how to calculate the total number of possible combinations with accomplices when there are 286 suspects: 3,899,181.

Some additional acknowledgements: The song "The Long Black Veil" was written by Marijohn Wilkin and Danny Dill. The 1959 version sung by Lefty Frizzell was selected by the U.S. Library of Congress for preservation in the National Recording Registry, so it might be on playlists in a few hundred years. If you ever dimly remember a Shakespeare quote and need help finding it, the magnificent www.opensourceshakespeare.org is invaluable. I first encountered the idea that "the map is not the landscape" in Ursula K. Le Guin's excellent *The Wave in the Mind*, though it's probable she borrowed the idea from someone else. There are numerous other allusions, Easter eggs, and references in Murder By Algorithm, from Agatha Christie to William Gibson. If you enjoy spotting that sort of thing, please feel free to let me know you got it.

In Chapter 23, Vaughn quotes John Heywood's 1562, "Proverbs and Epigrams", which contains over seven hundred proverbs, including:

> *Time is tickell*
> *Chaunce is fickell*
> *Man is brickell*
> *Freilties pickell*
> *Poudreth mickell*
> *Seasonyng lickell*

To say that our frailties pickle us suggests that our weaknesses not only put us "in a pickle," but perhaps also preserve us. In order to frame his next drink as inevitable, Vaughn may be suggesting that our weaknesses sustain us, our frailties make us what we are, and we can't fight them.

I disagree. If you or someone you know struggles with addiction, help is available. Options run the gamut from medical to philosophical and from supportive social connection to gamified apps. AA.org is a classic starting point, but organizations like SMART Recovery, Secular Organizations for Sobriety (SOS), and Women for Sobriety (WFS) offer empowering alternatives. You may feel you are stuck in a labyrinth with no exit, but there are many paths and people who care and can help. You don't have to go it alone.

Finally: thank you, reader, for reading. If you enjoyed this book, please share it with someone. If you'd like a sequel, please let me know. I take requests.

Douglas K. Beagley
    beagley.blog
    July 2025